T0366175

Solitaire, Sin, and Desire

CLAIRE MILES

PARTRIDGE
A Penguin Random House Company

To order additional copies of this book, contact
Toll Free 800 101 2657 (Singapore)
Toll Free 1 800 81 7340 (Malaysia)
orders.singapore@partridgepublishing.com

www.partridgepublishing.com/singapore

Maria Wright had been thinking about it for some time. She could not see much point in living any longer. All things considered, life wasn't that bad. She had lived reasonably comfortably for many years. She should have been content, if not happy. But happiness no longer existed.

She thought back to when she was a small child living with her mother and the man who was supposed to be her father. Not that she ever saw much of him. She tried to recall any overwhelming feelings of happiness or joy back then. She couldn't think of any.

Maybe she was never fated to feel happy. There was plenty of talk about the pursuit of happiness. She had done as much as she could to pursue it, but it eluded her. There were never any rapturous feelings inside her. Beautiful sunrises, flowers, furry animals and especially people had no effect. All those things that were supposed to uplift the spirit did nothing for her.

No, it was death she sought—delicious death.

Wouldn't it be wonderful if it just walked straight up to her and took her?

She'd originally had no intention of seeking death on that particular morning when she set out for her walk. The sun was another thing that was supposed to bring warmth to the dead, empty space inside her, especially in winter when the days were shorter.

She had her sunglasses on to protect her eyes from cataracts or destroying her macula. Her floppy hat was pulled down firmly on her head to keep her skin safe from cancers and wrinkles. She had even applied sunscreen.

She stopped at the bridge and carefully checked out the safety railing. It didn't look terribly substantial. It would be easy for a person to fall through. Maria thought the local council was very lax. They should do something about making it safer. After all, there were plenty of children in the area.

As it turned out, it was very easy to accomplish. *Look out, death, here I come.* She took one last look at her ugly hands. Pride filled her as she vaulted over the safety railing without scraping herself. She didn't remember looking down at the water. She sailed right off the edge, feet first.

On the way down, she started laughing uncontrollably. At last she felt happy. There was so much to laugh about. She was especially happy that she had fooled them all. All the monsters that had been on the periphery of her mind were beaten. They could no longer come into her dreams at night.

There was nothing she could do about the little monster during the day. He was always there, skulking in the bedroom.

What made her flight from the edge of the bridge all the more hilarious was the fact that she had done all she could to get enough sun to keep her bones strong. As she flew through the air, she was even aware of the oily lotion on her face. What a joke it all finished up being. Again, she had fooled them all.

Not even the elements could get the better of her now.

As she hit the water, she was a little shocked. She hadn't expected it to be so cold. But what the hell! Hadn't she put up with much more than a little cold water? Her final thoughts were that at long last she had accomplished something worthwhile in her miserable life.

A man who was looking out his living room window saw her jump. He was on the third floor and had a good view. He was astonished how quickly it had happened; one second she was walking across the bridge, and the next she had vaulted over the edge and disappeared into the murky waters below.

Another woman, who was walking her dog not far from the bridge, saw it happen. But what would forever live in her mind was the maniacal laughter. When she described what she had seen and heard, the police intimated that it was probably screaming, but the woman remained adamant that it was laughter.

For Rina Wright, the day her mother did not return would always remain firmly entrenched in her memory. It was a brisk winter's day, not too cold or windy; one of those lovely days when the sun shone warmly enough to make outdoor pursuits enjoyable.

When Rina returned home, the house was locked which wasn't unusual as Mother always kept the door locked whether she was home or not. Rina let herself in and glanced around. When she did not see Mother, she called out to her. Mother, of course, did not reply. This was not that unusual, as her moods were very changeable.

She went in search of Jude. Unlike Mother, Rina was often happy, especially when she came home. If only Mother could unlock the anger and bitterness in her heart. But it hadn't happened and wasn't likely to.

"Hello Jude," Rina called out, walking straight to his bedroom. As usual there was no reply nor did she expect any as Jude never spoke.

She walked into his room and there he was—the joy of her life. He looked up at her from big, brown eyes as she came in. She did not receive a smile from his small, pointed face. It had taken years for him to maintain eye contact. Rina often wondered just what went on in his funny, little brain.

"We'd better get you rugged up if we're going for a walk." Rina was already heading for the cupboard that contained his winter clothing.

His eyes followed her as she brought him a warm coat.

"Come on, Jude, you can put it on yourself. You don't need me to help you. And hurry up about it. I want to get you outside before Mother gets home. Goodness knows where she's disappeared to this time." Rina helped him with the buttons.

Once they were both rugged up, they walked outside. Jude always went to the mail box and waited for her while she locked the front door. When this was done, he would walk towards the shops. Rina remained behind him watching his strange, awkward gait. It was as if his joints did not connect properly, but the fact that he could walk was another of the great joys of her life.

This was an afternoon treat for both of them. They went to the convenience store where Jude got to choose. This was another breakthrough Rina was very proud of.

"What's it going to be today, Jude?" Mr Baxter, the kindly store owner, always stood behind his counter and pointed to the display of lollies that would entice the eye of a young boy.

Jude always took his time. He looked at all the displayed lollies but every time he chose the Minties. It was a ritual that never changed and Mr Baxter made a game of it.

"Where's your mother, Rina? I haven't seen her all day." The shop-keeper always made a point of asking about Rina's mother.

"She's probably still out walking. She should be back soon. She's not usually this late." Rina replied as she watched Jude very carefully unwrap his Mintie and place it in his mouth. He then went to the rubbish bin that Mr Baxter kept near the front of his store. Jude's eyes followed the wrap as he threw it in.

"The days are getting shorter," Mr Baxter said. "It doesn't do to be out too late. You never know when the weather might change." Rina waved briefly to Mr Baxter as they left his shop.

Rina could hardly blame the shop-keeper for always enquiring about Mother. It was easy to understand his interest. The whole family set up was strange, even to Rina. Mother was a very peculiar lady. In the years they had lived there, Mother had not once taken the least interest in Jude.

Rina brushed her black hair away from her face as she watched Jude play in the small park. He was now able to hop on the swing himself and hold on as Rina pushed him. He had never learned the art of swinging himself.

If Jude was going to avoid Mother, then it was time to leave. Rina always made sure Mother never had any contact with him. Mother had always hated him. In fact, it was more than hate. It was akin to absolute detestation.

This attitude always upset Rina. Their history was so chaotic that Rina was confused just thinking about it. She had difficulty remembering who she was at times as Mother always told her that she was two separate people. What a peculiar family they were. Peculiar they might have been but the resemblance between them was striking. The three of them had black hair and near-black eyes. Their skin had the same creamy texture and colour. Their slim builds were much alike.

Once home, Jude went to his room while Rina waited in the kitchen for Mother to return. As usual, she prepared their dinner. Jude ate while Rina waited. He always ate in his bedroom. Rina gave Jude food that he could pick up with his fingers. She cut everything up very finely so he could manage. He was a very slow eater, but if she gave him enough time, he would eventually eat everything on the plate.

Rina waited and waited as she did not want to disappoint Mother as she could become very angry, very quickly.

Rina had learned very early how to avoid the triggers. She knew if she talked too much, Mother would become angry. If she asked too many questions, Mother would become angry. Even any query about what was on television brought on anger.

Rina always spent time with Mother each evening watching Mother's favourite programs. Mother only enjoyed certain shows so Rina went along with it—anything for a peaceful life.

Tired of waiting, Rina ate her dinner. Mother's meal was left on the table as routines were rigidly adhered to. They ate at a certain time, went to bed at a certain time and arose at a certain time. The routines did not vary.

Rina quickly washed and dried the plate and cutlery she used and put them away. Hopefully, when Mother came home, she would realise that Rina had already eaten. Rina never knew what would set Mother off. She was unpredictable and a great hater.

Mother hated no end of things and was not averse to letting Rina know about them. Near the top of her list were men in general, but particularly the politicians and clergy who made people's lives so intolerable. She hated sportsmen who preened about on television showing off their muscles, prowess and tattoos. She had many and varied hates, but at top of her list was Jude.

Rina listened nightly to her rants, agreeing in general with everything Mother said. Life was much easier just to agree. Offering a different point of view only incensed her. So Rina waited in the kitchen for her return. She dare not turn on the television in case she was caught watching some program that Mother deemed unsuitable. It was very trying living with Mother and avoiding her outbursts.

Rina woke shivering in the cold, night air. She realised she must have dropped off. It was unusual that Mother had not come into the kitchen and roared at her as the meal she had prepared was sure to be cold. This would not please Mother.

After a discreet search of the house, it was clear that she had not returned while Rina was asleep. As she checked on Jude, she pulled the covers up over him. Not that she expected Mother to be in Jude's room unless she was planning to exterminate him. Mother never went into his room.

Rina had no idea where she could be. There was hope in her heart that Mother may have found herself a boyfriend, or for that matter, any sort of friend. She was such a lonely, sad and bitter person.

As there was no sign of her, Rina went to bed. She called it going to bed, but in fact she never slept in the bed in her room. She always slept on blankets on the floor.

Rina slept well. Jude never woke during the night or if he did, Rina never heard him. When she arose the next morning, she went in search of Mother. She was not in the kitchen or the living room. Gingerly, Rina opened Mother's bedroom door, certain she would be there. But the bed was empty.

Rina was astounded that Mother was still not home. Then she smiled to herself as she imagined that she must have found herself a boyfriend and had spent the night.

She had heard the students where she did vocational training speak about the nights when they never made it home. She felt a great sense of relief. Maybe Mother was at long last making a better life for herself.

Jude remained in his room. Usually he sat on his chair looking out the window at the birds that twittered in the small, garden shrubs in the enclosed area near his room. The endless cooing of doves and pigeons always attracted his attention. He listened intently to their sounds. Rina took his breakfast into him.

"You better eat up, Jude. I have to leave shortly. I've made some sandwiches for you. Don't leave them sitting too long or the bread will dry out."

Rina never covered his sandwiches with plastic wrap to keep the bread fresh as one day she returned home and found he had eaten the wrap. What pleased her was that he appeared to eat the sandwiches as there were none left on the plate. She knew he sometimes wandered outside into the enclosed courtyard and often left crusts for the birds. Just so long as the birds didn't get the lot, they were welcome to a few crusts.

After eating her own breakfast and packing her lunch, Rina dressed and then went again to check on Jude. She always left his clothes out, but sometimes he did not remember to get dressed especially if he saw the birds.

She left the pack of playing cards with him. It had been a long battle teaching him the basics of solitaire. It was another of the joyous moments in her life when he started to get the gist of it.

As Mother had not returned, Rina said goodbye to Jude and left to attend her vocational training. With everything she had learned raising Jude, she was certain she could manage a course on child care. He had been a very trying baby, hardly eating, never crying and very slow to develop. It had been very difficult learning to be a mother.

Rina felt guilty that Jude didn't get more developmental training but Mother was adamant they had to learn to be invisible people. Over the years, when Rina attended school, she had learnt to be invisible. There were so many children from so many cultures it was easy to go unnoticed. Rina was certain that no one would ever remember her.

Other than Mr Baxter and his wife, Rina doubted that there was anyone who knew Jude existed. He had never been to see a doctor as Mother would not allow it. He had never been immunised. When Rina was at school, he had remained in his room while mother prowled the rest of the house. The system worked. As long as Rina cared for Jude, Mother left Jude alone.

In one way, Rina sometimes thought it was just as well that Jude had next to no contact with other people as he never got sick. He didn't get any childhood illnesses that she knew the children at her school suffered from. If he ever became really sick, Rina had no idea what she would do. For certain, Mother would rather see him die than get any sort of medical help.

When her lessons for the day were completed, she hurried home, but again there was no Mother. She had mixed feelings about this. It was really peaceful to spend time in the house with only Jude for company. Not that he was at all stimulating but he was all she was used to.

But Mother had saved her, and Rina owed her, or at least that was what she had been told for as long as she could remember. Rina had made it part of her life's work to do Mother's bidding in return for having been saved.

Rina even got up the nerve to turn the television on. It was easy to get caught up in the numerous programs on offer. She was enjoying this new freedom so much that she almost forgot about dinner. She quickly cooked up a meal for the two of them, but kept enough for Mother in case she walked through the door.

But Mother never returned. Days went by, and then weeks, still no Mother. Rina was bewildered by this. She had no idea where she could be. She dreamed that Mother had eloped with some handsome man. She had seen a romantic program where this had happened.

Rina always had money in her purse. Mother had always been good about giving Rina enough money to get by. But her cash was now running out. There was still food to buy. Rina decided to take a chance and go through mother's bedroom in search of more cash.

This was an unnerving experience. She kept looking at the bedroom door fearful that Mother would walk through the door and catch her. But no one walked through the door as she kept searching. There were cupboards full of dowdy, old clothes which was Mother's choice of clothing. They were the same type of clothes that she made Rina wear which were supposed to help keep them both invisible.

She pulled out bags and old shoes from the bottom of the wardrobe. She kept searching while keeping an eye on the bedroom door. At the very end of the wardrobe, she pulled out a black backpack. It looked as though it had been there a long time.

Rina placed it on the bed and opened it up. What she saw caused her to gasp and sit back on Mother's bed which under any other circumstances she would never have done. But the shock of the contents of the backpack was enough to forget her mother.

The backpack was crammed full of one hundred dollar notes. The largest denomination Rina had ever seen was a fifty, yet here were bundles and bundles of one hundred dollar notes. Rina ran from the room calling out to Jude.

"I can't believe it. Guess what I found in mother's wardrobe. You should come and look at it." Jude looked at Rina, not understanding her excitement. Rina took him into the bedroom. Jude seldom went through the remainder of the house except for his afternoon walk, so he was reluctant to follow Rina.

She dragged him into the room. "Look at that, Jude. What do you think it means? How could anyone have so much money?"

Jude looked at the money on the bed. He showed little interest, preferring to sit on the floor where he could fiddle with the backpack. Rina started counting. Because of her excitement she often got mixed up and had to start again. She also found counting the money took extra time due to her missing finger. But finally, she had all the bundles in order. She kept a tally. When she was finished, she had counted one million dollars.

She remained in a state of bewilderment as she watched Jude pull out a piece of paper from the backpack. He was about to put it in his mouth, when she pulled it away from him. The paper was old and faded. Rina noticed that there was only one word written on it. She studied the word and read it out loud several times until she thought she got the pronunciation correct—*Tewantin*.

He stood alone at the grave site. The years had passed by very quickly. Gabriel Farraday remembered the day when both his parents had died, separately, and at almost the same time on the same day. He remained angry. The deep hurt lingered inside him. No amount of time had lessened the rage he felt towards the person or persons who had murdered his parents.

The curse he made on that day was still etched in his mind. He had promised to slit the throat of whoever had killed his parents. His father had been murdered while in jail. He would never believe his mother had taken her own life as her death certificate implied. Never in a million years would he accept this. She had been murdered just as surely as his father had been.

He didn't leave flowers. He could not see the sense in it. It was more of a female thing to do. If he had been more like his twin brother, Raphael, he would have said some prayers. That was all Rafe ever seemed to do these days, say prayers and do good works.

But Gabriel was not like his brother. He did not have his generous outlook. He was not into forgiveness. He was more of a revenge sort of person. He always told himself that one day he would find out who was responsible. But many years had passed since they had both died and he was still no closer to finding out who had murdered them.

He stayed at the graveside a while longer. He looked at their head stones and remembered how much they had loved each other as well as their children. Gabe and Rafe had struggled on without them, but their sister, Sarina, had been given no such chance.

She had been taken and murdered, her body never found, so that she could not be buried with their parents. His heart remained saddened at all that had befallen his family.

The day was overcast and a slight drizzle of rain had fallen. It was time for him to leave. He strode over to his SUV. Two big, ridgeback dogs waited patiently for him. He gave them a pat and then left the cemetery.

He returned to his home which was partially hidden away from the rest of the world. He drove over a small bridge, turned left until he came to a group of trees that concealed the entrance into his home. A high fence kept out the rest of the world and kept his dogs inside. He locked his dogs in the yard then went inside the modest house. He phoned his brother, Raphael.

"Hi, it's me. Feel like having a beer?"

He heard his brother's voice. "Not today, Gabe. You know what today is, don't you?"

"Sure I do. That's why I thought we'd have a beer together," he replied.

"Have you forgotten that Matt and Mia are expecting us?"

"I hadn't forgotten. There's nothing to stop us having a beer together first."

"You'll be three quarters gone before we get there, Gabe. If you start now, there'll be no stopping you."

"You're a prick and a wowser, Rafe." He was waiting for his brother to start in on him.

"And you have no respect for anything or anyone, Gabe," his brother replied.

"Get stuffed, Rafe," Gabe answered as he ended the call.

That put paid to those plans—so much for brotherly love. He hung around playing with his dogs then went to his laptop and played a few games of solitaire. This filled in the time until the day drew to a close. Then he hopped back into his SUV and drove to his first stop. He banged on the front door. He didn't have long to wait until it opened.

"Hi," he said, as Annie Webster opened the door.

"Hi. Where have you been?" she asked, letting him in.

"Here and there, working, what about you?" he asked, looking her up and down. She always did things to him.

"I guess the same as you, working. What do you want?" she asked, returning his look. "You need a shave and a decent clean up."

"How about it?" he asked. "Then I'll take you out for a beer."

"I don't believe you. I don't see you for weeks then you turn up here and ask me 'how about it' and then you tell me you'll take me out. What sort of a person are you?" She didn't try to sound disgusted. She was disgusted. The things he did and said often disgusted her. She could never understand what she saw in him.

"Well, if it means that much to you, we'll have a beer first." He was already coming towards her. She knew if he touched her, she would fall for his crude attempts to get her into bed all over again.

"Just get out. You're nothing but a selfish, unfeeling slob. Just go. I can't stand the sight of you." She turned her back on him. She fully expected to feel his arms sneaking around her, with his hands cradling her breasts. She waited for him but all she heard was her front door slam shut.

Annie was left feeling bereft that he had actually gone. Usually it made no difference what she said to him. If he wanted her, he just took her and she was only too willing to let him.

He was used to the games that Annie played. They had this thing where she would pretend he was so far beneath her, and the next thing she would be in bed with him, loving every crude thing he did with her.

There was more than Annie in the world. First he stopped for a few beers then moved on to a restaurant where he bought himself a decent meal. He put in some time by walking along the river.

It was always peaceful beside the river. It reminded him of his parents. He listened to the lorikeets squawking in their hundreds in the trees that grew beside the river. He looked in amusement to see that many of the cars parked beneath were already dotted with their droppings.

He kept an eye on the time. When it was late enough he went to the club where she worked. He was always in two minds about Lizzie. He enjoyed watching her gyrate around the pole and discard most of her clothing as much as any man, but on the other hand he felt a modicum of shame seeing his cousin like this.

Bad, beautiful Lizzie—was what the management and patrons called her. She was certainly beautiful. The number of men who feasted on her was proof of this. If rumours were correct, then the bad part might also be true. Of course, this depended on your point of view. Had she not been his cousin, he might well have been tempted to find out for himself.

He gave up drinking beer and started on whisky. He watched as the procession of pretty girls did their thing to keep the patrons entertained. Lizzie danced several times. She was very definite a crowd favourite. Even he began to get stirred as he saw her remove the tiny piece of fabric that hardly covered her breasts.

He turned his back on her. Memories flooded back. They had all been children together, living through the bad times, trying to get through to the other side where life might be better.

The whisky did nothing to lift the depression that seeped into his mood. Next thing he knew, Lizzie had more clothes on and was sitting beside him.

"Want a drink?" he asked.

"Water," she replied. "I haven't finished yet, one more to go." She regarded him in silence for some moments before adding, "How's Rafe?"

"Still on his knees praying," he replied. "He couldn't even come and have a beer with me."

"Don't be so hard on him. We all had to learn to cope in our own way." She watched as he ordered another whisky.

"You don't look so happy. What's the matter?" she finally asked while he sat nursing his drink.

"Do you know what today is?" he said, not looking at her.

"Same as every other day, I suppose, another lovely day in paradise." She sipped her water, looking with disdain at all the hungry male faces who sat in the club.

"It's the day they were murdered," he said. "Anniversary some people call it, some anniversary, not something to celebrate."

"Oh, Gabe, I'm sorry. I forgot. I almost forgot about dad as well. Sometimes it seems like it was yesterday." He saw the few tears that she tried to hide.

"We're a sorry pair, Lizzie. We're a sorry, damn family if you ask me. Do you ever feel as though we're cursed?" he asked.

"Yeah, I do," she replied. "Take me for example. What sort of a person is I, doing this for a living?"

"I don't see anyone complaining," he smiled at her, seeing again the pretty, young girl she had been when they had lived together as children. "Why do you do it then if you don't like it?"

"Life isn't that simple, Gabe. Sometimes there are no other options." She got up then and left him. He wondered what she was talking about when she said there were no other options.

He watched and drank. Lizzie did another dance. There were whistles and cat calls. Most everyone was drunk. He had seen men who sold illegal drugs. He was tempted but knew he might jeopardise his job in the mines if he got caught. Keeping out of trouble was his primary focus. His uncles had made it very clear that they were sick of bailing him out when he struck trouble.

He would not be given any more chances. They had stopped access to his parent's inheritance. He had to stay clean and keep on the good side of the law.

It was also the thought of his dogs that kept him away from the drugs. What would happen to them if he did land up in jail? He knew Rafe would not be able to take care of them as he was at university most of the time. He didn't think he could afford to keep them in kennels if he did get caught and cop a sentence. Keeping them in the kennels while he worked away was expensive enough.

But none of that really mattered. His mission in life was to avenge his parent's death and he wasn't getting very far with that. Lizzie was wrapping it up. He watched her walk away to get changed. When she returned, she walked back over to him. He asked again if she wanted a drink. She again declined saying she still had more things to do. He wondered what other things she had to do. He hoped it wasn't what he thought it might be.

Lizzie then said goodnight and left. He watched her walk away expecting her to leave from the front entrance. As far as he knew there were only two entrances. It was one of the things he did. He always checked out the exits. He guessed it was a carryover from his childhood.

Lizzie met up with a man. He was tall with dark hair and eyes. He was also much older than his cousin. Lizzie looked at him with what Gabe thought was hate. Then this man took her by the arm and walked her out the back door. She didn't object. He guessed it was Lizzie's business if she liked older men and what she did with them.

Gabe had expected the alcohol to make him feel better, but nothing helped. He desperately needed a woman, but Annie had annoyed him so much. He was sick of her games. He didn't feel like seeking out Josephina's company. She was probably booked solid for the night.

There was nothing left for him but to go home to his dogs. As he left the club, he heard taunts being thrown at him behind his back. They sounded like the same taunts that he had endured all those years ago. At first he thought it was just the alcohol causing him to become delusional.

But he again heard the words. They were the same words he had heard so often in his childhood. *Sons of child killers* were the cruel words that had filled him with rage back then and were doing exactly the same now. He tried to control himself. They were only words. They couldn't really hurt him.

He kept walking towards his vehicle. He could still hear his uncle Mitchell warning him what would happen if he got into strife again. But the taunting words kept on coming.

"Stuff Mitchell Farraday," he spoke the words out loud as he turned to confront the two men who were deriding his parents. He recognized them from his school days. They were probably as drunk as he was. In his mind it was morally wrong that anyone should get away with saying such things about his mother and father, especially today of all days.

"You want a fight? Then you come and get me." Gabe, like his father before him, had a history of brawling. He too had spent nights in the cells over the years. He had been before the courts. So far he had avoided a jail sentence. He was well known to police. But what the hell, these two had asked for it.

The fight was quick and savage. He always carried a knife but never used it. Instead he used his fists and legs. As one of the men went down, he hammered him again in the knees with his boot. The second man was too slow. Before he got over the shock of his friend lying groaning on the ground, he too had been savagely thumped in the jaw and abdomen before a kick to his groin finished him off.

Gabe walked away. For the first time that day, he felt a little better. He wondered again what this said about him as a person. Violence was never a good way to settle a difference but sometimes it was the only way. It had also sobered him up.

He continued to walk towards his SUV. The lorikeets had departed. They had obviously enjoyed their evening. Whether they ate the berries on the trees or were into mating, he had no idea. He wouldn't mind a bit of mating himself now that he had sobered up.

But the night had moved on. There was no Annie or Josephina to subdue his masculine urges. There was nothing for it but to go home. He listened to the sounds of the river, felt the soft breezes against his now heated body. He thought of his parents and his sister, all dead, all gone. The deep pain within him was his loneliness.

He sometimes envied his brother and his strong beliefs. Rafe seemed to have an answer for all the bad that had happened. Gabe didn't have this ability to see deeper into his humanity. All he had was his physical strength, his rage and his desire for justice.

He had almost reached his SUV. It was parked some way from the marauding lorikeets. He never parked it under any trees. This saved him from having to wash his vehicle to remove any bird droppings.

He never heard any sound. On later review, he realised this was probably due to the remnants of his alcoholic binge that impeded his senses. Still, he was proud to have shut up the two men who were denigrating his parents. Today was a day for remembrance and reflection. He had done that in his own way. He remembered his mother and father and how much he had loved them both. He had put paid to those who had dishonoured them.

The punch to the back of his head came out of the blue. He had not been aware of footsteps, noises, breathing, anything. All he felt was the blow that knocked him to the ground and rendered him senseless.

When he awoke he had no idea how long he had been lying in the half-dark beside his vehicle. He was cold and slightly damp from the drizzling rain. His head was on fire. He could do nothing but lie on the damp ground. He stayed where he was, breathing deeply, trying to overcome the pain that was like a hammer belting into his skull.

He lay there as long as he could until he realised that the pain was not suddenly going to disappear. He wanted to get home, to lie in his lonely bed and sleep. He knew he was in no fit state to drive. He felt in his pocket for his phone. Then he experienced a dreadful thought that maybe it had been stolen. When his hand clamped around it, he breathed a sigh of relief. At least it was one small mercy in his favour.

He touched the screen waiting for his brother to answer.

"What do you want at this hour, Gabe?" His brother's voice was full of annoyance.

"Can you pick me up? I'm in some trouble," Gabe said, as he held onto his thumping head.

"When are you not?" Rafe replied.

"Look, just come and get me. I can't drive." He told his twin brother where he was. Then he closed his eyes and waited for him to arrive.

He must have dozed off for the next thing he knew Rafe was shining a torch on his face.

"What have you done this time?" he asked, helping Gabe to stand.

"I did nothing," he explained. "Someone king hit me as I was about to get into the SUV."

"I find that hard to believe, more like the other way around," Rafe replied.

"Look, save the lectures, and just drive me home. If you can't do that for me just get the hell out of here. I'll find my own way home."

"Just quit it. Of course I'll take you home. You smell like a brewery. You should lay off the booze." Rafe helped him stand then assisted him into his own vehicle.

"Yeah, there are a lot of things I should lay off. Maybe I will one day if ever I figure it out."

The brothers sat in silence as Rafe drove his brother home. They both knew what Gabe meant. It was an obsession with him. All he wanted in life was to find the person or people who had killed their parents. Unlike the rest of the Farraday family, Gabe would never accept the explanation of how his parents had died. He remained convinced that there had been a conspiracy.

Rafe dropped his brother off. The house was difficult to locate. Unless, you were shown, you could drive around for hours and never find it.

Rafe watched his brother walk to his front door. He heard the dogs barking and then his brother's voice speaking softly to them. Rafe pulled away as Gabe staggered through the door. Both brothers were left with their individual thoughts and opinions of each other. But whatever their differences, they were identical twins. They would always look out for each other in spite of the different and changing paths their lives had taken.

Rafe drove back to where he lived with his uncle and aunt, Matt and Mia. He worried about his brother whose life seemed to overflow with anger. He was grateful for the two dogs. At least they provided a modicum of comfort.

4

Grandfather was excited. Life was good. He was living the good life. As good as could be expected as long as Uncle Lucas remained in the back ground. If it wasn't for Uncle Lucas, both he and grandmother would be twice as well off. But he had to be honest, if it wasn't for Uncle Lucas, their enterprise would not have been nearly as successful.

Their beautiful granddaughter, Luce, had been the catalyst for their success. It was such a stroke of luck that Grandmother had taken the girl all those years ago. It had happened by accident. What had started out as an act of kindness had turned into a bonanza? What was the expression—*no good deed goes unpunished*? This did not apply to either Grandmother or himself.

Grandfather had gone to school to collect his granddaughter. He was annoyed when the school explained that the students had gone on an excursion. He wondered what type of excursions disabled children needed to go on. What did the teachers think they were doing? They could have an accident, get lost, anything. He would have something to say about this tomorrow. An accident was the worst thing he could think of.

If anything happened to her, life as they knew it would cease to exist. There was also Uncle Lucas to be considered. He had more plans for her. He guaranteed that their granddaughter would not only be the goose that laid the golden egg, but the egg would be encrusted with diamonds.

The teachers told grandfather that he could either pick his granddaughter up from the school or wait at the railway station for her. Grandfather was so annoyed that he decided he would go straight to the railway station. Otherwise he would have to wait longer. He wanted to get home as quickly as possible.

The train stopped. He watched as the group of students got off. They took their time. They were fumbling around and talking in their strange ways to each other. He watched the hand movements, watched as they pushed and appeared to laugh with each other.

Then he spotted her. There she was, as lovely as a summer's day. Sometimes grandfather thought his heart would give out just looking at her. She was so lovely.

She was about to jump off the carriage. She had her bag in her hand. What he saw next enraged him. How dare she? After all the education, the teaching, the lessons and the consequences, she continued to disobey him. Here she was doing it again. He watched as a young man took her bag from her hands as she got off the train. As he did so, she collided with him and he put his hands on her to steady her. She looked at him shyly. Then she smiled at him.

Grandfather was incensed. He strode along the platform intent on confronting her. More than anything, it was the smile that set him off. She knew the rules. She knew what would happen if she did not obey them.

The students were heading towards the waiting bus that would take them back to the school. Grandfather pushed himself through the students until he stood in front of her. She looked up and saw him. She knew immediately he had seen what had happened. In a panic, she looked towards the young man who had helped her, but he was already getting onto the bus.

Grandfather then spoke to the teacher who accompanied the students. Luce watched the teacher nod her head which indicated she was in her grandfather's care. Then her grandfather returned to her. He took her by the arm and together they walked towards the end of the station where there was an overpass that would take them to grandfather's car.

He began to berate her. He told her that her time couldn't come quick enough. She had disobeyed the rules again. As soon as Uncle

Lucas returned, he would tell him they were ready for the next stage. When she heard him say this, she knew she could not take anymore. She heard more noise behind her. She recognised the sound. There was another train coming. She glanced around while grandfather held onto her arm, squeezing and pinching it.

Squeezing and pinching did not bother her in the least. She was well used to it. It was the rest of the punishment that frightened her. She waited until they were near the end of the platform, then she dropped her bag. The threats continued.

As she bent down to pick it up, she kept an eye on the train. It was still travelling at speed. When she gauged it was about to pass them, she quickly stood up and gave Grandfather a sharp nudge.

All she saw was his rotund, fat body falling over the side of the platform and the train coming at speed. She pretended nothing had happened. She put her bag over her shoulder and strolled off. Luce didn't look back. The bloated, ugly, old toad was dispatched.

Luce Potulski felt giddy with happiness as she walked home. Even the ugly boots she wore over her ruined feet did not bother her. She knew the way home in spite of the fact that her grandparents never let her walk anywhere by herself. She was never left alone when she was outside their home.

It was a long walk through many streets but she did not care. She experienced such a feeling of freedom that she started to whistle, then to sing. It was so wonderful to be able to use her voice outside the house. She took her time. There was still Grandmother to contend with.

Luce had no idea what her grandmother would do when she found out that Grandfather was no longer with them. She imagined she would scream out and then start crying. Poor Grandmother— how sad it would be!

Luce finally made it home. She was not at all tired. The euphoria she experienced at knowing Grandfather was no more, remained. As usual, the door was locked. She banged loudly. It took some minutes before the door was answered. Like Grandfather, Grandmother had become very fat over the years and was flat out walking very far. Luce watched as her grandmother opened the door.

"Where's Grandfather? He was supposed to pick you up. You're late."

Luce shrugged her shoulders. "I don't know," she replied. "He wasn't there to meet me. I had to walk home. I think I'll go straight to my room. It was a long walk and I'm tired."

Luce left her grandmother at the front door. She knew the older lady was perplexed, wondering where her brother could be. Luce went straight to her room, closed the door and then picked up black devil.

"She'll soon find out. I wonder how long it will take before he's identified." Luce spoke to the black, teddy bear that had been with her for what seemed like all her life. She looked at it as if expecting it to talk back to her. "Never mind," she continued, "he won't be able to hurt either of us again."

The bear lay propped up on her bed. The sight of him sometimes upset her. She looked at the arm that had been ruthlessly chopped off with a scissors by Uncle Lucas. Of all the consequences she had endured over the years, this was about the worst. She couldn't remember where black devil had come from or even how he had got his name. All she knew was that he was her most prized possession and only friend in the world.

There had been many threats made against black devil which was part of the reason why she tried to keep the five rules. The other reasons were too painful to think about. She looked down at her feet. No wonder they were so sore after her long walk. Consequences, consequences—how often had she heard this word and how often had she suffered them?

She remained in her room quite happily. She would have loved to listen to music or watch television but this was another rule she had to follow. To fill in time she played solitaire, until she was summoned by Grandmother. There was never a knock. Grandmother always marched straight in to tell her it was time to prepare the dinner.

Her glee was even greater when her grandmother worriedly explained that Grandfather had still not arrived home. For the first time ever, she asked Luce a question.

"What on earth could have happened to Grandfather? Are you sure you didn't see him?"

"No," Luce replied solemnly. "Maybe his car broke down."

"You better hurry up all the same. He'll probably be starving by the time he gets home." Grandmother turned to go. Luce followed her.

The young woman did not mind preparing their meals as she was quite an accomplished cook. There was an array of ingredients to choose from. Luce didn't care what she cooked as long as the meals she prepared were loaded with lots of salt, fats and oils which were in good supply in the cupboard. She never cut the fat off anything. It was left on and loaded into any dish that she cooked.

She did not eat the same food as her grandparents. This was not allowed. Luce had a special diet which consisted of next to nothing. That was another rule she had to follow. She only ate what her grandparents allowed.

She looked at her skinny arms and lean body. She was so thin she looked more like a young child than a young woman, which was the whole point of Grandfather's plan. He and Uncle Lucas wanted her to remain looking wraith like, to be more like a child than an adult. They both said there was more money to be made this way.

Grandmother ate her meat and vegetable casserole while she fretted and wondered about Grandfather. She asked for a second helping which Luce served up. The salt shaker was on the table in front of her. Luce asked politely, "Would you like more salt on your dinner, Grandmother?"

Grandmother picked up the salt shaker and gave her second helping a generous sprinkle. Luce sat beside her as she ate her apple and slice of cheese. She then drank a glass of water. She kept her elation well hidden.

Grandfather had not returned by the next morning. Grandmother was so used to having him tell her what to do all the time, she was becoming lost. Luce told her that she would walk to school. This would be one less worry.

All day Luce wondered what was happening at home with her grandmother. She scarcely paid any attention to the lessons the teachers had prepared. For once she could not wait to get home. Not even the boots she wore could slow her down as she hurried home. Again the door was locked. Grandmother let her in as soon as she heard her knock. One look at her face assured Luce that the worries hadn't stopped.

"I don't know where he could be," Grandmother wailed. "I'm just so worried. I wish Uncle Lucas was here."

"I'm certain that Uncle Lucas said he would be overseas for several more weeks on his business trip. Maybe Grandfather is taking a short holiday. He'll be home soon." Luce sounded very sympathetic and encouraging.

Again, Luce cooked Grandmother's dinner which she again loaded up with as much salt and fat as possible. Grandmother gorged herself while Luce ate her apple and slice of cheese. Grandmother had a second helping, before helping herself to Grandfather's meal. She said there was little point in keeping Grandfather's dinner if he wasn't home to eat it. Grandmother was beginning to sound quite annoyed at Grandfather's disappearing act.

Luce remained in her room upstairs wondering if there would be a knock on the door informing them that her grandfather's body had been identified. She kept imagining him chopped up like the minced meat she sometimes cooked up, but so far so good. There had been no knock.

Luce listened carefully for any phone calls concerning her grandfather. Again there were none. She came downstairs to find her grandmother sitting in their best living room chair gasping for breath.

"What on earth's the matter, Grandmother?" Luce asked in genuine astonishment. The older lady looked very unwell as she breathed rapidly and clutched her chest. She had expected Grandmother to be crying and wailing while waiting for Grandfather. Instead, she was groaning in pain.

"I think I'm having a heart attack," the older lady gasped. "The pain in my arm and chest is dreadful. Please call an ambulance, Luce. I can't stand this pain."

"Of course, Grandmother, you sit quietly. I'll call them right away." Luce hurried to the phone in the kitchen area which she was never allowed to use. In fact, she didn't think she had ever been allowed to make a phone call in her whole life, not that she didn't know how.

She returned to grandmother and said, "I don't know how to phone an ambulance. If you just tell me what to do, I'll do my best. You know neither you nor Grandfather ever included phone calls in my happy bedroom education." Luce looked gravely at her grandmother, trying her best to at least look concerned.

Grandmother was struggling to breathe as she held onto her left shoulder. "Oh, the pain, Luce, the pain is so terrible." Grandmother seemed to have forgotten about the ambulance and the phone call.

Luce patted her hand and said, "Poor, dear Grandmother. What could be wrong with you?" Grandmother's face was now turning a bluish purple. Luce kept squeezing her hand, watching her chest movements. They were fascinating to watch. They would be fast. Then they would slow down. Grandmother started making gurgling sounds in her throat. Her eyes were bulging as she looked again at Luce.

Luce was tempted to throw her a kiss as a sign of goodbye but thought this would be really cruel. She thought of all the other things she would like to do to Grandmother, such as push needles up under her toe nails and cut into the soles of her feet with branding irons. As well as all the rest of it that was too disgusting to even think about.

So she sat with her grandmother and watched while Grandmother clutched at her chest until her breathing stopped all together. It was only then that Luce felt for a pulse. She knew how to count a pulse and find a heartbeat. It was amazing the things you were taught at school.

When she was absolutely certain that Grandmother had breathed her last, she raced upstairs to black devil. She kissed him and hugged him, then told him that at long last they were free. If they could escape before Uncle Lucas got back, she and black devil could live happily ever after. Oh, what joy awaited them both!

Black devil was given the privilege of seeing Grandmother lying slumped over in the household's most prestigious chair; the one that was reserved for the most important visitors. VIP's was how Grandmother referred to them. But she was quite dead now. There would be no more VIP's ever coming to visit Luce.

She then sat black devil opposite Grandmother so he could have a long, last look at their captor. Luce sat beside him, watching evil float away. Then the unimaginable happened. Grandmother let out an almighty sigh as air escaped from her mouth. Luce screamed and grabbed black devil. She then took off up the stairs with him and slammed her door shut. She thought she might even be having a heart attack the same as Grandmother as her heart was beating so fast.

Black devil stayed in her arms. When she felt less frightened she sat him back on the bed. Of course he fell over to the side because of his missing arm. She sat looking at him wishing he could speak.

It remained very quiet down stairs. There were no further noises to indicate grandmother was up and walking around. She left black devil on the bed as she stealthily crept back down the stairs.

There was Grandmother, still slumped over in their best chair with drool coming out of her mouth. It was clear that Grandmother was now properly dead. Luce turned her head, not sure if she could stand to look at her any longer.

But courage was required. There were some simple ways she had devised to help her get through the bad times. She always talked to black devil. So she started telling him about what had happened to Grandfather, not out loud, but in her mind.

You just never knew what Uncle Lucas got up to. He had all those tiny, listening devices and cameras. As far as she knew, he kept all his equipment upstairs in the happy bedroom, but you could never be too sure.

After much discussion, black devil agreed with her that she would pull Grandmother up the stairs and leave her in the happy bedroom. Her big concern was that she would not be strong enough to do this as she was so thin and scrawny.

But she had to try. This was their chance to escape. She had tried several times before but always Uncle Lucas or grandfather found her and then there were the terrible consequences to endure. But this time she would be smarter and wiser.

There were plenty of thick blankets in the house. One of them she placed on the floor in front of grandmother. Then she stood behind Grandmother and pushed her off the chair. When she heard the thump as the dead woman hit the floor, Luce almost apologised. She laughed at how foolish she was and proceeded to tell black devil what she had almost said.

It was very gruelling and tiring work. Grandmother had become so fat which in some ways was a good thing as Luce could roll her across the living room floor to the stairs. It was far easier to roll a rotund butter ball than a bag of bones. But once she reached the steps, her biggest problem occurred. How was she to push her up the stairs?

She tried several times but was not strong enough. Eventually, she tied the blanket around Grandmother with ropes that were kept in the happy bedroom. These kept Grandmother intact so she wouldn't fall out of the blanket.

Luce used a heavy kitchen chair to hold grandmother's body as she pushed and pulled. The house was old and at each step there was a small raised edge which was deep enough to prop the chair legs against which prevented Grandmother from sliding back down again.

She tied one end of another rope around Grandmother's hands. Before she could do this, she had to untie Grandmother to get her arms out which took more time. She tied the other end of the rope around the stair-case palings which also helped prevent the body from falling back down the stairs.

Luce kept at it all night. It took all her strength. She stopped at each step and went to the kitchen where she drank some milk and ate a slice of cheese. Black devil stayed on the top step to give her encouragement. Eventually, she had Grandmother at the top of the stairs. Now all she had to do was roll her into the happy bedroom.

Then she had to somehow get her onto the bed. She knew this would be almost impossible. She sat and thought about how she might manage this until she realised that she would never be able to get Grandmother onto the bed; not unless she had a crane like those she had seen on building sites.

This was a great pity because she thought maybe she could make Grandmother suffer some more the way she had. A heart attack seemed very trite compared to what she had put up with over the years. Luce shrugged her shoulders in defeat. She gazed again at black devil. Then she told him that if she couldn't get her onto the bed then she would just make a bed for her on the floor—and that would be that.

Luce was no friend of beds. She had no good memories of either her bed in the happy bedroom or her own bedroom. So she always slept on the floor with black devil.

She rolled Grandmother into the happy bedroom. The doorway proved difficult but she finally managed it. When she looked at the bed which she hated with every vestige of her being, she was again frustrated that Grandmother would never have the same experiences as she had endured.

So she made a bed for her grandmother on the floor. She used the red satin sheet on the bottom and the black satin sheet to cover Grandmother. Luce left her in the clothes she had died in and then she placed the little, red head-band with the dainty, little horns attached to it on Grandmother's greasy, grey hair. She looked around the room and was finally satisfied with her efforts.

"Your turn to be red Lucifer, Grandmother," Luce looked to black devil as she said this, but he gave no indication he understood. *Just as well he had been spared the happy bedroom*, Luce thought.

Then she had another idea. She went to the box that Grandmother kept in the happy bedroom. She took out the long, sharp needles and the little, branding irons that were in the shape of an 'L'. These she placed across Grandmother's chest as a mark of goodbye. Grandmother could go to the great here-after with all her tools of torture.

Luce then went to the air conditioning control and turned it down as low as possible. The control to the happy bedroom was the only control she turned on. The rest of the house she left alone. She knew it worked very well in the happy bedroom as Uncle Lucas always wanted his clients to be as comfortable as possible.

There was no end of times when she'd heard him say that they always got hot and bothered. She shivered as she thought of all the clients who had been in the happy bedroom.

Luce was so exhausted that she went straight to her own bedroom and fell immediately asleep on the floor with black devil curled up in her arms. She woke that afternoon still feeling totally exhilarated. She no longer had the trials and abuses of her grandparents hanging off her shoulders.

She did her usual routine of telling black devil of her plans. There was no time to waste. For once she thanked her Grandparents for having sent her to a school for the disabled which had large numbers of hearing-impaired students even though there was nothing wrong with her hearing or speech.

For while she had been at the school she had learned many things, not least the ability to lip read. So while her grandparents had been having their important discussions with Uncle Lucas, she had put her education to use.

The hidden safe was carefully concealed behind an erotic painting of little children that hung on the wall in the happy bedroom. She was certain she knew the combination which would open the safe. She just hoped she had remembered the correct sequence.

Luce's hands trembled as she attempted to open the safe. She remembered the words spoken on the lips of Grandfather. She was quite sure she had the numbers correct but was not certain when to turn the lock clockwise or anticlockwise.

Her frustration was rising as she tried again and again to open it. Black devil sat at the door to the happy bedroom slumped to the side. She went and sat beside him. There were times when she became so angry with black devil that she would throw him at the wall or pinch him the way her grandparents would pinch and squeeze her when they thought no one was looking.

It was totally unfair what she did. She picked him up and slammed him against the door. When she looked at his fallen body she was immediately ashamed of herself. He was her best friend, her only friend. She apologised. Then she picked him up and cuddled him. After that she felt more relaxed. She went back to the safe and tried again.

She remained calm as she remembered the movements of the lips. She turned the lock right, then left, then right and finally there was a rewarding click. She pulled the door open. Her elation was almost as joyous as when Grandmother had dispatched herself.

Very carefully, she inspected the contents of the safe. She had always suspected there would be cash inside. What she wasn't prepared for was the huge numbers of notes she found. She pulled them out and shoved them into a pillow case that she found in the happy bedroom. She made sure she didn't use either a red or a black pillow case. She would count the money later when she was back in her own room.

She looked back down at Grandmother who unfortunately looked quite comfortable on the red, satin sheet on the floor. Luce realised she was becoming cold, so she went to her own bedroom and put on a coat. Black devil didn't seem to mind the cold. He remained slumped over at the door looking at her.

Next she mentally prepared herself before she pulled out the DVDs. Knowing what they depicted made it difficult for her to even touch them. So she returned to the kitchen and pulled on a pair of latex gloves. That was another lesson she had to learn about being perfect. She had to look after her hands. It didn't matter about her feet. Her Grandparents never gave a toss about them.

She took out the whole collection of DVDs. How often had she heard Uncle Lucas say they were his prized possession? They frightened her. They were her worst nightmare. As quickly as she could, she pulled out the bag where Grandmother kept her costumes. She tipped the costumes on the floor then shoved the DVDs into the bag.

After this was done, she stopped to regain her strength. She went back downstairs where she ate another apple, a slice of cheese and a drink of milk. The worst of her preparation was almost complete. All that was left in the safe were papers. She didn't think these would be much use to her but thought she had better sort through them.

There were pages of names, addresses and amounts of cash. She had no interest in these. She had almost gone through all the papers when she pulled out an old envelope. There was no letter inside. She held the envelope under the light where she could see the stamp more clearly. It was quite an old stamp. Stamps were one of the things that the school she attended was keen on. The stamp club was very popular. The rest of the papers and documents were thrown in the bin.

She looked at the stamp and tried to read what was written on it. The post mark was indistinct. She tried to make out the letters from where it had been posted. She slowly read them out to black devil. She told him she could see an e, a, t, i, t, n, w, and another n. She wondered where this place could be. She wrote any number of variations using the vowels and consonants.

Eventually she came up with the word *Tewantin*.

She lay outside in the sun. These were some of her best moments while she was alone, when she could feel the warmth creep into her bones. Lizzie Smythe did not consider that she had many moments in her life that were as good as what she was experiencing now.

She didn't want to think about her mother, certain she knew what she would be doing right at this very moment. She would be either eating or sleeping. Her mother was good at both. The only thing she was better at was opening her legs up for Leon.

But it was no good Lizzie having a dim view of her mother when she was no better herself. What was she good for? She wasn't much good for anything. At least her mother seemed to be good at being happy in her own vague way.

Maybe she should be grateful to Leon Jones for his contributions to her mother's few pleasures in life. Isn't that what her mother often told her when Lizzie gave into her outbursts about Leon's influence upon her? She told her daughter time and time again, that Leon was the only person who contributed to her happiness.

The sun was very warm on her back, so she rolled over and pulled a hat over her face. She opened her arms out wide so she could get her ten minutes of sun on the underside of her arms. It was important she looked trim and have an overall tan. Sprays weren't that good especially if it was very hot. Leon was adamant she always look her best.

She thought again of Leon Jones. She guessed contribution was as good a word as any for sex.

Lizzie would be a whole lot more grateful if she didn't have to be subjected to the contributions she received from him. They did nothing for her happiness. He had been contributing to her for so long now. She could not even remember when his contributions had first started. She thought she had been a little girl.

Her only redeeming thought was that he only visited her once a month. As regular as clockwork, in he came for his once-a-month contribution to her. She didn't know why it was only once a month, not that she minded. She didn't think she could have stood it if it had been any more frequent. Maybe her mad mother had some mystical means of keeping him satisfied. Or for all she knew, he had a dozen more women to whom he contributed.

Her ten minutes on either side was up so she went to her room. During the daytime, she did lie on her bed but she never slept in it at night, never—too many bad memories. She spent the next few hours reading. She enjoyed reading. It was another of the great pleasures of her life. She enjoyed all types of books, had even been into the heavy stuff like Shakespeare and the classics. When she tired of reading, she played solitaire.

Playing solitaire required little concentration. It was during this time that she thought of all the people in her life who owed her. Her uncles owed her, especially Mitch. They had left her with her mad mother and Leon Jones. But as bad as her uncles were, her older sister, Hope, came a close second. Horrible Hope was how she thought of her. Hope had left her alone with her mother when they had been little girls. She had never come back to share her mother's madness and abuse.

Her brother, Harry, who had been a toddler when Lizzie had been left alone with her mother, never came home either. Her uncle and aunt had kept him and raised him.

Then there was Arlo who was as much to blame for Hope's desertion of her as anyone. She knew Hope and Arlo had been *doing it* since they were young teenagers. If he and Hope had not been so obsessed with each other, then Hope may have come home and the burden could have been shared.

She had heard them once *doing it* when she had been left at Uncle Mark's house one time. No doubt they thought she was just a stupid, little girl who knew nothing about these things. What they didn't know was that Leon had been *doing it* with her for years. Cousin Arlo was not much better than horrible Hope.

She liked Uncle Mark. He was a nice man who had always been gentle and kind. The unfortunate thing about him was that he didn't seem to know what went on under his eyes.

He spent all his time with his motor vehicles, motor bikes and push bikes. When he wasn't working, he watched every documentary ever made. He never seemed to figure out that his only child, Arlo, had been screwing her sister, Hope, for years.

Hope and Arlo were definitely on the list, but near the top was Raphael Farraday. He was about the worst of the lot. His desertion had devastated her. All those years and he hardly saw her, let alone speak to her.

Gabe was different. He always spoke to her, always had. She even thought he was a bit sweet on her especially when he watched her dance when she was almost naked. But that was really cheating. They all were a bit sweet on her then. But Rafe was another question altogether. She always imagined that she was just that little bit more special in his eyes.

When they had all been young living together, when her cousins, Sarina and Lucia had disappeared, Rafe was the one who would lie next to her on the floor. He used to look at her as if she was some delicate flower. But the delicate flower looks he gave her had long since disappeared.

Now all he did was pray. Isn't that what Gabe had told her? He was still on his knees, still at it. It was understandable when his parents had died, but that was so long ago. He should have been over it by now. Instead he went off to university and was said to study theology and philosophy of all things.

There were two things Lizzie vowed to do as soon as she could. One was to have sex with Arlo to spite Hope and the other was to screw Raphael's brains out to cure him of all his pious ways and his desertion of her. It was even rumoured that he kept away from girls—probably hadn't even done it yet.

Then she had another fearful thought—maybe he was the other way. But her instincts told her that this was not so. She remembered again back to their childhood when his hand rested on her back.

She even knew where she would do it with Rafe. It didn't matter at all where she did it with Arlo. Anywhere would do.

The idea came to her when the family did their annual visit to the cemetery. On a particular Sunday every year, they all got together and trudged around looking at family head stones and pretending to be upset and pray. Maybe that was an exaggeration. Most of the family were genuinely upset, but Lizzie never was. The dead were as much to blame for what she had endured for all these years as much as the living.

It was when they visited her infamous, maternal grandfather's grave that the thought came to her. His head stone was very stark, nothing much written on it except his name, Alan Farraday, with the date of his birth and death.

She thought it was very quaint when she overheard one of her uncles say that the words *secrets, sex, and lies* should have been carved under his name. She had found the absolutely best spot in the world for Raphael's punishment. Once he got a taste for it, she would leave him gasping for more.

There was no time like the present to get even. She would start with Arlo. She contacted the club where she worked most nights and asked if they would send Arlo Farraday free tickets. Men were always buying stuff like that for their mates. Free booze and a bit of erotica was sure to get any red-blooded male through the door. After that, it was up to her.

But first there was Leon to consider. He kept a sharp eye on her activities. It wasn't easy to get away from him. But he did disappear sometimes. Goodness knows where he went. He wasn't like Rafe, that's for sure. He wasn't off doing good deeds or on his knees praying.

Leon dropped her off as he always did. Sometimes he hung around, other times he disappeared. Bad, beautiful Lizzie was heralded with the usual enthusiasm. She kept an eye out for Arlo as she gyrated around her pole. Sure enough, her lure had worked. There he was sitting by himself looking sheepish and no horrible Hope to accompany him.

She sidled up beside him. Of course he was embarrassed to have his half-naked cousin being so up close and personal with him.

"If you don't like it, maybe you shouldn't have come," she said as she leaned into him. She could see he was as hot and bothered as most of the men and some of the women in the place were.

"I didn't know you worked here, Lizzie. I honestly didn't realise that it was you who was bad, beautiful Lizzie." Arlo moved away from her but she leaned back into him and started nuzzling his ear.

"How many did you think there were, Arlo?" She rubbed her bare thighs up against his. Hope was an attractive girl with the dark hair and eyes and the slim build of the Farradays and Smythes, but in the looks department, Lizzie took the prize. He seemed tongue tied as she started touching him.

"You want to come upstairs, Arlo? I've always fancied you." She had taken his hand and was rubbing it around her upper thighs. She saw his arousal. "I think you better come upstairs with me."

She took him by the hand and together they disappeared through the partially obscured door that led them up to an empty room on the next floor. Lizzie didn't have to do much after that. Poor Arlo never stood a chance under her tutored hands and mouth. It had become easier over the years for Lizzie. All she did was go away to her grey world and after that it was all rote. Leon had taught her well, just the way he liked it.

When she judged he was about to contribute to her, she groaned and moaned and started to shudder. He landed on top of her with heavy breathing and sweat pouring off his face.

She looked at him with half-open eyes and was surprised at the effort he had put into it. No wonder Hope kept him busy in his bedroom while she pretended to be studying in the next room. Poor Uncle Mark, pity he couldn't get a bit of the same. It might cure him of his documentaries.

"Oh, Arlo," she groaned and bit onto his ear lobe. "That was incredible. Could we do it again, just one more time and very quickly? I have to be on again in a few minutes. Oh Arlo, that was so good."

Arlo was overwhelmed by the whole experience. He had only ever done it with Hope. They had been lovers since their early teens. He immediately felt guilty which she knew he would. This was exactly what she had been planning. They didn't call her bad, beautiful Lizzie for nothing.

She took false pity on him. "It's Ok," she said, "maybe we can catch up again next week." She tenderly touched his face then kissed him gently on the lips. He moved off her as he hurried to get his clothes on again. *Just as well*, she thought. *Taking chances with Leon around was risky business.*

But she had set the scene. Arlo had experienced his first taste of her. She could now call the shots. But in future she would try to avoid any more encounters at the club. There was a big, wide world out there and lots of secret places where you could indulge in sex, if only she could escape from Leon. Poor Hope.

She had just returned downstairs when she saw Leon reappear. She had just made it. He hung around until it was time for him to take her home. She hopped in beside him. He had a thing about black, powerful vehicles.

"What were you doing upstairs?" he asked.

"What do you mean, what was I doing upstairs? I have to get showered. It's sometimes necessary, you know." She replied, her voice impatient and angry.

"It's not your time, Lizzie. Have you forgotten that I know all about you? I know your cycles. I know every time you pretend with me."

She didn't reply. Of course he knew all about her. He planned her life. "At least your mad mother doesn't pretend, Lizzie. I don't know why you have to. There must be something wrong with you."

She almost choked at this—something wrong with her. Was he stupid? Of course there was something wrong with her. Didn't he know anything? She had lost her soul years ago when he came to her in the middle of the night when she was only a child. And what did he do with her now? He shared her with his friend, Bart. Neither of them was like poor, inexperienced Arlo. They were evil men. She could smell it on them.

Leon was more than evil. He was cruel as well. She still had the long, thin, white scar along the outside of her left hand to prove it, as well as whatever damage he inflicted inside her. She didn't want to think about that or else she would have to return to her grey world.

They arrived home. She did not speak to him again. She knew there would be some punishment. He knew the endless sex didn't hurt her any longer. He followed her inside into her bedroom. Her mother never woke. She was too drugged out with all the stuff she took to make out she was sane.

At first, she thought he wanted her on the bed but instead he went to her precious collection of books.

"Which is your very favourite, Lizzie? Is it this one, or this one?" He tormented her as he picked up book after book.

She didn't understand what he was doing. "If you want to read any of them, just take one. Take whichever one you want."

"What is your very favourite book in the whole, wide world, beautiful Lizzie?" he asked. This time he sounded concerned, even genuine in his interest.

"My very favourite is *The Catcher in the Rye*," she replied, unsure of the direction of his questions.

"Tell me about it, Lizzie?"

'It's about adolescents, about how they identify themselves, about life, being alienated, sexuality, belonging, all that sort of thing."

"That's very interesting." He looked along the shelves until he found it. He took it down and opened up the pages, glancing through them.

He looked up at Lizzie. She was incredibly puzzled. Then he took the book and ripped it apart. The pages fell out all over the floor. One after the other, he pulled them apart and down they fell. Then he turned and left her.

She slid to the floor picking up her precious pages. They were torn and ripped apart. She could not believe her eyes. Of all the things he could have done to her, this was about the worst. She lay down on her blanket in the corner of her room. She decided then and there that it was time again to relinquish her coloured world. As she closed her eyes, all her images and thoughts returned to grey.

Rina Wright knew it would take some planning. She had to be certain that Jude would be safe. He had never been out of the house except for the short walks they took each afternoon. It would be a great shock to be confronted by the big, wide world. It would be a shock for her as well, as her view of the world was probably not much wider that Jude's.

Rina Wright intended leaving the house that she had shared with her mother. Her only regret was that she would no longer be able to see Mr and Mrs Baxter at the convenience store. But she had been both an invisible person and two different people for as long as she could remember. There would be no one to miss her.

Another thing that her mother had drilled into her head was that there were monsters out there that would be still looking for them. Now Rina had a better understanding of why these monsters might be looking for them. It was probably due to the million dollars she had found in the backpack.

Her memories were confused. She remembered very vaguely about monsters that had been present in her childhood. She looked again at her left hand. She was fairly certain that it was monsters that had taken her little finger.

Rina was not a confident person but she was pretty certain that no one ever remembered her. Her teachers always forgot her name. Her neighbours never spoke to her, so it was doubtful anyone would remember that she had lived in the house with her mother and Jude for so long. Only Mr and Mrs Baxter would have any memory of her.

Now the time had come when she would have to bolster her courage and gain more confidence.

Mother never returned. Rina had no idea what had happened to her. Mother did keep a disposable mobile phone which she very seldom used. She often told Rina that you just never knew when you might need to phone someone.

She had phoned several hospitals in the area where they lived and enquired if her mother had been admitted. No one had any record of Maria Wright. What was she to do? Mother had disappeared, gone off with her boyfriend. So Rina came to the decision that she would leave the place where they now lived and go someplace where the winters were not so cold.

She worried about Jude. Not that he ever got sick, but during the winter the house was very cold and there was little sun to be found in the area where he played during the day. Not that he played exactly, but he did look around at the trees and shrubs and listen to the birds. As his development was delayed, Rina reasoned that a warmer climate might help him.

Rina was uncertain where she would go but the little scrap of paper that Jude had pulled out of the backpack had given her an idea. She looked up the place called Tewantin on a map that she had kept from her school days. Mother never allowed them to have the internet at home. She had found the place on a map. It would be a long journey for both of them. She decided she would look at it as an adventure.

The question remained about how she would travel to Tewantin. For years she had watched the big planes fly over their home. She considered flying but when she looked at Jude, she decided against it. He would most probably be frightened, not that she could ever really tell. Truth to tell, she would be the one who would be frightened.

Another thing she had to consider was the memory of her mother's words. She had to always remain invisible and be wary of monsters. She would travel by bus. Another thing she worried about was identification. She was sure that she would have to produce documentation at some point during their journey.

Rina never knew how her mother had managed to enrol her into her school or her vocational training courses. When she looked through the papers her mother kept, she could find no birth certificates for either herself or Jude. She knew enough that most people had birth certificates, Medicare cards, passports or credit cards. Neither Rina nor Jude had any of these.

She had found some papers regarding her mother. Again it was very confusing. Mother had several birth certificates. One was in the name of Maria Wright and the other in the name of Maria Farraday. There was also another birth certificate for Geraldine Wright. This was just another puzzle in her confusing life. There were also several, old bank-books.

Rina did not take any of the documentation that was with the money as she could make little sense of it.

Plans had to be made. They were not in the habit of keeping much in the house. Over the years, they had collected very few personal items. There were their clothes, some books and small electrical items. Other than this, there was only the furniture and fittings that were in the house when they arrived.

Rina had no idea how the rent was paid. No one had come to toss them out since her mother's disappearance, so she guessed the rent was not a problem.

She would leave the house much as it had always been in case Mother came home. She packed up their clothes, as much as she could fit in the bag that she had purchased in a second-hand shop. She didn't want to be burdened with too much luggage as she would need her hands free to help Jude.

She had one pull-along bag, the black backpack which she would keep on her person at all times and another handbag with small items. That was about as much as she thought she could handle. She had heard that it was possible to buy a ticket at the bus terminal. This sounded simple enough.

Her biggest regret was that she would have to say goodbye to Mr and Mrs Baxter. They were as near to a family as any. In the end, she decided she would tell them that she was going for a holiday up north. She said goodbye and that she would see them in a few weeks. Neither of them saw the tears in her eyes as she walked out of the shop.

The time had arrived for their big adventure. She used the disposable mobile phone to call a taxi. This in itself was an adventure because she could never remember having been in a taxi. The driver offered to put the backpack into the boot, but Rina declined. She looked at the house that had been her home for so long. It was a house of confused memories. She shut her eyes and hoped for the best as they drove away.

Purchasing the bus ticket was relatively simple. Very soon, they were on their way. She said goodbye to Sydney. The backpack was kept in the seat between herself and Jude.

Jude sat by the window. He stared out for hours at a time. Rina dozed but would wake with a start, feeling for the backpack and making sure Jude remained in his seat. They got out several times for meals. Jude did not appear frightened. Rina gave him sandwiches which she cut up into small pieces. As usual he was very slow to eat. So she had no option but to keep some of the sandwiches and pull them apart and give them to him as they drove along.

As they travelled north, she noticed that the weather became warmer. There were several stops at resort towns. Finally, the driver announced that they had arrived in Tewantin.

This was the part that Rina had not planned for. She had no idea what they would do once they got there. Here she was at last, with just one bag, a backpack with a million dollars in it, a handbag and Jude.

The next part of her life was about to commence.

There was a café close to where the bus stopped. Thankfully Jude was content to follow behind her. For once she was pleased that he was different. He didn't run off or play up on her. He didn't make a sound. They sat outside on the footpath looking at the town they would call home. She had no idea where she would stay for the night.

Gathering her courage, she asked the lady in the cafe where she might find accommodation for the night. The lady told her there was a tourist information centre at the other end of the street. Rina set out with her luggage and Jude in tow. Before she reached the information centre, she came to a hotel that offered accommodation.

Before she lost her confidence, she went inside where she booked several days accommodation. When she was in the room, she told herself to keep viewing the journey as an adventure even though she was racked with nerves. But she had survived this far. Now all she had to do was find a permanent safe place for them to live, some place where they would not be noticed, where they could continue to live as invisible people.

So far she had spent only a fraction of the one million dollars. She had a sudden thought that if her mother did return and find the money was gone, she was sure to be very, very angry. This was another reason why she had to remain hidden.

As well as the monsters that Mother had warned her about, there was also the chance that her mother might also turn into a monster. The anger that Mother sometimes displayed was monstrous in itself. Rina did not want to be subject to any more black rages.

The next day, she went in search of permanent accommodation. She was asked for references but she said she had none as her mother had recently died. Jude stood silently beside her, not saying a word and looking into space. The agent then told her he had several places for rent.

Looking at Rina, he was certain that she was on the poorer side of life. The boy with her looked as though there was something wrong with him. He didn't have to ask if she was a single mother. He had also noticed that she had a finger missing and that she looked nervous.

He showed her several places he thought might be suitable. Rina knew immediately which place she wanted. The house was situated back from the street and behind another house. It was almost impossible to see. It was small with a closed-in yard and close to a park and a small shopping centre.

While she checked out houses, she left Jude locked in the room at the hotel. When she returned, he was missing. Rina rushed down the stairs searching for him. Her heart was thumping in her chest as she combed the surrounding areas. She spotted him almost immediately, sitting under a tree not far from the hotel.

A man sat beside him. As Rina watched with fear in her heart, she realised the man was eating fish and chips and offering some to Jude.

"Jude, it's time to come inside." Rina was shaking in fear at the thought of Jude being at the mercy of some unknown man. She looked at the man. He looked rough with black hair and eyes.

"I hope you don't mind, but he seemed hungry. It was nice having some company." The man smiled at Jude as he spoke.

"Thank you," Rina replied. "But we really have to go. Come on Jude." Jude stood up to leave but before he joined Rina he looked back at Gabriel Farraday who waved to the boy. Jude lifted his hand in a return wave. Rina was astounded to see this happen.

The next thing she did was to collect her bag from the hotel. She then ordered a taxi which took them to the furnished house she had rented.

She had done it. She had a place to call home, a roof over her head and a haven of safety. She was so excited that she immediately took Jude for a walk through a bush track until she came to the park which contained playground equipment and dirt hills. Boys were riding bikes and skate boards. Rina was so excited. She walked around the park until she came to a sign that said Sundial Park. She felt safe at last.

7

Luce Potulski was almost ready to disappear. She had spent several days cleaning every spot in the rooms she had been allowed into. There would be no evidence of her left behind—just in case. She knew about finger prints. When she wasn't cleaning, she watched police dramas.

So she cleaned and wiped until her arms felt as though they might drop off. She also knew about hairs. The programs she watched taught her that a hair root was required for identification. So she swept and vacuumed again and again. Extra care was given to all those places she saw on television, like sink drains and doorways.

One thing she was grateful to her grandparents for, was that she had only ever been allowed in specific rooms. Her bedroom, the happy bedroom, the living room, the kitchen and the bathrooms were the only places she had been in.

There was no need to touch the rest of the house which would contain fingerprints belonging to her grandparents, Uncle Lucas and the VIP's. Well, too bad for them.

So far, her grandmother looked very intact and cold. She didn't smell although there were some fluids seeping out of her. Luce kept the door firmly shut. The air conditioning was blaring away at full bore. The room was almost freezing.

If her grandparents had a large enough refrigerator or freezer, Luce would have put Grandmother there. But she was too fat, so the happy bedroom would have to do.

Luce threw away all her clothes except three changes of the dullest grey or brown that she could find. Her costumes had already been disposed of. There would be no more red or black Lucifer costumes for her. She never wanted to see these ever again. She rolled up her spare loose, long-sleeved tops and long pants so that they would fit snugly in the bag she intended taking with her. Other than the bag with the cursed DVDs and the bag with the money, there was nothing else she would be taking from her old life.

Except for black devil, of course, but he could be squashed up in her shoulder bag. She marvelled at how tough black devil was. He had been through about as much as she had. No matter how many times she threw him at the wall, all he did was keep looking at her until she apologised.

Her regret was that she was not going to be able to say goodbye to the friends she had at school. She phoned the school and pretended she was Grandmother. She was quite clever at imitating other people's voices. Maybe it was because she had pretended to be deaf and dumb for so long.

She told the school authorities that she and Grandfather were taking Luce up north where the climate was warmer. Grandfather was getting on in years and wanted to live where the weather would be kinder on his old bones.

So that was that. Luce was ready to go. It was goodbye to Grandfather who was probably still in pieces in the morgue, waiting for someone to claim him. It was goodbye to Grandmother, may she rest in freezing torment for the rest of her life. It was goodbye to Uncle Lucas. May he have needles and branding irons shoved into every orifice of his body for as long as he lived.

Luce was on her way. When it suited her, she pretended to be deaf and dumb but when necessary she used her voice. The bus was on its way. She looked at the tall buildings, the cars and the people. She sat back in her seat and tried to keep the elation she was feeling from bursting out of her. Her next stop would be this place called Tewantin.

It really didn't matter where she went, just as long as it was far away from Sydney and from Uncle Lucas's wicked tentacles. He was never going to get the chance to take her to the next stage. What-ever that was. One thing she knew was that she would never have to find out now.

Luce was exhausted by the time she arrived. She held her bags close to her. It wouldn't do for any of them to be out of her possession. Now that she had reached Tewantin, she was at a loss to know what to do.

The bag with the DVDs worried her the most. She didn't know what she would do if it was ever lost or stolen. At the very least, she was sure she would be jailed. She didn't know much about the world, but she knew enough that what was on those DVDs was very wrong and illegal.

As she sat drinking a cup of milk and eating an apple at a small café close to where the bus dropped her off, she realised she knew next to nothing about herself except for the horrible years spent with her grandparents.

They had told her very little about herself. She didn't know where she was born or how old she was. She was sure that her name wasn't Luce Potulski. She knew very little about her grandparents other that than they had both been evil. She doubted that their name was Potulski. She had once heard Uncle Lucas calling her grandparents by different names.

She dearly wanted to discuss her situation with black devil. But knew she would look foolish if she did. She looked strange enough as it was without talking to a black bear. She had cut her hair short and dressed in a baggy, grey hoodie and track pants. Her black boots kept her feet covered and protected.

As she watched the various people drinking coffee and eating cakes, she made another discovery. She had never eaten cake in her whole life, nor had she ever had a cup of coffee. It was one of the things she would have to do now that she had her new life.

But then she remembered the five rules. They were deeply entrenched in her subconscious. She would never be game enough to break any of them, except maybe the one about talking. She had broken it plenty of times since her escape.

Some of the people were beginning to stare at her as she had sat there for so long. So she got up and began walking up and down the street, looking at the shops and the various items that were for sale. She walked up and down, first one side then the other, until the shops began to close and the sun was disappearing.

What was she to do next? She had no idea. She looked at the buildings around her. There was nowhere for her to stay. It wasn't the money. She had plenty of that. She had walked past a hotel, but there were so many men there. They were drinking and gambling. This frightened her. They reminded her of Uncle Lucas and his VIP friends. Not that she thought they were the same type of people. There could not be other people in the world like her grandparents and uncle.

She had to be certain that she was safe. She hadn't done the things she had done and travelled as far as she had to fall into the same traps she had escaped from. A lot of the people she had seen as she had walked past the hotel magnified the memories of her grandfather and Uncle Lucas.

Some were old, fat men who were bloated up like toads or else they were slimy looking. She felt a shiver go through her. She would never go through that again. She would rather sleep on the street or under a bridge than be subject to evil people.

She was beginning to feel sorry for herself. She had a fortune in the bag that hung over her shoulder. But what good was it when she was too frightened to make use of it? She felt in her shoulder bag for black devil. Momentarily she became angry with him.

Why the hell didn't he talk to her, tell her what to do, tell her how to be safe? Instead, black devil stayed in her shoulder bag and did not say a word. Had she more time, she would have thrown him into the gardens that she walked past on her useless trip up and down the main street of Tewantin.

The night was closing in quickly. Luce realised she could not keep walking up and down the street so she kept right on walking west. She rationalised she must come to a park or someplace where she might be able to hide out for the night. If she could survive nights in the happy bedroom, she must surely be able to survive a night out in the open.

She walked past a school which was well lit. She could see cars parked close by and lights on in some of the buildings. It would not do to sleep there although the chances of finding a quiet bench were good. She kept walking, slowly taking her time. Eventually, she came to a cemetery.

Cemeteries didn't frighten her. Luce thought they were exactly what they were supposed to be—places of rest. She wondered again how her grandparents were resting. Not peacefully, she hoped.

Not wanting to be noticed, she quickly walked into the cemetery while there was a lull in the traffic. Her bags were becoming heavy so it was a relief to sit behind a head stone that was so large it would block any one from seeing her if they happened to walk the same footpath she had left.

She was very tired and hungry, not that she felt hungry very often. She was so used to keeping the five rules that not eating did not worry her too much. It was just when her strength began to ebb that she knew she had to eat. She pulled out two apples and a packet of processed cheese that she had bought at a small shop on her bus trip from Sydney.

As usual, black devil did not reply when she asked if he was hungry. She pulled him out of her bag. He came out looking squashed up as he was a big bear. To get him into her shoulder bag, she had to push him down until he was bent out of shape. It was a tight squeeze keeping him in her bag. Of course he slumped over as he leaned up beside her. He didn't seem to mind the head stone.

The night became quite cold as she lay on top of a grave which was at least smooth. It was better than the grass as it did not prickle her. She could have sheltered in the small open shed, but it was obvious from the road where she would easily be seen.

As the night cooled down further, Luce opened up her bag and took out her two extra sets of clothes and pulled them on. She laid her head on black devil and went to sleep. She had bought a piece of rope with her that she had removed from the happy bedroom which she used to tie the other two bags to her wrist.

She got the idea to do this from when she had tied grandmother's wrist to the palings on the step railings. She felt quite safe as she had all her worldly possessions within her reach.

Voices woke her. It was deep into the night. Voices and footsteps were quite close to where she lay. She could not imagine who would want to walk around a cemetery at night. She pulled herself up into a sitting position and sat quietly.

She grabbed black devil and shoved him into her shoulder bag. The other two bags remained tied to her wrist. If she had to run for it, they would prove awkward. But she could not lose either of them.

The voices came closer. Luce was frightened. They were male voices. They were not old and high pitched like grandfather but were younger. There was so much vile swearing. This did not bother Luce as she had experienced every awful word in the English language while she had been kept in the happy bedroom.

They had made her use some of these words herself. But they were only words and could not physically hurt her. They may hurt her in other ways, but it wouldn't be the same as having needles shoved up under her toenails or branding irons on the soles of her feet.

Torch light was being flung around. She saw glimpses of light on the head stones close to her. She could hear the voices reading out the names on the head stones. The voices were getting closer. There was no doubt that she would soon be seen.

Luce had to make a decision. She could stay and brazen it out with whoever was roaming the cemetery or she could make a run for it. After a few moments consideration, she knew there was only one option. Never again would she allow herself to be at the mercy of anyone. She would rather be dead.

She pulled on the handles of the two bags attached to her wrists, slung her bag up over her shoulder and ran for her life towards the footpath she had left before she had sought shelter in the cemetery.

The men who had been swearing and shining their torch around were as startled as she had been. She could not run very fast due to her fragility and the uneven load she pulled behind her.

She could hear them calling out. Their footsteps were gaining on her. She was getting closer to the main footpath. It crossed her mind that if she got rid of one of her bags, it would improve her chances of escape. The bags were hindering her speed. But the question remained in her mind, which bag would she choose? Would she give up the money, the DVDs or black devil? She knew she could never give up any of them.

She kept running as fast as she could. But one of the men caught her. His hands grabbed her arms. She swirled around and tried to kick him but he was too big and strong. Two other men looked on.

"What are you up to?" The voice was gruff and fuelled with alcohol.

Luce could not reply because she was so terrified. The man started pulling at the bag on her shoulder. She started to scream. Another man who was trying to grab her pushed her over. As she landed in loose grave, she heard a vehicle pull up not far from where she had landed. The scream of brakes broke through the night.

Then there was a fourth man coming towards them. He was running in her direction. She knew her chances of escape were next to nil.

As she lay on the ground, she tried to roll out of the first man's way. She felt her shoulder bag being kicked into her from the boot of one of the men. Black devil came to her rescue and took the brunt of this battering. She was tangled up in the bags she had tied to her wrist.

The man from the vehicle arrived. She saw his dark shape quickly approach. The second and third men were standing back watching the first man try to pull her bags away from her.

The man from the vehicle began cursing as he spun the first man around and belted him hard across the face and then his stomach. As the first man backed away, he was hit again. The other two men began to move away. The first man was now on the ground nursing his injuries while the new man began shouting at her.

"Get into the vehicle—hurry."

Luce was winded but knew she had to move if she was going to escape. She pulled the two bags which were still tied to her wrist into her grasp, then grabbed the shoulder bag and managed to stand. The new man had pulled the first man up off the ground and was again thumping into him.

Luce struggled to stand. When she found her balance, she started running again towards the footpath. She saw the vehicle the fourth man had spoken about. She was uncertain what to do. Did she get in this vehicle with some unknown man or did she take her chances and keep running? She decided she would keep running.

Running was very awkward with her three layers of clothes and her boots. She was almost at the footpath when the bag which contained the money became caught on the brick fence that circled the cemetery. This slowed her down. Then she heard more footsteps behind her.

"I said hurry up. Get in the bloody vehicle or else these louts will have you." Luce looked towards the voice. She expected to be in further trouble. The bag was well and truly caught. Luce watched in dismay as he reefed the bag off the fence, picked her up, then grabbed the three bags, opened the back door of his SUV and threw the lot inside.

The back seat was soft enough but there was a strong smell attached to it. She was unsure what the odour was. It reminded her of animals. She lay panting and frightened as the vehicle sped away from the cemetery. The driver initially said very little as he was intent on getting off the main road.

"Tell me where you live and I'll take you home?"

Luce didn't know what to say to this as she had no home to go to. She could make something up but had no idea where to direct him. Instead she just groaned as she felt pain in her back as she rolled forwards towards the voice of the driver.

"What, don't you speak English?" the man asked as she didn't reply. This gave her an idea. Maybe she would pretend she was deaf then she wouldn't have so many questions to answer.

She kept groaning. If she kept it up he might get sick of her and let her out again. She lay across the seat still tangled in the rope that held her bags.

"Shit," she heard him say. "What's the matter with you? Are you looking for trouble?"

How could she reply to this? Trouble seemed to be her middle name. Her rush for freedom was not working out as smoothly as she would have liked. So she kept on groaning and trying to sit up. Eventually, she untangled herself and managed to sit upright. Her back still hurt.

He said no more until he pulled up. It was very dark with little street lighting. Next thing she knew, he was out of the vehicle and had opened the back door. She looked at him, too frightened to move.

"Are you getting out or do I have to lift you out?"

Luce began shaking her head. There was some faint illumination from the cabin light. She commenced signing. Auslan was almost as natural to her as English. She used her hands and fingers. Initially, she indicated that she wanted to be left alone, just in case he did know Auslan which was very unlikely. When she saw the astonishment on his face and heard him again say "Shit", she knew he had no idea what she was trying to tell him.

She was totally unprepared for his next action. He hauled her out of the back seat with her bags dangling after her. He carried her up some stairs and then dumped her on an old, dilapidated two-seater. Her back and rib cage were again painful. She could not stop herself from groaning.

"What on earth did you think you were doing roaming around a cemetery in the middle of the night? You're just a scrawny kid. Where are your parents? And what's with these bags you've got dangling around your arm?" The man directed his anger at her.

If she had been game she would have told him where to go, but common sense kicked in. She was literally at his mercy. So far, he had done nothing more than haul her around and swear at her. She started signing furiously again.

"Stop," he said, "I don't have any idea what you're trying to tell me. I get it that you're deaf. But it still doesn't explain what you're doing out alone at night. Are you homeless? Is that it?"

She stopped signing and looked at his lips. If he could get the hint that she could lip read, she might be able to fend him off. She stared at his lips then pointed to them. "You want me to slow down and speak. You lip read, is that it?"

She nodded her head. "You mean you lip read or you're homeless or both?" he asked.

Luce kept nodding her head.

"That's too bad," he was regarding her intently. "Have you got bad parents? Is that why you're homeless?" He made sure he spoke slowly and pronounced his words evenly.

She nodded her head again. If she could, she would have told him that her parents were non-existent. As far as she knew, she had never had any parents. All she ever had were her evil grandparents and wicked Uncle Lucas.

"Well, I don't know about you, but I'm knackered, so I'm going to bed. You can either sleep here or inside where there's a spare bed. Take your pick." He unlocked his front door, and gestured for her to enter.

She shook her head and pointed to the two seater chair. "Suit youself," he said, as he turned and left her.

There were a few noises coming from inside. She waited until it was quiet, then she lay down on the hard floor boards of the front veranda. She had no love of sleeping on beds or soft chairs. Luce looked up at the stars and wondered what her life was now coming to.

She must have fallen asleep because the next thing she knew was that he was standing over her. Again fear ripped through her. There was more swearing before he threw a thick blanket over her. Then he disappeared again inside.

She was determined to stay awake. Her most precious possessions were in jeopardy. He must be wondering why she had two bags tied to her wrist. She listened until she was certain that she heard steady breathing. Then she crawled out from under the blanket and went back down the stairs.

There were few benefits from being so thin but one was that she could fit into small spaces. Before she lost the little courage she had left, she took her two bags and crawled as far as she could under the house and left these bags behind one of the posts that supported the house.

She was filthy. Her body still ached from her encounter with the men at the cemetery and from being thrown into the back seat of the SUV. If she had more sense she would flee again but she was too exhausted. She lay down again on the floor and pulled the blanket up around her bony shoulders.

The cold had seeped into her bones. The blanket had slipped down below her shoulders. She opened her eyes and almost screamed. It was all she could do to stop the horror erupting from her. Her mouth opened and shut. Her life was getting worse. She was staring at two great monsters. She thought they must be wolves or lions. They were enormous like some fearsome giants of the jungle.

She scrambled back towards the railing. Had she enough strength she would have vaulted over it and ran for her life. The man was standing beside the two beasts—the three of them staring at her. She stared back. She didn't have to worry about words. She was so alarmed she didn't think she would have been able to speak even had she wanted to. Any words she might have had would have stuck in her throat. She started signing right away.

He put his hand up in the air and said, "Stop, enough of that. Watch my lips," he spoke slowly. She nodded her head as if in understanding.

"Say hello to James and Boag. These are my boys. They won't hurt you." Then he muttered under his breath. "At least I hope not."

She didn't know what she was supposed to make of that. Did he mean they might attack her or worse, eat her? She nodded her head in greeting at the two, massive dogs that stared menacingly at her. "Pat them, its best you get to know them slowly."

She couldn't help herself. She started signing again. "Why do I want to get to know them?" But he was shaking his head at her again.

"No, just point or make some gestures that I can understand. No more of these hand signals. You'll frighten the dogs."

She didn't think there would be anything on earth that could frighten them. So she pointed to herself and then to the dogs.

"Yeah, that's right, you say hello to them." He seemed adamant she make some contact with them.

Her nerves were frayed but she slowly moved towards the giants. She shut her eyes as she put her hand out to touch one on the head, half expecting her hand to be bitten off, but nothing happened. She rubbed her hand into its coat. It didn't feel so bad with her eyes shut. She opened her eyes and then touched the next one. Neither of them did anything but look her in the eye.

Then she thought of her evil grandparents and Uncle Lucas. No one or thing could be as frightening as they had been. She bolstered her courage and patted them again. It was much easier the second time around.

He sat on the stairs and watched her become more acquainted with his boys. The dogs seemed to be responding to her. They didn't bark or growl which had to mean something. Unless they were just being cunning, sucking her in before grabbing her by the throat or something equally as terrifying. But they didn't seem to mind when she touched and patted them again.

"That's good. You're making progress. How about we have some breakfast and we can get to the next part? That's if you're interested, of course?"

He walked inside the house. The dogs followed him. She didn't know what to do. She should run for her life, but her precious bags were shoved under the house. She picked up her shoulder bag which kept black devil hidden and followed him into the house.

It was very stark with little furniture. The dogs went straight to the back door and lay there quietly. "You want something to eat?" he asked.

She shook her head. He shrugged his shoulders and said, "Suit yourself."

There were several wooden chairs around a small table. She sat down as she watched him pull packets out of a cupboard and milk out of the refrigerator. He placed half a dozen weetbix into a bowl and covered them with milk. Her eyes almost popped as he started shovelling them into his mouth. He looked at her again and then gestured to the weetbix packet. She again shook her head.

"If you don't eat something, you'll be a scrawny kid all your life." He kept munching. "Those men who were after you, did you know them?"

She shook her head. "You were lucky I came along when I did. A pretty, young boy like you, Goodness knows what they might have done to you."

She gulped at this and avoided his eyes. Then she realised it was probably for the best that he thought she was a pretty, young boy, as long as he himself didn't like pretty, young boys. After her experiences in the happy bedroom, it was hard enough being a pretty, young girl. God help her had she been a boy.

When he finished his weetbix, he started on toast and vegemite. Her stomach was telling her it was time to eat, so she opened her bag. There was nothing for it but to pull out black devil. The man's eyes stared in amazement at poor black devil. He was again scrunched up. The man just shook his head.

Her supply of apples was diminishing. She pulled one out of her bag as well as her packet of cheese. She started eating. He again shook his head.

"Doesn't look like you'll eat me out of house and home," he commented.

She pointed to the milk bottle. "Sure" he said, "go ahead." She went to the sink and took the cleanest glass she could find and poured herself a glass of milk. He watched as she drank it down. "That's it. Is that all you eat?"

She nodded. Then she washed and dried her glass. She put the milk back in the refrigerator. She picked up black devil and held him while she watched the man.

"If you like you can stay here, on one condition." She looked at him enquiringly. "You look after the dogs when I'm gone. Do you think you could do that?"

This confused her. She had seen a biro at the window sill near the sink, so she picked it up and wrote on the weetbix packet, "Gone where?"

He read what she had written. "Work—I work in the mines. Fly in and fly out. Two weeks on and one week off, that means you would have to look after the dogs for two weeks by yourself. If that suits you, and you don't have a home to go to, then we'll call it a deal. I can't pay you much, but I'll give you what I can. By the way, how old are you? I don't want to be getting into any more trouble for having underage, homeless boys living with me."

How old was underage? She was about to write the first thing that came into her head that she imagined was legal. Sixteen was the number she intended writing on the weetbix packet.

Before she had a chance to write anything, he said, "No, it doesn't matter. I really don't want to know. You look about twelve. If you decide to shoot through, you better let me know so I can get someone to look after the dogs. I'll get you a disposable mobile. If anything happens and you decide to shoot through, I'll want to know. To be on the safe side, I'll phone your mobile each morning. If you don't answer it, I'll know you're gone. But if you are here, you tap on the phone three times. If something bad is happening, say one of the dogs gets sick, you tap six times. You got that."

Luce nodded her head furiously. All her dreams were coming true. She was beginning to get excited. If he was gone most of the time, then she would have a roof over her head. Surely she could learn about dogs and put up with him for one week out of three. Maybe her life was turning around after all.

He didn't frighten her nearly as much now that she knew a little about him. The only things he seemed to care about were his dogs. The dogs would be her next challenge. She thought of Uncle Lucas and knew that a couple of monster beasts could not come close to him.

Lizzie Smythe always had numerous worries. Not least was her mother. There was no doubt that her mother was quite mad, just as Leon Jones always said. She was probably as big a psychopath as he was. Lizzie knew a little about these conditions. She was an avid reader and made it her business to learn about such things.

Had her life been different, she may have been a psychologist or a psychiatrist or a doctor of some kind like her aunt Zaylee. But her life wasn't different and wasn't likely to become different.

Mad her mother may be. Mad Maryanne was what Leon called her. But she was her mother after all, and she did feel responsible for her. No one else cared about her in spite of Leon's pretence of looking after her. Spending as much time as he wished between her legs didn't really count as being looked after.

Her sister Hope certainly never took any interest in Maryanne. Her only interest was the time she spent with Arlo between her legs. Lizzie did what she could for her mother. She bought her clothes— nice clothes that were practical and reasonably fashionable. Her mother had become quite fat so that Lizzie had to buy from the big women's section.

Not that her mother ever went anywhere. Lizzie took her for an occasional drive in her mother's car. But she seldom went far because good old Leon took notice of everything. Maryanne could care less if she never went anywhere as long as she received Leon's regular contributions.

He always knew what mileage was on the car. That was how he gauged what Lizzie got up to. She did her best not to anger him.

He always threatened that he would have no hesitation in harming her mother.

Lizzie often looked at the scar on the outside of her left hand. She was certain he would keep his word. She had read often enough that psychopaths could inflict pain without the slightest hesitation. She also knew that they were usually very clever people.

Her mother was clever. She had no doubt of that as she had been fooling the mental health people for years. She had fooled her brothers as well. They all said she was progressing well as long as she took her pills. As far as Lizzie was concerned that was the biggest joke of all—progressing well. Her mother progressed all right, but only into the labyrinth of Leon's brutal schemes.

She recalled when she was a little girl she used to sneak into the granny flat where Leon lived. There was a loose plank on the floor boards where she could slip through. She could then check on Leon and learn his secrets. It was tit for tat as there were plenty of times when she had caught him looking through her mother's house. He kept a box in his drawer where he had all sorts of papers and documents. But one day her mother had spotted her jumping out the window of his bedroom.

Did her mother keep her secret, of course not? The first chance she got she blabbed to Leon. Then the two of them had a very important discussion. Her mother loved to have important discussions with Leon. She called them very important business meetings. As far as Lizzie could tell, the only meetings were cups of tea and more food and then into the bedroom for her morning's entertainment.

Her mother was very proud that she was included in Leon's important business plans. Her contribution was to agree with everything he said.

When he suggested Lizzie be punished, and punished severely for entering his home without his permission, her mother instantly agreed. Lizzie had to pay for her disobedience. The big question was what the punishment should be. She had already been at the receiving end of his knife. He frequently sexually violated her. She didn't know what else he could do to her.

But he had another punishment that he knew she would never forget. He made her sit at the kitchen table beside her mother. Then he told her mother to lift up her dress. Maryanne did as she was told.

Lizzie looked at her mother's big, fat belly falling over the top of her panties. Leon went to the kitchen cupboard and chose the fish-filleting knife. Then he pulled her mother's pants down further and then cut a cross right across her abdomen.

It wasn't a deep cut but it was enough to draw blood. Lizzie watched in horror as her mother's abdomen was smeared with blood. Her mother laughed and screamed out at the same time.

"You see that, Lizzie? See your mother's big, beautiful belly and her lovely, red blood. That's what will happen to you—bad, beautiful Lizzie. Only it won't be a shallow cut. It will be right through you. Now clean your mother up and the pair of you get out of my sight."

Lizzie helped her mother to her bed. Maryanne was by now cackling like a rooster, as if it was a great joke. Lizzie got washers and towels to staunch the blood. He had said it was shallow but Lizzie thought she could see yellow fat where the knife had penetrated the big, overhanging belly.

How could she ever forget something so horrific? Lizzie knew he would do the same again to her mother as well as herself if she ever did anything to upset him. So Lizzie never went near his granny flat again.

There came a day when she found a key in a drawer in the kitchen. She wondered what it would open. After trying unsuccessfully to open all the doors in the house, there was only one place left—the granny flat. Would she ever be brave enough to see if she could unlock his front door and enter his home?

She didn't think it was worth the risk, but temptation was very strong. One day when he was gone for the weekend, she took the key to try his front door. It opened on almost the first try. But still she was not brave enough to enter his dwelling.

He uncles never had much to do with her as she was growing up, but they did insist she learn to drive. The scowls on Leon's face convinced her that he was less than happy with this idea. But her uncles insisted she be taught to drive and get her driver's licence.

Lizzie privately thought this was a cop out for her uncles, so that they wouldn't have to do anything for her or their sister. They said it was important she know how to drive in case she needed to get help for her mother in a hurry. If she was brave enough to learn how to drive, then she should be brave enough to ferret around in Leon's belongings and see what he got up to.

She was much older and wiser now. She would be meticulously careful. She knew his movements and time tables. The day she chose was a Sunday. He had taken her and picked her up again after her night of display in front of the eager gentlemen at the club where she worked. He would be gone all day and not return until the Monday morning.

Even though she was tired, she pulled herself out of bed very early. Her mother would not arise for hours yet. Her head had hardly hit the pillow before she crawled out in the early morning dawn. She took the key. Then she walked the path to the granny flat. The door opened easily. She was very careful in case Leon left any traps for her. She was probably being paranoid, but he was a very cunning man. She wouldn't put anything past him.

She glanced around. Everything was much as she remembered. She quickly went to his bedroom, pulled out the bottom drawer and looked for the box. Instead of just one, there were now two. So be it. She took out the two boxes, closed the drawer shut and then left the granny flat being careful not to leave any sign of her presence. She was trembling with fear as she started up her mother's car and travelled towards Tewantin.

Her impatience was wearing thin as she waited for the library to open. As quickly as possible, she started copying all the documents, opening up each page while trying to keep them in the order she had found them. She did not stop to read any of them. At long last she had them copied. She paid what she owed, then quickly returned to the car and drove home.

She briefly checked to see if her mother was still in bed. Maryanne always said that Sunday was for sleeping in—as if she didn't sleep in every day. Lizzie put the copied pages in her room then returned to Leon's granny flat.

Her hands were shaking as she replaced the two boxes exactly as she had found them. She locked the door and returned to her bedroom where she fell into bed with absolute relief. Her excitement prevented her from going back to sleep. Leon's secrets would not let her rest.

Disappointment flooded through her. She had expected to find out all sorts of malicious deeds. Instead there was nothing that seemed to be of much value. Many of the papers she had copied were quite old. There were birth certificates of different males and some females. She did not recognise any of the names.

There was mention of Mitchell Farraday and his daughter. Well there was nothing unusual about that because he did have a son and daughter. But why Leon would be interested in this, she had no idea.

Lizzie was very disillusioned with her find. After all her stealth, this was all she had to show for it. She hid the papers in the bottom of her wardrobe under her shoes. She decided she would find a safer hiding place for them at a later date. It was possible that they might come in handy one day.

She had found out one piece of startling news, and not from Leon's boxes. She had found this out at her place of work last evening. It was to do with poor, sad Uncle Mark. Not that she wanted to hurt him because she really liked him even though he never helped her out with her mad mother and Leon.

But if Arlo and Hope ever got really nasty with her, then she would have something to light a fire under the pair of them. Turns out, Arlo's mother, the traitorous Tiffany, who had been with her own father when they were both killed in a traffic accident, had been on with some other man when she was supposed to have gotten pregnant by Mark. Now, wasn't that a revelation? Just who was Arlo's father?

To cover herself, she asked her mother very politely if she would like to go for a drive. Maryanne replied that seeing as it was such a nice day she would enjoy a drive. Lizzie drove down the road a little until she estimated that she could easily account for the mileage she had clocked up going to the library.

She pulled over under a tree and pointed out all the familiar landmarks until she hoped her mother would be able to remember to tell Leon if he asked what they had done for the weekend.

Lizzie had more plans for the day. Once her mother was settled back at home and had stuffed herself with left-over pizza from the night before, she was happy to head back to bed where she would probably stay until Lizzie prepared her dinner for the night.

Lizzie was off. If she timed it correctly, she would be out on the road and would catch a ride with the neighbours. There were only a few properties further along.

She vaguely knew these people as she had gone to school with some of their children. They always drove along each Sunday afternoon, regular as clockwork, off to some church event. They were good-living people and were generally kind to Lizzie even though they seemed leery of her. No doubt they had heard what she did for a living.

She only ever got a ride to the entrance of the next property which happened to belong to her uncles. The family she hitched a ride with never questioned what she was doing there. She had told them previously that she liked to return there so as to remember her grandparents.

Again, this was a great joke. Hadn't her maternal grandfather been some type of criminal and her grandmother had been odd, if not downright strange? There was nothing about them she wished to remember but she was fascinated by the house they had lived in.

The property was called Sunshine which always seemed to be a most incongruous name for anything that belonged to the Farradays. Sunshine should denote some sort of happiness or good fortune. As far as Lizzie could tell, most of the Farradays were a bunch of mixed-up oddities.

Lizzie thanked the neighbours. Then she ran down to the house. She couldn't waste too much time as she wanted to be back in time to prepare her mother's dinner as she was sure to tell Leon if Lizzie was late.

The window opened easily. There was no trouble gaining access to the house. Everyone thought it was securely locked up. Little did they know. The room she climbed into was very stark as were most of the other bedrooms. She avoided the spook room. This had been the bedroom used by her grandparents.

She quickly glanced at the ugly, old, iron bed. It gave her the creeps. It was the prayer room that intrigued her the most. She didn't know why it was called the prayer room. Probably something to do with her peculiar grandmother who was said to have been quite religious and even had visions. Not that Lizzie believed the vision part. She did believe the religious part though. The prayer room was testimony to that.

Lizzie curled up in the big lounge chair and stared out the wide windows. She heard the creek gently flowing and the wind causing sway in the big gums that surrounded the property. All told, Sunshine didn't look that bad considering no one lived there, or hadn't done for years. The garden and maintenance service her family employed kept it in good shape. Why her uncles kept it, she had no idea?

This was a peaceful time for Lizzie. As she lay on the chair, she stared at the statue. Everyone called it the blind statue because it had no eyes. Lizzie wasn't too sure about that. She often thought she saw the statue looking at her, as if it knew all her sins—the ones she had committed and the ones she would like to.

Another thing that took her eye was the peculiar cross that hung on the wall. Someone had once told her it was a Celtic cross. Most of the smaller statues, holy pictures and icons that had been in the room had been smashed to pieces by her cousin, Gabe, in a fit of rage when he found out both his parents were dead. But that was years ago. Lizzie didn't want to think about that bad time.

The cross seemed to call to her. When she visited Sunshine, she always took it off the wall and put it around her neck. It was held by a string necklace. She lay back on the lounge chair and whiled away the time until she estimated she would have to leave.

The walk home always took her a good hour whichever way she chose to go. She could go up over the mountain or back along the road. She chose the mountain because she didn't want to risk

Leon being told by inquisitive neighbours that they had spotted her walking along the road.

The following Sunday she decided she would go to Sunshine early in the morning to spend the day there. It was better than being at home with her mother all day. If she stayed home all she would do was either read or play solitaire. She made her mother sandwiches for lunch as she explained what she intended doing. Her mother made no reply. Lizzie doubted she would even remember.

She took the track over the mountain. When she reached the Big Rock, the highest pinnacle on the track over the mountain, she stopped at a hidden cave at the base of the mountain to ensure another one of her secrets was still there. Finally, she was at the house. She climbed through the window, checked out the rooms before curling up in the lounge chair in the prayer room.

She needed some peace, because very soon, it would be the time when Leon required her. He was so peculiar. Lizzie could almost believe he enjoyed it and wanted her to enjoy as much as he did.

If she didn't put on a good enough act, he would carefully smack her around. Not so that anyone would notice. He was very discreet with his punishments. If she did not pretend well enough, with moans and groans and do all the things he wanted, then bam, she would cop another one.

Lizzie lay on the lounge chair with the Celtic cross around her neck. She must have dozed because the next thing she heard was the front door opening. Initially, she thought she was dreaming, but then she heard footsteps walking through the house. She was petrified. What if it was Leon?

She looked around for a hiding place. Her eyes went to the statue. It seemed to be calling to her. She hurried towards it and slid in behind the wooden stand that it stood on. It was doubtful that it would hide her fully. She held her breath, shut her eyes and held onto the cross.

The footsteps were now in the room. Whoever it was did not care about making noise. Eventually the footsteps moved away. She heard the front door slam shut. Lizzie breathed a sigh of relief and opened her eyes.

As she was about to move out from behind the stand, she noticed a key hole. This was very odd. What could possibly be inside it? She was twiddling her fingers around the string neck lace, when she felt the cross. She looked down at it and then at the shape of the key hole. It was hardly possible. Could the cross be the key to the stand?

Lizzie was very cramped so she scrambled out from behind the stand. She was desperate to find out who had entered the house. She stood up and stretched her cramped body.

"Hello Lizzie," the voice caused her to scream out loudly. He jumped almost as much as she did. "What are you doing here?"

Raphael Farraday was standing in the room, curiously observing her.

"I could ask the same of you, Rafe," she replied. She was still shaken. "You scared the daylights out of me." She put her arms around her shoulders to stop the goose bumps.

"Why were you hiding?" he asked.

"Why do you think? You're the last person I expected. I heard the footsteps. I thought you might be someone else. I was frightened. So I hid."

"Who did you think I might be?" He continued looking at her with curiosity, not having seen her for ages. It was unbelievable how she had changed.

"No one specific, maybe a ghost, I don't know. You frightened me. I didn't expect to find anyone here, that's all." She tried to keep her eyes off him. He was just as she remembered. He still had that aura about him. She wasn't sure quite sure what it was. Maybe it was kindness.

"Would you like to come outside and sit on the front steps? You seem to be cold. Are you feeling all right?"

"I'm fine," she replied. "It's just that you startled me."

"I'm sorry if I frightened you. I was surprised to find you here. Do you come here often?" he asked.

"Sometimes—I find it soothes me. What about you? You didn't say why you're here."

"Same as you, I suppose." He said as she followed him outside. They sat together on the front steps.

"Do you mean that you find this place soothing? I thought no one in the family found anything soothing about Sunshine. Isn't that why they shut the place up?" she asked, listening contentedly to the gentle flow of the creek. The sun was warm against her skin. The goose bumps had disappeared.

"It's got some bad memories. That's for sure. But I like to come here. It helps me get my head straight."

"Why would you, of all people, need to get your head straight? I would have thought that you would be the last person to ever feel the need for solitude or whatever it is you're looking for."

Raphael was confusing her. What did he have to be concerned about? His life seemed about perfect. He was at university. He was staring down the face of whatever he wanted to do in life. He had brains. He had looks. He was respectable. He was so far removed from her world he could have been a god.

"Life isn't always what it seems, Lizzie," he replied. "We all have our demons."

She burst out laughing at this. Demons, what did he know about demons? She lived with two of them. "You are so funny, Raphael Farraday. You always did make me feel better."

They sat together in comfortable silence, listening to the creek, looking out at the hills and mountains, feeling the slight breeze on their faces.

"What say we go for a walk? We could go up to the Big Rock. That's if you remember the way." She stood up and was off. She smiled to herself when she heard him follow her.

The house Rina Wright rented was just about perfect. There was a fenced-in back yard for Jude to play in—if standing and staring could be called play. There were three bedrooms, a lounge and dining room and a small kitchen. There was also the luxury of small patios at the front, side and back entrances.

The room she chose for herself was not the main bedroom but one of the single rooms. The attraction of this room was the single bed it contained. There was plenty of room where a person could crawl underneath. Old habits die hard. The main bedroom was left empty.

Rina could still hear her mother's voice telling her to beware of monsters. She wondered about Mother, if she had ever returned or if she was off enjoying herself with some man. She had pangs of guilt about the money. What if Mother had returned? Surely she would want it back.

The best aspect of the house was the gate at the back of the yard that led into the reserve area. If she followed the bush track that ran through it, she would eventually come to the playground area of the park. This became the main focus of her day. Rina would take Jude to the swings every day where he sat on the swing for as long as she would push him.

The front area consisted of a driveway to a single-door garage as well as a short foot path to the front door. Rina had so few possessions she had no idea what she would ever use the garage for. Her main problem was that she would have to keep the front door locked at all times in case Jude escaped. Not that this was likely as he seldom went too far away from the areas he was familiar with.

Every second day Rina took Jude to the shopping centre. She was careful to go each afternoon after school was finished. She always knew she had done the wrong thing in not getting specialised help for Jude. But she was too frightened to leave any clues behind. There was invisibility and monsters to be taken into consideration. Besides, she taught him as much as he could cope with.

She always took a taxi back and forth because she was sure Jude would not be able to walk that far. His strange gait was too awkward to cover long distances.

Rina badly missed Mr and Mrs Baxter. They had been her only friends in the world. They were the only people she had ever conversed with on any level. She had spent so many years being invisible and avoiding monsters. Her loneliness was more intense than ever.

Because she wanted to minimise any trace of her whereabouts, she did not get the electricity connected to the house. This would have necessitated paper work and accounts to be paid. It was one thing going to the estate agent every month to pay her rent in cash, but if she had the electricity connected, there would sure to be a paper trail.

Rina did not know how long one million dollars would last so she was forced to be very frugal. She scouted around the second-hand shop where she bought clothes and other small items for the house as well as toys or any educational tools that might assist Jude to develop some more. She had the great hope that one day he might speak. That he might call her mum.

Her purchase of a large collection of candles and kerosene lamps provided lighting. She also bought a small gas stove and a gas cylinder. Cooking was taken care of.

Refrigeration was her main problem. But then she decided she could do without this. She would use tinned and packet foods. It was challenging making up meals but she soon overcame this.

She had just finished cleaning up after giving Jude his dinner when there was a sharp rap on her front door. Candles illuminated the house as it was already dark outside. The knocking on the door continued. She took Jude to his bedroom and told him to stay there while she answered the door. There was no reason for anyone to be knocking on her door at night as she knew no one.

"Yes," she asked, "what do you want?" She did not open the front door due to her feelings of alarm.

"I was wondering if your power if off?" The masculine voice was loud and clear.

"What do you mean?" she asked. As there was no power connected to her house, she had no way of knowing.

"My electricity isn't on. I live next door. I checked the power box and there doesn't seem to be anything wrong. Then I noticed your lights were out. I phoned the electricity company and they were checking for faults. So I was wondering if you had lost power as well."

Rina did not know what to make of this. All sorts of things went through her mind. Could this man be one of the monsters that mother had warned her about. But then she chided herself. She must not become totally paranoid.

"I don't have the power connected, but I could lend you some candles if you like." She hoped this might satisfy him and he would go away.

"What do you mean you don't have the power connected? Everyone has the power connected." The man remained outside her door.

"Well, obviously not everyone. Look, I'll give you some candles then will you please go away."

"Why don't you have the power connected? Can't you afford it?" he asked.

Rina was now less frightened. Instead she was annoyed. "I can well afford it," she replied in what she hoped was her most disdainful voice. "I don't have it connected because it's against my beliefs." She hoped that would satisfy him. She was going to say she was allergic to it, but was pretty certain that electricity didn't bring on allergies.

"Heaven help us," the man muttered softly thinking she would not hear him, "Just what I need—another nutter." Then he spoke in a louder voice. "Well, sorry to have bothered you, madam. I won't be taking up any more of your time. I'll leave you to your beliefs."

Rina then opened her door as she heard him walking away. "Here, take these with you. It's also part of my belief not to be unkind to my neighbours." She had two candles in her right hand. "Have you got any matches? I could lend you a box if you like."

He turned around when he heard her voice. She was in the half-light. From what he could see, she had dark hair hanging around her face. She was dressed as though she had rummaged through a garbage heap. But he was taken aback by her sudden appearance and her offer of the candles and the matches. Before he knew what he was doing, he had taken the candles from her.

"Thanks, I'll return them when the power's back on," he said, trying not to be too obvious as he stared at her.

"No need. I've got plenty more." She put her left hand behind her back so he would not see her missing finger.

"I guess you probably do," he replied. He continued looking at her which made her feel very uncomfortable. She turned to go back inside when he said, "How do you get on with cooking, washing and all that sort of thing if you don't have any power?"

"You learn to do things differently. It's not that hard," she answered, turning to leave again. She didn't want to be rude. Her contact with men was very limited. The only males she had ever had contact with were Mr Baxter and the male students and teachers who had been at her school. Other than Mr Baxter, none of them ever took any notice of her which is how she liked it.

"You'll have to give me some lessons one day, or at least my children. My power bill is enormous. They don't know how to turn off a light, the TV, anything. They cost me a fortune," he was talking just for the sake of talking. The woman intrigued him. It hardly seemed possible that a woman could live without hot water, let alone a hair dryer. His daughter alone used up so much hot water, not to mention his son. There was no such thing as a ten minute shower for either of them.

"I'm sorry to hear they cost you so much. As I said, keep the candles. If you need more, please just ask. Now I really must go." She turned again and walked inside.

As she went to shut the door, he called out, "Good night."

When the door was safely locked, she felt relieved. The man had upset her carefully planned existence. She wanted to go unnoticed. Now here was a man knocking on her door at night. She wondered then if he had been telling the truth about his power being off. She looked towards his house, and sure enough, there were lights blazing everywhere.

He had duped her. How easily she had fallen into his trap? Her thoughts returned to Mother. She had warned her so many times about monsters. Had she not told Rina that they could turn up at any time unannounced? She would have to be more careful in future, especially as she had almost one million dollars hidden in her wardrobe.

Rina checked that Jude was asleep. Then she went to her own bedroom. One of the things about the house that had attracted her was that the bed was quite high off the floor. If necessary, she could always squeeze under it. She took the duvet off the bed, threw it on the floor, and grabbed a pillow as she lay down to sleep.

Her daily routine was becoming nicely established. She had not seen the man again, which pleased her. He was a big man, similar to the types that she saw in magazines, the sort with muscles everywhere. She even thought she had seen a carefully hidden tattoo on his upper arm. Men with tattoos frightened her. She was certain they were less than upstanding.

Jude played in the back and side yards unhindered. At least he walked around, listening to the birds in the reserve area of the park. When he walked inside holding a ball, Rina was dismayed as she had no idea where he had found it. She walked outside, looking around.

"Hay, Lady, is my ball in your yard?" The voice was that of a young man. She looked around and realised it was coming from the house next door.

"My friends and I have been having a bit of a kick around. Do you mind if I come and get it?"

"No, I don't mind. I could throw it back over the fence if you like," she replied, horrified to think she might be confronted by someone else from the house next door.

"No need," the person replied. "I'll just open the gate and come and get it." Before she could object, the gate separating the two houses was flung open and in marched a young man. He was a replica of the big man who had taken the candles from her, only much slimmer.

"Hi," he said. "I'm Tom, pleased to meet you." He held his hand out to shake hers.

Rina was taken aback. No one had ever shaken her hand before. She quickly put her left hand behind her back, and put her hand in his. He shook it several times.

"I'm Rina," she managed to say. She was overwhelmed by the friendliness of the young man. "I'll get your ball." She turned to go back into the house when Jude came stumbling out with the ball in his hands. Jude looked blankly at the young man. Rina went to take the ball.

"Hi," the young man spoke to Jude, "How you doing?" Jude continued to stare blankly at Tom. It became an awkward moment.

Eventually Rina spoke. "This is Jude. He doesn't speak." Then she took the ball from Jude and handed it to the young man. She was careful to keep her left hand behind her back.

"That's too bad," Tom replied. "Maybe he might like to play some ball."

Before she knew what was happening, the young man was trying to throw the ball to Jude. At first, the ball hit him on the chest. Then Tom lifted Jude's hands up and told him to hold his hands open. He again threw the ball at Jude, very slowly. Jude held onto the ball more by accident than design. They did this again several times.

Tom turned to Rina and said, "Maybe he just needs a bit more practice. When I have time, we'll do it some more." He turned to go back through the dividing gate. As he went, he said cheerfully, "See you later, and thanks."

Rina went inside the house, sat on a chair and began to cry. Other than the attempted wave at the man who had given him fish and chips, Jude had responded to another person other than herself.

It didn't stop with Tom playing ball with Jude. The next thing Rina knew there was a girl as well, not much older than eleven or twelve, who came through the dividing gate to talk to Jude.

It didn't seem to matter that Jude couldn't speak, the young girl chatted away to him like they were old friends. She was full of questions, asking Jude this and that. When he didn't reply, she didn't seem to mind. She went onto the next subject. She told him about school, about the boys she didn't like, the teachers that she did like and how she hated maths.

Her name was Amanda. The relationship started with Rina offering her a glass of cordial and a biscuit. Amanda was not in the least shy. She sat inside and ate her biscuit. Jude followed her in and ate his biscuit while he stared blankly at her. It became an afternoon routine. In she would come and together they would have their chat and biscuit.

Rina was finding out so much about Amanda and Tom. She knew that their mother had died. She knew that their father was a pain and never let her do the things her friends did. Jude began to follow her around when she went to check out his toys.

Tom came to play ball every now and again. If she didn't know better, Rina could swear that Jude almost smiled when Tom came over. Rina's life was taking gigantic steps since she had become acquainted with these young people.

She often listened to the radio she had purchased at the second-hand shop. It used up a lot of battery power but it was about her only means of communication with the world at large other than the local newspapers which she read avidly.

She wanted to know if Mother might have returned or if there was any indication that the monsters might be roaming around. How she would ever be able to figure this out, she had no idea but she needed to be careful at all times.

There was another loud knock on her front door. "Not again," she muttered to herself, quite sure it would be the man again. She had not seen him since the candle episode.

This time she opened the door straight away. "Yes, how can I help you?" she said as she looked at him.

"I wanted to return the candles and ask a favour of you." He handed her the candles and a box of matches. She quickly put her left hand behind her back.

"You didn't have to. I have plenty, but thanks." She found him disconcerting and his presence was overpowering. She wished it had been Tom who had returned the candles. She found him far less intimidating. He could have sent them back with Amanda. Instead here he was looking grim and dangerous, standing at her front door.

"What did you want?"

"Aren't you going to ask me in?"

This took her aback. "Why would you want to come in?" she asked, again very sceptical of his presence at her door. Bad memories returned to her. What had her mother warned her about?

"I don't know why you would want to come inside," she repeated.

She thought he was swearing under his breath. "Oh, forget it," he said as he walked away from her. He returned back through the dividing gate and slammed it hard just to be sure she got the message that he was annoyed.

That night, after the man from next door had stalked away from her, was the first night that her nightmares returned. As she lay curled up on the floor, awful images returned to her. She woke several times, feeling upset and distressed. She sometimes had difficulty remembering what the dreams were about. There were fragments that remained in her mind. She checked on Jude several times, but he lay asleep in his bed.

The following day after she had returned by taxi from the shops, Amanda was sitting on her front steps waiting. Rina noticed that she was not her usual cheerful self. The young girl followed them inside as she watched Rina put her few groceries away in the cupboards.

"What's the matter, Amanda?" Rina asked as she brought out the biscuits and poured some cordial into three glasses.

"Dad's really upset. We told him that you wouldn't mind keeping an eye on us, well on me anyway. Tom doesn't need any looking after. I don't either really, but dad won't have it. But Tom wants to stay overnight and Dad has to go out, so that means Dad will have to stay home or leave me at home alone and he won't allow that. I promise you I won't be any trouble if you let me stay. Or if you like, you could come and stay at our place."

Rina immediately felt ashamed. These children had been so kind to Jude. It was the least she could do to look after them. "Of course I'll look after you. Your dad really didn't explain what he wanted. He left in a huff. Please tell him that it will be okay. It's the least I can do after all you've done for me."

"Oh, thank you Rina, thank you." The young girl put her arms around Rina and hugged her. This was another intrusion into her attempt at being invisible. "I'll let Dad know straight away. Maybe we can have pizza. I'm sure he won't mind."

Amanda rushed back to her home and returned again a few minutes later. "Dad said to thank you very much and that pizza will be fine as long as it doesn't interfere with your beliefs—whatever that means. He'll bring one home with him."

Her life seemed to be twisting and turning. It was not what she had envisaged. It was becoming more difficult to remain invisible. There were more and more people coming into her life. She thought back to her dream and wondered if it was all connected.

Again her life changed. Amanda organised for them to go to her home as she said she didn't think she could survive one night without television. She was so enthusiastic that Rina found she did not have the heart to disagree. Again, this was a huge step for both Jude and herself. She had never been in any one else's house. She explained to Jude that they were going to another house for a few hours. He looked blankly back at her.

Challenge was hardly the word for it. She summonsed her courage before taking Jude by the hand. Together they walked back through the dividing gate. It was like taking a walk into another world. Amanda was waiting for them.

She introduced them to a very ancient-looking dog. She said the dog's name was Cupid. Rina thought it was a ridiculous name for such a big, old dog. Jude again just looked at the dog. But after Amanda showed him how to pat it, he voluntarily touched its head. In spite of this nerve racking experience, Rina was again excited that Jude had made some response.

Amanda's father was inside waiting to greet them. Not that it was much of a greeting. He merely nodded to her and then thanked her for looking after his daughter. He took his time looking at Jude. Rina kept her left hand behind her back. The way this man looked at her caused her to feel uncomfortable.

Rina watched as he kissed his daughter goodnight. Tom was already gone. As she watched the man kiss his daughter, her fear of him lessened. Surely, a man who could show affection towards his daughter could not be all that bad. But she had been warned and warned, time after time by Mother. *You never could tell where monsters might be hiding or what guise they may be hiding in.*

They ate pizza and watched television until Amanda said she was tired and went to bed. Jude lay on Tom's bed, sleeping soundly. Rina stayed sitting on the lounge chair waiting for the man to return. He had not said what time to expect him. She would have preferred the floor but knew the man was suspicious of her already. If he found her asleep on the floor, it would only strengthen his belief that she really was a nutter.

The dreams returned. There were faces, knives, hands, beds, black boots and all manner of frightening images. Rina tried to wake up, to escape from the nightmare. She knew in her dream that she was terrified, was screaming, her world was collapsing. She woke with a fright and hoped she had not screamed out.

She looked up. The man was standing there in the half-dark staring at her.

"Are you all right?" he asked, sounding concerned.

"I will be. It takes a few minutes. I'll have a drink of water. I'll be better then." She stood up to go to the sink. Before she could do this, the man filled a glass and gave it to her.

She was still shaken. Her right hand was against her chest because she could feel her heart still racing. She took the water in her left hand. As soon as she held the glass to her mouth, she knew she had made a mistake. The man looked at her hand, to the area where her little finger should have been.

He waited while she drank the water before taking the glass from her. "What happened to your hand?" he asked.

She didn't look at him as she knew he watched her every move. "This is the way I was born," she replied. "I need to go. I'll get Jude. Thank you very much for asking me to be with Amanda. She's a lovely, young girl. But I have to go now."

She hurried to get Jude from Tom's bed. The man followed her. She shook Jude trying to wake him, but he was deeply asleep.

"I'll carry him," the man said.

Rina did not want this. She did not want him coming into her home. Before she could object further he picked Jude up in his arms. There was no option but to follow him outside the house and through the dividing gate. She ran ahead and unlocked her side door. Very quickly she lit a candle. There was enough light to show him to Jude's bedroom. The man placed Jude on his bed and covered him over. Jude did not stir.

"Thank you again," she said. "You've been very kind." She held the candle in her right hand. She did not look up. She did not want to meet his eyes.

She was mortified when he took her face in his hands. "You have the most incredible eyes," he said. She looked up at him then. They stood looking at each other. Then he turned and left.

10

The dogs still frightened her although she was becoming more relaxed with them. Luce Potulski thought handling them was like taming a lion or a tiger. She was thankful that the man had a television in his house which she avidly watched. Every second show showed huge animals much like what she was dealing with.

While she had been with her grandparents she had not been allowed to watch any programs. So it was bliss to view so many different shows. The ridgebacks looked a bit like lions. They were almost as big and much the same colour.

It took time, but she gradually became used to their haughty ways. They were so big that she didn't think she would have the strength to take them for a walk as she had been instructed.

She was not very strong and had it not been for the fact that she yelled at them, or gave them firm commands, as her employer had advised, she would not have been able to handle them. Because he thought she could not speak, he had told her to give them a hit on the rump if they disobeyed.

Fear kept her from doing this. They were so big she thought they might eat her, so she used her voice to control them. It took a good part of her day to walk the two of them twice daily. She found a route that suited both her and the dogs. It took her through several streets until she came to Sundial Park. There she would rest before returning to his home.

As promised, he phoned every morning. She gave three taps which satisfied him. He usually hung up straight away but sometimes she heard him talking to others. She kept an eye on the calendar so that she would be aware of when he was due to return. Her first two weeks had been very enjoyable once she got the hang of caring for the dogs. He had left money. So she did not have to drag out the bag from under the house which held the cash.

Her needs were few. After the dogs had been exercised, she sometimes walked to the shopping centre. She had found a second-hand shop where she was able to purchase more clothing. Everything she bought was loose and dark in colour. Not black or red—never in her life would she ever wear black or red. Dark greys or browns were fine, but not the colours that had wreaked such havoc in her life. She did not want the man who owned the dogs to realise that she was not a boy. Her world felt much safer this way.

She bought apples and cheese which was all she needed, other than several cups of milk each day. The dogs required much more than she did. They were so huge and ate far more than she did.

The time was drawing close for his return. There was little housekeeping to do as there was so little in the house. The dogs were well cared for. The house looked ship-shape. She was asleep curled up in her blanket on the floor when suddenly the bedroom light was flicked on.

"What the hell are you doing on the floor?" he asked.

Again she almost forgot that she was not supposed to speak. She almost shouted out in fright as she sat up and looked at the man who reminded her of black devil. His black hair was curling around his shoulders and his face was covered in black whiskers. She grabbed black devil closer to her.

"What's with the bear? Geez, what have I got here, a kindergarten?" He groaned in frustration. "If the coppers get me for this, I'll be heading back before the magistrate. I don't know about this set up. I think it would be best if you leave. You better find someplace else to stay as soon as you can. I'm knackered so I'm going to bed. Enjoy your bed," he pointed back to the floor.

Luce Potulski became incensed. She had done everything he had asked. He was just like all the rest. He was going to throw her out, just when everything was going smoothly. She stood up and threw black devil at him with all the strength she had. It hit him in the back. It was probably no stronger than a pin prick, but he swirled around and grabbed her.

"What was that for? What did I ever do to you? I saved your butt from those hoodlums. I put a roof over your head and now you hit me with this mangy, looking bear. If you weren't such a scrawny, little kid, I'd put you over my knee and spank you."

As far as she was concerned, calling black devil a mangy, looking bear was the worst thing he could have done. He was her only friend in the world. She kicked him in the shins with her black boots that she never took off. She kicked and kicked and kicked and lashed out at him with her small fists.

He looked at her in both amazement and amusement. "What's the matter with you this time? Cut it out. You kick me again and I'll . . . ." He grabbed her hands to stop her feeble blows.

She mouthed the words, "You'll what?" Never again, never again—if she could, she would have killed him. She swallowed heavily as she backed away from him.

He saw the fear in her. He shook his head, "No, I didn't mean that. Is that what's happened to you? You've been abused." He let go of her. As he stepped away from her, their black eyes clashed.

"I'm sorry. I get it. I can understand you better now. That must have been terrible for you." He rubbed his hands through his hair. He seemed shocked. "Look, we'll talk about this tomorrow. You go back to sleep. Sleep on the floor. Sleep with your bear. Sleep where you like? This is all too much."

He turned and left her. Luce lay back down on the floor with black devil curled up in her arms. She couldn't help the tears and sobs. She knew her plan was not to speak, just as her grandparents rules dictated, but no one had said anything about crying. She couldn't help herself. All the bad kept coming back at her.

Her eyes were closed as her sobs kept coming. The next thing she knew there was a body lying down beside her. She could feel the body heat. He tapped her on the shoulder and she opened her eyes and looked at him. There was light coming from the lounge room.

"Just stop crying, will you? You can stay as long as you like. You don't have to be frightened. I told you I won't hurt you. Now pull the blanket up and go to sleep. I'll stay here with you until you're settled down. I know you can't hear me, but I know what it's like to be hurt and to feel as though the rest of the world is against you. It's the loneliest feeling in the world. Now go to sleep."

It just made her worse. They were about the kindest words anyone had ever said to her. She kept crying, not loud sobs as previous. She kept black devil close to her. She knew he was still awake. She could tell by his uneven breathing. He was still disturbed by her crying. Eventually, she slept.

She was outside with the dogs when she looked up and saw him standing on the stairs watching her. His staring unnerved her. She looked to him and was about to start signing, when he put his hand up to stop her. "Whatever it is you want to say, come inside and write it down"

She went inside. He had a pen and writing pad on the table. He tapped her on the arm and pointed to his lips. "What is your name?"

She had thought about this. She did not want to be known as Luce Potulski anymore. Uncle Lucas remained very firmly in her mind. She wrote 'Lu' on the pad.

"Do you mean you name is Lew short for Lewis?" he asked very slowly.

She shook her head and mouthed, "Lu."

"OK, Lu it is, but Lu who?"

She shrugged her shoulders and shook her head.

"I get it. You don't want to be found. You don't want anyone to know who or where you are. Was it that bad?" He seemed very genuine in his concern.

She looked away. "You poor, little bugger," she heard him say.

She turned back to him. She was on the verge of tears again. She pointed at him, wanting to know his name. "You" she mouthed.

"Gabe," he replied.

She stumbled and would have fallen if he hadn't grabbed her. The name jolted all her senses. He helped her sit on a chair. But she got up immediately and went to get black devil. She held him close to her chest. She pointed to the bear and then pointed to him. She was unclear in her mind why she did this. All she knew was that the name Gabe had disturbed her.

He laughed at her, "What, you think I'm a bit of a mangy, old bear? You're probably right. I feel like one sometimes."

She couldn't help herself. It was the same as the sobs she couldn't hold in during the night. She looked at him and smiled. He looked at her as if he was transfixed. He looked as though he wanted to touch her face. But he stopped himself then said.

"You remind me of someone. You better not smile like that too often. You look like a girl when you do. There are plenty of perverts around, so you be careful."

He turned away again to get his breakfast. "I suppose you won't join me," he asked. She shook her head. "Thought not, I tell you what, you have the day off and I'll take care of the dogs."

Lu, as she was now calling herself, did not know what she was supposed to do with a day off. The dogs and this house had become her life. She nodded her thanks and went to her room. She heard him leave with the dogs but he did not walk them around Sundial Park like she did. Instead he took them in his vehicle. It was several hours later when he returned.

She was sitting on the bed in her room. He stood at the door for a moment, and then knocked. She knew he was there so she looked up, pretending to be surprised. It was all she could do to prevent herself from smiling at him.

"Are you playing solitaire?" he asked, as he noticed the cards displayed on her bed. "That's a coincidence. That's what I do in my spare time." He looked ill at ease. "I was going to ask if you would like to have lunch with me, just to be sociable, so we could get to know each other better."

She shook her head and pointed to the apples on the kitchen table. Again he looked exasperated. "Okay, then, just thought I'd ask. I'll see you soon. I'm off to buy some lunch. I won't be home at all tonight. Just so you know."

He returned at lunch time. She was unsure what he had bought, but it smelt very enticing. She stayed in her room most of the time while he was away. Several times she went out to see the dogs, but returned to her room to play solitaire.

He banged on her door. There was no knocking, just his fist hammering either on the door or the wall. She didn't see his lips but she heard his word. "Come and get it."

She didn't want to be ill-mannered, so she came out to the kitchen where he had opened the pizza box and was already eating. As she joined him, she placed her apple and piece of cheese on a plate. She also got herself a drink of milk from the refrigerator. He was drinking beer. She looked at the label and could not help herself. The beer was James Boag.

She started giggling and looked again at him and smiled. He did not know what to make of the sounds she was making. But her smile stopped him in his tracks again. She kept pointing to the beer. He finally got why she was smiling.

"Yeah, not very original, I know. But that's the beer I drink. It seemed the right thing at the time. The beer is almost as precious to me as the dogs." He lifted his bottle and said, "Here's to James and Boag."

She lifted her glass of milk and clicked his bottle. She couldn't help but smile and laugh.

He was very quiet after that as he ate the pizza. She slowly ate her apple and cheese. They were both constrained. Then he stood up, went to the refrigerator and pulled out a tub of yoghurt.

He took the lid off and started eating. "You want some?" he asked. She shook her head. She had already broken another rule. She had smiled and laughed. Both grandfather and Uncle Lucas stood on the outskirts of her mind. But still she watched him eat. It smelled so good. It looked so good.

"Have some," he invited. Again she shook her head. The rules came back to her. *You must not talk, you must not laugh, you must not touch, you must not eat, and you must be perfect, unless Grandfather gives his permission.*

The demons were in her mind telling her to have a taste, but Uncle Lucas was also there, doing things to her, branding her feet and sticking needles into her.

He could feel her watching him. He took his time, licking his lips and salivating over the mango-flavoured yoghurt. "Boy, but this is good," he said again.

He lifted his spoon and brought it to her mouth. She could smell it. She could see the magnificent colours blended together. She was so very tempted. She looked at her apple core and the wrapping that her cheese had been in. Both her grandfather's and Uncle's voices returned, telling her she must not eat without permission.

Then he put the spoon back into his own mouth. She followed his movements. Her eyes became moist as she was on the verge of tears. Temptation was very strong. She was dismayed as he put the next spoonful into his own mouth. It was mesmerising. The smell and sight of it invaded her senses.

"You do have my permission to share it. If you like I'll get you your own spoon," he said.

Again she shook her head. She had to be perfect or else. Then she thought *or else what*. Neither of them was here to know if she was not being perfect. She watched as he ate another spoon full. Then she opened her mouth and licked her lips.

He had not taken his eyes off her. Her mouth was open. He brought the spoon to her mouth. She took a tiny taste off the end of the spoon. Her eyes closed as she tasted it. Then she made a noise as if she had reached heaven. He put the spoon further into her mouth. She still had her eyes closed. She closed her mouth over the spoon and swallowed.

As soon as he saw her swallow, he filled the spoon again. As she opened her eyes, she took another swallow. She nodded her head. He filled the spoon again, she swallowed. Then he had a spoon full. She watched the spoon enter his mouth. She nodded her head again. He gave her another spoon full.

She had a spoonful. He had a spoonful. They did this again and again. She watched the tub of yoghurt empty out until there was nothing left except for the excess around the sides. He scooped it up on his finger and gave it to her. She licked it off his finger. All the time their eyes held fast.

When she realised what she had done, she knew she had now broken every rule. He had touched her or she had touched him. She could still feel his finger in her mouth. Now every rule had been broken. Her mind was so full of conflict. It was if her grandparents and Uncle Lucas were watching her. She was no longer perfect. Her feet started to tingle in her black boots.

She had to leave, get outside. Get away from him as fast as she could. She pushed her chair back and ran outside. James and Boag were lying at the foot of the stairs as she rushed past them. She didn't know where to run to or where to hide. The dogs were alarmed and followed her. She went to the end of the yard and hid behind the dog kennels. She put her head between her knees and hid her face.

Gabe was again astonished. He had not initially set out to deliberately tempt her. The pinched, thin face with the big, black eyes had been his undoing. The boy was just skin and bone. No one should be that skinny while living in a world of plenty. He had wracked his brain how to get him to eat better. He had seen the look on Lu's face when he had started on the yoghurt. It was a look of desire.

Then when the lad had licked his finger, he felt a jolt go through his body. He thought of his sometimes girlfriend, Annie. What he felt was almost sexual. The sooner he got Annie into bed, the better he would be.

He picked up the chair that had been knocked over when Lu had rushed outside. He saw the dogs down the back of the yard. They were whining and standing proud and tall at the back of the kennels. Gabe went to his dogs. He saw Lu crouched down hiding her face.

"Look, I didn't mean anything by giving you the yoghurt. It's just that you're so thin you look like a skeleton. I know you can't hear me, but if you don't start eating better, you might get sick, starve or even die. You won't have enough strength to hold the dogs. I like having you here. You're a strange lad, but I'm fond of you in spite of all your weird ways."

She heard his words very well. She would like nothing more than to tell him that she liked being at his home, that she was becoming fond of him as well. But she had started her deceit of pretence and knew she would have to continue it. She kept her head down until she felt him tap her on the shoulder. She looked up at him.

"You don't have to hide. Come back inside. I'll be leaving soon and won't be back tonight and maybe not tomorrow. You don't have to be frightened. There's more yoghurt in the refrigerator if you want some. You did seem to enjoy it. I just wanted to fatten you up a bit."

He turned and left. When she finally returned to the house, he was gone. He did not return the next day as he had said. She looked after the dogs. She remembered what he had said about eating more. When she walked them, it sometimes felt as though her arms were being pulled out of their sockets. If she wasn't strong enough to do this, then she would be no good to him. He might kick her out.

He would be returning to his job very soon. His week was almost finished. She was curled up asleep on the floor when she heard the front door open. The time was close to midnight. He was making a lot of noise. She heard him stumble, then start swearing. There was the rattle of bottles. She was certain he was drunk.

Drunken men were not to be trusted. Not that Grandfather or Uncle Lucas ever had to get drunk to do the things that they had done to her. But she knew enough to be wary. He was quiet for a time. She thought he must have been sitting down.

If he fell over, it would be too bad, serve him right. But then she heard him moving again. His footsteps were outside her door. The door was open as she was certain he would not return during the night. Yet here he was, at the door to her bedroom.

She watched him walk to the bed then held her breath as he stepped over her. He lay on the bed. She could see him lying there. Then he started to talk.

"Bloody women, Lu, you can't trust them. When you grow up, you're better off just loving them then leave them. Bloody Annie, she drives me crazy. One minute she wants it. Then when she's had it, she gets all contrary on me. I think she's on with someone. And Josephina, she's not much better. No matter what you do, there's no pleasing them."

Lu could not give two hoots about his women troubles. As long as he stayed right where he was on the bed, he could carry on all he liked about his women. When she thought he was asleep, she sighed, pleased that at all long last he was quiet.

Then he started again, "I know you can't hear me, but I think I'd rather spend my time here with you, crazy and as skinny as you are, then waste my time with bloody Annie."

This pleased her. She was not quite sure why. She supposed it was because she was gaining a sense of belonging and security. She had a roof over her head, a bed on the floor, two dogs for companionship and now a man who thought she was crazy but wanted to spend time with her. At last there was someone who cared enough about her to feed her yoghurt and to fatten her up a bit.

When she woke the next morning, he was sitting on the side of the bed again, just staring at her. She had taken her boots off the previous night. She pulled her feet up under the blanket when she realised they poked out the bottom of the blanket.

"I've already seen your feet. What on earth happened to you?" he asked. Again he was very puzzled.

She pulled the blanket up over her head and curled up. She didn't want anyone to know about her feet. It was too humiliating. The next thing she knew he pulled the blanket straight off her, leaving her curled up in a ball. She felt utterly naked under his gaze.

He sat down on the floor beside her. "They look like burns, Lu, like you've been branded. Little 'L's' all over your feet. You've been tortured, haven't you?"

She put her face into her hands as she could not bear to look at him. Her feet were again pulled up under her. She wanted to scream at him, tell him to leave her alone. He poked her again in the shoulder. She shifted her hands from her face and looked at him. There were tears in her eyes. As she looked at him she realised he, too, had tears in his eyes.

"Come here," he said. Before she could move away from him, he pulled her into his arms. "You poor kid," he was genuinely shocked. "Who did this to you? What sort of hell have you lived through?"

She was sobbing again. He held her bony frame in his arms. They sat together on the floor until she stopped crying. He took her face in his hand and made her look at him again.

"I'll look after you, always. No one should have to live through what you have. When you feel like it, you can tell me what happened to you. But you're safe. I won't let anyone ever hurt you again." He rocked her in his arms a while longer. "Come on, it's time for breakfast. Then I have to be going. You remember the plan. I'll phone every morning. Remember to give three taps if everything is okay and six taps if there is something wrong. I'll be back in two weeks."

He left soon after. She sat at the table thinking about all that had happened. Then she went to the cupboard and took out the weetbix.

The keeper of secrets—that was how Lizzie was beginning to think of herself. She had so many odd things in her head that no one else was aware of. She had her secret liaisons with Arlo. It had been more difficult to manage than she had imagined because of Leon. He kept such a close eye on her that the only times she could be alone with Arlo was when he came to the club and Leon did one of his disappearing acts.

She was beginning to think it was a useless exercise, because horrible Hope had no idea that Arlo was being unfaithful to her. Maybe she might have to push *the getting back at Hope issue* along.

"Do you have a girlfriend, Arlo?" she asked after one of his very enthusiastic encounters with her. She kissed and nuzzled him but was finding it was becoming tiresome. She hoped he might confess about his feelings for Hope. They both thought no one knew about them, but Lizzie had always known.

"Kind of," he replied. "But it's not that serious." She almost burst out laughing at this. Not serious, when they had been having it off for years and years. Maybe it was his seven year itch time. But if she pushed him a bit further, he might feel obliged to tell Hope about his encounters.

"Does she know about us?" she asked, giving him another peck on the cheek.

"No, she'd kill me if she found out." He certainly sounded alarmed.

"Maybe you should. It's always best to be honest in a relationship." She let him digest this. Who was she to talk about relationships, but if it got under Hope's skin, who cared? "Where does she think you are now? It can't be very easy for you, having to sneak around."

"I tell her I'm having a night out with the boys. She thinks it's good for us, you know, to have time apart."

"What's her name?" she asked innocently. She could tell he was about to splutter. Poor Arlo, she then took pity on him. "I've got to go. See you when I can." She gave his backside a little squeeze as he was pulling up his jeans.

Lizzie was becoming used to the timings of Leon's disappearances. The night concluded and he was as usual waiting to take her home in case she did what—flirt, play up with some man.

"It's almost our time, Lizzie. So don't be going to work tomorrow night. I'll need you. I'll put Maryanne to sleep then it's my time. So be a good girl, and put on your best pretence for me."

"Why do you do it, Leon? It can't be much fun for you knowing how much I hate you?"

"Lizzie, it just makes it all the sweeter, your hatred. You don't seem to realise just how delectable you are, my bad, beautiful Lizzie." He put his hand on her knee as he drove.

"I don't understand you, Leon. I don't know why you stay. Why don't you just pack up and leave? If it's just about the sex, there are hundreds of women out there. You're not too bad-looking. You could have your pick." She looked at his dark hair, now with flecks of grey. "I will never understand either why you say that my family owes you. What do they owe you?"

"At least a million fucks, Lizzie. That's the very least your family owes me. Once a month from you takes a long time to add up to one million." His hand sneaked further up her leg.

"You're as mad as my mother, you know that. You make a good pair." She shifted his hand and turned her back on him.

They were home at last. She was about to get out of the car when he grabbed her by the throat. He squeezed hard. She could not get her breath. But she knew he would time it just right. When she started to shake, he let go. She breathed in heavily until her respirations were normal.

"Good night, Leon," she struggled with her words. "I'll see you tomorrow night then."

Lizzie waited for her night with Leon. It was as ugly as usual. He really seemed to love to humiliate her on these monthly occasions. He had her do all the things she hated. There was no such thing as straight forward sex for Leon.

After these nights, she often looked at her wrists and imagined how easy it would be to slice them open. Add some hot water and bingo, it could all be over. But then she thought of her mother. She would be totally at Leon's mercy. But then again, why should Lizzie care? Her mother never seemed to care about her. It was all about Leon. But responsibility was responsibility.

Lizzie was very depressed. She remembered that he said he had further plans for her. He had her service another man from time to time. Service—the word boggled her mind. It was like she was a bull in a cow yard. She serviced this other man periodically. There was no specific time frame, not monthly like with Leon. But her servicing was still carefully calculated by Leon.

When she had to see this other man whom Leon called Bart, he always took her to another house in Tewantin. As far as Lizzie was concerned, the house had a bad feel to it. She called it the house of dread. It was quite spacious, but very stark. It could have done with a woman's touch.

Leon was very at home in it so she guessed it was where he went on weekends. She had no idea if he owned it or if it was rented. There was also a large shed at the back which looked like a granny flat.

Her one small piece of respite following her ordeal with Bart was that Leon let her have time to herself. He was happy for her to get away from the house after her interludes with Bart, the unbearable, as he had business to discuss. So Lizzie was dismissed and allowed to go for a walk in the park at the back of Leon's house.

She was quite familiar with the tracks that wound through the bush land. At the northern end of the park was a play area for children. She would often find herself here, sitting on the swings, contemplating her miserable life. She looked at her watch. She had an hour until she had to return to Leon.

It was as she sat on the swing that Lizzie first saw the huge dog. She had scant knowledge of dog breeds, but it looked far too strong for the person trying to handle it. The dog was making straight for her. She didn't like the look of it. It looked as if it was capable of taking a piece out of her. It was enough that she had to put up with Leon and his buddy, Bart, without having to do battle with some out-of-control dog.

She left the swing and hopped up on top of the stand that led to the slippery slide. Unless the dog could climb, she would be safe. But who knew what such a giant creature was capable of? She felt sorry for the skinny person who was hanging onto its leash for dear life. The dog reached the playground equipment and began sniffing around. Its handler looked exhausted.

"Why don't you tie it up and have a break?" Lizzie directed her question to the dog's owner. She was unsure if she was addressing a male or a female.

"It would probably just pull free," the person replied. The dog had stopped and was observing Lizzie on top of the stand. "I'll just sit for a while and have a rest."

"You don't look strong enough to be walking such a big dog." Lizzie was beginning to think that she was talking to a young female who was dressed as a male.

"I'm getting better at it. It's not as hard as it used to be. The dogs are better behaved now."

"You mean there's more than one?"

The young woman laughed, "Only one more, thank goodness." It felt good to talk to another human being. "My name is Lu. Do you come here often?"

"Lizzie. Not that often," she replied. "What about you? Do you live around here?"

"Yes, not far from here. I like to bring the dogs here when there are less people around. Just in case they get away. I don't think they would attack anyone, but you never know."

Lizzie climbed down and sat beside Lu who was sitting on the ground watching the dog.

"What's the dog's name?" Lizzie asked, noticing the unattractive, baggy clothes and the boots the woman wore.

"This one is called James. The other one is called Boag. It's kind of funny naming your dogs after a beer."

"Sounds like something my cousin would do. He loves his dogs, and his beer. Do the dogs belong to you?" Lizzie asked.

"No. I just look after them while the owner is away." Lu was pleased the dog remained content to lie still. "What about you? What do you do?"

How did she reply to this? "I'm in the service industry," she answered, thinking of Leon and Bart—satisfied customers, both. She had just come out of her grey world and joined the coloured world, but talk of *what she did* almost had her escaping back into grey.

They sat in silence, feeling the sun warm their bones. The dog was equally content. Another woman with a child entered the park. Both women watched as the third woman walked slowly towards the swings. A boy followed behind, much like a well-trained poodle.

The woman helped the boy onto the swing and started pushing him. It was an awkward few minutes as none of them spoke. Then the third woman said, "Nice day."

"Yes, no rain as yet," the taller of the two women replied. "Your boy seems to enjoy the swing."

"Yes, he does. It's good for him to get out of the house. I usually come here every day about this time." Rina surprised herself at how freely she was opening up to these two women who sat on the grass near her.

"My name is Lizzie. This is Lu." She indicated the thin woman. The third woman said her name was Rina and that her son was called Jude. The three women chatted on, talking about superficial things. The weather and the dog made for safe conversation.

The boy stayed on the swing. "Would you like me to take over?" Lizzie asked, noticing that Rina was becoming bored with pushing the boy up and down.

"If you like," Rina replied. Lizzie took over this chore, wondering what was wrong with the boy who gave no indication that he was being pushed by someone else.

The skinny woman called Lu began patting the dog which appeared to be almost as big as she was. Rina and Lu chatted on about the dog. Rina was somewhat disconcerted as her world had taken another leap from invisibility.

She did her best to keep her left hand out of sight, but it was hard to push a swing one handed. But neither of the other young women mentioned it. She had inadvertently let more people into her life. Not that she would probably ever see either of these women again.

Lizzie looked at her watch. "Got to go," she suddenly said, leaving the boy still swinging. "See you again sometime." The other women watched her disappear in a hurry through the trees.

"I guess I'd better be going too," Lu said, as the dog was becoming restless. She had to hang onto him with all her strength as he started to pull away from her. "It was nice meeting you and Jude. Maybe I'll see you again sometime."

Rina watched as Lu and the dog went in the opposite direction to where Lizzie had disappeared. Rina resumed pushing Jude on the swing. She suddenly felt a powerful desire to leave this place. It was when she had seen Lizzie disappear into the trees that strange images came into her mind. Sundial Park did not have a good ambience about it this day although she had enjoyed her few minutes of conversation with the other two women.

Lizzie returned to the house of dread. Bart, the unbearable, was gone. But Leon was waiting impatiently for her. "What were you doing, Lizzie?" he asked.

"What do you think I would be doing in a park? I was sitting on the swing thinking how much I despise you, Leon. In fact, I enjoyed it so much, I might bring mother for a drive one day and we can both sit on the swings and think about how much we both despise you."

"Your mother doesn't despise me, Lizzie. She loves me, you know that. I'm the only person who makes her happy. You must have heard her say that a thousand times."

"Well, that's the thing about my mother, Leon, she can be unpredictable. She might be as mad as a hatter, but the day might come when she could turn against you. If she ever finds out what you do with me, she could become very jealous."

Leon had locked up the house and opened the door to his vehicle, "If you don't shut up and get in the car I'll take you back inside the house, Lizzie. I could always make it more than once a month, you know. Anyway I have more plans for you. Between us, Bart and I have extended our business plan and you're the major player, Lizzie. We can make more money out of you than having you swing around a pole."

Lizzie had no idea what he was talking about. Whatever it was, she knew it wasn't anything good. She longed to be home, so that she could hide in her room, play solitaire and dream of a better world. The sooner she could get out of Leon's sight the better.

She thought of Raphael Farraday, about the walk they had taken up to the Big Rock. They hadn't talked much. He wasn't nearly as talkative as his twin, Gabe. But it was soothing to be with him all the same. It had been nice just to walk, to throw stones in the creek, to climb the hills.

Then her rage at him returned. He had left her just like everyone else, left her to Leon's evil desires. Her guilt and sin about what her life was all about sickened her. As soon as she was home, she picked up the cards again, shuffled them, and mindlessly let her game of solitaire continue.

She thought back to the day when Rafe had scared the living daylights out of her. Then she thought of the blind statue which had been sitting on the stand for so many years. It was the stand which had a lock hidden in the back of it. The Celtic cross that she had taken from the wall hung around her neck. She was sure it was the key that would unlock the stand.

Lizzie then thought of all the little secrets she knew about. She had found pictures, an old mobile phone and a recorder hidden under the granny flat many years ago. As far as she knew they still remained there. There had to be a story involved otherwise why would someone have hidden them?

Leon was not around. Hopefully he was at the other property he was supposed to look after, although Lizzie didn't think he did too much looking after. He was too busy poking his nose into her family's business. She went to the granny flat where she knew these items remained. She never crawled under the flat any more, as she had grown too big. But she was able to wriggle far enough under to reach her hand up to where she knew the pictures and other items were kept wrapped up.

Very carefully, she undid her find. The pictures were old but still in good condition. She looked at them carefully. What she saw shocked her. They were of a man and a woman. The woman looked terrified. The man had his hands around her throat trying to throttle her. The phone was old fashioned and dead. If she bought new batteries for it maybe it would still work. She had no idea who these two people were, but the woman did look familiar.

Right then and there she decided she would return to Sunshine and see what was in the stand that held the blind statue. On the way she would check out her other secret—the majorly, big one, the best one of the lot.

But there were also Leon's documents. It was not so long ago that she had copied them in a desperate dash to get to the library before being discovered. She pulled out the documents that she had hidden under the shoes in her wardrobe. She took her time studying them. Most of them meant nothing, but then she saw her Uncle Mitch's name. This time she looked at it more carefully.

Uncle Mitch had married a beautiful woman called Francine. They now had two children, a son, Finbarr, and a daughter, Roza. Francine was something of a recluse. The ring finger on her left hand was missing. She still owned several dress boutiques but left the management of them to others.

Her uncle Mitch had been in the military for many years but after another uncle and aunt had died many years ago, he left his career and was now basically in charge of the Farraday business enterprises. His brothers, Mark, Malcolm and Matthew were also highly involved in the business.

Of all her uncles, it was Mitch who she had no time for. Of all of her uncles, he was the one who was the best equipped to help her. But no, he was too involved with his wife, his two children and the business. He had let her rot in her own part of hell.

To further her humiliation, he had paid her a visit not so long ago. Not because he cared about her but to berate her about her choice of career. He implied that she could do better than to swing around a pole half-naked in front of a bunch of randy men.

She studied all the documents she could find which concerned Mitchell Farraday. Why Leon should have information about him she had no idea? She carefully perused the document which mentioned his daughter. This was when she made a momentous discovery. The daughter, that the document alluded to, indicated that she been born many years ago. How bizarre was this? His daughter was in primary school.

Well, how about that? Lizzie's thoughts were on overdrive. Was it possible that Uncle Mitch, the military hero, had another daughter? She read further and came across another name she recognized. *Oh, Uncle Mitch, what have you been up to? Shame, shame, shame on you—and you would dare lecture me.* Her thoughts were going wild.

Lizzie was determined there would be payback for mighty Mitch. She considered how she would achieve this goal. Then she had a second thought. *Why not kill two birds with the one stone?*

Look out Uncle Mitch and look out Sister Hope. Lizzie became animated. She had not felt this good since—she could not remember. But caution was now second nature to her. Leon and her mother had taught her great lessons about caution. She had to plan and execute this very carefully.

She took all day to put her plan together. She was very careful. There would be no evidence pointing back to her. Rafe still lingered on the outskirts of her mind. But he could wait till later.

She pulled on her latex gloves, carefully prepared the two letters, put them into the stamped, addressed envelopes and hay presto, she would wait for the fallout.

On her next free day when Leon disappeared, she decided to return to Sunshine to try out the Celtic cross key. She walked the long distance over the hill from the Smythe property which took her to the Big Rock and the cave.

The family sometimes referred to this as the haunted cave. It had once been used as a tourist attraction by her parents as a skeleton had been found there years ago. But her father was dead now and her mother was very mentally unwell and totally dependent on Leon.

The haunted cave also held her greatest secret. Weariness caught up with her as she reached the cave. She sat outside for some minutes to catch her breath before venturing in further. It was very dark at the back of the cave.

She could see discarded tins of fruit and soups which had been taken their most probably by her cousins when they were youngsters. There were also the remnants of old blankets and sleeping bags.

But it was none of these that took her interest. Instead she crawled to the back of the cave and felt around until she found the backpack and the gun. They had both been carefully hidden. But Lizzie's lonely childhood had given her ample time to thoroughly search the cave. She even left a torch there permanently. She did not want to be carrying a torch with her every time she went for a walk. Leon was suspicious enough of her without giving him more ammunition.

Of course she had opened the backpack. Her shock at the time was immense when she saw what was in it. It was full of one hundred dollars notes—packed full. She had never counted them but common sense told her that there was a lot of money. It was her secret. If she ever truly needed some cash, she would have bundles of notes right at her finger-tips.

But again, fear held her back. It was the gun that frightened her the most. Whoever had put the money there, must have owned the gun. She might have wanted to slit her wrists at times, but she had no plans to be confronted by whoever had planted the money in the cave. Her family had deserted Sunshine years ago. As far as she knew, no one had lived there since her uncle and aunt had died and her cousin Sarina had been murdered.

She kept on until she reached the childhood home of her mother and her brothers. Again she pushed the window open in the second, biggest bedroom and climbed inside. Everything looked the same. She walked past the spook room—her grandparent's bedroom with the old, ugly, iron bed.

Lizzie had often suspected that Leon visited Sunshine. She had no clear evidence to prove this. It was his furtive behaviour that caused her to think this. If he did go to Sunshine then he had no business being there. His job was to look after the Smythe property and Miriam's Place which was where her grandmother Miriam had lived when she had married old doctor Sam Calhoun.

The doctor had been dead for many years and her grandmother remained at the aged care facility at Cooroy, in a severely debilitated state. In Lizzie's opinion, she was not much more than a vegetable, but she still recognized people. She could no longer speak or walk and spent her time in a wheel chair.

But it was the prayer room that was her main focus today. She went to the stand and pushed it out from the wall. The blind statue held firm as she did this. Lizzie quickly took the key from around her neck and put it into the lock. She turned the key but nothing happened. She tried several more times until finally she heard a noise and the door swung open.

The musty smell was the first thing she noticed. Then she looked down into the bottom of the stand. Again she was shocked. Dollar notes were bundled up. They looked old but were dollars and not pounds. Lizzie tried to remember when decimal currency had come into being. She recalled the date—14th February, 1966.

Was this how long the notes had been there? Lizzie had no idea. She sat back on the floor and wondered about the mysteries of her family. Who would have hidden this money in here? Her grandfather was quite infamous. The rumours were that he was some sort of tyrant and criminal. She imagined it was probably his doing.

She did not count the money because time was passing. She had a long walk to get back to her home. So she locked up the stand, pushed it back, gave the blind state a wink and a nod and told it to keep the secret safe. She kept the Celtic cross on a cord around her neck.

If Lizzie ever wanted a perfect hiding place, then she had found it. She vowed as she walked back past the cave at the Big Rock that she would transfer all her best kept secrets to the stand. The blind statue had done a good job so far. She just hoped there was enough room for the backpack, the gun and Leon's documents that she had photocopied.

Her mind tried to come out of its black fog. It was like there was a light beckoning her, but it was just out of reach. No matter how many times she tried, the light faded and she went back into the black fog.

Maria Wright had lain unconscious for many days in the quiet room in the hospital where she had been taken when a brave bystander had dived in and brought her to the surface of the river where she had desperately tried to end her life. It was unlucky for Maria that the man who had saved her was a very experienced life-saver.

He was a strong swimmer and one of his missions in life was saving people from death by drowning. So unfortunately for Maria, she hardly stood a chance at finding death. She was brought to the surface, not breathing. But cardio-pulmonary-resuscitation was started and continued until an ambulance arrived and paramedics took over.

After that, Maria never stood a chance. There were ventilators breathing for her. Oxygen was administered. Heart and oxygen rates were measured. Blood pressure was kept elevated whenever it dropped. Her coma level was constantly monitored.

Maria was eventually able to breathe by herself. She was fed through a tube into her stomach. Her life was probably as happy as it could have been. She was alive but not alive. She had no thoughts of monsters to bother her.

But the light kept flickering, like a finger gesturing to her, giving her a signal to return to the light. No matter how hard she tried to extinguish the light, it did not happen. So eventually, she opened her eyes. As soon as that happened, there was great excitement going on around her.

Her memories were hazy. The people who attended to her were so cheerful and pleased to see her. They kept saying things like, "It's so good to have you back with us".

Then the questions started. It was all done with great care and sensitivity.

"What is your name?"

This was the question she was asked time and time again. She said nothing, because in truth she did not know if she could even talk, let alone say what her name was. So they used all sorts of devices to help her remember her name. But she could not remember. She did start to talk though.

At first she just nodded or shook her head when questioned. But then her voice gradually returned and she was able to say a few words. She had so many therapists come to see her. She was a wonderful challenge for all of them. Everyone wanted a piece of her. She would be their success story.

The health professionals who were the keenest were the ones who wanted to get into her head, to find out why she had wanted to end her life. Maria's memories were returning slowly. But she had decided she would be very guarded with what she revealed about herself.

There were many questions about her hands, especially about her missing fingers. Maria always said she did not remember what had happened. There were fuzzy memories there but nothing definite. What she was certain about was that losing her fingers was not a pleasant experience.

Gradually Maria improved. She was able to eat, so the tube was removed from her stomach. Her mobility had improved to the extent that she was able to walk with a walking frame. The care givers were very confident she would soon be able to walk unaided. With the achievement of all these things, the next big issue was—what would happen to Maria?

She remembered that her name was Maria so she was referred to by this name. There was nothing else known about her. Searches for missing persons in the area where she had been rescued had been fruitless. What was known though, was that she had given birth.

She said she had no memory of having born a child. If anything might bring back memory, it was thought this might be a trigger. All it brought was some agitation which was put down to the fact that she must be subconsciously missing her child.

The time came when Maria was well enough to be transferred to a secure living unit. It was a place where she could learn to be independent while having the security of on-site people to ensure she was coping. For a person with limited memory, this was a crucial step to take.

They told her it would take time for her memory to return. If she was more relaxed, this would most probably help. Maria had difficulty interacting with the other people who lived in the same building as herself. She remained in her room as much as possible, watching television. At lunch time, she was forced to join in with the other residents. This was an ordeal for her as she had to attempt to make conversation.

Conversation proved to be very difficult with her limited memory. The art of conversation was another skill she had to learn. She could not hide her hands as she ate her meals knowing people were drawn to her ugly hands. Good manners prevented them from asking what had happened. Maria remained as unobtrusive as possible. She preferred her solitary world.

Uncle Lucas returned home from his business trip all fired up to visit the Potulski's and the lovely Luce. He had made many contacts overseas. He flagged down a taxi and asked to be taken to the house that he had set up for the Potulski's. He could not wait to get started on his next project.

The house was in darkness when he arrived. This caused him some annoyance as it was part of the deal he had with Grandmother and Grandfather that the lovely Luce also cook their meals. Grandmother had become very obese and was not much good in the kitchen at the best of times, but Luce had proven to be a god-send when it came to meals.

As long as she remembered the five rules, he was happy to give her free reign with her cooking skills. In fact, it seemed to make her more relaxed. He had a sudden thought that he might be able to incorporate her cooking abilities into his DVD collection. After all, cooking shows were all the go.

She knew what she was allowed to eat and she also knew what would happen to her if she ever put on weight. Little, skinny, prepubescent girls were central to his operation. He was unsure how old she was, but she had to be much older than the DVDs portrayed. As long as she looked like a young girl, he didn't care how much time she spent in the kitchen.

The dark and closed-up house intrigued him. He could not imagine where the Potulski's could be. They had better be home with Luce. He had set strict rules for both Grandmother and Grandfather.

He needed a good, hot meal, a good sleep and then he was ready to introduce the next stage.

He knocked but there was no answer so he retrieved his key and let himself in. There was an eerie feel to the house. He was not sure what it was that disturbed him. He switched on the lights and noted that everything was as it should be. The hum of an air conditioner was working somewhere in the house.

He walked up the stairs. The first thing he did was to check Luce's room, but she was not there. There was no sign of her. He next went to the Potulski's room but it was also empty. That left the room he sometimes slept in and the happy bedroom. A check on his room, revealed nothing. The happy bedroom was usually kept locked. He opened the door and, as he did so, the smell hit him. It was like nothing he had smelt before.

The room was cold. It almost felt like it was freezing. Uncle Lucas covered his nose and mouth. Then he looked down on the floor beside the bed. He was unsure what he was seeing. There was a mass of dark movement. It seemed to be shifting from side to side. It took him several moments to realise what he was looking at.

Maggots, what seemed like millions of them, were hungrily moving and swaying over a bloated, smelly lump of what looked like flesh. In spite of the cold, they were busy. Lucas Cowell was overwhelmed by the sight before him. He backed out of the room, slammed the door shut and ran back downstairs.

He ran into the kitchen and stood over the kitchen sink as his stomach revolted. Quickly, he poured himself a glass of water. He took his time, sipping it slowly. What he had just viewed had been about the worst thing he had ever seen in his life. Nothing in his varied experience had been like it.

He had to clear his thoughts, get over the horrific scene he had escaped from. He sat in the living room which was the room he had carefully furnished to welcome his guests. After a time when his head cleared, he realised that he had been looking at Grandmother, or what was left of her. He had yet to understand what had happened to her or how she came to be lying on the floor. The remnants of fluid-filled black and red sheets remained on the floor with her.

Many thoughts passed through his mind. He understood she was well and truly dead. Her body was being consumed by maggots, in spite of being in a very cold room. How had she died?

How had she managed to die in the happy bedroom on the floor beside the bed that had to date been integral to their schemes? The maggots with their busy movements as they devoured her body, was something he would never forget. It was as if Grandmother had been moving in a sea of black, putrid fluid.

All it took was one blowfly.

After a time, he managed to get his thoughts in order and tried to make sense of what had happened. It was clear both Grandfather and Luce were gone, but where? Then he had a second thought. He ran to the safe in the happy bedroom. Grandmother and the smell were temporarily forgotten. He removed the erotic painting of the little children. He fumbled as he tried to open the combination lock. It took him several attempts as his hands were shaking so much.

The door swung open. He looked inside but there was nothing there. No money, no documents and worst of all—no DVDs. He stared at the empty safe not believing his eyes. How was it possible that this had happened?

He became so angry that he picked up the painting and slammed it against the bed-head. Pieces of it flew across the room and landed on the remains of Grandmother. If Grandmother had been in better shape, he would have slammed it into her as well. But the wriggling, writhing mass on the floor again became too much for him. He slammed the door shut and returned to the living room.

He worked on all the scenarios he could think of. Had Grandfather taken off with Luce to satisfy his own cravings and left Grandmother home alone? Or had he killed Grandmother, disposed of Luce and gone his own way? If this was the case, Grandfather had enough money to last him two lifetimes and all of it was due to the diligent hard work of Lucas Cowell. Grandfather would not be allowed to get away with this.

He thought further. Where was Luce? That was the major question. Luce was the cash cow. Was she dead? Had Grandfather absconded with her? Lucas had many questions. But first of all he had to decide how he was going to get rid of the mess upstairs. He could no longer think of her as Grandmother or Mrs Potulski or whoever she had been. Their liaison had been merely financial. Now that financial association had disappeared.

How do you get rid of a body, not a normal body but a body swarming with maggots and falling to pieces, not to mention the smell? Lucas Cowell was almost at his wit's end. The major source of his money-making enterprise had disappeared as well as the money itself. He could hardly believe that Grandmother and Grandfather had cheated him of his life's work. And where was his prize possession, Luce?

Before he got started, he sat down with pen and paper to work out just how he would get rid of Grandmother. He was no mathematician or physics professor, but he did consider he had common sense. How hard could it be? To check on his plan for disposal, he would do a test run.

He looked in the refrigerator. There was not much in there other than some rotting tomatoes. He put some in a plastic bag, tied the bag tightly and dropped them into a bucket of water. They did not sink but floated on the surface. He next added a few stones from the garden. Again, they did not sink.

Next he tied the tomatoes into one of grandmother's head scarves. He dropped them into the bucket. They did sink but not to the bottom. So he added more stones to the mix, retied the head scarf and dropped them into the bucket. Hallelujah—straight to the bottom—grandmother had passed the test.

The tomato test was the way to go.

Darkness was his friend. Most of his best dealings were completed in darkness. Lucas went shopping. He bought overalls, thick gardening gloves that went past his elbows, several tarpaulins and lots of face masks. He also bought a supply of bricks. He had plenty of sheets in the cupboard. He had never disposed of a body before so it was a first.

But he was good at firsts. Luce had been a first in his particular type of business and how profitable had that been? Even though the profits had now disappeared—but first things first.

He was glad of the very cold room. By the time he had spread out the tarp and placed lighter, plastic sheeting over the top of it, he was already warming up. Two sheets came next. The next part of his chore was to somehow shift what was left of Grandmother onto the layers lying beside her.

Doing this soon cured his penchant for red and black satin sheets. He used a shovel to manoeuvre the remains onto the sheeting. The maggots didn't seem to mind this disturbance. They kept up with their avarice. He kept his eyes shut as much as he could while he shifted Grandmother. The clang of metal that he heard as he shifted the body was another puzzle.

Eventually he had the whole mess shifted. He shovelled the two sheets which had originally housed Grandmother onto the plastic sheeting as well. The floor could be cleaned up later. He pulled the cloth sheets around the remains as firmly as he could. Then he secured them with safety pins. He would have to undo the messy bundle later on to insert the bricks.

He was sure he would be unable to manoeuvre Grandmother into his vehicle if she was weighted down with bricks. His next move was to secure the blue tarp around the cloth sheets. He tied the lot together with ropes. He had no shortage of these. When this was done, he rolled the whole bundle onto the heavy tarp.

Getting Grandmother into the back of his SUV was not as difficult as he had imagined. He worked as quickly as possible. It was the dead of night when Lucas headed off towards the river. He knew of a spot that was out of the way.

He pulled up as close to the riverbank as possible. Grandmother came out with a thud. He quickly untied her of all her covers. Then he undid the safety pins and put the bricks into the fluid mess. He thought he might be sick but he was almost finished. He just hoped she would sink.

With the light from two strong torches, he heaved Grandmother into the black waters below. He shone his torch down onto the bundle and watched as it slowly disappeared.

The tomato test had proved to be successful.

Lucas Cowell was sure he would never eat another tomato for as long as he lived.

The next part of his plan was to locate Grandfather. He had searched the house. Curiously, Grandfather's clothes remained while Luce's clothing had disappeared. He wondered why this should be. Maybe Grandfather had decided to purchase a new wardrobe.

He was also puzzled about what had happened to Grandmother. Why had she died? The body was too decomposed to tell if Grandfather had hit her across the head to finish her off. Anyway, it no longer mattered. She was in her watery grave.

Lucas phoned the school. He said he was checking to see how his niece was coping. The school told him that Luce was no longer a student there. They explained that Grandmother had phoned and said they were shifting up north for Grandfather's sake, to a warmer climate which was more suited to his failing health.

Lucas tried to put all these pieces together. His only conclusion was that cunning, old Grandfather had taken off with the delectable Luce after doing away with Grandmother. Well, Lucas would be coming after Grandfather, of that he had no doubt.

The nightmares did not lessen. They were coming almost every night. Rina Wright was getting to the stage she did not want to go to sleep when night had fallen. But for the fact she had to be alert enough to take care of Jude, she would have slept all day and stayed awake all night.

As well as the nightmares, she was also experiencing visions or maybe they were hallucinations. Sometimes she saw a young girl, very pretty with golden hair. She had no idea who this person was. At least these visions weren't frightening like the nightmares.

She often reviewed how her life was changing. How it had become almost impossible to remain invisible. There was the family next door. That was one thing, but now she had met two other young women in the park. Maybe she would never see them again. But it had been a nice interlude talking to them. They were different from the people she had known in Sydney. It was as though they held an abundance of secrets between them.

She woke with a fright, her skin covered with goose bumps. The images in her dream were as terrible as ever. Just fragments remained of ugly, black boots, beds, and women screaming. Rina got out of bed then checked on Jude who was sleeping peacefully. This was one thing she was grateful for. In spite of Jude's disability, he never seemed to suffer from poor, sleeping habits.

There was little point in trying to go back to sleep, so she got off the floor, threw the blanket around her shoulders and walked outside. The night was very crisp so she gathered the blanket closer around her. She sat on a camp chair she had bought at the second-hand shop and looked out at the night sky. She had read in the newspaper that there was to be a super full moon, where the sky would be brighter than usual.

As she looked around, she realised that it was so bright she could almost read the newspaper. She settled down and made herself as comfortable as possible in the canvas chair. Her eyes closed as she reviewed the barren state of her life. All she really had was Jude and her nightmares. She had no family, no parents, no brothers or sisters, no cousins, no aunts or uncles.

Her biggest fear was what would happen to Jude if she should get sick or worse—die. He would be totally alone. There would be absolutely no one in the entire world who could care less about him. She must have dropped off to sleep. The next time she woke she was screaming. Then she started crying. The futility of her life increased her tears to sobs.

"Why are you crying?" The male voice came out of the blue.

Rina stifled a scream. Her eyes flew open and there in front of her was the man who lived next door. Her emotions were so open and raw she imagined he could almost read her mind. "Oh! You startled me. What are you doing here?"

"I saw you sitting there on your chair. It's not too hard to see in this moonlight. Then I heard you crying. Sounds are often magnified at night."

"I'm sorry if I disturbed you. I didn't mean to."

"You didn't disturb me. I wasn't asleep either."

"Do you have trouble sleeping?" she asked. He remained in front of her. She felt bad mannered. "There's another chair back on the patio if you would like to sit down." She hoped he would just go straight home. She was not up to talking to anyone, certainly not this irritating neighbour.

He grabbed the chair and placed it beside her. "Why can't you sleep?"

She shrugged her shoulders. "It's because of the dreams. It's sometimes better to stay awake. What about you? Why can't you sleep?"

"The usual reasons, I suppose. Worries, work, that sort of thing, but I don't usually wake up screaming."

"Oh, did I do that?" She felt ashamed. It was enough that he had seen her crying. She didn't always know when she screamed out.

"Yeah, you did. It must have been one hell of a dream. What was it about?"

"I don't usually remember. You know how stuff just disappears. It all gets mixed up. All I know is that the dreams leave me feeling wretched. I wish I didn't have to sleep. If it wasn't for Jude, I would sleep all day and stay awake all night."

He said nothing for some time. "What if I sat with you? Do you think that would help you sleep?"

She couldn't help herself. She laughed. "Why on earth would you want to do that?"

"Think of it as payment for helping out with Amanda. She's become very fond of you and Jude, as has Thomas."

"I enjoy having Amanda and Thomas visit. They are both so good to Jude. It's me who should be grateful." They sat in silence before she added. "Don't you think you should be going? You can't stay here all night. What about your work?"

"I suppose I should be going. As long as you're sure you're all right." He stood up to leave.

"I'll be fine. I'll go back to bed now." she said. "Thank you for your kindness. By the way, I don't even know your name, let alone what you do for a living."

"My name is Andy, Andy Brown and I'm the sergeant of police. Goodnight," he said as he left.

Rina would have collapsed onto the ground had she known this. Instead, she gripped the sides of her camp chair and tried to steady her breathing. Of all the people in Tewantin, he had to be a policeman. How could she remain invisible? His job surely was to find things out about people. Had he checked up on her? He already thought she was a nutter. Now he had more ammunition. He knew she had nightmares and woke screaming in the middle of the night.

She went to bed. To her amazement, she woke the next morning feeling refreshed. There had been no more nightmares. Maybe she was safe. There was no reason why she would ever be confronted by him again.

Rina continued to go daily to the park with Jude trailing behind. She met up again with Lu, the young woman with the dogs. Rina did not know one dog from the next. To her they looked identical.

Jude had been introduced to the dogs and, like the old dog that lived in the house next door, he slowly began to pat them. The dogs retained their haughty ways, but surprisingly they allowed Jude to sit in front of them when he would occasionally pat them and look straight into their eyes. It was a strange bonding.

The other young woman called Lizzie joined them on occasions. They were an unusual trio. Over time, a friendship began to form. None of them spoke of anything personal. Each one was totally unaware of anything much more than their first names and what they liked to eat. This was about the extent of their conversations, but the silence that held them together made the bond stronger.

Rina's life was changing even more. She hated that her private world was being invaded. She still woke each night. To reduce the stress of the nightmares, she always sat outside. Had she more sense, she would have braved the horror of her dreams and stayed in bed. Instead she went out into the night. And every night, when Andy Brown saw her sitting outside in the dark, he would appear through the gate that divided their homes.

As he sat beside her, he would always ask. "How are you tonight, Rina? Did you have another dream?"

She would answer, "Yes, but not as bad as last night." The nightmares never got any better but she could hardly tell him that.

Then they would talk, again about nothing of importance. They would sit and look out into the dark night. The conversations always ended the same way.

"I'd better go back to bed now," she would say.

"Are you sure you'll be okay," he'd say.

"Yes, I'll be fine and thank you for your kindness."

He would get up to leave and say, "Goodnight, Rina."

Then she would sleep soundly. She hoped that one day she would have the confidence to ask if he ever went back to sleep after their nightly talks. But maybe asking this would take her into more personal realms and she didn't want this. The whole set up confused her. She had no idea why he came over to her every night. She also supposed if she did not go outside, he would not come. But the dreamless sleep she experienced after he left was well worth it.

One night as they sat side by side, he asked, "When is your birthday, Rina?"

She was immediately alarmed. "Why do you want to know that?"

He had to think quickly, "Amanda wants to know. She thought she would like to buy you a gift for all the times you keep an eye on her."

"Oh, please, she doesn't have to do that. I love Amanda. I love having her here."

"It's important to her. It's something she really wants to do."

After some time she replied, "I don't have birthdays."

"Why not, everyone has a birthday?"

"Well, I don't," she replied firmly. He knew she was annoyed. But he had come this far, so he pushed her further.

"What, is it against your beliefs, like the electricity?"

She stood up quickly, "I think it's time I went to bed. Thank you for your kindness. Goodnight."

She tuned to run inside but he grabbed her by the arm. "All I asked was when your birthday was. Is that so bad? I didn't ask how old you were, just when you were born."

"Let go of me," she said, trying to pull her arm out of his grip. The blanket had fallen off her. He saw her in what he thought was an old-fashioned nightie, but at least it wasn't black or brown like everything else he had seen her in.

She was almost crying again. He felt her tremble. He couldn't help himself. He pulled her into his arms. "It's no big deal, Rina. It doesn't matter when your birthday is. Amanda can buy you a present. I'll just make up a date, any date will do."

Rina's emotions were in tumult. This man held her in his arms. She had never before felt arms around her, not in comfort, not in anger. "You don't understand," she said.

"What don't I understand, Rina?"

"It's all confused in my head. I'm two people." He could feel her shuddering breaths.

"Tell me about being two people, Rina?"

"You already think I'm a nutter. I can't talk about it."

He sighed, "I don't think that at all. I didn't know you heard me that first day I saw you. It's just that I've never met anyone quite like you." She seemed to have relaxed a little, so he kept holding her. "You can tell me anything, Rina, anything you like."

She thought about this. But he was a policeman. If he knew she had near one million dollars shoved in the bottom of her wardrobe, he would think she was much more than a nutter. But she knew he wasn't going to let her go without some sort of explanation.

"I used to be one person when I was very young, then I became another person. That's all I know. I have to remain invisible. That's why you should not come over here anymore."

He absorbed what she had said. "I don't think I can do that, Rina." He took her face in his hands and briefly kissed her on the lips. Then he said, "Goodnight, Rina. I'll see you tomorrow night."

*

Andy Brown was mesmerised by the young woman who lived in the house behind him. He didn't know how it had happened. But she was like a magnet. After that first night when he heard her scream out and then start sobbing, he had been drawn like a moth to a flame—or to a candle.

He had grilled his daughter, Amanda, as unobtrusively as possible about what she knew about Rina and Jude. But his daughter was not the least interested in finding out the finer details of Rina. Amanda was a born chatterbox. She could chat on for ages about school, music, sport and her friends. Andy Brown was certain that Rina Wright was too clever to let slip any personal details. It would be more like the other way around. Rina most likely knew all about his family.

He told himself he had to respect her privacy. If she didn't wish to talk about herself, then she didn't have to. But her mystique would not leave him. After his last conversation with her, he had to break his promise to himself. He looked her up in the police data bases. Nothing—no history at all, not that he had expected any. She didn't look like a big time criminal, but you could never tell.

Thinking where else to look, he phoned the real estate agent who handled the rental house she lived in. He explained that there was a problem with the fence that divided the two properties. The real estate agent told him the house was rented by a Rina Wright.

It was one of the homes that Michael and Denise Farraday had left in their estate to be used by the less fortunate. He said that as the lady had a disabled child and was a single mother, she fitted the bill. As to the owners, he would have to contact the Farraday family who handled all these matters, specifically Mitchell Farraday.

Farraday—how often had he heard this name over the years? But it had not popped up in any nefarious deeds for ages. They were now the soul of respectability, at least the older ones.

Gabriel Farraday was anything but respectable. He had numerous convictions, going back years. Being drunk in a public place, hooning, driving while under the influence, unlawful use of a motor vehicle, driving while being disqualified, drug possession, affray, even breaking and entering, although this was contestable. He was so drunk when picked up, it was questionable he knew what he was doing.

Detective Senior-Sergeant Andy Brown was at a loss. He did not know where else to turn. He told himself it was because of his son and daughter that he was interested in her background. The young woman, who called herself Rina Wright, had in effect trapped both his son and his daughter. They couldn't seem to keep away from her. He excluded himself from this scenario. He only saw her during the night because she was upset, crying and screaming. No way had she trapped him.

He did not know where else to turn. It was really none of his business. After all what had she done—nothing really? His daughter and son had befriended her. It was not the other way around. His children had made the first approaches. She had a son who was disabled—but so what? There were numerous, disabled children around.

He contacted disability services and announced his title. He asked about a child called Jude Wright and was told they had no information about a child called Jude Wright. He went further, interstate, requested information about a disabled boy called Jude Wright. There were no results. How obscure was that?

He also tried the electoral roll, but again there was no Rina Wright. He contacted the Registry of births, deaths and marriages but was given no information. He tried not to appear too intrusive while making these requests. He had no real legitimate reason for doing so.

*

Rina Wright was again in despair. She had not only let her next door neighbour hold her, but he had kissed her as well. She had also told him things about herself, things that she had vowed never to tell anyone. But he had this knack of getting past her defences. She would have to be more guarded. She thought briefly that it might be safer if she packed up her few possessions, grabbed Jude and took off again on a bus and go wherever it took her.

On further thought, she rationalised that Andy Brown would have even more reason to be suspicious of her if she disappeared. She was sure he would find her. No, she would stay put and learn to be more vigilant.

That night when the dreams came, she remained inside. She sat on the small lounge chair and waited for the terrors to pass. She lit a candle and played solitaire. Solitaire was the only safe game for her to play. She would avoid Andy Brown at any cost and the games that he was playing with her.

But staying inside did not stop him. She heard the soft knock. There was no one else that it could be. If she didn't answer the door, then maybe he would go away. He knocked again and again. Defeated, she opened the door and he came straight in.

"What are you doing here?"

"I just wanted to apologise for last night. I'm sorry if I was too pushy. I won't get personal again. If you don't believe in birthdays or you're two different people, or that you want to be invisible, that's fine by me. But you have to understand, my children think the world of you. It's only natural that I'd want to know something about you."

She picked up the cards and put them back in the pack. He sat down beside her. The double seated lounge chair meant that he was very close to her. She wanted to get up and run away from him. But she steadied her nerves and remained where she was.

"I can understand that you want your children to be safe. That's what I want for Jude. I want him to be safe, always. You must know that your children would always be safe with me."

"I do know that, Rina. You have a kind heart." He was sitting on her left. She was very startled when his big hand reached down and took hold of her left hand. She tried to pull away, but he held on. "You don't have to hide your hand from me, Rina."

"It's very ugly," was all she said.

"There's nothing about you that's ugly, Rina." He brought her left hand to his lips and kissed it. "Would you let me hold you again, Rina?"

She would have escaped to her room, only he still held her hand. "I don't know anything about being held or kissed," she said. The memory of the previous night was strong.

He almost asked her how her son had been conceived but stopped himself in time. He didn't want to lose the steps he had gained. Not waiting for a reply, he pulled her into his arms again and kissed her gently on the lips. That was all. She didn't try to push him away. She stayed sitting beside him with his arms around her.

They must have both dropped back to sleep. What woke them were the faint noises coming from Jude's room. Andy Brown woke with a start due to the weight across his chest. She had slumped down almost onto his lap. Somehow his hand was around her breast. He left it there while she awoke. She pulled back from him. Their eyes met and held.

"You'd better go," she whispered. "What about your children?"

"What about their father?" he whispered back. They stood up together. Before he left he took her in his arms again, and kissed her properly. This time she opened her mouth and kissed him back. She found that she was experiencing feelings that she had never known before.

The weetbix packet was almost empty. She knew he would be home the next day so she proposed to walk to the shopping centre and purchase some more. Lu was becoming used to eating first thing in the morning.

Gabe had been back many times. His usual habit was to disappear for several nights on his week home. Most days he also went off with the dogs. Where he went she had no idea? They had settled into a routine.

She even sat down with him and ate. He still fed her pieces of the foods he ate. Sometimes he fed her ice cream, more yoghurt and also pieces of meat. Lu had cooked plenty of meat dishes for her grandparents, but she had never partaken of any. It had been apples, cheese and milk for her and only in small portions.

The weather was beautiful in spite of there being a hint of coolness during the day. The days were as near as perfect as possible. Lu was beginning to relax. Her life followed a pleasant routine. Up early, eat breakfast, which was a new venture for her, feed and exercise the dogs which took up most of her time.

She sometimes saw the young women in the park. She enjoyed their company although none of them ever said anything about their personal lives. She did not find this unusual because she had never spoken to anyone about her most private thoughts or her life.

She knew she was putting on weight. This played on her mind. She had been so conditioned to remaining in an emaciated state that she sometimes thought she might vomit up the extra food she had eaten.

But she had heard about eating conditions such as anorexia nervosa and bulimia—she didn't want to fall into these categories. She had come too far, had escaped from one hell and she didn't want to fall into another.

So she let her stomach become used to the extra food. Very gradually, she was able to eat a little extra. When she had her shower, she never, ever, looked in the mirror. Her body was nothing but a source of shame to her. But when a picture of a scantily-clad female which was taped to the bathroom mirror fell down, she felt obliged to pick it up and put it back again. This was when she was forced to look at herself—naked.

The five rules were back in her head. It was rule four that she broke again and again. What she saw was a body that was no longer as emaciated. She turned her head away. This was not her. But curiosity made her look again. Her face was the same but it was fuller. The bones were not as prominent as previous. There was a covering of what she supposed was muscle or fat over her limbs. Even her hair looked different. It was not as dry and scraggly.

But as she looked, the worst of all was that she now had small breasts instead of a faint swelling with a nipple in the middle. She turned away and hurried into her clothes.

The warm sun seduced her. She had walked both dogs, talked to Rina in the park as Jude sat with the dogs. Then she walked to the shops to purchase more food supplies.

She had developed a brazen plan in her mind. If it was good enough for the dogs, surely she could manage it. She had watched them on countless occasions, lying like lords of the realm in the sun. The yard where they were kept was totally enclosed. Lu decided she could do the same. If they could enjoy nature's glorious benefits, then so could she.

She whipped off her clothes and lay naked on a towel under the warm sun. In her fanciful imaginings, she thought maybe the sun might melt off some of the fat that had settled on her skinny frame. Then rule four would not be seen to have been broken.

She lay on her stomach with the dogs close by. She could hear them panting. She heard them stand and move, but lethargy kept her lying in half-sleep. It was such a warm, delicious feeling having the sun on her back and legs. The dogs were making more noise. She lifted her head. There he was sitting on the back steps staring at her with a dog on either side of him.

He did not speak. She did not speak. She was unable to read his face. All her old fears come back. He was her grandparents and Uncle Lucas all rolled into one. She was not being perfect.

She screamed out, looked around in alarm, grabbed the towel and ran down the back to the dog kennels. She heard his footsteps behind her, could smell the dogs. They were with him as he ran after her.

She ran behind the kennels, pushing herself as far back as she could until she was wedged up against the kennel and the back corner of the fence. She pulled the towel up over her and hid her face in her hands. The dogs were now barking at her. She could feel him standing there.

How long he stood there before he spoke, she did not know? It seemed like an age. "You don't have to stay there. You can come out."

She had always liked his voice. It was not high pitched like Grandfather or evil like Uncle Lucas. She kept her face hidden in her hands. "Please don't hurt me, please don't"

"I'm not going to hurt you. I just want you to come out of there." He had spoken slowly. She imagined he might have been shocked. He had plenty of reason to be.

"I'm not a boy," she said. She pulled the towel up further. The breasts that had come from nowhere were beginning to bother her.

"I can see that," he replied. "You can also talk and hear."

Slowly, she shifted her hands and looked at him. He was standing at the end of the kennels. From where she sat crouched down, he looked very big and menacing especially with the two dogs standing on either side of him. "Please don't hurt me. I'll be good, I promise. I won't break any more rules. Just don't hurt me."

"I thought we talked about this. I'm not going to hurt you. You know you can trust me. I said I would look after you. Just because it turns out that you're a girl and you can both hear and talk, doesn't mean I'm going to turn into some sort of monster. Please come out."

The dogs were beginning to tire of this new experience. They went back to lying in the sun. She did not move. "Look, if I get your bear then will you come out?" She nodded her head.

He was back with the bear and held it in front of him.

"Promise you won't hurt him either. He's the only friend I've got." Her voice was not much more than a whimper.

"I promise." He held it out to her. She stood up with the towel still in front of her. She slowly moved along the fence and took the bear from him. She clutched it to her chest.

"I'll go back to the house. I want you to come inside and put your clothes on. Will you do that for me?"

"Yes." She watched him return to the house. When he disappeared into the house, she ran to her room where she slammed the door firmly shut. It took only seconds to get back into her clothes. She didn't know what to do then. So she sat on the floor holding black devil. He knocked on the door. She didn't answer, so he opened the door and walked in. He sat on the bed.

"Tell me about the rules?"

"I don't know if I'm allowed to repeat them just to anyone. Uncle Lucas will be very angry if he finds out."

He swallowed heavily before he spoke again. "Uncle Lucas isn't here. I'm the only person here. You know you can trust me so you are allowed to tell me about the rules."

She tried to keep Uncle Lucas out of her head. Slowly, she began to tell him. "There are five rules that must be obeyed, otherwise there are consequences." He sat and watched her.

"Go on," he said.

"I must not talk, I must not laugh, I must not touch, I must not eat, and I must be perfect unless Grandfather tells me otherwise." She said the rules in a hurry. "I've broken them all." She was almost crying.

"What are the consequences, Lu?"

"You know what they are. You've seen my feet. There are needles being pushed under your toes and having your feet branded, as well as the rest of it. But I can't talk about that, not to you, not to anyone, not ever."

She was openly crying now. He slid down off the bed and pulled her into his arms. They sat together like this for a long time. He didn't ask her anything more. She didn't tell him anything more.

Gabriel Farraday could not imagine what had happened to this girl who had duped him so convincingly. After a time, he asked, "How come you can sign and read lips so well?"

"I went to a school for the disabled. That was how I could keep rule number one."

"What about rule number two?"

"That wasn't hard. There was never anything to laugh about."

"And rule number three?"

"I don't talk about three, not ever".

"Number four?"

"You get used to not eating."

"Number five?"

"I just did as I was told. My grandparents and Uncle Lucas made sure of it. Most of the time I was perfect."

"Where are your grandparents?"

"Grandmother died of a heart attack."

"And Grandfather, what happened to him?"

She took her time answering this. "He fell under a train."

This intrigued him. "How did he fall, Lu?"

She put her face in her hands again in embarrassment before answering, "I pushed him."

This definitely surprised him. "Good for you," was all he said.

She wouldn't look at him. "Do you think I'm wicked? It was a great big sin. I didn't intend doing it, but there were going to be more consequences so I just did it. I couldn't live through anymore consequences."

"I don't think you're wicked. And I don't think it was much of a sin, as long as you got rid of him altogether. You were very brave doing what you did." He pulled her tighter into his arms before asking.

"What about Uncle Lucas?"

He could feel her tense up in his arms. "He'll come after me if he ever finds me. He'll probably kill me. I took some of his stuff."

"What sort of stuff?"

She looked up at him, again in embarrassment and shame, "The bad stuff."

He pulled her closer. "Is that the stuff under the house in the two bags?"

"How did you know it was there?" She was very nervous knowing this. She started ringing her hands in dismay.

"I live here. You had the two bags with you that first night. Then they disappeared. They had to be somewhere. They weren't too hard to find. I take it this stuff is important to you."

"No one can see it, no one. I would rather die than have anyone see it or else I'd go to jail."

"No one's going to jail, Lu." He was quiet in thought before he said. "What's your real name?"

"They called me Luce Potulski, but I don't think that was my real name. I think I've had many names but I don't remember. I don't ever want to be Luce Potulski again."

"Maybe we can change your name. Do you have a birth certificate or any form of identification?"

"I don't have anything. All I remember are my grandparents and Uncle Lucas."

"I'll have to think about this. So you don't know your real name. Do you know when you were born or where?"

"No. All I know is that they wanted me to look like a young girl, to never grow up. It was better for business. That's what Grandfather and Uncle Lucas always said."

They stayed sitting on the floor together. Black devil sat with them. The dogs remained at the back door. After a time, she spoke.

"Why are you home so early? You weren't due back until tomorrow."

"I had an injury, hurt my back, but it seems to be better now."

"That's good. I'm pleased you're better." She felt better herself, so she shifted out of his arms. "Maybe I could cook you some dinner. That is, if you're not going out."

"That would be nice, Lu. I didn't know you could cook and I'm not going out, not tonight."

She stood up and headed towards the kitchen. He followed her out.

"How about I get take-out for tonight and you can cook tomorrow. I don't think you should be cooking tonight after all you've been through. Would you like to come to the shops with me and we'll pick something up? We'll get Chinese. The owners, Mr and Mrs Lee, live across the road. They're nice people."

She nodded shyly. She hopped into his SUV. It was the first time she had been in his vehicle since the night he had come to her rescue.

When they picked up the Chinese, he introduced her to Mr and Mrs Lee. He told them that she was his friend. They shook her hand and said she was very lucky to have such a nice man for a friend. Gabe looked uncomfortable and quickly left.

She set the table with the best crockery and cutlery that she could find in the cupboards. They ate together. He gave her a glass of beer. She had never tasted alcohol before. After half a glass she started laughing at his silly jokes. When she laughed and smiled, he could not stop looking at her. She looked so pretty. Her brilliant smile kept reminding him of someone.

He was tired after his trip. His back still ached although the beer had smothered the pain. He went to his bed. She lay on the floor in her room. She could not sleep as she listened to his uneven breathing coming from the next room. After a time, she heard his footsteps come into her room. She pretended she was asleep. He lay on her bed. As she lay on the floor, she heard his breathing slowly even out. She soon dropped off to sleep.

When she opened her eyes the next morning, he was awake sitting on the side of her bed watching her. Her feet were sticking out the bottom of her blanket. She hurriedly pulled them back out of sight. He pretended he hadn't noticed.

"I hope you didn't mind that I slept in your bed. I thought you might be frightened and wake up."

"I don't mind and thank you for being so thoughtful," she mumbled.

"How about we have some breakfast and then we'll take the dogs for a walk?"

"You mean together," she asked, surprised.

"Sure. We'll go for a drive."

Neither of them felt quite as comfortable as they had the previous evening as they ate weetbix together. The dogs were fed, then he ushered them all into his SUV. It felt strange to be sitting beside him. He travelled along lonely roads and pulled up outside a locked gate. She saw a sign that said Sunshine.

"We'll walk from here." She watched him unlock the gate. She followed him and the dogs into the property. There was little to see other than an old house and some sheds.

"What is this place?" she asked.

"It's just a place where I bring the dogs. No one lives here. I walk along the creek and up into the hills. Do you think you could walk that far?" He pointed up into the hills. She could see a craggy rock. Now that she was eating more, she hoped she had the energy to get that far.

"I'll try," she said. He let the dogs off their leashes and they raced ahead. She followed him, trying to keep up. He stopped and waited for her. Sometimes he took her by the arm where the track was rough and steep. At first she flinched when he touched her, but then she became used to his help. When they reached the top, they sat together looking out at the countryside.

"This is a very beautiful place. Why doesn't anyone live here?"

"They say it's a sad place. No one has lived here for years." He pointed out the track they had followed before asking. "Do you want to see a cave?"

He was up and moving again. She hurried after him. The cave was partially hidden by an overhanging rock. The dogs were already ahead of them. They didn't have a torch, so they remained at the entrance of a deep cavern.

"This has a spooky feel to it," she said. She grabbed him by the hand. They stood staring into the dense darkness of the cave.

"You stay here," he said. "I just want to check on something." She remained with the dogs while he went further into the cave. He returned a few minutes later. "We'd better be getting home," he added, as he noticed the clouds were thickening.

Again he helped her down. She sometimes even took his hand voluntarily as she stumbled down the track. When they reached the area where the house was, he put the dogs on the leashes again. They returned back to his home. She was quite tired and hungry. She shyly asked him if he wanted some lunch. He smiled at her and said, "Sangers and beer, what do you think?"

She made sandwiches, using salami and onion for him. She sliced up some apple for herself and put it on a piece of bread. They are together. She drank her second beer of her life. Again she started laughing. The second rule lay dormant in her mind.

"I've been thinking about your situation, and about my situation." He didn't want to be too crass by mentioning all that she had been through.

"What's your situation?" She couldn't imagine what sort of situation he might have other than his sore back. But considering how he had climbed up and down the steep hill, there didn't seem to be too much wrong with his back now.

"It's not so easy to talk about. But you've told me your secrets, so here goes. I've been in a lot of trouble with the law. I have to front up to court soon. I've done some stupid things. I have a long history of traffic demeanours and other things. I could be facing a jail sentence. It would not have bothered me once but that's all changed now." He almost said *now that I have you.*

Instead he added. "I said I'd do my best to protect you, but if I cop a jail sentence I won't be able to do that."

She looked at him in bewilderment. How was it possible that he could go to jail when her grandparents and Uncle Lucas had done all those things and they had never even been visited by the police? They had been free to roam the earth unhindered. Or for that matter, look what she had done, pushed Grandfather under a train and let Grandmother die from a heart attack, as well as all the other stuff.

"You can't go to jail. You of all people don't deserve to go to jail." She sounded alarmed.

"It's my track record. But anyway, what I was thinking is this— that's if you're prepared to go along with me. What say I marry you?"

She started laughing and asked for another bottle of beer. He loved to hear her laugh and watch her smile. "I mean it. If we got married, it might help my case, especially if you pretended to be deaf and dumb, you know, like how you fooled me."

She had stopped laughing as she realised he was serious. "If I went to jail, it would mean that I would have to leave a disabled wife with no carer and no income coming in. If I can avoid a jail sentence, you could continue living here with me and the dogs. If Uncle Lucas ever turns up, then I will be here to deal with him and you'll be safe."

"Marry you. You mean like a wedding. That would mean I'd be your wife." She could not believe what he was proposing. "Let me get this straight. We get married. I go back to being deaf and dumb when you go to court. You avoid jail, and in exchange I get to live here permanently and you keep me safe. Is that about it?"

"It's the best I can come up with. Have you got any other ideas?"

"No, I don't," she remained thoughtful. "Say I agree to this, the marriage part, what else would it involve?"

"Are you talking about sex?" She avoided his eyes as she nodded. "Not if you didn't want it." He kept his voice even. He was not certain himself how he felt about this part of the marriage, not that he wouldn't be tempted—but she was too fragile. Her bones looked like they might crack. He still had Annie and Josephina to fulfil these types of needs.

She turned her head away from him before saying. "I don't think I could stand it. Not after everything that's happened."

"So, do you agree?"

"I guess I do," she replied, "but I think I'm going to need another one of those beers."

He stood up and brought two back from the refrigerator. "Here's to the engagement," he said. She giggled again as he charged his glass.

"So when do we have the happy event?" The beer was going down at a fast rate.

"We have to get you a birth certificate first and a name. But leave that to me. Then we have to get a marriage celebrant to do the deed.

After that, we're home and hosed." He took the ring off the bottle top and put it on her finger. "It's not much of an engagement ring." She looked at her finger. As she lifted her hand, the ring fell off and tumbled under the table. She was down on her knees looking for it. He got down on his knees as well to help with the search. They were both slightly drunk; she more so than he. They were now both under the table when he found it and slipped it back on her finger. She looked up at him to thank him. She smiled.

The smile was his undoing. He took her face in his hands and kissed her. It was brief and gentle. This time she didn't pull away. Rule number three did not come back into her head. She shut her eyes and felt the tenderness of his lips on hers.

It was another intimate yet embarrassing moment. He helped her out from under the table and then said he had some business to attend to. He left in his SUV. She told him that she would take the dogs for their afternoon walk. She took them one at a time because she was still not strong enough to hold the two of them.

As she walked with the dogs, she kept feeling the beer bottle ring on her finger and the sensation of his lips on hers. Nothing in her life was making much sense. Her life had taken another big leap.

Gabriel was uncertain if he was doing the right thing. This person, Lu, who turned out to be female, had intrigued him from the first night he had picked her up. Even when he thought she was a boy, he had wanted to keep her with him.

Now he had made another proposal. It was a plan that would keep the pair of them safe, or so he hoped. He then thought of his father who had died a lonely death in a jail yard. Then he thought of his mother, who everyone said had taken her own life, but he wouldn't believe this, never.

He didn't believe in prayers or anything else much, but if his parents were watching out for him from wherever they were, he hoped they would give him right guidance. More than anything, he just wanted to keep her with him. Then, just maybe, he might find some peace.

He seldom visited his uncle Malcolm. There were too many sad memories. But he didn't know how else to achieve his plan. His uncle still lived in the same house when he was married to his first wife, Carrie, who had been murdered by persons unknown.

It was also the place from where his uncle's daughter had disappeared. She had been a very young girl and was never seen again. It was not known if she had been murdered or taken and sold into slavery. Her body had never been found. Malcolm had never been quite the same after this.

When Gabe rang the front door bell, it was answered by his Aunt Zaylee, Malcolm's second wife.

"Hello, Gabe. How nice to see you. Come on in." His aunt welcomed him in. She always looked so young, too young to be a successful, medical practitioner. He followed her inside. They walked through the house into a spacious living room. "Mal's not here at the moment. He's taken Emmet to basketball practice. He shouldn't be long."

"How's he doing?"

"Who—Malcolm or Emmet?" she asked, motioning for him to sit.

"Well both, but Malcolm, I guess."

"He's not too bad. He pretends a lot, makes out that everything is okay. He still doesn't sleep much. I guess that will never change. Nothing will ever make the memories go away."

"I guess not." They chatted on. She asked about his work. She studiously avoided any mention of his numerous clashes with the law.

"I was wondering if you wouldn't mind if I visited Lucia's room. I often think of her. I can't stop thinking about Sarina either. They were such close friends. There's nothing to remember Sarina by. It helps seeing Lucia's room. I feel embarrassed asking such a crappy thing. But it's like you say, the memories never go away."

"Of course I don't mind. You go ahead. I'll make us some tea." He waited until she was out of sight then he went to Lucia's room. He had seen her birth certificate in a folder of mementoes that Malcolm and Zaylee had compiled years ago of the missing child.

He quickly took it out of the folder, then replaced the folder exactly as he'd found it. He stayed a little longer, looking at the dolls and toys that had belonged to his cousin. It was a sad and lonely place. Malcolm had never given up his search for his daughter.

He returned to Zaylee. He didn't want to seem ungrateful, so he drank the tea down in a hurry and then said he had to leave. He explained he would come back later with a six pack for his uncle. He would love to have a beer with him. Zaylee was somewhat taken aback by his abrupt departure. But then she thought it was a nice gesture that he was going to return to have a beer with his uncle.

Dr Zaylee Lang had always been fond of her husband's twin nephews. Their lives had not turned out as expected. Great things had been expected of them. They had been bright, highly achieving children but when their parents had died, all that changed. Lots of things had changed when their parents had died, not just for the twins.

Gabe drove as inconspicuously as he could to the nearest photocopy shop. He made a copy of the birth certificate. He was very pleased with the results. It was almost impossible to tell which one was the original copy. He then bought a six pack. Not that his uncle needed any excuse to drink. It was well known that he hit the bottle pretty hard.

When he drove back to his uncle's property he saw that Malcolm had returned with his young son. Gabe played around with Emmet, putting the ball through hoops. Then he went to see his uncle.

The sadness never left him. No matter how hard he tried to cover it, the pain remained in his eyes. Malcolm Farraday remained a handsome man. He was trim and charming. They sat together and drank the beer. Gabe was pleased he didn't receive another lecture about drinking and driving. They talked about sport, Emmet, the weather. The Farraday business was not mentioned.

Gabe was on the outside when it came to the Farraday fortune. He had not yet redeemed himself, at least, not in Mitchell Farraday's eyes. When he thought about it, Gabe didn't really blame any of them. He was no shining example of respectability. It was Rafe who was the shining light.

Before he left, he asked to see Lucia's room one more time. Again, he said he had recently been upset about Sarina as well as Lucia. He had even been dreaming about the two of them. Malcolm just looked away and told him to go ahead. He kept it as a shrine to his daughter.

Gabe slipped the photocopy of the birth certificate back into the memento folder. He took one last look at the room. He had really loved his little cousin. She had been a beautiful, sweet, golden-haired girl.

When he left, Zaylee spoke to her husband. "I really like Gabe. I really, really like him. He's a fine, young man."

Her husband looked at her quizzically. "He's always in trouble of one sort or another. I just wish he could get his act together and do something decent for a change."

Gabe returned to his own home. Lu had attended to the dogs. They had been fed and groomed. They stood together on the back veranda admiring the dogs when he said. "It's all fixed. We can do it in a month. That will be before my next court case. Are you sure you still want to go through with it?"

"As long as it keeps Uncle Lucas from finding me, I don't care what we do. How did you manage to get a birth certificate for me? You don't even know who I am."

"I got one. You don't need to know all the details. It should get us through all right as long as no one looks too closely. The date of birth on it should be about right, if you can make yourself look a bit older. As for the name, it might prove a bit tricky but we should be able to bluff our way through it."

"As long as I'm not called Luce Potulski, I don't care what name I use."

She wished she were a fly on the wall. That way she would know exactly what the reactions were. Lizzie Smythe had set part of her plan of revenge in motion. She did feel a little guilty as she was well aware that what she was planning was bad. But that's what people called her—bad, beautiful Lizzie.

The beautiful part had never got her anywhere, so maybe she's test out the bad part. Her first object of revenge was the mighty Mitch. Next on her list was her sister, horrible Hope, and last but not least, Raphael. But the biggest revenge of the lot was for Leon Jones. But so far, he had proved to be too smart for her. He was always two steps ahead.

Lizzie estimated that it would be about now that they would both be receiving the first letter.

*

Francine Farraday was totally in love with her big, handsome husband. He took care of her. He loved her and he loved their children. She had tried to overcome the loss of her finger, to pretend that she was a full and whole person. But she was not.

Something bad happened to her which her mind refused to remember. Not only was the ring finger gone, but part of her memory as well. She had given up trying to fathom what had happened. Her husband told her very little of what had occurred that day. Just that she had been abducted and then returned.

Mitch was now quite the accomplished, business man. Long gone were his days as a military hero. He continued the business empire that his deceased brother and sister-in-law had commenced. Along with Dax Webster, the family's trusted accountant, their business continued to branch out and prosper.

He did most of his business from his home. Their children were at school. His wife seldom left their home. She still took an interest in her boutiques, but only by phone or email. She had staff employed to run her business.

The mail was delivered. Mitch collected it. This gave him a break from his every day duties. He would walk to the front of their acreage property, stretch his legs, and smell the fresh air, the blossoming trees and shrubs before returning back to his office. Coffee came next, then the mail. There was usually very little other than householders, advertising and the odd request for donations.

Today he received a letter in a plain, white envelope addressed to him. He pulled out the folded sheet of white paper and opened it up. At first, he could make no sense of it. There were letters cut from newspapers and magazines. He held it one way then the other until he had it right way up. The message was disturbing.

He read it out loud, "Shame on you, big daddy—shame."

He had no idea what this meant. He sat in thoughtful silence until he slipped it back into the envelope and hid it in the bottom of a drawer. Of course his thoughts returned to the daughter he had never met. She was the daughter whose name he never knew and who had been born when he was just a teenager. The daughter whom he had run away from and joined the military.

It was the same daughter whom he had sent money to for years to help with her care. He had sent it to his deceased brother, Michael, who then sent it onto the mother of the child. The identity of this child had been lost when his brother died.

He had no idea where the mother of this child now lived. She had left the area years ago. It was doubtful that the child involved ever knew of his existence either as she had made no effort to contact him over the years.

He thought of his own two children, Finbarr and Roza. They were wonderful, healthy children, growing fast. His loved them dearly. He thought his heart would burst with love for them. His life was very blessed. Other than his wife's reclusiveness and reticence, he was leading the perfect life.

His beautiful wife, Francine, and his two children were the joy of his life. What the letter meant, he had no idea. He put it out of his mind.

*

Hope Smythe sat with her uncle Mark watching a program about ancient Rome. She could never understand what he got out of watching these shows about monuments built to some old Roman ruler who had lived centuries ago.

Uncle Mark always said it was the architecture that got him in. Couldn't Hope understand the absolute genius of the slaves who had built such things? Hope never really got why he was so intrigued, but the big, old things certainly did look impressive, even if they were falling apart—pity about the poor slaves.

No one in Mark's household was interested in mail deliveries. So that when the letter arrived addressed to Ms Hope Smythe, it lay in a bundle with the rest of the householders, old newspapers and magazines. They were living in a modern, electronic world.

*

Lizzie was unclear in her mind about what she expected would happen when either of these two parties received their letter. When it was obvious there was no big upset in either Mitch or Hope's lives, she decided it was Raphael's time.

How to do it? How to entice him to the cemetery? She held onto her desire to screw his brains out. She had vowed to do this and on the grave of the big Farraday kahuna himself, her grandfather Alan Farraday, even if he had been dead for years.

From the stories and whispers she had heard, vague though they were, it seemed he was the ultimate bad man. Everything that had happened to her was in some way connected to this dead man. She had heard talk of his secrets, sex and lies—all those things that she was now a recipient of.

Doing it on his grave, was it sacrilegious? She certainly hoped so. It would well and truly serve Raphael right for his abandonment of her and for seeking redemption or whatever it was that he was looking for. If sex on a grave, let alone a cemetery, didn't put a shiver up his spine, nothing would.

Lizzie put a lot of thought into how she would go about getting her revenge on Raphael. Leon could wait for later. He wasn't going anywhere—unfortunately. Her next victim was Raphael, her childhood . . . what? She wasn't sure what to call him, certainly not friend. They had been too young for boyfriend and girlfriend. They were cousins. They had been children. She was younger than he, but there had always been something there, something more than friendship.

She recalled the times they had lain on the floor watching television or playing games like solitaire. He would contrive to lie next to her and as the night wore on, he would put his arm across her back.

There was never anything more than this, but Lizzie still remembered the feeling of being special—about the only person in her life who had ever made her feel this way. She was special to Leon, but in a totally different way. But that special feeling of belonging had disappeared when all the really bad things in their families had started to happen.

Lizzie remembered back to the time when her little cousin, Sarina, had disappeared. Then her aunt and uncle had been arrested for her murder. Then her own father had been killed in a traffic accident along with her aunt Tiffany. It was close to the time when another aunt was murdered and another young cousin, Lucia, had disappeared.

There was no end to the turmoil and to cap it all off, her aunt and uncle, Denise and Michael, had died. Her mother had lost her mind for a time, although Lizzie considered that she had never really got it back properly, in spite of everyone saying her mother was doing fine. What a lot of crap—everyone else had no idea?

The biggest issue was how to get away from Leon. Granted he disappeared on weekends during the day, but he was always around at night when she was at work, always hanging around keeping an eye on her. She belonged to him. Escape at any time was difficult but Leon could wait till later.

Raphael was next on her list. As luck would have it, her revenge was very simple to achieve. She knew Raphael was home from university. As usual he was staying with her Uncle Matt and Aunt Mia. Lizzie often phoned them to check up on her little brother, Harry. From these conversations, it was very easy to find out if Raphael was home.

Harry was the lucky one of her family. He had been cared for by Matt and Mia ever since he was a baby. It was doubtful that he even realised that they were not his birth parents. Matt and Mia still had their child care centres. As well as this, they often fostered children. Harry would never know it, but he was one lucky boy, in spite of the fact that Mia was somewhat vague and goofy.

Mia loved children and Harry was at the top of the list. Lizzie often wondered why they had no children of their own. Rumour had it that Mia thought she would never make a good mother as she was too much of an air-head. Not that Harry or any of the other children ever complained. Mia was dearly loved by all who come across her path.

Lizzie tripped while walking out of the club with the ever-present Leon. It was the high heels. They were so high they were an accident waiting to happen. Just as she went over, she knew she had found a way. She grabbed her left ankle and struggled as she tried to stand up, wincing with the pain.

While she sat beside Leon on the way home, she complained bitterly about her painful, swelling ankle. Thank goodness it was dark. As far as she could tell, there was no swelling evident. But Lizzie had been taught by a master how to pretend. If she could be that convincing while having sex with Leon, then she should be able to carry off a twisted ankle.

Maryanne could not have cared less as Lizzie stayed in bed the next day with a bandage wrapped around her ankle, moaning in pain and discomfort. The only thing that upset Maryanne was that Leon was paying attention to her daughter. Maryanne disliked any competition when it came to Leon.

Lizzie had shoved a sock around her ankle to make sure it was larger than her right ankle. The elastic bandage covered the sock successfully. To add authenticity to the twisted ankle, she rubbed some dark eye-shadow above the bandage. If no one looked too closely, there was ample evidence of bruising. When Leon visited her mother, Lizzie made a point of hobbling around. She took pain killers every four hours to be convincing. Leon agreed she should rest her leg.

Lizzie looked upset when she said she doubted she would be able to work at least for the next day or so. When Leon was within earshot, Maryanne conceded that it was a great shame that Lizzie was incapacitated, but Leon knew best. Lizzie needed to rest.

Entrapment—what a good word? Raphael received a call late at night from a distraught Lizzie, begging his help. Her car had broken down near the cemetery. Could he pick her up?

"What's up, Lizzie? What's wrong? It's late." He sounded very surprised to be receiving a phone call this late.

But Lizzie was a night person, maybe not by desire, but certainly by design. Nights didn't bother her. "I need your help, Rafe. I didn't know who else to turn to. I know it's late. It's mum's car. It's broken down."

"Can't you phone for road-side assistance?"

"I could, only my mother doesn't have any type of car insurance. Please, Rafe. I'm stuck here by myself. Please hurry." Lizzie did her best to sound disturbed. To fulfil her plan, she would have to get the car back before morning. Just in case her mother woke up; not that it was likely.

She saw vehicle lights then his small Hyundai pulled up behind her mother's car. She guessed he was puzzled as she was nowhere to be seen. She called out to him.

"Over here, Rafe." He made his way towards her.

"Come on, Lizzie. Get in the car. What are you doing way back here?" She stood on the marble slab that kept the ghost of Grandfather Alan Farraday from escaping.

"Waiting for you, Rafe," she replied. She could see him reasonably clearly from the dim lights that came from the street.

"Well, I'm here. How about we get going?"

"Don't you want to spend a few minutes paying your respects to Grandfather?" She sat down on the grave. She tapped the marble beside him, inviting him to join her.

"What's got into you, Lizzie? I thought you wanted a ride home." He sounded annoyed When she wasn't about to stand up, he sat down beside her. She conceded he had every right to be annoyed. Hopefully, she would banish his annoyance and replace it with something more satisfying.

"Why don't we just sit a while and enjoy the night?"

"Are you off your head, Lizzie? In case you haven't noticed we're in a bloody cemetery in the middle of the night and its damn near freezing."

"Stop whinging, Rafe, and relax. Are you frightened of ghosts, ghouls, all those creepy things associated with cemeteries?" Lizzie edged up close to him. Her hand was on his arm. She noticed he didn't attempt to shift it. "That's the beauty of cemeteries, Rafe. They are usually quiet places, restful and peaceful. Everyone here has had their time. It's now our time, Rafe. We shouldn't waste it."

Raphael was more than intrigued with his cousin. He briefly wondered if she was becoming like her mother—losing it. She was acting weird. But when she put her hand on his crotch and started rubbing it, these thoughts was forced from his mind.

"Geez, Lizzie, what the hell are you doing?"

"What does it feel like, Rafe? Does it feel good?" Lizzie was now doing more than rubbing him. She was kissing him, applying little nips to his neck and chest. Somehow she had opened his shirt. Her hands then travelled inside his shirt, pulling at the hairs on his chest.

In spite of his instant reaction to her, he was astonished by her behaviour. Lizzie was the little girl he had played with years ago. Now all these years later, here she was in the midst of seducing him. By the way he was beginning to feel, she was right on track. He started kissing her back. She took his hands and placed them on her breasts. Somehow her top was also unbuttoned. There was no hindrance of a bra. Raphael was beginning to think paradise might just well exist in a cemetery.

"Make love to me, Rafe," she whispered. She was flat out on the cold, marble slab, but there was no coldness being felt by either of them. She had slipped her hands inside his track pants. She heard his little gasp of breath as she held him. Her world was still coloured but she was preparing herself for when she turned it grey. Raphael—here we come.

She was prepared for him, waiting for him to enter her. Instead, she heard him whisper, "Lizzie, we shouldn't be doing this. We're cousins."

Damn! She didn't need him to suddenly develop a conscience. "So what, do you think cousins haven't done it before? We wouldn't be the first." She had expected he might turn all religious and say it was against his beliefs or some such thing, but never did she think he would bring up the cousin angle.

"You don't need to do this Lizzie. I don't know what your game is, but you're better than this, Lizzie Smythe." He pulled himself out of her arms, and started to do up the buttons on his shirt. He removed her hand from inside his track pants.

"That's the thing, Rafe," she said, as she attempted to pull him back. "I'm not better than this. This is just what I am, Rafe. You know what they call me."

"I know what they call you—bad, beautiful Lizzie. I've seen you. I know what you do to men. There's not a male around with red blood running through him who wouldn't be flattered by having you seduce him. But I don't want that for you, Lizzie."

Lizzie again felt a failure. She clasped her arms around her legs as she watched him straighten his clothes. "I'll never forgive you, Rafe. You're just like the rest of them. You all left me, every last single one of you. I should hate you. Part of me does hate you. Of all of them, it was you who I thought would save me."

He could see her in the half-light. If he didn't know better, he would think she was starting to cry. "I don't understand you, Lizzie. I don't know what I've done to earn your hatred. I always thought there was something special between us when we were kids. But we both had to grow up and go our separate ways. That's life, Lizzie, nothing stays the same."

She could have said a thousand things to him; that for her everything had stayed the same. She was still at the mercy of Leon; had been ever since she was a young child. She had always been his victim. She stood up suddenly, pulling her clothes together.

"Well, stuff you, Raphael. You don't have a clue, do you? You live in your ivory world, off studying all those fancy subjects, trying to learn about life, or whatever it is you're trying to do. Well, life is right here in front of you. You want to do good deeds—well you just missed your chance."

She stormed off. He hurried up to catch her, grabbing her arm. "What is it with you, Lizzie?"

"Just go home, Rafe. Go home and pray or whatever it is you do." She shook him off. She was almost at her mother's car.

"Hop in with me, and I'll drive you home. Maybe you might simmer down by the time we get there."

"I'm not going anywhere with you, Rafe. In fact, I hope I never see you again. Goodbye." She opened the car door and hopped in.

"I thought your car was broken down," he said, again perplexed.

"Well, I lied. That's what my whole life is all about—secrets, sex and lies. Then there are more lies, a lot of lust and worst of all, the silence. All this family ever does is to keep silent. So go and keep yourself occupied with your fancy courses at university. Leave the sin and desire to me, Rafe. You know what you are, don't you? You're the king of hearts, broken hearts, Rafe. Keep up the good work."

Lizzie left an astonished Raphael to wonder what the entire interlude had all been about.

Two days spent in bed, mending her twisted ankle and her latest failure left her feeling despondent. Nothing she ever did turned out right. Raphael remained on her mind. What a fool she'd been? Had she really though she could seduce him? For a while it felt like she could.

She had even been tempted to do it all in colour. Come to think of it she had never had sex that wasn't in grey. Even though it had been in the middle of the night, colour had surrounded her. But this latest try at revenge had been a spectacular failure.

It was no good lying in bed feeling sorry for her. Leon was back again poking around, pretending to care about her. Maryanne was less than happy when Leon paid attention to Lizzie. She finished up telling him in no uncertain terms that she would take care of her daughter. There was no need for him to concern himself.

Leon gave her mother one of his enigmatic looks, winked at Lizzie when Maryanne was not looking and went on with his business.

Lizzie made good use of her time of being incapacitated. She wrote some more letters to Mitch and Hope—deserters both. If the mighty Mitch had remained in the military and allowed his troops to be treated the same way as Lizzie had been, he would have been court martialled.

But he could desert his family and what happened to him— nothing. He just got richer, had the beautiful wife and the two wonderful children. As for horrible Hope, she got to keep at it with Arlo, day in and day out and went on her merry way.

The letters were written and posted. Lizzie's ankle miraculously got better and she was back doing what she did best—being bad and beautiful.

Mitch could not forget the bizarre letter he had received, so that when he picked up the mail each day, he very carefully sorted through it. As soon as he saw the white envelope, he knew what to expect. He quietly retreated to his office. His lovely wife was busy on the phone with her boutique managers. He spent some minutes looking at the envelope. It was no good putting it off.

Before he slit the envelope open, he thought about his past deeds. He again thought of the daughter he had never met and whose name he didn't know. All that information had died when Michael was murdered. He had no idea where the mother of this daughter had disappeared to. It had been so long ago. The daughter would be well and truly grown. He wondered what she looked like. What she might be doing at this very moment.

The other perplexing issue was who it was who had kidnapped his wife? He was more than certain they were the children of his father, Alan Farraday, which would have made them his half-brothers. He remembered back to that fateful day when he and his sister-in-law, Denise, had killed three of these men.

Then his three brothers and Denise had buried the bodies. They all agreed they would never speak of it again. Not even when Denise and Michael died did the brothers speak of the three men they had entombed.

He often wondered if there had been at least one other who had been involved in the abduction and torture of his wife. He had no idea who this person could be. As it had happened so long ago, there was no reason to believe that any further threats remained against his family.

The biggest question was what had happened to the two million dollars ransom they had paid for the return of Francine. Presumably, the first million had been taken by the men whom they had killed, but the missing second million was a mystery. He wondered now if any of these deeds were coming back to haunt him.

He donned his latex gloves and slit open the envelope. He pulled out the letter, again written on common white A4 paper and with letters cut from magazines and newspapers. He felt his heart start to beat more rapidly as he read.

"Big daddy, are you still enjoying her—shame?"

There was only one person he had been enjoying for years and it was his wife. The letter disturbed him more than the previous one. There was only one explanation—the letter must refer to his wife. He felt a black rage rise inside him. Never again would he allow anything to happen to her. Hadn't they almost killed her once before? Hadn't she been damaged for life? Not only had they taken her finger, they had destroyed part of her mind as well as part of her spirit.

There was only one conclusion he could draw. There had to be another of Alan Farraday's illegitimate sons who was back. No amount of investigation all those years ago had discovered any further trace of half-brothers. He vowed if he found any more, they would suffer the same fate as the three they had buried.

Mitch brooded about the deceased men. He had always thought they were his father's illegitimate children. Alan had been married to their mother. But what if he hadn't been? What if he had been married to some other woman? Maybe Miriam's children were the illegitimate ones. He asked himself if this could be why they had been so intent on vengeance.

Mitchell Farraday did not want to cause undue alarm to his family, but common sense dictated that they take extra care. He phoned his brothers and casually said they should meet. When he explained about the two letters, the only rational explanation was the connection to what had happened all those years ago at Sunshine.

They had never spoken of the slaughter and the buried bodies since the day it happened.

Decisions were made. More protection was needed. They would have to be more vigilant. Two girls in their family had disappeared years ago, probably murdered. Now there were more children and they had to be kept safe. The worst case scenario was that the evil predator had returned.

When Hope Smythe received her letter, she opened it immediately and was totally perplexed. It took her some minutes to work out what the letters said.

"Do you know if he enjoyed it as much last week?"

Hope had no idea what it meant. She thought of Uncle Mark. He enjoyed his work with his bikes and his cars. He loved his documentaries. As far as she could tell, he was a fairly happy man. Sure he had lost his wife who had died in the same traffic accident as her own father but that had been years go.

No one knew if the rumours were true. Privately, Hope thought they probably were. She could vaguely remember her mother being upset when her father used to come home very late at night. It didn't take a genius to figure out what he had been up to.

That left Arlo. What was it that he had enjoyed last week? They had been to dinner with a group of friends. They had both enjoyed the night out. Arlo went out with his mates during the week. As far as she knew he went to the gym and then to play pool at one of the hotels. The easiest way to find out was to show him the letter and ask him. It was very puzzling why it had been written using those ridiculous cut-out letters.

Ostensibly, Hope boarded with Uncle Mark. She had lived with Mark and Arlo almost since the time her mother had returned from hospital after her father died and her two cousins had disappeared. People said they had most probably been murdered. Her mother had never been the same since her father had been killed.

Hope had never gone back home to live. Her great relief was that her mother had not wanted her. She had only wanted Lizzie. Even Harry had escaped, thanks to Uncle Matt and Aunt Mia.

Arlo slept in the next bedroom, or made out he did. They had been having sex together for years, ever since they were young teenagers. As far as they knew, no one was aware of this relationship. After all, they were first cousins. It would not be a good look if they were found out.

When Arlo returned home from the gym, Hope crept into his room.

"Have a look at this and tell me what you make of it?"

"What's going on?" he asked. He had expected her to be in his bed. They hadn't been together for a few days.

She showed him the letter. Like Hope he was initially bewildered. But then he took a closer look.

"Well, what do you think?" She had not missed his stunned expression.

"I have no idea," he mumbled. He avoided looking at her.

"What's the matter with you? You must have some idea."

"Why would I know what it means? It was addressed to you, wasn't it?"

Arlo was not much good at bluff. He knew he had reddened in the face. "What have you been up to, Arlo? Who is she? Don't lie."

He sat down on the bed. "It was nothing. Just a couple of times, I swear it won't happen again. I'm sorry, Hope."

She turned away from him, but not before he'd seen her tears. "I want to be adult about this. It's not as though we're married or anything. Even boyfriend and girlfriend, it's just that we've been together for what seems like forever. You're all I've got, Arlo."

He put his arm around her and she leaned into him. "You're pretty much all I've got, Hope, other than dad. It was just one of those things."

"Was she very beautiful?" she asked.

Arlo could never tell her it was bad, beautiful Lizzie. "It was just some girl. I was half drunk. She kind of just picked me up and I fell for it."

"What's going to happen to us, Arlo? I don't think I could survive without you. You've always been part of my life. I love you Arlo."

"I love you too, Hope. I don't know what will happen to us. Maybe when we're finished with our studies, we can shift away. Go and live someplace where no one knows us."

"What about your dad?"

"I think there's something going on with him."

"You mean a woman?"

"Not a woman, but I wish he could get himself a girlfriend. No, he's been right on my case about being careful. He seems to be agitated about something."

"That's funny. He's said much the same to me. As a matter of fact, I've seen a security firm doing checks on the house. They leave those little slips under the front door. I wonder what's going on."

"Maybe we better cool it for a while. Not that it will be easy. I promise it was just a fling. I can't lose you, Hope."

She looked at him mournfully and wondered what was happening to them.

*

Lizzie couldn't help herself. She was overjoyed, especially after they had received a visit from the mighty Mitch. He was being very obscure, but his main focus seemed to be on safety. Of course, Lucas had to find something of urgency to do at Miriam's Place, so he disappeared when Mitch arrived accompanied by Malcolm.

Maryanne made much of their visit, saying that of course she was always mindful of being careful. She was well aware of the hazards that could befall people. Lizzie was bamboozled. Safety and security wasn't the concern she intended. It was his conscience. Either he was a very good actor or he didn't give two hoots about any moral code.

Lizzie remained in the background—pretending. All was well, what a happy family they were! But something was up for why else would her uncles be visiting. Even so, she could tell that they couldn't wait to be gone from their sister, their only sister, who at times in her life was more than a bit crazy.

Lizzie was baffled as to why they were worried about security. All she wanted was for Mitch to cop some of the same horror that she'd been enduring for years. She did have a conscience, though, when it came to his two children, Finbarr and Roza. No way did she want to harm either of them, or for that matter, the lovely Francine.

However you looked at it, mighty Mitch was rattled for some reason in spite of trying to pretend otherwise. Pretend, pretend, pretend—Lizzie knew all about pretence. She was the queen of pretence.

But all was not lost. Lizzie became excited after speaking to Hope, which didn't happen very often. Hope was part of the pact of three who had put her into her untenable situation.

As she spoke to her sister, the anxiety was not hard to miss. Lizzie asked what was wrong. Hope replied that she was feeling depressed. Lizzie sounded sympathetic and offered to have coffee with her. Hope replied that she would love that. Lizzie kept pretending. When the call was ended, she was overjoyed—two down and two to go.

The three young women met on occasions. Rina and Lu saw each other often, but it was only about once a month that Lizzie was able to join them. Where did they meet? Of course it was at Sundial Park.

Lu was now strong enough to bring the two dogs, James and Boag, at the same time. The dogs were aware she was their master. They obeyed her commands. If they had to, they could easily over-power her. But she was an intelligent, kind and firm handler. The dogs never gave her any trouble

They always sat at the children's play area. Jude mostly stayed on the swings, with Rina and Lu taking turns pushing him. He could never get the hang of how to swing himself. The dogs stood by in dutiful watchfulness. When the two young women were sick of pushing Jude up and down, he sat with the dogs. It was a strange relationship. He touched them on the head and under the mouth a few times, but then the three of them would just sit in the shade together.

The two women talked, generally about nothing of importance. It was pleasing to both of them when they saw Lizzie walking from the southern end of the park to join them. Lizzie looked strained although she tried to be upbeat. They talked trivia.

Lu often studied Lizzie carefully. She knew from the nuances in her speech, her sometimes overly forthright opinions, and her furtive looks that Lizzie had problems. From her experiences of old, she could feel Lizzie's suffering. In spite of Rina being present, she suddenly said to Lizzie.

"What's he doing to you, Lizzie?"

Lizzie was taken aback. It was usually she who was the forward one, posing the questions, being abrasive. But here was little, skinny Lu asking intimate questions that she should have no knowledge of. "I don't know what you mean." Lizzie looked to Rina for support. Rina said nothing as she was equally intrigued by Lu's question.

"I know, Lizzie, I know what it's like. You don't have to pretend. What you have to do is escape." Lu had this disconcerting habit of saying little but looking you straight in the eye.

"Is this a trick question?" Lizzie was becoming uncomfortable.

Lu took Lizzie's hand in her own, bringing the scar that ran down the length of her left hand into focus. "You don't have to pretend. Look at Rina. She never says anything either, but I know bad things have happened. I'll show you my bad, if you like."

Rina and Lizzie looked at Lu as if she were touched. Lu bent down and removed her boots. Her boots were old and worn. The dogs stood by, looking on in as much amazement as the two women who watched Lu stretch out her legs.

Then her feet were on display. It was the first time she had ever voluntarily shown anyone her feet. The two women saw the scars burnt into her feet with dozens of little letter 'L's' scattered all over the soles of her feet. They saw the bunched up toe nails that had been brutalised.

No one spoke. The horror of this sight took away their speech. They could only stare in silence. For the first time, Rina voluntarily held out her left hand with the missing fifth finger. This time she wasn't as ashamed. The ugly red scar was prominent against the smooth skin of the rest of her hand.

Lizzie stretched out her left hand, and traced the scar that ran from the finger tip of her fifth finger to her wrist.

None of them asked about how these horrors had occurred. They sat in silence. There was only the sound of the gentle breeze swaying the palm fronds, the panting of the dogs and Jude playing with a stick.

Eventually Lizzie broke their silence. "How do I escape?"

"You could push him under a train," Lu replied in all seriousness.

"Or you could put your hand over his mouth and smother him." Rina had no idea where this had come from, but the words were out before she could consider their origin.

Lizzie sat staring out at the trees before she started giggling. Before she knew it, she had burst into full-blown laughter. She laughed so hard that she had tears in her eyes.

Lu asked, "What's so funny?"

Between paroxysms of laughter, she said. "We don't have any trains around here and he's too big to put my hand over his mouth. What an odd bunch we are?"

The women laughed together. The dogs looked on. Jude kept playing with his stick. It was so good to laugh, even if it was about how to murder someone. When their laughter subsided, Lizzie looked at her watch.

"I've got to go, but they're both good ideas. I'll let you know what I come up with." Lu and Rina watched her hurry away through the bushes.

Lu took her time putting her boots back on. Rina didn't know what to say. She wanted to ask how such terrible things had happened to the skinny, young woman who sat beside her. But words wouldn't come to her. It was Lu who eventually broke the silence.

"Do you think you could help me choose a dress, a nice dress? I don't know much about dresses. I've never worn one."

"I'm not too sure I'd be much good to you. I don't know anything about fashion either as you can see from the way I dress, but I'd love to help out." Rina looked down at her dark and loose clothing.

"I thought I might go to the second-hand shop down at the shopping centre. When do you think you could come with me?"

"Why not now, we're half-way there already? Jude should be able to walk that far."

Lu was very excited, "I'll take the dogs back home and then I'll meet you there."

There was no good reason why she should be so excited, as it was only a marriage that would save both their hides. But a marriage of convenience or not, it was an awesome event to get married. Lu would have loved to tell Rina all about it, but the less people who knew the safer she would be.

The two women went through all the dresses on the racks. There were dozens of sizes and styles. Rina asked what colour she would like. Lu said definitely nothing in red or black. She thought for a few more minutes and said, "Nothing in white either."

They went through all the racks. The majority of the dresses that Rina pulled out were too big. Lu was still very thin. The more they looked, the less certain Lu became. Rina was getting into the swing of looking at pretty, coloured dresses, even if they were second-hand. Lu tried on several, but the dresses with tight skirts were too fresh in her mind. It wasn't just that she was so skinny. It was the memory of Uncle Lucas and his video camera.

Lu eventually settled on a multi-coloured dress with a full skirt. It was the colours that got her in. That was what her world needed, a lot of colour. She didn't care if she looked like a rainbow. It was better than looking like a devil. It was probably a child's fancy dress, but it fitted her perfectly.

Rina surprised herself as she also purchased two coloured dresses. Not that she ever had any intention of wearing them. If she were to remain invisible, she would have to keep to her dark, drab clothing. But like Lu, there was something happy about having coloured clothing.

The two women prepared to return to their respective homes when Rina asked, "By the way, what do you need the dress for? Is it for a special occasion?"

Lu was again on the verge of blurting out her news but contained herself. "Nothing important, just for taking the dogs for a walk—in case I take them somewhere flash."

Rina was left to wonder why Lu would want to wear a dress to walk the dogs. Or why she would be taking the dogs to walk somewhere flash. She didn't think the dogs could care less where they walked. But strange things happened all the time. If she wanted to walk the dogs in a multi-coloured dress, then so be it. The dress seemed to make Lu very happy.

After their dresses were parcelled up, Rina returned home with Jude.

Amanda came each afternoon for her daily visit. Tom also came when he could and coaxed Jude outside where he would play catch with him. Jude was a little quicker now, and knew to lift his arms to catch the ball. Rina was eternally grateful to Tom for his efforts with Jude. These were pleasant times in Rina's life.

The dreams kept coming, equally as bad. Andy continued to visit during the night. If she was inside or outside the house, he still came. If she was inside, there would be a soft knock on the door and she would let him in. He would sit beside her and hold her hand. She was no longer embarrassed when he did this. He often ran his hand along the scar where her missing finger should have been. They often fell asleep, sitting side by side. She was even becoming used to his kisses. He would kiss her goodbye every time he left.

Eventually he asked for a key to her house. He told her it was important that someone else had access especially as she used candles all the time and because Jude was so vulnerable. She thought about this for several days. She knew it was for more reasons than the dangers from candles and Jude, but they were very valid reasons all the same. So she gave him her second key.

Andy Brown didn't know how long he could keep it up—sitting beside her, holding her hand. He should have taken advantage of the secretary employed in his office. She was more his age and obviously as hot as a fire cracker, if the looks and enticements she gave him were any indication

She wore low-cut and body-hugging dresses, really not very appropriate for her position, but his colleagues appreciated it. He hoped she would get the message of his disinterest or maybe one of his colleagues might take her off his hands. The secretary might be interested in him, but she wasn't the type to be interested in a teenage son and a young daughter.

The dreams had not yet woken her. Her sleep was sound, but some noise disturbed her. She lay quietly on the floor beside her bed. She pretended sleep. She knew her sounds. It was not Jude in the room next door. Nor was it the wind or the trees. It was a different sound.

She sat up suddenly, groping for the candle. That was when she saw him standing at her bedroom door.

"Why are you sleeping on the floor, Rina?" he asked softly.

She tried to calm herself. His silent presence had frightened her. After all, it could have been a monster.

Before she could stop herself she blurted out, "I thought you were a monster."

"Is that why you sleep on the floor, because of monsters?" He remained standing at the door.

She was comfortable enough with him now to be honest. "Yes."

"What are the monsters like?"

"I don't really remember, but more than likely they will come for me again, so I have to be ready to hide."

"Do you mind if I sit down beside you?" He didn't wait for her reply. He came straight into the room and sat on the floor beside her.

"Where would you hide, Rina, if they did come for you?"

"Under the bed," she replied simply, "where else?"

He looked at the bed and sure enough the bed was high enough for a person to get under. Andy Brown was more perplexed than ever. He should run now, get right away from her. He had initially called her a nutter. Now he was almost sure he had been right. What sort of an adult person sleeps on the floor so that they can hide under the bed if the monsters came?

"Do you think of me as a monster, Rina?"

"No, of course not," she answered quickly. "Your boots are different."

That stumped him. He didn't know what to ask her after that. He drew her into his arms, and started kissing her. She had admitted to herself that she loved his kisses, loved being held by him. She even loved kissing him back. More than anything she wanted to feel his body against hers.

It was the floor that was both their undoing. There was no little two-seater lounge chair or single-bed to stop the assault on their feelings. He was overcome with good old-fashioned lust for her. She didn't seem to mind as his hands sought her breasts. In fact, when he shifted them to move himself over her, she grabbed them again and brought them back onto her breasts.

Rina could not stop herself. This was better than suffering nightmares, or worrying about monsters and her endless concerns about Jude. This desire she felt for this man was insane. Every plan she had made, every step she had taken to remain invisible was falling away.

She even surprised herself when she put her hand down and touched him. She could feel him rigid against her through the thin fabric of the ugly, old nightie she wore. Ugly or not, the nightie wasn't stopping him.

He thought of the old expression—a standing prick has no conscience. Well, neither his prick nor his conscience was making any difference to the incredible desire to be inside her.

She was moaning and pulling him closer as if she might eat him up. Her kisses were ferocious. Her tongue sought his. There was no stopping either of them—except there was. He had entered her, but that was as far as it went. She kept pulling at him and murmuring, "More please, more."

Again he was stumped. At first he could not work it out, could not believe what was happening. This young woman, who he was making love with, had given birth. There was no rationalising what was happening, so he pushed all the harder and then he was inside her.

She blew his mind. Their coupling was intense, fast and furious. When he thought she had experienced enough, she pulled him back to her. He kissed her, loved her again and again. Eventually they slept in each other's arms. He woke first, put his clothes back on, covered her up and left her.

Detective Senior Sergeant Andy Brown had a lot to think about, much more than he had bargained for when he had first sat down on the hard floor beside Rina Wright.

He thanked his lucky stars that it was a slow day at work. If anything major had happened, he doubted he would be able to keep his mind on it. The office secretary even gave up sending out her messages. He was too preoccupied to even notice her. He would have to be very selective with all his dealings with the secretary. He didn't want her thinking he was interested.

Of course he was back the next night and of course, she was only too happy to have him on the floor beside her. This time he was more prepared. He hadn't expected what had occurred the previous night but nothing was going to stop him. Of all people, in his position, he should know the results of unprotected sex.

It was initially fast and furious again, but settled to a more leisurely pace as the night wore on. But discipline was called for.

As he held her close, he asked, "Tell me about Jude?"

She immediately stiffened in his arms. "What do you want to know?"

"Tell me about when he was born, that sort of thing."

"I don't remember it that clearly. You tend to forget, but I know it hurt like mad. The pain was terrible. Then there was all that blood. When he was born, he was covered in all this blood and slime. It took me ages to wash it off him. Then I thought there was another baby coming, but it was the afterbirth. I had to cut the big rope that tied the afterbirth to Jude. I cut it with a knife, but he wouldn't stop bleeding so I took the rubber band out of my hair and tied it around the rope. The bleeding stopped then."

He tried to absorb all she had told him. It seemed to be so clear in her mind. He didn't know what he was dealing with. It had been a virgin birth—impossible or another immaculate conception—again impossible.

The thought of more sex with her for this night was abandoned. He was at a loss. The way she told the story of Jude's birth was very convincing, at least to Rina. It was obvious everything she had told him was the truth as far as she knew it. There was one more question—dare he ask it?

"What about Jude's father? Who is he?"

That was the finish of the cuddling and expectations of any more loving. She pulled herself out of his arms and said. "I think you should be going now."

There was little point in arguing. The way she said it was final. He was not going to find out any more, especially about Jude's father. He didn't want to risk alienating her any further. He kissed her again, put his clothes back on and covered her up.

As he was about to leave the room, she said, "Thank you." If she had added 'for your kindness' he thought he might have throttled her.

It was almost more than he could bear. Was she a total fruit loop? It would seem so. But conscience had a funny way of catching up with a person. One minute he vowed to keep away from her all together. The next minute, he knew this would never happen. She had him right where she wanted him, whether she knew it or not. Whether she had planned it or it was just one of those things that happened.

He had to know more. He knew she left the house every day with Jude to go to the park. He returned home, checked she was gone then used his key and entered her home. He did a quick search of the kitchen and lounge room, but found nothing that added to her mysterious past.

Then he entered the bedroom. The bedding that she slept on at night was carefully rolled up under the single bed. Just to be on the safe-side, he checked under the bed. Her tale about the monsters had spooked him. It was sheer fantasy, but the genuineness of her telling, remained with him.

As quickly as he could he searched her few belongings in her bedside table. He almost knocked over the candle she kept there. Then he looked through her clothes—all ugly, dark looking tops and loose pants. He noticed that there were two brightly, coloured dresses, which was a surprise.

He looked down at her shoes. Again they were dull and uninspiring. He saw a black backpack. It was carefully hidden under more old, dilapidated shoes. He pulled it out and opened it up.

Everyone who directly sees large amounts of cash is astonished by it. Andy Brown was no different. Had she walked through the door at that exact moment, he would not have been able to take his eyes off it. She would have caught him red handed.

His thoughts were in turmoil. What was this young, bizarre woman doing with a bag full of huge amounts of cash? She was living like a pauper with no electricity, wearing the worst of clothes, cooking with a small gas burner, having no sort of life. Yet here she was rolling in money.

He doubted he would have time to count it properly. So he did a quick calculation of counting the bundles, and multiplying them. He was again in disbelief. There had to be up to a million dollars in cash in the backpack shoved into the bottom of her wardrobe.

His brain was in overdrive. He worked as quickly as he could, putting everything back as he had found it. He was not sure how long he had been in the house. Time had slipped away. He did one last quick check to make sure everything was as he had found it, then he relocked the house and slipped back through the dividing gate to his own home. His old Alsatian dog looked at him curiously as he hurried inside.

Andy Brown needed more than a glass of water to help get him over his surprise. He never drank in the middle of the day, but this day was an exception. He poured himself a good drop of whisky.

He stood at his back window and waited for her return. It wasn't long before she was back with Jude trailing behind. He looked carefully at the lad. Yes, he had the same dark hair and eyes as well as the same skin texture and colour. Any other resemblance was impossible to tell due to his slow gait and awkward movements.

He wondered again what had happened to the boy, what had caused the catastrophic damage that was clearly evident. Would he ever know? Was it even his business to know?

He watched her come through the back gate from the park. She waited for Jude to come through, and then saw her close it. They both came around to the side of the house that joined his. She opened the dividing gate and the old Alsation trotted through and went straight to Jude. Jude touched its head. Then both Jude and the old dog sat down on the lawn—not doing anything, just sitting side by side.

Andy Brown knew nothing about this intrusion into his life. No one had mentioned that his old dog was best buddies with the odd boy who lived beside him. He didn't know that the mysterious Rina let his dog out to be with her son. He would have to question his children about how this had occurred.

He tried to be angry with her, wanted to be angry with her. But then he rationalised that he let himself not only into her yard, but into her house, her bed—actually it was the floor—and her body.

Letting the old dog be with the boy was mild stuff compared to what he did to and with her on a daily basis. He knew he was being petty. But of all the things in his life, his two children and his old dog were his most cherished possessions. She was skilfully worming her way into every aspect of his life. Worst of all, was the way she had wormed her way into his mind.

She suddenly looked up and saw him standing at his window watching her. She gave him one of her Mona Lisa smiles. His knees almost buckled. She took his breath away. She looked like an old bag in her dark-grey loose top and pants. But that smile blew him away. It held all the mystery and enticement of a siren. He knew he would visit again tonight, the next night and the next.

The mystery of one million dollars hidden away in a black backpack in the bottom of her wardrobe did not hold a candle to the enigmatic allure of what was Rina Wright.

Much as Lu tried, she could not help but feel excited. It was to be a sham marriage, not made to last or to be real except to satisfy their individual requirements.

He would be home soon. The month was up. It was almost time for the marriage. He had organised it all. She didn't ask too much, thinking the less she knew, the safer she would be. She had her pretty dress to wear. She had never been to a wedding. All she knew about them was what she had read in magazines when she had been at school.

But hers would not be anything like those exotic weddings where the bride looked stunning in a sequinned, white gown, with hair done up with pearls or flowers. At least, she hoped he hadn't planned anything elaborate.

The more she thought about it, he didn't seem to be an elaborate sort of person. He was a loner. That much was obvious. He never talked about any family, so they were much alike. No family, no friends, so no guests at the wedding.

Just for a minute, she thought she would have like to asked Rina, Jude and Lizzie. But no, the less people who knew of their liaison, the safer she would be. There was less likelihood of Lucas finding her.

One thing she wanted to do was to buy him a present. She had no idea of etiquette, but it seemed like good manners. She knew how to use the internet, so she used his laptop which he left at his home. The costs and formalities of weddings blew her away. There was just too much involved. So she gave this idea away, deciding to use her common sense instead.

She returned to the second-hand shop as she still had money left over after purchasing the dress. She closed her mind to the money hidden under the house.

As she looked around, she wondered what he would like. He loved his dogs and his SUV but there wasn't much for sale about either of these. There were books about dogs and vehicles but they were tattered and worn. Next she looked at the figurine section. Nothing stood out.

The toy section contained all sorts of items. This was where she spied what she hoped was the perfect present. As she walked home with her small purchase, she looked up at the clear sky with its gently warming sun and thought how perfect her life was becoming.

She fed and walked the dogs and was left with time on her hands. She pulled out her cards and started playing solitaire. The cards she used were very old. It seemed she had been using them forever. She wondered when she had first got them.

As she played away, sitting on the bed in her room, she noticed that none of the kings ever turned up. Her game was fruitless. She wasn't a superstitious person. She had no idea really what superstition was, but it was odd that on this day when she expected him home, there was no sign of any king. He had become the king of her heart.

His vehicle pulled up outside. She had rehearsed in her head any number of times what this greeting between them would be like. It was to be the last night of her life as a single person. Tomorrow they were getting married.

She opened the front door as he reached the top step. He looked at her; she looked at him. He smiled. She smiled back with all the brilliance of her wonderful face. Their eyes held for a moment, before discomfort overcame them.

He didn't know whether to touch her, kiss her or what. So he just said "Hello" and came inside. She followed him in. He asked how the dogs were. She said they were fine, getting bigger and eating like horses.

She asked would he like her to cook him a meal. He replied that he would, that he was tired and hungry. She knew he liked beef, so she cooked him rump steak, with chips and green salad.

"Have you been eating enough?" he asked, as she sat beside him with very little on her plate. She didn't want to admit that she was feeling all churned up having him home and sitting beside her.

"Trying to," she replied. "It takes time getting used to eating so much. But I'm much stronger now. I can take the two dogs at once. I don't get nearly as exhausted."

"That's good." He got himself another James Boag. "Are you ready for tomorrow?"

She nodded. "But I'm a little nervous about it all."

He held her hand in his. "It will all turn out okay." They smiled at each other. He left her then and unpacked his bag.

They sat beside each other watching television until she said it was time she went to bed. He heard her pull out her blankets and make her bed on the floor. He drank some more beer. He hoped she was asleep when he came and lay on the bed beside her. Instinct told him she was awake.

"Why do you sleep on the floor and not in a bed?"

"Why would I want to do that?" she asked, looking up at him from her position on the floor.

"Because it's what most people do." He almost said normal people.

"I guess then I must not be most people."

"It's more comfortable."

"Not to me," she replied.

"Be honest, Lu, tell me why?"

She rolled onto her back, looking up at the dark ceiling. "All the bad that has happened to me, happened in a bed. Why would I ever want to sleep in one again?"

This saddened him immensely. "Do you mind if I sleep on the floor beside you tonight?"

"No, I don't mind. It will be kind of nice, you know, before tomorrow."

He lay down on the hard floor beside her, certain he would never get used to it. He took her in his arms and held her. He thought he heard her crying.

They were both very shy around each other the next day. He hoped he had all the paper work in order. His application for a wedding ceremony from the local council had been approved. The wedding celebrant was hired and identical rings were purchased. He had even bought a new pair of jeans and shirt. The ceremony was to be held early in the day because Mr and Mrs Lee, who were to be the witnesses, had to get to their Chinese restaurant by midday.

The morning flew. Before he dressed, he knocked on her door. She was sitting on the bed playing solitaire. He cleared his throat before speaking. It was incredible that he was so nervous.

"I bought you a present," he said. She smiled at him as he came over to the bed. He gave her two medium-sized parcels. "Open them now. They might come in handy."

"No one has ever given me a present before," she said. This time she cried openly. He looked away as he knew his eyes were wet as well. She opened the two parcels which contained two pair of new boots, one brown and one cream. She ran her hands over them, feeling the soft leather.

"Thank you," she whispered. "They're beautiful. Which pair will I wear today?"

"What about the cream pair." She nodded in agreement.

"Do you mind if I help you put them on?" He wiped his eyes at the joy he could see in her.

She shook her head as he gently took her left foot in his hands. He sat at the bottom of the bed. She looked tremulous as though she would pull her foot back at any moment. He lifted her foot up and kissed it. Then he slipped on the soft boot. He did the same with her right foot. Then he held her feet covered in the soft, cream boots.

It was a spiritual moment for both of them. She was crying again when she flung herself into his arms. He held her, stroking her hair, feeling her thin body against his own.

"Thank you," she whispered, trying to stem her tears. "I have a present for you too. I hope you like it. It's not as nice as what you gave me." She put her hand under the pillow and pulled out a small parcel wrapped in brown paper.

"Whatever you give me is something that I'll always cherish, Lu." He took the parcel from her and opened it up. She was looking down at her boots, embarrassed, in case he didn't like it. It had been such a stupid idea. "I already love him, Lu. I'll keep him with me always."

Shyly she looked at him, and saw the genuine, gentle expression on his face. "He's the same as my black devil, only he's much smaller. I hope he will be as good a friend to you as he has been to me."

They sat looking at each other, in awe of the big step they were taking. After a time, he said he had to get dressed and get the dogs ready. He told her he would wait for her out the front when she was dressed and they would walk to the park together.

The dogs sensed there was something important going on. They stood with their haughty heads held high. Lu walked down the few steps to meet him. Her rainbow dress flared out around her slim legs. The cream boots fit perfectly. Her dark hair with golden highlights was in gentle waves around her face. She smiled at him; the smile that went up to her eyes and lit up her face. He thought his heart would burst with love for her.

They walked arm in arm with the two dogs to the park. She held her black devil in her thin, delicate arms while he carried his small black devil in his shirt pocket. Mr and Mrs Lee and the marriage celebrant were waiting. Mrs Lee was a vibrant, dynamo of a little lady. She placed a garland of frangipani flowers around Lu's head. They stood on a small bridge while the celebrant, an older man, commenced the ceremony.

There were children in the park, mostly boys on their bikes and skate boards. There were also several, young girls. When they realised there was a wedding in progress, they gathered around. No one ever got married in Sundial Park. This was much more exciting than sitting on a swing or a see-saw. The two dogs stood at either end of the small bridge, looking regally in charge.

The celebrant commenced. He started with kind, caring words. Gabe would have liked to have said the verse that had been read at his parent's funeral about the whole dynamics of love but their wedding was different from most couples. He was somewhat tongue tied as he tried to say the words he felt in his heart. The celebrant asked him to repeat his words.

"I, Gabriel Michael Farraday take you, Lu, to be my lawful wedded wife. I promise to cherish you, care for you, protect you for as long as we both shall live, so help me God." He slipped the gold ring on her finger. As he did so, he noticed she wore the ring from the beer bottle top on the thumb of her right hand—the engagement ring.

Then it was her turn. She could hear the young girls in the background, could hear them whispering about how beautiful she was. It was all so alien to her. There were scruffy-looking boys leaning against their bikes with caps on back-the-front. Other boys held their skate boards in their arms as they watched on.

She held black devil close to her. He had been through the worst with her and now he was going through the best with her. She could see Mrs Lee out the corner of her eye, smiling as if it were her wedding. The celebrant asked Lu to repeat after him.

"I, Lucia Farraday," she nearly stumbled at these words but managed to keep talking, "take you Gabriel, to be my lawful wedded husband. I promise that I will always care for you, cherish you, treasure the life that we will have together for as long as we both shall live, so help me God."

Mr Lee gave her the ring and she placed it on his finger. They waited for the celebrant to pronounce them man and wife. Then they kissed. The young girls present thought it was the most romantic thing they had seen. The boys started clapping, banging on their skate boards. Then there was hand shaking. Boys with grubby hands and dirty knees shook his hand.

She received embarrassed pecks on the cheek from both boys and girls. All the young girls were crying with the beauty and simplicity of it all. Someone shoved some hibiscus flowers into her hands. She shrugged her shoulders at her new husband, and threw the flowers over her shoulder.

There were squeals of delight as one young girl caught them. Lu heard the girls laughing as a girl called Amanda was teased about catching the flowers.

Mr and Mrs Lee signed the relevant documents as witnesses to the marriage. James and Boag looked on with amused disdain. Gabriel had a few moments of sorrow as he wished his deceased parents and sister could have been with him. He had wanted to call his brother, Raphael, but he was back at university.

Besides, Rafe would only try to tell him he was making another mistake as usual. It didn't enter his head to ask any of his uncles. They had little time for him because of all his clashes with the law. The only person he thought he might have asked was his aunt Zaylee. But had he asked her, he would have had to ask his uncle Malcolm.

So the wedding guests were his neighbours, Mr and Mrs Lee, and the children who used the park, as well as the two dogs, James and Boag, and the two black devils.

But as weddings went, it was as good as any. His bride was radiant in her rainbow dress and cream boots. She couldn't stop smiling. The frangipani in her hair brought out its golden highlights. The sun shone warm against them. It was their golden moment in time.

Mr and Mrs Lee presented them with a red basket filled with chocolates and treats. Mrs Lee laughed and giggled as she pointed to a red-painted egg. "Fertility," she smiled. Lu looked down at her cream boots in embarrassment.

The ceremony was at an end. The children dispersed. Mr and Mrs Lee went off to their restaurant. The celebrant was thanked and then the newlyweds held hands and with one dog each, walked back through Sundial Park to their home.

When they reached home, he said, "What about the wedding feast? We should shout ourselves."

She was only too happy to agree. They put the dogs in the back of the SUV. He drove to the shopping centre. Together they went into the baker shop. They made their choices. He slipped into the bottle shop and bought a six pack. Then they drove off, totally happy.

"Where are we going?" she asked. The road seemed familiar.

"I thought we would go out to that place we went to before called 'Sunshine', sit on the creek bank and have some lunch. How does that sound?"

"Wonderful." She was too happy to think anything more about it. This time he unlocked the gate and drove in. He handed her the bag containing their lunch while he got the dogs out. She followed him to the creek bank. He spread a plastic sheet on the ground then started to unpack their wedding feast. She placed the two black devils up against a tree. Of course, the one-armed black devil fell over against the smaller one. She left him where he was.

Lu watched in fascination as he pulled out the pies and mud cake. They sat together, "Two meat pies for me, one bacon and cheese for you, one each for the dogs. Then we can attack the mud cake. Let's get started. I'm starving."

He opened a bottle of James Boag for each of them. She knew she'd be giggling after the first few mouthfuls, "I though dogs weren't supposed to eat pies or mud cake—or drink beer?"

"They are allowed to on special occasions," he said, as he raised his bottle to hers. "Here's to you, Mrs Farraday."

"And to you, Mr Farraday," she said. They sat together watching the water run smoothly in the creek. The day had turned warm. She shifted back into the shade. She was reluctant to get her rainbow dress dirty. Her cream boots were now about her proudest possession. She kept rubbing off any bits of dirt that appeared on them.

"Do you want to have a swim?" She watched as he started stripping down.

"I don't think I can swim. In fact, I don't think I've ever been for a swim."

He turned his head before she could see his dismay. Her life had been stolen from her. She had never had a present before, never been for a swim. Her best friend was a one armed, worn-out black teddy bear bearing the obscure name of black devil.

Before his heart broke for her any further, he dived in. She watched him cavorting around in the creek. She couldn't take her eyes off him, especially as he came out of the water. He was magnificent with his bronzed, muscled body and his black, wild hair hanging around his shoulders

He sat down beside her as he let the sun dry the water on his body. "You are a very beautiful man," she said, unable to look him in the eyes. Her words pierced his whole being. Never had anyone thought he was good for anything, let alone beautiful, even though it was an odd description.

"Look at me, Lu. You don't have to be shy. If you like, you can touch me. It's allowed. We're married."

"I will one day. I can't, not yet. But one day we'll come out here again and we'll make love at this very spot, on the bank of this creek." She looked at him then, her brown eyes meeting his. "That's if you want to."

He couldn't keep looking at her any more. She knew there were tears in his eyes. She pulled his face towards her and wiped away his tears. She kissed him gently on the lips and took his hand in hers. The dogs had been for a run but were back again, panting under the tree next to the two black devils.

"Where did you get the name from? I liked the name Lucia," she finally asked, breaking the silence between them.

"I managed to get a birth certificate. Doesn't matter where? It was a bit tricky both of us having the last name. But the celebrant cleared it after I told him it was just one of those chance things that happen."

"Do you want to call me Lucia?"

"No, you're Lu, my Lu." He was tempted to tell her about his missing cousin, presumed dead or sold. But it was not the day for sadness. It was their day—their wedding day.

He was hungry again so he cut the mud cake. She watched him keep eating. He stopped every now and then and gave her a bite. It wouldn't be his fault if she didn't fatten up. Her bony body still embarrassed her, but she looked better than she had. He kissed her between bites of mud cake. They drank more beer even though it was now hot. She giggled and laughed. He couldn't stop looking at her in her rainbow dress and cream boots.

But every day must end, and so did theirs. They slept together on the floor. Several times he had to get up and leave her when he was overwhelmed with desire. He knew he could never go back to Annie or Josephina. He would have to do the right thing by them and tell them he was no longer available. Not that either of them would probably care too much.

They had one more day together before he had to go to Court. They made the most of this day, walking the dogs and grooming them. She cooked him a meal. He did his best to get her to eat more. She told him she couldn't eat another bite. On his court appointed day, they were both nervous. They took a taxi to the court house.

She wore her dark, drab clothes accompanied by her new brown boots. She left black devil at home but she could see his small black devil in his jean's pocket. She followed him into the court house. As they walked through to the room where his case was to be heard, she started signing. They were an odd couple. She didn't have to pretend that she was nervous. She was. The Auslan kept her busy. Gabe looked at her as she signed away, pretending he knew what she was doing.

His charges were read out. He already had a number of charges under his belt, but there were more. There were more traffic offences—driving while under the influence, speeding, driving while being disqualified, hooning and others.

As they were read out, he realised the futility of his life. No wonder his uncles were disgusted with him. Due to his history, his court-appointed defence lawyer had told him he faced a jail sentence. He quite believed him.

His defence lawyer did his best. He told the magistrate that Gabriel Farraday had a wife with a severe disability. She was profoundly deaf and would not be able to cope without her husband's help. Lu signed to Gabe throughout this speech. He nodded and kept writing words on a piece of paper so she could understand the proceedings.

She started crying. Again, she didn't have to pretend. She could not bear the thought of him not being with her. It was bad enough that he had to go away to work and leave her. In the end, she was sobbing.

Gabe again thought of his mother and father, how they had both been jailed. He couldn't imagine how they had felt. How terrible it must have been to leave their children? As he looked at his wife, he felt absolute desolation at the thought of not having her by his side. There was no worse feeling.

It was Lu Farraday's quiet sobs that swung the magistrate's opinion. That and her endless Auslan. Gabriel Farraday stood holding his breath as he was given a sentence of two years, wholly suspended. He was fined and given community service. His driver's licence was revoked for eighteen months. The judge gave him a stern lecture.

He was being given an opportunity, but he had to prove himself, remain in employment, to not lose his job. He was told to keep working in the mines if he did not wish to breach his sentencing conditions. He had to report to police when he was home. It was over very quickly.

They left the court house holding hands. Lu was still crying. When they were well away from the court house, they kissed. He hailed a taxi and they returned home. What neither of them knew was that a certain Lucas Cowell had watched the entire proceedings.

They only had a few days left until he had to return to the mines. He needed money as he had a hefty fine to pay. He would no longer be able to drive his vehicle, so he would be dependent on taxis for all transport. This would not be cheap.

He told his new wife that he had to go out for a while. He didn't say where. Gabe knew where there were substantial amounts of cash. Sunshine was his next destination. He should not have been driving, but it was another risk he had to take. The dogs were with him.

As quickly as he could he made his way up the hilly track to the Big Rock. This time he brought a torch. He went straight to the dark, back areas of the cave and pulled out the black backpack that he had left there years ago.

He never knew why his mother had a gun and a backpack full of one hundred dollar notes in the bottom of her wardrobe. He had found these just before his mother had been murdered. Even though everyone said she had taken her own life, he didn't believe it. She had been so happy, planning to leave Sunshine and get his father out of jail. Then the worst had happened. Within a couple of hours both his parents were dead.

He pulled the backpack out into the sunlight. The notes felt old and smelt musty. He had never touched this cache before even though he had been tempted over the years. Well, it was now or never. He had a wife. Didn't she deserve more than living in obscurity? They would have a honeymoon, go somewhere flash. See some of the world.

He counted out one hundred thousand. These notes were pushed into the bottom of a plastic shopping bag. He put the rest of the notes back into the backpack and returned it to the back of the cave.

When he arrived home, the dogs were skittish. He tried to calm them, but they kept growling and were agitated. There was no sign of Lu. He called out to her, but there was no reply. He checked out the house and yard. She was nowhere to be found. As it was getting late, he began to worry. He let the dogs out and told them to, "Go find". They ran off towards Sundial Park. He followed them, running to keep up with them.

The dogs soon found her. She was crouched under the small walk bridge where only a few days ago they had been married. The dogs stood guard while he caught up with them. Again, he was bewildered. Why was his new wife hiding under a little walk bridge in Sundial Park?

He knelt down in front of her. He could see she was terrified. "What's the matter, Lu? Why are you frightened?"

"I saw him down at the shopping centre. He was just standing there, looking around. It was him. He's come back to get me." She was trembling with her feet curled up under her. The ground was wet beneath her. Her clothes were wet. He was fearful for her well-being, uncertain how long she had been hiding under the bridge.

All at once his fears about her returned. "Who's come back, Lu?"

"Uncle Lucas. He must know I live here. I can't live through any more consequences, Gabe, I just can't."

"You won't have to, Lu, I promise you. I said I will protect you and I will. Please come out now. I'll take care of you and I'll deal with Lucas."

"No, I'll have to leave. He'll find me. Then he'll find you. You know what he's like? You know what he's capable of. I can't put you in danger. I would never do that to you."

He sat on the damp grass trying to talk her out. He had no doubt of her terror and no doubt that she had seen, or thought she had seen her Uncle Lucas. The dogs stood guard which was a great consolation. If Lucas was around then he would have to get past the dogs first. As much as he tried, he could not coax her out. In desperation, he phoned his aunt Zaylee.

Dr Zaylee Lang was totally surprised to receive a phone call from her husband's nephew. He never came to them for anything. He never came to any of his relatives for support or assistance. He had been a wild and unpredictable boy who had not changed as he grew into his teenage and then his adult years. After his parents and sister had died, he had changed and not for the better.

"Hello, Gabe, how can I help you?" She had been quick to note the anxiety in his voice.

He was becoming very desperate as he spoke to her. "I need your help. Please help us. I don't know who else to turn to."

"Where are you Gabe? How can I help?" He told her he was at Sundial Park and he had a friend who was in trouble. Dr Zaylee Lang didn't ask what sort of trouble. It was enough that he had reached out to her.

She told her husband that she had an emergency. She didn't know when she would be back. Malcolm had called on his wife plenty of times during the first months of their rocky courtship. If she said it was an emergency then he never questioned her.

She arrived at Sundial Park to find an agitated Gabriel and his two massive dogs sitting beside a small walk bridge. His relief was palpable as he saw her approach. He thanked her for coming so quickly. When she asked what the trouble was, he was only too happy to tell her.

"It's Lu. She won't come out from under the bridge. She's terrified. Other than drag her out, I don't know what to do."

This was not the same reckless man she had known since she had married into the Farraday family. This was a man who was deeply concerned. She looked under the bridge and saw a frail-looking, young woman crouched in a huddle in the wet soil. She was trembling with her arms clutched around her legs.

"Hello, my name is Zaylee. I'm a doctor. Gabe is very worried about you and has asked for my help." Zaylee again was unsure about what she was doing. The circumstances were much the same as when she was confronted by Gabe's mother, Denise, all those years ago when her daughter had disappeared. She didn't know exactly what she was doing then and had no idea how this current situation had come about.

The young woman didn't look like she was going to shift any time soon. It was getting dark. All she could think to do was to start talking. "I've known Gabe for a long time. He's a wonderful young man. How did you meet him?" Gabe looked at the doctor and raised his eyebrows in scepticism. He assumed that doctor talk must have mysterious powers.

The young woman was nodding her head in agreement. "At the cemetery," she finally said. The doctor looked at Gabe for confirmation. He nodded his head.

"Well, if you met in a cemetery, it must mean something special, something restful or something good. Is that how it is for you and Gabe?"

"Yes," she replied. "It is for me. I think it is for him as well."

Gabe stood back from the doctor as she sat crouched down in front of the frail, young woman. "You're my life, Lu. I'm no good without you."

Doctor Zaylee had never thought she would hear any man speak so sincerely.

"You mean everything to him, Lu—may I call you Lu? If you come out from under the bridge, then you and Gabe can come back home to my place, get dry, put some warm clothes on and have a cup of tea. Will you do that for him, Lu?"

Lu had lost some of her fear. Gabe was there as well as the dogs. The lady who called herself a doctor seemed very genuine. If Lucas was nearby then he would have to be very quick and fast to catch her. It would be more than just herself that he would have to fight off. There were two, massive dogs as well as two other people. She reasoned that if he did not know where she lived, then he would have no chance of finding her.

She crawled out from under the bridge. She was now dripping wet and cold. She flew into Gabe's arms. He held her tight while they trudged towards the doctor's car. The dogs followed him. But when they got to the car, it was clear the dogs would not be able to come with them.

'Stuff it," he said. "I'll take my SUV. You go with the doctor, Lu and I'll be right behind you."

She looked at him beseechingly, already shaking her head, not wanting to be separated from him.

The doctor spoke to her gently. "It will be all right, Lu. Please trust me. Gabe knows where I live. If you like we can sit in the car and wait for him. That way you'll know he's just behind us."

Lu nodded in agreement as she sat beside this next new person in her life. The doctor seemed to be very familiar with her husband as she started asking questions, nothing too personal, just if she was cold, would she like to put the doctor's coat over her shoulders. Lu was beginning to shake, so she thanked the doctor and told her she would like her coat.

They both kept watching for Gabe to pull up behind them. He was not long. Lu began to relax as the doctor drove away from Sundial Park towards her home. The doctor had her own fearful memories of Sundial Park.

They arrived at Malcolm and Zaylee's acerage property one after the other. Lu was immediately out of the car and went straight over to Gabe and the two dogs. She nearly started crying again when she saw he had brought black devil with him. The doctor was left to watch the bizarre procession of two adults and two, large dogs follow her.

They had pulled up at the back of the house. They walked up the few steps to a back veranda. Gabe and Lu stayed there with the dogs. Zaylee went into the house where she found her husband peering out at the gathering that his wife had brought home with her. When he saw his nephew, he said to his wife.

"What's he doing here and who's that scrawny-looking scrubber he's got with him? What's he want this time? What's going on?" She could smell the alcohol on him.

"I'm not altogether sure. They need a bed for the night and to get cleaned up. But something is up with the pair of them."

"Look, I know you're fond of Gabe, so am I, but he's nothing but trouble, you know that. I don't want them staying here for the night, especially with those great, vicious-looking dogs. What about Emmet?" Malcolm Farraday kept staring out at the bedraggled couple on his veranda.

"It's only for one night, Mal. It's the girl I'm worried about. She's terrified of something."

"Well, she can be terrified somewhere else. They're not staying here. She looks like there's something wrong with her. If you don't tell them to go, I will. They're your emergency."

"What's wrong with you, Malcolm? Why are you being like this?" Zaylee was more than hurt by her husband's attitude. She was becoming angry with him. "Look, don't you remember what it's like to go through hard times? You should, you went through enough of your own?"

"That was a long time ago. They've got to go and that's all there is to it." He went to the back door and called his nephew over.

"You can't stay here, Gabe, not with those two, great dogs of yours. Take your little girlfriend somewhere else". He glanced at the young woman who stood to the side. "What's wrong with you? You should be able to pick yourself up something a bit better than that scrawny, little piece."

This was more than he could take. His uncle had insulted his wife and had refused to help them. Gabriel hauled off and smacked his uncle across the face. Malcolm looked at his nephew from the floor of the veranda in utter astonishment.

"When did you get to be such a mean, miserable prick of a man, Malcolm? You can keep your fancy house and your millions."

Lu was again quaking in fright. She pulled the doctor's coat closer around her. Gabriel grabbed his wife by the arm, whistled his two dogs and got them all into his SUV. Licence or no licence, speed limit or no speed limit, he would not spend another second on his uncle's property.

24

Zaylee Lang was a successful doctor. She also considered that she was a successful mother and up until recently she would have thought she also had a successful marriage. But the recent behaviour of her husband was causing her to question this.

When they had married, they were totally in love. She still loved him but his cruelty towards his nephew and the frightened, young woman had upset her greatly.

She looked around at all they had. Every material possession imaginable was in front of her eyes—the fabulous house, the modern and expensive furniture and fittings, the pool, the gardens, the cars and the successful businesses they had developed over the years. They also had the clever and good-looking son, Emmet. All the trappings that rang out success were there for the world to see.

Malcolm had never been mean. He had been through his bad and sad times when his first wife was murdered and his only daughter, Lucia, disappeared all those years ago. She knew he still had many moments of sadness when he thought of his missing daughter, wondering what had happened to her, if she was dead or alive. Of all people, he should have been the first to help out someone in need.

After all, Gabriel's father, Michael, had ended up in jail for him years ago. This was after he had been raped by his father's half-brother. Michael had taken revenge for Malcolm against their father's half-brother. He had belted him up and had done six months in jail for his trouble.

To add insult to injury, Michael and Denise had been charged with the murder of their daughter, Sarina. Eventually Michael pleaded guilty to this alleged murder so that Denise, his wife, could be released so as to care for their twin sons, Gabriel and Raphael. But Denise Farraday had died the day after her release presumably from her own hand after hearing that her husband had been murdered in the yard of the jail where he was incarcerated.

So many tragedies had occurred. Zaylee was hoping against hope that her own husband was not turning into another one.

To take her mind off her own troubles, she drove the short distance to Miriam's Place. This was the property where Miriam, Malcolm's mother, had lived with old Dr Sam Calhoun. The doctor had died from a fractured neck of femur and Miriam had suffered a stroke when told of the demise of Denise and Michael. Miriam had been living in an aged care facility ever since, not speaking and not walking.

Zaylee had fought tooth and nail to hang on to Miriam's Place when there was talk of selling it. It was an outstanding property, kept in excellent condition and was used to host charitable events. Several times each month, some charity used the house and gardens for fund-raising purposes. The Farradays had enough money to keep the property for such events. No one lived there permanently, but the family employed a man to manage it.

The doctor found it always soothed her to visit Miriam's Place. She had to get away from her husband to clear her thoughts and emotions. She liked to sit out on the bench under the Poinciana trees and enjoy the day or else she would wander around inside the house enjoying the art work and the graciousness of the home which had been decorated by Sam Calhoun's first wife, also deceased.

She sat at the red-cedar desk in the study. This was a spacious room with wide windows that looked over spectacular, rolling hill-country. There were very few personal items left in the house. It was now a display home for the various charities that ran their events. Zaylee was proud of this for there was no end of people in need—those with cancer, obscure conditions and diseases, and the disabled. These fund-raising events were amongst her most crowning achievements.

Idly, she started to open the top drawer to the desk but there was something stopping it, so she tried again. She put her hand inside as far as she could to see what the obstruction was. There was nothing there so she pulled on the drawer again but it still did not fully pull out. She took a ruler from the top of the desk and again tried to free whatever was hindering the drawer.

There was nothing to be felt but she did hear the rustling of paper. In exasperation, she put her hand into the drawer again and felt around the sides. There was nothing on the bottom or sides of the drawer. The only other place that could hinder the drawer from opening was the top. She knelt down on her knees as she reached her arm in.

She felt paper, so she pulled as carefully as she could. It was obvious that it had been kept there by sticky tape. Cautiously, she managed to remove the paper by breaking off the crumbling tape. With nervous hands she lifted it out of the drawer. It was a piece of A4 paper with words written in black ink. It looked very old.

The doctor was intrigued by this find. She sat back on the office chair to read it. It read like a lament.

I know I cannot give him what he most wants—which is his desire for children. But I have never tried to stand in his way. I know he has a son and a daughter. I know he sees his son on occasions and is very proud of him. I do not know what has happened to his daughter. I pray to God that she is well taken care of. I love him so. All I want is his happiness.

Zaylee was astonished by these words. She knew what they meant but then again she didn't. She asked herself if this 'he' was Dr Sam Calhoun or someone else. When she thought about it more, it had to be him. As far as she knew, Sam Calhoun and his wife had built the house years ago. No one else had ever lived there except for Miriam Farraday when she married Sam Calhoun. Was the writer the doctor's first wife?

She was in pensive thought when there was a soft knock on the study door and a quiet voice said, "Is there anything I can help you with, Mrs Farraday?"

Zaylee jumped in fright. She thought she was alone but here was the manager, Leon Jones, standing not far behind her. She had met this man several times over the years. She was not sure how to take him. He seemed quite charming and was a good worker. Miriam's Place always looked immaculate.

There was something about him she could not take to, but all things considered, he was good to her sister-in-law, Maryanne. This was something that the entire family was grateful for as Maryanne could be quite a handful. Her mental health problems were under control but had not always been so.

"No thank you, Leon, everything is fine. I was just looking to see if there were any personal items that Miriam might enjoy. She hasn't got much in her life to brighten things up." Zaylee hoped the man would disappear as silently as he had arrived. She watched as he bid her farewell and walked away.

The doctor had no intentions of finding any personal items for Miriam. She doubted there was anything of significance left in the house after all these years that Miriam would find interesting or stimulating. But having spoken these words, she felt obliged to at least make some pretence of finding something of interest for Miriam.

She carefully folded the old letter and put it in her bag. Then she proceeded to the main bedroom that Miriam had shared with the old doctor. The built-ins were bare so this search took very little time. She had the experience now of feeling under the tops of drawers for hidden documents so she opened up all the drawers in the mahogany chest of drawers that was near to antique as possible. They were all empty as she expected.

She opened the bottom drawer and did the cursory check of feeling under the bottom of the drawer above. Never in a million years did she expect to pull out another piece of paper. This time she got down on her hands and knees and was able to see what was held there. It was a white envelope, very yellow with age.

Again, she carefully pulled the sticky tape off the envelope and pulled it out. There was the letter 'M' written in fading ink on the front. She remained sitting on the floor as she warily opened up the flap of the envelope. She pulled out the paper. Her amazement grew as she saw words written in neat handwriting on what looked like the pages of an exercise book.

She felt like she was a snoop of the worst kind delving into the secrets of another person. But she had come this far, so she might as well forge on. Though the ink was faded she could still read the letter. Zaylee had to hold back her tears as she read on. It was probably a love letter of sorts from Alan Farraday to his wife, Miriam. It was very personal. It explained a lot about the person who was Alan Farraday.

Then she came to the part about her deceased brother-in-law, Michael. The doctor was again taken aback by Alan Farraday's assertion when she read the words—*'I know he is mine, Miriam, I can see the resemblances and traits there, just a few of them that are like me. He would defend all those he loves to the death'.*

All these years and she had never known that there had been a question about the paternity of the second son of Alan and Miriam Farraday. She was sure none of the rest of the family had known either. What did it mean? She sat on the floor pondering these questions. She knew Michael had fought for and defended his mother and his siblings all his life. He had reared his youngest brother, Matthew, while Miriam had been ill. He had gone to jail for her own husband.

Granted, the entire family looked much alike with dark hair and eyes, and with tall, strong builds. From what she remembered the only person Alan Farraday had defended was his no-good, half-brother, Jack Smith. When the going got really tough and Jack Smith was shot dead by Michael's wife, Denise, Alan Farraday had hung himself.

What a strange bunch she had married into? So many secrets, so many lies, so much sex and lust which she had to admit, included herself as she remembered the encounters she had indulged in with Malcolm on the floor of her consultation room at the medical practice. Most of it was kept quiet—the big silence that enveloped them all.

She decided it was time to leave. She would take the two letters with her and try to make sense of them. She locked up, waved to Leon Jones who was busy at the back of the house and drove back to her own home.

Driving the back, quiet roads to her home gave her time to think. Was there a connection between the information in the two letters? What else had the second letter said—*'I can't blame you for turning to the doctor. He is everything I wasn't or could ever hope to be'.*

So it was possible that Michael had not been Alan Farraday's son but was in fact the son of Dr Samuel Calhoun. But after all this time what difference did it make? The first letter said there had been a son and a daughter. If Michael had been the son, then who was the daughter?

She let her mind travel in all sorts of directions. How many years had she been searching for her birth parents? Was it even remotely possible that she was the daughter of Dr Sam Calhoun? If the first letter had been written by Samuel Calhoun's wife, then it was possible she may be his daughter—someone had to be. All her searching over so many years had been futile. She thought of the woman's words—*'I pray to God that she well taken care of'.*

Zaylee had certainly been well taken care of. She had the best of parents and enjoyed the best of childhoods. She should be satisfied with her life but that nagging, endless desire to know her roots never left her alone.

What was she to do about it? Sit on it for the rest of her life and do nothing more or keep going until she found some resolution. In her heart she knew she could never let it be—she had to know. There was only one thing for it. She had to find Gabriel Farraday.

She knew where he lived or at least had a vague notion of the location of his home. She tried to remember what he had once told her about his home. *It wasn't much of a place but it was good enough for himself and his dogs.*

She wondered about the young woman who had been with him, concerned if they had found a place to stay, that she was warm and not the bedraggled, wet, terrified, wreck of a young woman she had been. After taking wrong turns and streets, she found where Gabriel lived. It was exactly as he had described—it wasn't much of a place. But it did have a high fence around it. No doubt to keep the dogs in and intruders out.

She didn't consider she was an intruder. She was his aunt by marriage and if what she surmised might be the truth, she may just be his aunt by blood. She felt a tingle of excitement that she may have at long last found a living, blood relative.

She opened the front gate and was about to walk up the few stairs to knock on the front door when a man stood up and confronted her. He had been concealed by sitting down low on a chair that sat on the front veranda. Zaylee was taken aback to find a stranger sitting as comfortably as you like at the front of Gabe's home.

"Can I help you?" he asked casually.

"I'm looking for Gabe," she replied. "Is he here?" She noticed he was of medium height with bland features. There was nothing remarkable about his appearance.

"No, he's not. I've been looking for him as well—some unfinished business," he said. "You don't know where I might find him, do you?"

Zaylee had an uncomfortable feeling about this stranger. She knew very little about Gabe's personal life, but this ordinary-looking man put a shiver up her spine. "I have no idea," she replied, "but if I find him, I'll tell him you were looking for him. Who shall I say you are?"

"Just an old friend, I'd like to surprise him. I'll catch up with him some other time." The man stood up as if to leave. Zaylee said a quick goodbye and was out the front gate and was driving away as she saw the man also leave.

She was at a loss as to where to look next. Knowing that Matthew, her husband's youngest brother, might have some idea how to contact Gabe, she drove to the property which he shared with his wife.

Matt and Mia were an odd but happy couple. Mia was several years older than Matt. They had no children of their own but they fostered children from time to time. They were also heavily involved in the running of several child-care centres.

Mia's mother had disappeared many years ago and her body had been found buried under a shed on the Farraday property 'Sunshine'. Mia had been raised, or more like dragged-up, by her grandmother. She had no relatives until she married Matthew. She then became part of a large, extended family. It was thanks to Mia and Matt that the children of Matt's brother and sister, Michael and Maryanne, had not been put into foster care when numerous tragedies had occurred years ago.

If anyone knew how to contact Gabe, it would be Matt and Mia. The home they owned was big—meant for a large family. As Zaylee pulled into their front yard, she recognized Gabe's vehicle. She breathed a sigh of relief at having found her nephew.

She knocked on the front door, but as there was no answer, she walked around the back. There she found Gabriel and Lu in earnest conversation with Matt and Mia. As she approached, they all looked at her at the same time. The two large dogs she had seen the previous evening were being held under control by Gabe. The young woman still wore the doctor's coat and was being partially held up by Gabe.

Mia, being a generous and kind soul, immediately flung her arms around her sister-in-law and was on the verge of tears. "Oh, thank goodness you're here, Zaylee. Poor Lu, she's so unwell. I've been trying to convince her to come inside, but she refuses. All she wants to do is lie down in the back shed. Not even Gabe can get her to come inside."

Zaylee took one look at the young woman who was breathing rapidly beside Gabe. She spoke gently to the young woman, "Do you have a headache? Have you been coughing?"

The young woman nodded. Her eyes were glazed over. She felt hot to touch. Zaylee recalled all she knew of Gabe's friend. She knew they had met in a cemetery. The first time she had seen this thin, bedraggled woman was under a damp, walk-bridge in Sundial Park, shaking and terrified. Then her husband had refused to offer any assistance when they had come seeking it. She felt immensely guilty about this young woman's present condition.

"She should be lying down, Gabe. If she won't go inside, then get her a mattress and put it in the shed. By the sound of that cough, she's probably got a rip-roaring chest infection. By rights she should be in hospital, but from what I know of you lot, she would probably object."

Zaylee took the young woman by the hand and guided her to a stool that was inside a three-door shed. There was one garage space empty.

Matthew immediately went inside his home and carried out a mattress which he placed on the cement floor of the shed. The young woman did not need any coaxing to lie down. The doctor quickly listened to her chest sounds. Lu did not object as she was feeling too ill. Gabe was kneeling beside her, concern etched on his face.

"I'll start her on some treatment right away. Hopefully, that should clear the chest. You'll have to make sure you keep her temperature down and give her fluids. This isn't the best place for recuperation. Make sure you keep her warm."

Mia was already upset and beginning to cry at the plight of the young woman. "I'll stay with her tonight. Matt can bring out another mattress and one for you as well, Gabe."

"Well, if you're all sleeping out here, I might as well come too. It will be like old times, Gabe, like when you were kids. Not that I mean to detract from Lu's illness. She'd be much better inside." Matt went in search of more mattresses.

Zaylee felt immensely better knowing this woman would be taken care of. She remained puzzled why the woman called Lu would not go inside the house. Everything about her was a puzzle. Her relationship with Gabe was also perplexing. For a while the doctor had forgotten the real reason for her desire in locating Gabe.

It seemed very crass to be asking him for a blood sample in view of all that was happening to his friend, but she was on a mission. She took Gabe to one side. *Another lie, another secret*, she thought, *what's a few more going to matter?*

"Gabe," she commenced. "It might be just as well if I take a blood sample from you to make sure you're not at risk of contracting any contagious diseases, just to be on the safe side. We don't want Lu getting any other bugs in her systems. What with whooping cough, influenza and pneumococcal and who knows what else, it's just as well to be prepared?" Gabe did not question her advice. "I'll take a sample from Lu as well. Then I can be satisfied that I'm treating her with the correct antibiotics."

Neither Gabe nor the very sick and sleepy Lu gave second thought to having their blood sampled. The doctor was ecstatic. She did have a few pangs of conscience but nothing that she could not live with. She had done far worse over the years.

It was done. She had her nephew's blood, whether it was her own nephew or her husband's was the issue. She felt in her very being that she was on the right track in locating her roots.

She made sure that Gabe's friend was in good hands. She was resting more comfortably with the medications she had given to her. There were ample people to care for her during the night. Before she left, she told the assembled group that she would be back the next day to check on her new patient.

Zaylee sent away four blood samples, which included her own and her husband's. She told her husband she was worried about him due to his moodiness and was concerned he might be anaemic. He replied that he felt quite well, but his wife was adamant he was not himself. It was as well to check. When he saw her concern, he apologised for his behaviour of the previous day. He realised it was a pretty mean thing to do to his nephew and his friend.

Now it was a waiting game.

The next day she returned to check on her new patient. The young woman remained in the shed with the two, large dogs lying beside her like sentries. To her surprise, Gabe had gone back to his work in the mines. He had left his vehicle with Mark for a service where it would stay until his return. Zaylee remembered that she had neglected to tell her nephew about the man who had been sitting on his front veranda.

None of the family realised that Gabe's licence was suspended and that he had avoided a jail sentence. For once, the Farraday name had not attracted the notice of the media.

Mia was tending to Lu, trying to encourage her to eat. "I know it's fashionable to be thin, but there's thin and there's too thin. Gabe would never forgive me if I let you lose more weight. That's the last thing he said to me before he left—'Make sure she keeps eating, Mia.' He's a great guy, Gabe. He's just like his father, Michael. Did you know that Matt and I took care of Gabe and Rafe after it happened? But I can't talk about that episode in our lives. It's still too painful."

She looked down at the young woman and saw she had again shut her eyes. "I know I talk too much, and I talk a lot of rubbish, but it's the way I was born. Sometimes I don't know what's wrong with me. I have a crazy brain."

Lu enjoyed listening to Mia ramble on. She was starting to feel relaxed with Matt and Mia especially since Gabe had left. The presence of the two dogs also made her feel more secure.

Mia chatted on. "We have a son, called Harry, but he's not really our son but we think of him as our own. He's at school at the moment. We never had children of our own because I really don't think I'm capable of looking after my own children. But it doesn't really matter as we seem to look after everyone else's children."

Mia's rambling conversation was interrupted by the arrival of another vehicle. When she heard the voice of Dr Zaylee Lang, Lu again opened her eyes and attempted to sit up. Black devil fell out of her arms and onto the cement floor. She hastened to pick him up.

She pulled her feet up under the blanket that covered her. Someone had removed her boots, probably Gabe.

"How are you feeling today, Lu?" the doctor asked. "Do you mind if I listen to your chest again?"

The young woman made no attempt to assist the doctor. She couldn't bear to have another person touch her. "I promise I won't hurt you," the doctor spoke kindly to her. Lu immediately felt chagrined at her reluctance to let the doctor examine her, especially after all her kindness the previous day. Slowly she acquiesced.

The doctor knelt down beside her on the mattress and asked Lu to lift up her loose, dark, drab top. She was loath to do so but with some more encouragement, the doctor was able to persuade her to let her listen to her chest sounds. Lu shut her eyes tight. The doctor pretended not to notice how painfully thin she was. As she pulled Lu's clothes back into place, Lu pulled the blanket up further to cover her bony appearance. As she did so, her feet became exposed. Before she realised this had occurred, the doctor noticed her feet.

This time, the doctor could not pretend she hadn't seen. "What on earth has happened to your feet?" Before Lu could pull away, Zaylee held her feet in her hands, studying the bulging toe nails and the numerous letter 'L's' burned into the soles of her feet. "You've been tortured, haven't you?"

The young woman pulled the blanket up over her face and pulled her feet back up under it as she curled into a ball. Mia and Zaylee gazed at Lu in astonishment as she hid under the blanket. For once, both women were lost for words.

The dogs still stood sentry beside Lu, but were no longer content to just stand by. They looked menacingly at the two women. When she heard them growl, Lu slowly pulled the blanket down from her face and sat up.

"I can't talk about it," she said. "I'm very ashamed, not only about my feet but about all of me." She looked appealingly up at the two women. "You can see what I look like. It's not easy being a freak."

Mia burst immediately into tears. "Oh, Lu," she said. "Please don't say that. You're a beautiful, young woman. You just need to put on some weight and that's my job now. Do you think Gabriel Farraday would have anything to do with you if you weren't good looking? He has a reputation, you know. All the Farraday men do, for that matter. They only go for good-looking women. You fit the bill exactly." Mia was up and running with her mindless chatter.

Lu couldn't help herself. She looked at Zaylee and despite her illness and embarrassment, she smiled. Zaylee Lang thought she had been hit by a bullet. The smile was so much like that of her husband's. But then the more she looked at Lu, the less certain she became. It was just that first smile then there was no other resemblance. She put her foolish judgments aside.

Mia decided it was time for banana milk-shakes. She left Lu and the doctor alone.

"Mia talks a lot, but she is the kindest and most generous person I know. You couldn't be in better hands," the doctor said. More than anything she wanted to ask about her feet but feared the young woman would clam up.

"I'm very grateful to her, to all of you. I'm sorry about before. That was very ungracious of me." Lu clutched her black bear to her chest. "Matt and Mia have been nothing but kind and generous. What happened to Mia? What's wrong with her?"

"Nothing's wrong with her, nothing that I know of. Why do you ask?" The question about Mia was totally unexpected, especially coming from this sick woman.

"It's just that she's so much like someone I used to know." Lu was remembering one of the children she had been at school with. Mia was so much like this girl.

"In what way," Zaylee asked, intrigued by Lu's observation.

"It's not important," she replied. "It's none of my business."

Just then, Mia returned with a jug of creamy milk. She poured a glass for each of them and kept topping up Lu's. Mia started rambling on. The doctor caught the same smile on Lu's face several times as the conversation jumped from subject to subject. But the facial resemblance evaded her. All she could think was how pretty Lu was when she wasn't being so secretive.

The time came for Zaylee to depart, but wild horses would not keep her away from the intriguing woman who was lying sick on a mattress on the cold, cement floor of a shed, being guarded by two, huge dogs.

Gabe phoned his wife twice a day as promised. His concern about her was intense as he left her, but he was comforted to hear her sounding better. He would be forever grateful to Matt, Mia and Zaylee for looking after her. He knew they had many questions about her. He did as well.

One day he hoped she might feel confident enough to tell him all that had happened to her, even though she vowed she would never talk about it. He wondered again about the two bags she had shoved far under his house.

He suffered pangs of guilt. Without her knowledge, he had retrieved one of the bags, the one that was closest to his reach. While he respected her desire for privacy, he rationalised that if he could see the bag from outside the house, then other people could as well. The second bag remained well out of sight under the house. The first bag was now carefully buried under the dog kennels. He had insulated it with more plastic and hoped it would be safe for whenever she felt the need to retrieve it.

Mia and Matt stayed each night in the shed with Lu. Mia was in and out of the shed throughout the day, making sure medications were taken and that Lu was eating. Matt took care of the dogs. Lu was still too weak to be looking after them. Harry was introduced to Lu and the two dogs. There was an instant rapport established, not only with Lu, but with James and Boag as well.

Like Zaylee, they were all intrigued with the young woman. They had endless conversations about her. Where she had come from? Who exactly was she? What was her relationship with Gabe?

Most of all were the questions about her feet. Zaylee had surmised she had been tortured.

Try as they might, they did not get another peep at her feet as Lu kept her boots on at all times, except during the night when she made sure they were covered by her blanket. They had given up persuading her to live with them inside their spacious house with its numerous bedrooms.

When Matt asked Mia if she knew how Gabe and Lu met, Mia told her husband in no uncertain terms that it didn't really matter how they met, the important thing was that they were in love. Matt looked at his wife in puzzlement and asked, "How do you know that?"

"Haven't you got eyes in your head, Matt? Can't you tell?" Matt took his wife's word for it. It was beyond him how women knew these things.

As Lu improved, Matt and Mia left her alone on the property for short periods as they attended to their business. Lu was asleep on her mattress with the ridge-backs sitting on either side of her. She was unaware of the vehicle that pulled up at the front of the house. She did not know that a man had got out of his vehicle and walked up the front stairs of Matt and Mia's home. She slept on, regaining her strength and overcoming her illness.

The first awareness she had of anything different was when the two dogs began growling and left her side. Lu became frightened. She knew Matt and Mia were away, that she was alone in the shed. She stood up and quietly pulled down the roller door where she had been asleep.

She could hear the dogs barking and growling so she surmised that there was something or someone there that had attracted their attention. Her thoughts went straight to Uncle Lucas. Had he found her again? It could not be Dr Zaylee as the dogs now knew her and were used to her. If indeed it was a person? It could well be a kangaroo, wallaby or simply a goanna. The dogs were inclined to become agitated at any type of intruder.

To be on the safe side, she went to the back of the shed and climbed up onto the top of a tall ladder that lay against the wall. She crouched down on it and cuddled black devil to her. Being perched on top of a ladder was far better than landing back into the hands of Lucas. She missed the security the two dogs provided as they could not get back into the shed as all the doors were closed.

She had no idea how long she sat perched on top of the ladder. She could hear the dogs stirring outside the shed, but she dare not let them in. She became tired and cramped but lacked the courage to shift from her hiding place. Her illness, though improved, still remained.

She became sleepy. She knew the doctor had prescribed her medication to help dry up her chest secretions which also had the effect of causing drowsiness. Lu was terrified to come down from her hiding place and yet was equally terrified that she might fall asleep and tumble off the top of the tall ladder.

She woke with a start. She had been asleep. Thankfully she had not fallen off. The sound of the dogs barking and the roller door being pushed open again caused terror to course through her. She closed her eyes as she could not bear to look into the face of Lucas.

"What are you doing up there, Lu?" Matthew asked, bewildered at seeing the young woman perched precariously on top of his highest ladder. Mia was close behind him. The dogs scampered in and began whimpering at the base of the ladder.

Lu looked down at them all. She again felt very foolish. What must they think of her? She was sure they already thought she was unhinged. How could she tell them that she thought her uncle was coming for her? Who would believe such a story? If she told them about Lucas, then she might have to reveal what had happened to Grandfather and for that matter, Grandmother.

Lu, who had not told these kind people who had taken her in, anything about herself, found herself facing more shame and embarrassment.

"I thought I heard a vehicle," she stammered. "I was frightened so I hid. I'm sorry if I alarmed you. I couldn't think what else to do."

"You're right, Lu. There was a vehicle here. I saw the tyre tracks as I drove in. I'm not sure who they belong to, but there's no one who would call here who would hurt you. Let me help you down." Matt helped the shaking, young woman down off the ladder.

Thankfully, his wife started chatting, telling Lu about all the healthy food she had bought for her. By healthy, she meant everything that was guaranteed to fatten her up. Mia winked at the young woman as she told her about the food that was now in her kitchen. She concluded that they might just have to have a party to welcome Lu to the family.

Matt was equally concerned by the vehicle that had driven onto his property. Mitch had warned them to be careful, that he thought that even after all these years, there may be someone else coming after them.

It brought back the memories of the three bodies that the brothers had buried in the tunnel under the home at Sunshine. Matthew would never forget the crackling of the bones of another skeleton that had already been entombed there as he dragged the three bodies deep into the tunnel. How long this first skeleton had lain there he had no idea?

Mia was bubbling with excitement. She had decided they would have a girl party, nothing big or elaborate, just something in the shed. She was of the opinion that Lu needed cheering up, something to help her get over her illness. She told her husband of her plans. His only response was that as long as he didn't have to attend with a bunch of chattering females, he didn't really care what she did. If it helped the young woman, he was all for it.

Mia was on the phone to her sisters-in-law Zaylee, Malcolm's wife, and Francine, Mitch's wife. She thought about asking Maryanne, her husband's sister, not that she really wanted her to come, but she couldn't be ill-mannered. Nevertheless, she hoped she would refuse as Maryanne always frightened Mia. Fortunately, when she phoned, Lizzie answered. When Mia explained her plans, Lizzie said her mother was not feeling up to it, but she would come instead.

As Lizzie made her way in her mother's car, she felt relieved to be able to escape. Leon was, as usual, listening into the conversation. Lizzie explained that she was going to visit her little brother, Harry, as well as her extended family. Leon did not object.

Like Francine, Lizzie was more than surprised to find they were having a girl's morning tea in the shed and not in the house like most normal people would. But thinking about it, she should not have been surprised. It was something that only Mia would do. Lizzie made her way down to the shed, carrying cups and cakes.

Lizzie's astonishment only grew as she saw her friend, Lu, sitting on a mattress which lay on the floor of the shed. "Lu, what on earth are you doing here?"

Lu was equally surprised to find her friend from Sundial Park sit down on the mattress beside her. She was tongue tied. Her list of acquaintances was growing rapidly, too rapidly. The more people who knew about her only increased the risk of Lucas locating her. She was feeling trapped. But she was in no position to escape. She was reliant on these people, at least until she felt stronger.

"I'm sick, Lizzie, and these kind people offered to look after me. What are you doing here?"

"Oh, it's just Mia being Mia. She thought it was time for a get-together." As Lizzie looked at Lu, she thought that if it was possible, she was thinner than ever. "Are you feeling better, Lu?"

"Yes," she replied, "but I'm not up to any get-togethers. I just want to disappear."

"Don't worry, I'll look after you. Besides, I see you've still got your two, monster dogs for protection. There will only be a few people here."

Just then, Mia arrived with Francine and Zaylee carrying more party food. "I see you two have met," Mia announced.

The two young women glanced swiftly at each other. Neither knew why they did not already explain that they had already met. Was it the comradeship of the torture of damaged souls?

Zaylee immediately went to Lu to check on her progress. Francine stood to the back staring at the young woman who sat on the mattress. Lu suddenly looked up at this other woman. Their eyes met and held. Lu knew immediately that she had found another damaged soul, another person who had felt the wounds of inflicted cruelty.

Neither spoke. Lu smiled at the beautiful woman who stood in front of her. She had noticed she kept her left hand behind her back. Without saying a word, for the second time ever, Lu voluntarily took her brown boots off in front of a group of people. She spread her feet out in front of her. She heard Francine gasp. Then Francine brought her left hand from behind her back and spread it out in front of her.

The silence of suffering was on display. Lizzie held up her left hand with the thin scar that ran from the tip of her little finger to the outside of her wrist.

Mia burst out crying. Zaylee could do nothing but stare. Her desire to locate her ancestry diminished in comparison to what she was seeing. Lu again began to feel ashamed for treating Mia's efforts to brighten up her life so deplorably. A pall of sadness now hung over the group

She forced herself to speak. "Thank you for the party, Mia. I'm sorry for what I did. Maybe we better start eating."

Lu grabbed some cake and forced it into her mouth. Mia dried her tears and commenced chatting. Zaylee made small talk with Francine. Their children were of a similar age so they had a lot in common. Lizzie sat on the mattress beside Lu and fed titbits of the party food to the dogs.

"Can you look after Rina, please Lizzie?" Lu eventually asked after she had managed as much food as she could.

"Sure, I will, Lu, not that I see her very often. Why do you ask?"

"I'm not really sure, just a feeling I get." Before she could make any more explanations about her feelings regarding Rina, Francine screamed out and began to shake.

"Francine, what's the matter?" Zaylee was aghast as she watched her sister-in-law begin to fit. As quickly as possible, she had Francine on her side. She began shouting out to Mia to call an ambulance.

Mia was again crying, trying to follow Zaylee's instructions. Mia looked imploringly to Lizzie who grabbed Zaylee's phone and requested an ambulance immediately. Zaylee held Francine while they all waited in anguish for the ambulance to arrive.

In the meantime, Lizzie phoned her Uncle Mitch to explain what was happening to his wife. When she heard the concern in his voice, she immediately felt a ton of guilt for what she had done. No one deserved what was happening to Francine, not her husband or their children. Lizzie told Mitch that she would organise for their two children to stay with Matt and Mia.

Lizzie and Lu watched with deep concern as they saw Francine being taken away in an ambulance. They would never forget the terrible sight of the seizure. Nor would they forget the way that she held her head in pain as the fitting ceased and consciousness began to return.

Lizzie breathed a sigh of relief as she returned home. For once she was pleased to be home even if it was to be met by Leon. Francine and Mitch's children, Finbarr and Roza, were collected from school to stay with Matt and Mia along with her young brother, Harry.

It brought back memories of the times when she had stayed with her cousins at Sunshine when they had all been young children. She briefly wondered where Rafe was. She wished he would return home as she badly needed someone to talk to. There were so many strange events occurring.

Leon was, as usual, full of questions about what had taken her so long. She had no patience with his endless need to know every aspect of her life. But rather than have him grab her by the throat or twist her arm behind her back, she gave him an exact description of the seizure that Francine had suffered.

She elaborated how the ambulance siren's screamed out as Francine was carted off to hospital. Lizzie did not have to pretend or act when the tears came to her eyes as she recalled Francine's back arching up in spasm, her head shaking and froth coming from her mouth.

Lizzie went straight to her room, shut her door and pulled out her cards. If there was a time for solitude and for solitaire, it was now. As she pulled out her first card which was the three of hearts, she looked out her bedroom window and sure enough it was raining.

Was it karma that often when bad things happened in her family, it would rain. She remembered the stories she had heard when she was young, about how there was a dreadful storm at Sunshine, how the creek waters raged and a shed had been washed away and there lay the bones of Mia's mother.

The next card she drew was the five of spades—swords and fire. She wished someone would put a sword through the worst of the lot, Leon Jones, and set him on fire.

Lizzie did have a few qualms about her homicidal thoughts, but not too many. Some people deserved to die, people like Leon. But nothing bad ever happened to them. It was only people like Francine, good people, who had seizures and had to be carted off to hospital. Lizzie felt sick to her soul.

She went back out to the kitchen where her mother sat giggling with Leon. She announced that she would not be working tonight. She was too upset at what had happened to her aunt. For once, her mother was in agreement. Maryanne thought a good rest would do Lizzie good. Leon did not make any comment, but raised his eyebrow and told Lizzie he would see her next week.

As she left them, she heard Leon tell her mother that he had big plans for the following week—big plans that would bring them all good fortune. Maryanne began her maniacal laughter as she told Leon that she hoped she was included in the big plans. Lizzie turned around and saw her mother looking at Leon as if he were a saint. She gave him her most hateful look. He merely smiled back at her and while Maryanne was looking elsewhere, he licked his lips.

Lizzie was intrigued to know what the plans were. She had no doubt they would be anything but good. He had hinted previously about his plans and strategies. She was thankful she would be spared going to the cursed club where she had to swing around a pole and expose her body for the world to see.

Would there ever come a day when her body need not be seen as an exhibit, when some man might see her for a human being of feelings and emotions? Lizzie could not see her plight changing.

Because she was feeling so low, she picked up her phone and contacted Mia and Matt. This was a legitimate call due to what had happened to Francine. Of course, Leon kept track of her calls, and would grill her about any unknown number she contacted. Lizzie knew better than to speak to anyone outside his approved list of contacts.

To her eternal gratitude, Raphael answered. She almost cried when she heard his voice. "Can I see you?"

"Sure, when and where?" his response was immediate.

"Tomorrow, at the cave—early," she replied. Had it not been raining she would have said, "Right now".

"See you then." That was the end of the conversation.

It was a long night for Lizzie. Her sleep was fitful. There was so much on her mind. She heard Lu's words asking her to look out for Rina, but how was she to do this. She was kept so under the thumb by Leon. It was almost impossible to evade his powerful hold on her.

She was up bright and early the next morning. The rain had stopped. She told her mother she was going for a walk. Maryanne ignored her as she rolled back over in her bed. Lizzie heard her snoring as she left the house.

She had freedom at last, freedom from her mother, her responsibilities, freedom from the nightmare of her job and best of all freedom from evil Leon. She had two whole days of freedom before next week, before he commenced his next big plan, his next strategy—whatever that might be.

Lizzie even packed lunch. The sun was warmly shining. It felt good to be walking up the track to the Big Rock. She didn't care if he didn't arrive for hours. She was alone, by herself, walking up through the trees and rocks.

As she strolled up into the hills, she vaguely remembered her grandmother singing an old hymn about Amazing Grace. The morning was so beautiful and she felt so free, that she thought grace must be dripping off all the glistening leaves that had been drenched the day before.

When she reached the top of the Big Rock, she walked over to the side and looked down at the long drop to the bottom. Then she looked over at Sunshine, the place where she had spent a lot of time as a child. It was a beautiful sight. She couldn't help it, she started singing Amazing Grace.

The breezes gently swayed the glistening leaves on the tall gums. The sound of this was so soothing that she sang out the words— *Amazing Grace, how sweet the sound, that saved a wretch like me.*

It was a euphoric moment for Lizzie. Her cares were blown away. She had no doubt she was a wretch, but the sound of it was uplifting—that is until she heard the rustling in the grass and the hiss of a large lizard, a goanna, that stood up on its legs just a few metres away from her. Lizzie took a step closer to the edge of the cliff. As she did so, she screamed out.

The goanna was as frightened as she was. She pulled herself back from the edge of the cliff, her heart beating rapidly. The goanna was equally frightened by her scream. It disappeared with little to no noise back into the grasses. Lizzie did not stop to consider what could have happened if she had stumbled over the side of the cliff and fallen to the bottom of the Big Rock.

She took off, back down the track onto the next property, Sunshine. She arrived at the bottom of the Big Rock and went straight to the cave. She was still shaking as she entered. That was when she saw him. She went straight into his arms.

She buried her face in his chest and could not stop herself from crying. The incident with the goanna had unnerved her. She tried to explain to him how close she had come to falling off the cliff. It was not so much the goanna but the image of falling that had her most upset. Raphael held her until she stopped crying. Then he sat her down on a plastic sheet that he had brought with him.

"Hush, Lizzie, you're safe now. Tell me what happened." He loved the feel of her in his arms. When she didn't attempt to shift, he didn't attempt to let her go.

"I was singing Amazing Grace, you remember, just like Grandma. She was always singing that hymn. It is such a beautiful day. It just makes you want to sing. I was standing on the edge of the Big Rock and suddenly there it was—the biggest, ugliest goanna you're ever likely to see. I thought it was going to come right for me. All I could think to do was to scream as loud as I could. So that's what I did. Otherwise I might have gone right over the edge with fright. I don't know what happened to the lizard, but I ran as fast as I could down to the cave. It frightened the daylights out of me."

"I can understand how frightened you must have been, but you're safe now." He continued to hold her. Lizzie was content to be held in his arms. But arising feelings and passions had to be dampened. It was too early in the day. So Lizzie pulled herself away from him. Together they sat on the plastic sheeting.

"Maybe you should christen the goanna, Amazing Grace," he said. "It was pretty amazing that he was there in the first place, considering the time of day. He was probably sunning himself or else was after smaller lizards. It was also pretty amazing that you didn't fall over the cliff. What do you say we drink to Amazing Grace?"

Lizzie was so overwhelmed that she burst into giggles. Raphael pulled out some cans of coke and handed one to Lizzie. Together they drank and ate the lunch that Lizzie had brought with her. It was far too early for lunch, but Amazing Grace had changed the circumstances of the day.

"What did you want to talk to me about, Lizzie?"

"I wanted to know how Francine is."

"She's better, improving. No one knows why she had the seizure. It's never happened before. The children are staying with Matt and Mia. Just as well they have a big house. It's starting to fill up. That's another funny thing that's happened. There's a frail, young woman staying in the sheds. Mia said she's been sick. That's why she's staying there. I don't know why she won't stay in the house. She's got two, huge dogs with her as well. They look a lot like Gabe's dogs." He saw her looking intently at him. "Do you know anything about her, Lizzie?"

"No, I only met her when Francine had the seizure." Lizzie was unable to explain why she was reluctant to reveal that she already knew Lu. Then she thought of the other woman called Rina that they had met in Sundial Park. Lu had begged her to check up on her. But it was not possible to escape Leon without causing him suspicion.

"Would you do me a favour?" she asked.

"Sure, if I can," he replied.

"I have a friend who has a young son who is disabled. I worry about her, so I was wondering if you wouldn't mind checking up on her sometime. She's often in Sundial Park about midday. You won't be able to miss her. She gets around looking like an old bag and the boy is always with her. You know where Sundial Park is, don't you?"

"I remember it well," he replied. "Why not go and see her yourself?"

She knew this was the obvious solution. "I'm pretty busy what with mum being the way she is. I can't always get away."

He made no comment. He knew very well that her mother was more than a handful. But it was the last thing in the world he wanted to do. He did not have good memories of Sundial Park, let alone check up on some old bag with a disabled son.

They sat side by side on the plastic sheeting at the entrance to the cave. The sun shone warm upon them. Suddenly, Lizzie whipped off the shirt she was wearing and proceeded to take off her jeans.

"What do you think you are doing, Lizzie?" He tried not to look at her, but it was next to impossible.

"Getting some sun—what did you think I was trying to do, seduce you?" She stretched out on her back beside him and shut her eyes. "Why don't you try it? You're looking a bit pale." He had never looked pale in his life. He was the picture of good health.

She kept her eyes shut tight. She could sense him beside her and was dying to know if he had stripped off. But knowing him, he was probably on his knees praying. But whatever he was up to, it was just nice to be lying in the warm sun beside him, to forget her troubles, forget her mother and Leon Jones and his big plans.

She heard him clear his voice. "Do you mind if I touch you, Lizzie?"

This was the last thing in the world she expected to hear. She had given up on her seduction plans. She was with him just to talk, but if he wanted to touch her, who was she to object.

"Do you want to hold hands?" She put her hand out to the side so he could hold it. It was her right hand for which she was grateful. Her scars were her own business, whether they were physical or emotional. She kept her eyes shut tight.

"I want to do more than that, Lizzie." She couldn't believe what she was hearing.

"What's stopping you then?" She was breathing more rapidly than a few moments previously. She thought she felt his breath near her face.

"Open your eyes, Lizzie."

She slowly opened her eyes. There he was with his near-black eyes staring down at her. She opened her mouth. He kissed her then. This was beyond her imaginings. She kissed him back. He touched her breasts. She gasped as she felt him play with her erect nipples. She again sought his lips. Their passion ignited. She was pulling at him, drawing him close onto her. It was then that she realised he had shed his clothes. It felt so good. It became very frantic. He wanted her. She wanted him. He entered her. She rejoiced in the feel of him. Their coupling was intense, so intense that she felt millions of coloured stars burst through her brain. When it was over, she lay in his arms, crying.

"Why are you crying?"

"There was no grey, not one speck of it. I never thought it could ever happen like that for me."

"Are you saying it was good?"

"Raphael Farraday, sometimes I think that you are so dense. Of course it was good. Was it good for you?"

"It was so good, Lizzie Smythe, I'd like to do it again—if you'd let me."

She smiled at him, and pulled him back down on top of her. The sun made its slow trek across the sky of Sunshine as their love intensified. He had a few chocolate bars in the pocket of the jeans he had shed, so he fed these to her as he continued to taste her, to feel her, to love her. He was mesmerised by her beasts. He could not keep his hands or his mouth off them. But days must end and so did theirs.

"Why are you looking so sad when this has been the happiest day of my life?"

"There's something I have to tell you. We can't be doing this anymore, Lizzie."

"Doing what, making love? You just said it was good. I don't understand." She had thought he was as enthralled as she had been. "Just because we're cousins doesn't mean we can't make love." She could never use the word sex when it came to him. It had been so much more than sex.

"I've made a decision." She looked at him in anticipation. "I'm going to join the priesthood."

She could not speak. Words failed her. She just stared at him, seeing his downcast black eyes. "You can't be serious. What on earth do you want to do that for?"

"I've done things in the past, bad things."

Lizzie then knew he was joking. "Raphael, you have never done anything bad in your life. If you want to know about bad, just look at me. You know what they call me—bad, beautiful Lizzie. For a minute there, I thought you were serious."

"I am serious, Lizzie. I mean it. That's why today has been so wonderful, being here with you, making love to you."

She sat in silence beside him, shaking her head in disbelief. In a quiet, hurt voice she said. "So it was just a quick one to say hello and then another to say goodbye. Is that all it meant to you? One day of fun before you become celibate, and I was the lucky winner."

She ran her hands in dismay through her messed-up hair before she continued. "There was no grey, Rafe, not one shade of it. It was full of colour—all the most beautiful colours on the planet. That's what it was like for me. Now I'll never see those colours ever again. That's what you've done to me, Raphael."

"I don't mean to upset you, Lizzie. I hardly ever understand what you're talking about. But I've got to make up for what I've done somehow. It was my fault, you know, all of it, everything that happened."

"No, I don't know. Like you, I have no idea what you're talking about." She was trying to keep the tears from her eyes. "What was your fault?"

"Sarina and my mother, and subsequently my father—I could have prevented it. With Sarina, I woke up and heard noises, but I was too frightened to do anything about it. If I had been braver, like Gabe, I would have done something, woke my parents, called out, instead of lying there in bed. It was the same with my mother. I should have stayed with her, but I went with Matt to Tewantin to buy pizza. It was her first day home. All she wanted was to be with her sons."

"You were a child, Rafe. You couldn't have known what would happen. You don't have to run away again. If you want to run away, you can run away with me. We could pack up right now and just go. All we have to do is put our clothes back on and just disappear. Please, Rafe, don't do this."

"It's done, Lizzie. Another week or so and I'll be gone. I should apologise to you for today. It shouldn't have happened, but I'll never regret it."

"Well, that's big of you—you'll never regret it. Do you want to know what I'll regret, Rafe?" Her disdain of him was cutting. He did not reply. He knew what she had to say would not be nice.

"I now regret every second of the time you spent with me, every touch, every kiss, you being inside me, all that feeling. I wish it had never happened. I wish you had never come into my life. You are no different from him. At least all I have to do is pretend with him. He never really expects me to be honest. But I was honest with you, Rafe. I never had to pretend. Did you know that I've been pretending all my life, Rafe, since I was a little girl?"

He was worried about her. She was talking crazy. Nothing she said was logical. "Settle down, Lizzie, you're not making any sense. Let me help you with your clothes." He handed her the crumpled shirt that they had thrown onto the dirt beside them in their frantic bid to unite their bodies.

"Don't touch me, Raphael, don't you ever touch me again. After I find out what the grand plan is next week, if I don't like it, then it's all over for me. That will be the end of it. You've done that to me Raphael Farraday." She was almost at screaming pitch. "But don't worry. You can spend the rest of your life doing more penance. Me, I won't have a care in the world. Goodbye, Raphael, have a great life, Padre."

Raphael was left standing at the entrance to the cave as he watched her run down the other side of the Big Rock, with her black hair streaming out behind her. He heard her sobs as she ran through the tall gums, scrambled over the rocks and disappeared out of his view as the sun was setting.

He had never felt so miserable in his life. What had she said? It had been the happiest day of her life. Now it was about the worst day of his life and seeing the pain in her eyes, he guessed it was probably the same for her.

Lizzie knew her mother had any number of pills. There were pills to slow her down, to lift her up, to stop her eating, to help her sleep. She grabbed the bottle that would help her sleep. Her mother was in bed asleep, so she took three of the little white tablets, pulled the duvet off her bed and threw it on the floor. She curled herself up in it and fell into a dreamless sleep.

She could not believe the night had passed without dreams, without tears, without sensual feelings overcoming her. Even though she felt slightly groggy, somehow the plan had come to her during the night. There was so much for her to do this day. For two days, she had been free of Leon Jones. She refused to think of that other man, the one who was giving her the final push.

Whatever Leon's plans were, she just knew they would be evil and she would be forced to partake in them. If by some miracle, his plans happened to be of a different persuasion, then she might reconsider. She would make her final decision by using her cards. She would see what they told her.

She saw to her mother, gave her breakfast and watched as she shoved tablet after tablet down her throat. Before she proceeded any further, Lizzie went to the granny flat where Leon Jones lived. She crawled underneath it as far as she could. It was not often she cursed her breast size but this was one time that she did.

It was very difficult slithering under the floor boards so as to retrieve the items that had lain hidden for who knows how long. There they had remained, wrapped in protective plastic, on the beams under the granny flat. She gathered them up as well as the photocopies she had taken from the hidden cache in Leon's draw. She was almost prepared for her journey.

She grabbed some biscuits and water then set off again up the hill to the Big Rock. She kept an eye out for Amazing Grace. There he was standing up on his stubby legs, looking at her with menace in his eyes. He was a monster, almost two metres in length, looking for a feed.

There were enough monsters in her life. Trying her best to ignore him, she threw a stone at him and missed. He shot up the nearest tree, but it didn't stop him hissing and eyeing her off with evil intent.

She went straight to the cave. Memories of the previous day's interlude were banished from her head as she went through the entrance to the dark areas at the back. She found the torch she left planted there.

The bag and the gun remained in the same place. She was unsure if she should take the gun, but in the end she couldn't see what difference it would make, so she shoved it into the shopping bag with her biscuits.

Lizzie found the backpack heavy going, so she slung it over her shoulder as she trudged down the track to the home at Sunshine. For once in her life, she was grateful for all the exercise she got from swinging around the pole in front of all those hungry eyes.

She went straight to the window of the bedroom where her deceased aunt and uncle had slept. As she pushed open the window with the broken latch, she again thought of her little cousin, Sarina, who had been taken and murdered all those years ago.

But Lizzie was not in any mood for sad memories. She remained angry at the nightmare that was her life. Once inside, she went straight to the prayer room. The Celtic cross hung around her neck. She pulled the stand that the blind statue stood on away from the wall. Then she inserted the Celtic cross key into the back of it. The door swung open instantly. She looked down at the bundles of notes that lay stacked at the bottom.

Unable to help herself, she started laughing. She laughed so hard that tears were streaming down her face. If anyone had seen her, they would have thought she was as crazy as her mother—all that money just lying there, waiting for some lucky person to take it and run.

But Lizzie was not a lucky person. Besides she had nowhere to run and no one to run with. But maybe it would make some person happy.

She carefully put the backpack on top of the notes. Then she squeezed in the plastic-wrapped contents of the video, the recorder and photos she had found under Leon's flat. Lastly, she shoved Leon's photocopied documents on top. It was a tight squeeze.

The one thing that she found most interesting was the strange, wooden circle with the imprint of a lady on it. It looked religious. It did not look like something Leon would cherish. She was sure he would never miss it. So it went in with the rest. The stand was almost full. Her last task was to put the gun on top of the backpack. When she tried to close the door, it refused to shut.

This was exasperating. Something she could do without. She made a quick decision to remove the backpack. Lizzie returned back to the room that she had first climbed into where she had seen a man-hole. The problem of how to reach the ceiling was solved when she found a solid, tall stool. She balanced on this as she pushed the man-hole cover open and threw the backpack in as far as she could. All she now had to do was to replace the cover and return the stool to its former place.

She returned to the prayer room and restacked it with the gun on top. The stand was still very heavy. Again she was thankful for the strength she had gained from the pole-dancing. The stand and statue were finally in place.

She sat on the lounge chair as she stared at the blind statue, half expecting it to open its eyes and look at her. She ate her biscuits and drank some water. Then she went outside, found some white lilies that had survived out near one of the sheds. These were placed in a vase which she filled with water. The vase sat on the floor in front of the blind statue. Someone had once told her that lilies represented death. They seemed very appropriate.

She almost asked the statue to look after Raphael as he went in his pursuit of redemption, but thought better of it—*serve him right*.

The lilies looked very soothing sitting there in the old room. They brightened the whole atmosphere but the emptiness of feeling in the unused house and the myriad of terrible memories did not diminish.

But Lizzie could not linger. She had lots more to do. She had relished her previous day of happiness until it fell apart, but she put this behind her. She had much to achieve. It was still reasonably early. As quickly as possible, she hiked back to check on her mother who by now was sitting in the kitchen drinking tea.

She told her mother she had errands to run. Maryanne made no comment but continued to eat last night's left-overs and drink tea. Lizzie did not ask permission. She took her mother's car. Too bad about Leon—he could check the fuel gauge and the distance travelled all he liked. He could belt her, rape her—at this stage she didn't care. She had things to do.

First she went to visit her father's grave at the cemetery at Cooroy. She barely remembered him now, but she knew he had loved her. He had also loved her Uncle Mark's wife as well, or so rumour had it. She briefly went to see her grandmother Smythe who by now was very old. She spoke a few words of encouragement to her as she watched her trying valiantly to get around on her walking-frame. This saddened her.

Next she went to see her other grandmother, Miriam, who remained in the aged, care facility. Again, the sight of her was very upsetting. Lizzie remembered back to the day when Miriam had been notified of the deaths of her son, Michael, and his wife Denise.

It was the day Miriam had suffered the devastating stroke that had taken away her speech and her mobility. It was also when her second husband, Dr Sam Calhoun had fallen and broken his neck of femur which ultimately caused his death.

It was also the day when Lizzie began to realise that her own mother was far from normal.

There were so many to visit, both living and dead. Next she went to the Tewantin cemetery. She spent a few minutes with her uncle Michael and his wife Denise, her aunt Carrie, Malcolm's first wife, and then Tiffany, her uncle Mark's wife. She did not have good feelings towards Tiffany, as she had been in the accident that had claimed her father's life.

Lastly, she went to Alan Farraday's grave. Her recent thoughts of her time with Raphael were painful. So she spoke to her grandfather and told him that although she never knew him, they did have one thing in common which was that she would join him in hell. She added that she would probably see him very soon.

She was in two minds whether she should visit her sister, Hope. Arlo would no doubt be there, not that this worried her. But she was fond of Uncle Mark, so she drove on. Mark was surprised to see her. He told her that Hope had shifted out, that she was back living with Matt and Mia. Arlo was still in bed asleep after a heavy night. Lizzie only stayed a few minutes—just to say hi and goodbye. Mark gave her a quick kiss on the cheek. He could not fathom young people. They were full of surprises.

She couldn't face mighty Mitch. Not after what she had done. She kept away from the hospital where Francine was. She liked Francine and her children, but she was sure she would probably run into Mitch there.

When she considered her young cousins, Finbarr and Roza, she realised that they were perfectly normal children. This gladdened her heart. In spite of her dislike of Mitch for leaving her to a life of sexual slavery, she had no ill feelings towards his wife or children.

Sundial Park was next on her list. It was almost midday. Rina and the boy should be there. It took her only a few minutes to locate them. Rina was pushing Jude on the swing. The boy stared blankly out at the trees in front of him, oblivious of everything else except the pleasure of being pushed up and down.

Rina was surprised and pleased to see her. They hugged and briefly kissed. Lizzie had many acquaintances but very few whom she would call a friend. But she felt close to Rina even if she did look dull and uninspiring in her dark, drab clothes. An old, Alsatian dog accompanied them. It lay on the grass beside the swing and watched Jude swing up and down.

Lizzie made some excuse that she was just passing by. They only spoke for a few minutes. Excuses—Lizzie said she was busy and had to rush off. She turned and left before Rina could see her tears. As she walked the path to her car, Raphael pulled up. As much as she wanted to avoid him, she knew she couldn't.

They both stopped, avoiding each other's eyes. Their greeting was stilted. All she wanted to do was to get away. Her eyes were still tearful as she said, "Thank you for seeing Rina. If you can, will you please keep her in your prayers, or whatever it is you say? Goodbye Rafe."

Lizzie was openly crying as she drove away from people she loved, or could have loved. It was all so overwhelming. There was just one more stop. If she could get through that, then she might just do it straight away, and not wait for Leon and his grand plan.

As it happened, her next stop was even enjoyable. Mia was in full flight, talking endlessly as she mothered Finbarr and Roza. Her Aunt Zaylee was there with her son, Emmet. The gathering was moving down to the shed where Lu remained with the two, great dogs.

Lizzie was caught up in the fun of it all. Lu even looked happy and was beginning to look better. Lizzie thought she may have gained a few ounces. She could no longer hear the racking spasms of coughing that had previously sapped her strength.

There was Hope, her traitorous sister, happily ensconced in the safety of Matt and Mia's home. She had a brief moment of remorse, but it was very brief. Hope could have come back to her own home, to share some of the burden of responsibility of caring for her mother. She could have shared Leon as well if she happened to be missing Arlo.

Leon could most probably contribute to the whole town. For all she knew, he may have done. They kissed and hugged like loving sisters, but that was as far as Lizzie was prepared to go. No small talk, no chit-chat—Lizzie's heart was not soft enough for anything else.

Seeing her young brother, Harry, was almost her undoing. He was a mix of everything that had been good about her mother and father. She loved Harry. She was going to give him what she hoped would be a blessing and not a curse.

"Harry," she called him to one side. "I've got something for you. It's very important and I want you to have it. But you have to promise never to lose it, to always keep it safe." Lizzie produced the Celtic cross that hung around her neck. Harry looked at it with curiosity.

"What is it?" he asked.

"It's a key. A key to a great treasure; it's my gift to you. But you have to promise you won't tell anyone you have it—promise."

"I promise, Lizzie. What sort of a treasure?" Harry was intrigued by her gift. "Should I wear it around my neck?"

Before she could reply, Gabriel walked up behind her. She was so happy to see him. Next to Harry, he was her favourite relative. She didn't include Raphael as a relative, and certainly not one of her favourites. They talked for a few minutes before he was called away.

Lizzie talked to them all. Emmet seemed to have befriended Lu. Lizzie could see that Lu had been teaching him solitaire, but as the conversation gathered pace, Lu gathered up her cards and put them back into a very, well-worn pack. Lu had the old, half-worn bear within her reach. Lizzie wondered why she kept such a decrepit-looking toy with her.

Lizzie and Lu often looked at each other, their expressions telling of their concern, but were unable to speak any close words. Today, they were two young women enjoying a family gathering.

It was time to go. Lizzie was experiencing feelings of euphoria. She asked Zaylee to send her best wishes to Uncle Malcolm. Matt kissed her goodbye. She waved goodbye to all of them as she left. As she drove away she noticed that Gabriel was sitting close to Lu. She felt glad about this. The two, huge dogs haughtily surveyed the happy gathering.

It felt good to be alive this day. Maybe it was the cake and coke she had devoured. Whatever it was, her sadness abated, her spirits lifted. She felt she was ready for the release that she knew was coming the following week.

Three young women brutalised and traumatised as children, trying to live as normal people, trying to live normal lives. Thought patterns and processes were constantly challenged.

It was not like you woke up each morning and thought that this would be another ordinary day in paradise. No, every thought and action was a battle for normality. A battle to see the world as others saw it, to not be frightened of every different sight and sound, of every new experience. But some old experiences were too indelibly entrenched in their minds.

Rina Wright fought her daily battles, avoiding the monsters, being invisible, being two people while trying her best to appear normal. Andy Brown came to her every night. Their love-making had settled into total pleasure.

When she slept, he would lie awake looking at her, wondering about her. He never asked her any more close questions. He knew she would alienate him as quickly as she let him into her bed on the floor. If he pushed further with his questions, it would be soft beds for him forever. He wondered if he would ever know anything more about her.

He knew just when she would wake, shaking each night with terror. He became so good at predicting when the screaming would start, that he would kiss her and wake her. He would wipe the sweat from her brow, and hold her until she was calm. He was becoming used to living with night terrors and living by candle-light. His children never said anything to him, but they had to know when he returned each morning to get them up for breakfast and school.

Had he not known she would refuse, he would have suggested she shift in with him. But there was little point in such a suggestion. He was fated to spend his nights on a hard floor, but if he wanted her, he had no option but to put up with the discomfort. And he wanted her, of that he was certain.

His children still visited her. Amanda was there every day, playing with Jude, chatting to Rina. Thomas was also under her spell. Not that she did or said anything that caused this enticement. He told his dad that she made him feel calm. Andy Brown suspected that his teenage son had a crush on her, not that he could blame him.

Most of the time, she did have that effect on people—to make them feel calm, except in the middle of the night, when there was anything but calm. Part of him was envious of his son. Thomas saw the daytime Rina. His son had come to know this daytime person, whereas Andy Brown only knew the night time Rina—the Rina who lived her nights with monsters.

But then there was the love-making. This trumped everything. He knew he would take night time Rina with her monsters any day over the daytime calm that had enthralled his son.

Amanda always told Rina of the things that captivated and enriched her life. She had told her about the wedding she had seen in Sundial Park, how it was so beautiful and oh, so romantic. How the great dogs had stood guard while the happy couple had made their vows.

But her most memorable moment was when the bride had thrown her bunch of hibiscus flowers over her shoulder and she had caught it. She asked Rina what this meant. Rina had no idea, not ever having attended a wedding, but she assured the young girl that it meant life-long happiness. The absolute enthusiasm on Amanda's face made the lie so easy to relate.

Rina was very happy. Her life was running smoothly. Jude was happy and doing well. He seemed to be more stimulated every day. There were people he was becoming familiar with. There was the old dog and there were the people she met in the park. Best of all were the nights she spent with Andy Brown. She could live with the terror nightmares, but having him there compensated for all the terrible things that occurred in her sleep.

She did not understand her dreams, would never be able to. Instinct told her that she had experienced them her whole life at one time or another. Not much about them made any sense. But when Andy Brown held her in his arms and made love to her, this made complete sense. Rina Wright was living in a world of contrasts. One minute she was terrified, the next she was experiencing utter bliss.

Amanda Brown returned home from school. She changed out of her uniform and headed through the back gate to see Rina and Jude. Rina usually had some simple treat waiting for her, like a biscuit or a coke. As she came into the yard, she thought it was strange that Jude was not sitting outside with their old Alsation dog. Not that he was waiting for her in particular, but Amanda chose to believe that the odd boy looked forward to seeing her.

She found herself briefly annoyed that their dog was not there to greet her. Then she rationalised that as he was very old, he was probably curled up under their house.

Amanda was past the stage of knocking. She was so familiar with Rina and Jude that she just barged right in through the back door. But there was no Rina and no Jude. Amanda called out several times, looking for the two of them.

She knew Rina often went to the shops in the afternoon but usually by this time, she was back. Amanda shelved her disappointment at not finding her two favourite people. She reluctantly went back through the adjoining gate to her home. She watched several programs before returning to Rina's home.

There was still no sign of Rina or Jude. Thomas was staying overnight with his friends. Her father would not be home for ages. Amanda looked around the house. She began to worry. Rina never went anywhere other than the park and the shops. Where could she be and where on earth was Jude?

She went out through the front door to check if either of them returned. She had never noticed before but the front door rattled and squeaked. It was then that she heard the fine, intake of breath.

Amanda was puzzled. She was certain it was breathing she had heard and it was coming from inside the house. She was mindful of being intrusive. She had never been inside Rina or Jude's bedrooms. Her domain was the kitchen and living room. This was the area where they enjoyed their afternoon teas and their fun conversations.

She felt like a leper when she went first to Jude's bedroom. He was nowhere to be seen. Rina's bedroom was the next place she checked. She knew her father secretly visited Rina during the night.

One night she had seen him go through the adjoining gate and sit beside Rina outside on her patio. She suspected that he still visited her during the night although he never said anything. Why he bothered creeping into his bedroom as the sun was breaking each morning was beyond her.

Rina's bedroom was empty. Amanda sat on the single bed, wondering where Rina and Jude were. It was then she realised that the bed only had a spread on it, no sheets, no duvet, no blankets to keep out the cold of night and no pillow. Amanda thought this was very strange. Why would Rina have such an uninviting bed, especially if her father was sharing it with her?

One thing about her father, he loved his creature comforts. He loved his good food, his wine with dinner and his comfort. They had the best of lounge-room suites that spread from wall to wall. They had the most modern of electronic equipment.

Why would he spend the night with Rina in a tiny, single bed when he had the biggest and most macho king-sized bed of his own? When her mother had died, her father had decided on a make-over of their home. Everything was new and ultra-modern.

Amanda sat on the small bed pondering all these things. There was a slight noise. It was only because she had been sitting so quietly that she heard it. It was the sound of a breath. Amanda was startled. Where had the breathing come from? She listened again, and sure enough she heard it once more. There was definitely breathing going on and it seemed to be coming from under the bed.

The young girl was alarmed. She was not sure what to do, so she phoned her father and told him he had to get home right away, that there was something terribly wrong at Rina's house. Andy Brown did not stop to question his daughter further. He told her to return home and he would be there to take care of things.

He knew he could not feel more scared if there was a cyclone coming. His daughter might have been an endless chatterer about all sorts of trivial things, but she never phoned him unless it was absolutely important. With his heart beating at a pace more than was healthy, he entered Rina's home and did a quick check. There was no Rina and no Jude. He remembered his daughter saying she thought she had heard breathing as she sat on Rina's bed.

But Andy Brown was privileged to more intimate information about Rina's sleeping habits than his daughter was. He went straight to her room and leaned down to check under her bed. His heart was breaking as he saw the curled-up figure in a foetal position covered by the blanket that they shared each night.

"Rina," he spoke gently. Whatever was happening to her was obviously very serious. "Rina, it's me, Andy. I want you to come out now. There are no monsters. It's just you and me. Please come on out."

He watched as she covered her head. He swore that she was sucking her thumb. He was baffled. Here was the woman whom he made love to every night, the woman whom he loved, curled up under her bed sucking her thumb. She made no attempt to move or to respond to him. He spoke to her several more times but with no response.

He was at his wit's end. He knew he should phone for an ambulance and have her carted off to hospital. But he had to try something else before he reverted to this. There was still the question of the whereabouts of Jude. Andy Brown felt a responsibility for the two of them. In desperation, he made a phone call. He knew there was a doctor in the district who didn't ask too many questions. He phoned Dr Zaylee Lang.

As was her usual practice, Zaylee Lang answered on the second ring. He gave his full title of Detective Senior Sergeant Andy Brown and said he required her assistance immediately. Of course, Zaylee was instantly alarmed and intrigued as to why the top police person in the district would be phoning her in mysterious circumstances. Of course she agreed. She told her husband she had another emergency.

Zaylee arrived at the home of Rina Wright shortly after receiving the call from Andy Brown. She entered the house to find a quietly, agitated man in obvious distress. He explained briefly and accurately that his neighbour, Rina Wright, was under the bed in her bedroom and would not come out. He also explained that she had a young son who was missing.

He did not elaborate on the rest of her disturbing history. It would be up to the doctor to get her out and find out what had caused this break in her behaviour. Before he instituted more drastic steps to find Jude, he needed to be clear about what was happening with Rina.

Zaylee was becoming very used to the strange requests for assistance from the public that she occasionally received, but this was as bizarre as any. She sat on the floor beside the bed and lifted the spread that hung down the side of the bed. Sure enough, she sighted the curled-up body of what she presumed was a woman who was partially covered with a blanket and sucking her thumb.

"Hello, Rina," she commenced. "My name is Zaylee and I'm a doctor. I would like to help you if I can. Will you please tell me what's bothering you?"

Andy Brown remained outside in the lounge room. His heart was pounding. Here was the woman he slept with every night in some sort of fugue state. Her son was missing. He recognised that he was a mess. His wits seemed to be deserting him.

Zaylee Lang persevered. As usual she was unsure and unclear of the right direction to take, of the right words to say. How many times over the years had she been in a similar situation? She again remembered the words of her old professor telling her it was sometimes not so much the words, but the presence of someone who cared. His expertise was in loss and grief.

Here goes, she thought. She sat on the floor beside the bed. She did not speak for some time. Her hope was that the woman under the bed would feel comfortable enough to talk to her.

"Rina is a lovely name. I don't think I've ever met a Rina before. Can you tell me how you came by such a beautiful name?"

Rina Wright heard the words and wondered why anyone would be interested in her name. It was such a simple question for which she had no answer. She took her thumb out of her mouth and said, "I don't remember. I don't think I've always been called Rina."

This was a breakthrough. Andy Brown breathed a sigh of relief, but it still did not explain where Jude was or why Rina was acting so peculiarly.

"If you haven't always been called Rina, what do you think you were once called?" Zaylee was not sure how long she could keep helping tortured souls. It was sometimes just too much for one person to deal with.

"I don't remember. But I was once another person. Now I'm two people."

Zaylee cast her mind back to all that she had learned over the years. She knew there were well-documented cases of dissociative identity disorder. Was this what she was hearing?

"Can you tell me about being two people, Rina?"

"No," the reply was firm and swift. "I don't understand it myself. But I am two different people. I must remain invisible."

"Why do you have to remain invisible?"

Zaylee heard the exasperated sigh. "Because the monsters will find me and then you know what will happen again."

"Can you tell me what will happen to you, Rina, if the monsters find you?" Zaylee was treading in dangerous waters of which she had little experience. Andy Brown listened with dread.

"What do you think? They cut you up, put you in a garbage bag and throw you in a dumpster. I don't know why you can't understand what monsters do. But they do more than that. You just ask the other woman. She'll tell you. She was there. She suffered. She knows what monsters do."

Zaylee was doing her best to remain sitting upright on the hard floor beside the woman who was rolled up in a ball under the bed. She wanted to flee, to be away from the words that were tumbling out of this woman's mouth.

Andy Brown was cringing as he sat on the lounge chair where he had sat many a night beside Rina Wright holding her hand, just wanting to make love to her. But here he was, listening to the most horrifying words he had ever heard in his experience with the police. Not even the worst-case scenarios that he had studied compared with the words he was now hearing.

Zaylee was just hanging on, trying to pretend she was the professional. "Who is this other woman, Rina?"

"You know who she is. She became my friend. She loved me and I loved her. When it was safe, I would crawl out from under the bed and we would lie together on the bed and comfort each other. It was harder for her than for me because they had her tied up. She became very ill. Then the monsters took her and she never came back again. I think they killed her."

Zaylee almost vomited when she heard these words. What was she dealing with? She screamed out in her head for help. Andy Brown looked into the bedroom at the doctor. They were both crying with quiet tears that streamed down their faces.

"Do you want to come out now, Rina? What's say we have a cup of tea? Would you like that?"

"No," Rina's reply was slow and sleepy. "I'm very tired. My brain is very sore. It's never been like this before. I just want to sleep. I think Jude is in the park with the old Alsation. Would you mind making sure he's put to bed? And thank you for your kindness?" Rina Wright put her thumb back in her mouth and appeared to go to sleep.

Zaylee stumbled as she stood up. Her hands were shaking. She went out into the lounge and sat beside Andy. Neither could speak. The sun was fading. Then there was a noise, which was the back door being opened and Jude walked in followed by the old Alsation. He walked past the two people sitting on the lounge and went straight to Rina's bedroom. He lay down on the floor beside her. The old Alsation followed him. Together they lay side by side beside Rina.

The next thing Zaylee was aware of was Andy Brown on his phone, telling someone that both Rina and Jude were safe. He would be home soon. Stunned was hardly the word for how she was feeling.

It had only been a short time ago when she had to coax a terrified, young woman out from under a small walk-bridge. Then her sister-in-law had suffered a major seizure right in front of her, but this latest experience beat all.

"What does it all mean?" she asked Andy Brown.

He shook his head. "I don't know, but whatever it is, it doesn't sound good."

"She should be in hospital, you know, with psychiatric help."

"I don't think she would agree with you. If you did that, she could hardly remain invisible."

Zaylee stared at him, thinking he was almost as touched as the woman under the bed.

"Are you saying you think this is the right thing to do—to leave her lying there under the bed?"

"No, I'm not saying that. But if you force her to do something against her will, she'll be gone. She'll disappear and none of us will ever see her again. Who knows what could happen to her then?"

She again felt like she had failed. Here was another person who should be receiving proper care. "Oh, I see, I think. What about the boy? Who is he?"

Andy Brown felt as though he was talking in riddles to the doctor. "She says he's her son."

"You don't think so, is that it? She looks too young to have a son of that age."

"That's what she tells me," was all he said.

"So you know her then?"

"I live next door," he replied, evading her probing eyes. "She looks after my daughter from time to time."

She did not respond to this. She knew Andy Brown was much more than just a neighbour. His tears and his reactions told her this. He was much older than the woman under the bed, but it was none of her business. "What happens now?"

"I'll stay with her tonight. I'll put Jude to bed. She has these terror nightmares, every night. She usually sleeps after them. But there's never been anything like this. This time it's happened during the day. What do you think has caused it?"

"There must have been some trigger that set her off. Has anything changed?"

"Not that I know of, but she's very secretive and she has all these weird ideas. You heard her—talking about being two people, being invisible and about monsters. She says electricity is against her beliefs. I can't figure her out. Most times she's the sanest and calmest person I've ever met and then this happens. Do you think you could come back tomorrow to see how she's doing?"

"Of course I will." Even though the whole episode had unnerved her, Zaylee knew she would not be able to keep away. "You must love her very much."

Andy Brown was shocked to hear the words spoken by the doctor. She was a very perceptive and forthright woman. He remembered her from long ago. She had been at the Farraday property, Sunshine, after Michael and Denise Farraday's daughter had disappeared. It was later alleged that the daughter had been murdered. Her father had eventually confessed to the crime.

The detective had seen her again when Maryanne Smythe had gone off her head following the death of her husband, Danny Smythe. He recalled that the doctor had later married Malcolm Farraday.

The Farraday name again seemed to be popping up everywhere. So many memories and not many of them were good. With this family, it was as if every dozen years or so, the genie got out of the lamp and all hell began to break loose.

The doctor took her leave. The woman under the bed was sleeping soundly. The entire episode had been so bizarre that Zaylee felt spooked. But she had trust in the big detective. He would not abandon the woman. Never in a million years would Andy Brown cause hurt to the woman called Rina. He was equally trapped by the woman's nightmares. The doctor hoped the detective sergeant would be smart enough to figure out what was happening.

He left Jude on the floor with the Alsation while he went home to his daughter. She was sitting very quietly watching television. He reassured her again that Jude and Rina were both okay—at least he hoped they were. Amanda was not surprised when he said he would stay the night with Rina as she was sick. His daughter did not ask what was wrong with her and he did not offer any explanation.

Andy told his daughter that it would be a good idea if she slept at Rina's house just for the night, as he did not want to leave her alone in their home. Amanda nearly laughed at him then as he left her alone for the most of every night as it was.

At some time during the night, Rina Wright crawled out from the bed and lay beside Andy Brown. She kissed him and then made love to him quietly and slowly. They both then slept.

The next morning, Andy took his daughter home. Together they ate breakfast, neither of them saying much. Before he left for work, he noticed the doctor's car outside Rina's home.

The scene the doctor walked into was perfectly normal. Rina was preparing breakfast for her young son. She welcomed the doctor with grace and charm. It was as if nothing had happened. They chatted away pleasantly about any number on inane things—such as the weather, the price of food, anything other than what had occurred.

Eventually when they had run out of pleasantries, the doctor asked. "How are you feeling today, Rina?"

"Perfectly fine, thank you for asking. And you?"

She could hardly tell this young woman that she had sat up half the night, looking up case studies about various people, mostly women, who had suffered from dissociative identity disorder.

"A little weary," she replied.

"Oh, I'm sorry. I should have offered you some refreshment. Would you like a cup of tea?" Before the doctor could respond, Rina was boiling water on a small gas stove. This reminded her of Mia, her sister-in-law, making tea, being gracious. It was while she was pouring the water into the cup that she noticed her left hand with the missing fifth finger.

Dare she ask? Again this reminded her of her other sister-in-law, Francine. This was so coincidental. "What happened to your hand?"

Rina Wright immediately put her left hand behind her back. "Oh, that," she answered. "Just something I was born with."

The rough, angry scar didn't look like something that one was born with, but the doctor didn't pursue it. Zaylee watched the quiet smile appear on the woman's face as a boy came out and sat at the table.

"This is Jude, my son," she said with obvious pride. When the boy did not speak or look at her, Rina Wright explained simply. "He's disabled."

"Oh, he's a lovely boy." She thought of her own son Emmett, so full of life and fun, so different to this sad, tragic figure. When she studied him further, she was puzzled by the facial resemblance to her own son. There were the same dark eyes, black hair and slim build. If the child did not have awkward, kinetic movements, they might have been brothers.

"Was it a difficult birth?" the doctor asked.

"Yes, you could say that. It was hard, very hard." Zaylee could see that Rina was reaching back into her memory. Then in an instant, the subject was changed. Rina was asking the doctor about her own life. What it was like to be a doctor? How difficult a profession it must be? It was as if Rina had shut out any more information about herself.

Zaylee was not to be put off so lightly, so she came straight out with it. "What happened to you last evening, Rina? What has happened to you?"

Rina was caught. She did not want to be ungracious to this woman who had come to see her. She only wanted to be left alone but she had to be careful. Now there was another person who knew about her. It was becoming more and more impossible to remain invisible.

Not only was there the policeman who slept with her every night, but now there was a doctor as well. Both of these people were important in the community. One was a well-known and popular doctor. The other was the man in charge of the police district. It was becoming impossible to remain invisible and to keep out of sight of the monsters.

Rina felt trapped, so she did her best to explain it to the doctor. "It's all about to happen. I will probably have to leave very soon. If I don't make it, would you look after my son for me? Find him a good home. Promise me. That's what you do, right, look after people?" Her near-black eyes were totally serious as she held Zaylee enthralled once more.

"What's about to happen?" the doctor asked, again feeling unnerved.

"All of it—the end game, for all of us."

"Who is all of us?"

"There seems to be so many—including you. It's a lot to keep in your head. That's why my brain was so sore yesterday."

Zaylee Lang watched her own hands shake as she tried to drink her tea. This was like talking to a shaman or a witch. She knew all about people suffering headaches, but had never heard of a 'sore brain'. Maybe this is what happened if you were two people.

She had heard about her husband's mother, Miriam, with her strange predictions, but she had never experienced it. This young woman who sat at the table with her was scaring her witless.

As a doctor, she had planned to ask Rina Wright many questions to get to the bottom of her strange behaviour. She was busting to take some blood from her. She had a thousand excuses in her head for doing so. Were her bloods out of whack? Was she lacking essential vitamins and minerals? Did she have a brain tumour? Was she suffering some kind of blood disease or was it as it appeared to be—a mental disorder?

But the doctor had changed her mind. All her well-intentioned plans had flown out the window as Rina Wright spoke her grave words. All she wanted to do now was to get out of there. Hardly anything ever fazed her, but this young woman did. "I have to go now. Maybe I'll check up on you later."

"You don't have to. There's nothing anyone can do for me until it's over. But thank you all the same."

Zaylee was almost through the door when Rina Wright spoke again. "You didn't promise me."

"Promise you what?"

"That if something happens to me, you'll look after my son," Rina Wright was deadly serious.

"Of course I will, I promise." Zaylee took one last look at Rina and her son before running out to her car. She took off at speed. When she was out of sight, she pulled off to the side of the road and sat there, shaking, as she waited for her nerves to calm.

Gabe decided he would not tempt fate or the local police. So he left his vehicle with his Uncle Mark and used a taxi to take his wife back to their home. He called it their home now, not his home. Lu remained anxious about going back but Gabe promised he would not leave her side for the duration of the time he was home. It would be a brave Lucas who was prepared to take him on.

Except Gabe did not have the guile of Lucas Cowell. Nor did he have the same murderous intent except when it came to the person or persons who were responsible for the deaths of his parents and sister.

It was his first day back. He tried to express his gratitude to Mia, Matt and Zaylee for taking care of Lu, but there were too many of his relatives at their house.

He briefly spoke to Lizzie. She was as happy as he had ever seen her. *Must be a new boyfriend* was all he could think. She was sometimes very subdued.

As he waited for the taxi, he asked Matt to drop the dogs off when he had the time. He signalled to Lu that the taxi had arrived so they returned together to their home.

They got as far as the front veranda where he immediately dropped their bags. He took her in his arms. They kissed and kissed. Gabe knew he would have to sleep on the bed this night and not on the floor beside her. It was becoming very difficult for him to continue to wait until she was ready.

He unlocked the door. Then he picked her up in his arms and carried her into the lounge room. He kept kissing her while she remained cradled in his arms. She still felt as light as a feather. He could have held her forever except for the figure he glimpsed out the corner of his eye. He let go of Lu out of sheer surprise. She was giggling as her feet hit the floor.

It was the expression of sheer surprise on her husband's face that made her turn around. Her worst fears had come true. There was Lucas as large as life, sitting on the lounge chair, with a look of amusement on his bland features.

She would have immediately burst out screaming except Gabe pushed her behind him. "Who the hell are you and what do you want?" he asked, knowing that in all probably it was her feared uncle.

"I'm the person who has come to relieve you of your burden and to claim back my gold mine." The man was so insignificant in looks it was hard to believe the cold venom that he projected in his voice. You could have sat beside him on a train or a bus and have never noticed him. He appeared so insignificant.

Gabe could hear the frightened, mewing sounds coming from his wife. "Go outside, Lu, go over to Mr Lee's house and call the police."

"Oh, I don't think you ought to do that," Lucas Cowell lifted up the hand gun that had been hidden on his lap out of sight, "not unless you want to see a hole put through sweet Luce's hand, or foot or for that matter, her head. It's up to you, Gabriel, where the next piece of decoration occurs. Probably not the feet, I've overdone them already. It might be time to start on the hands. What do you say?"

"I'd say you better put down that gun and get the hell out of here before I kill you."

"Under the circumstance that might be difficult, given that your choices seem very limited." He waved the gun around for impact, then stood up and held it straight at Lu's forehead. "It only takes a minuscule of a second to pull the trigger."

Gabriel's mind was in overdrive. He was not sure what to do in spite of his brave words. He thought then of his father dying in the yard of a jail, and of his mother and all the battles they had fought. If he could, he would have shot Uncle Lucas straight through the forehead the same as his mother had done all those years ago when she had shot Jack Smith.

But he had too much to lose. He had to find another way to subdue this man who was threatening to take away all that was dear to him. He could feel Lu quivering behind him. He now fully understood her fear.

He had a knife which he kept in his boot. Ever since he and Raphael had been attacked as lads, he kept one on his person at all times. He knew how to use a knife. His memory returned to the time when Rafe had almost been abducted by unknown men in dark clothes and who drove black, menacing SUV's. He had to use his knife then to save his brother.

He also knew how to fight. This was one thing he had to thank his Uncle Mitch for. They had been taught as children how to both defend and attack. Now all he had to do was to find a way out of this dilemma and to protect his wife.

That had been his promise to her. That he would always protect her. It had sounded so easy. But now he faced a different reality—a psychopath with a gun.

"Keep behind me, Lu." He put his hand around his back to make sure she was out of view of the gunman. Uncle Lucas smiled as the display of affection and protection.

"Very touching," he said. "But you like being touched, don't you, Luce? Did you know that touching or should I say, being touched, is where she excels? But naughty Luce, I can tell you've broken the rules and you know what that means—consequence—and here's the first consequence."

Lucas Cowell lifted the gun and shot Gabriel Farraday. Gabe looked at the shooter in astonishment. Then he looked down at his left hand. He lifted it up and could not understand why he could see the floor through the hole in the centre of his palm. Then the hole began to disappear as the blood streamed out.

Lu would have screamed if she were not in so much shock. She should have been used to consequences, but they had always been applied to her, not to other people. Gabe was now on the floor trying to staunch the blood streaming out of his hand. He had nothing but his right hand to keep the blood from seeping out. Lu was on the floor beside him. She was now crying and trying to think what to do.

She had worn a cardigan all the time since her chest infection. All she could think to do was to pull her cardigan off and wrap it around her husband's hand. Lucas Cowell looked on in fascination at the two people who now sat on the floor in front of him.

The pain he saw in Gabriel's face was what fascinated him the most. He loved the way he groaned, held onto his hand and tried to staunch the blood that was already soaking through the grey cardigan. All that was required now was some screaming—oh, what joy it would have been.

Lucas had been unsure what to expect when he finally caught up with sweet, half-girl, half-woman, Luce Potulski. He had set up his little cameras—just in case. But he had never expected to catch another Farraday for his little movies. At the moment, screaming was out of the question. This was no sound proof room

But he couldn't indulge himself for too long. He had found out that here were so many of these Farradays. You never could tell who might be next to walk through that front door.

He walked over to Gabe and kicked him in the ribs. "Get out of the doorway and get over to the other side of the room. Hurry up about it."

As Gabe stood up, he was overcome with dizziness but Lu held onto him, directing him towards the kitchen. As they moved across the room, she grabbed a towel that lay on the back of a kitchen chair. It was an old towel they used to dry the dogs down with. She quickly removed the cardigan and wrapped the towel tightly around his hand.

"Get over near that cupboard and sit down," he gestured towards the floor. "Not that I expect you feel like dancing with your little girlfriend, or should I say wife."

Lucas then produced handcuffs and with his gun still pointed at Lu, told her to cuff Gabe's right hand and attach the other cuff to the handle of the cupboard.

He continued talking while he watched Lu. "Naughty, naughty, who would have thought little Luce Potulski would not only be sleeping with her cousin, but she'd marry him as well. Goes to show, anything goes with you Farradays."

Gabe was having difficulty making sense of what Lucas was saying. Lu thought he was being his usual vile self.

"What are you talking about?" Gabe said, as he lifted his left hand to staunch the pain. Had it not been for the extreme pain he was experiencing, he might not have taken any notice of the words the madman in front of him had said. But his whole body was sensitised. He was on hyper alert.

"What am I talking about, as if you don't know? I know all about you Farradays. But what I want to know is—where is grandfather? What have the pair of you done with him?" He looked around the room before he spoke again. "But that's enough talk for now. I have to sort out little Luce." He grabbed Lu by the hair and hauled her up off the floor.

"Now before we go any further, you go get a cloth and a dish of water, anything you can find and clean up that bloody mess near the front door. I can't stand messes."

Lu did as she was told. She grabbed some towels and cleaned up the floor as best as she could. Lucas watched her work in her loose, drab clothing.

"By the way, it's good to see you can still pass for a little kid. You haven't filled out any." He winked at Gabe before adding, "There's better money in kids, especially young girls."

He ushered Lu back near Gabe. As she went past, she threw Gabe another towel which he wrapped around his hand. Lucas pushed her down onto one of the kitchen chairs. He put the gun down and tied Lu's hands to the slats at the back of the chair. Then he pulled her feet back and tied her angles together with plastic ties. He did the same with Gabe's feet. They were both trussed up with no means of escape.

"Now we might get some answers. So we'll start again. Where is Grandfather?"

"I don't know," she whispered. "He just disappeared one day."

He eyed her with disbelief. "I don't think so, Luce. Not after what I saw was left of Grandmother. I think you lie."

He was rummaging around in a bag. Then he walked over to the gas stove and lit one of the burners. The flame erupted in brilliant orange and red. He was behind both of them, out of their range of vision. Gabe could smell the gas. He was fearful this madman might be going to burn the house down. He was in an impossible situation.

Lucas Cowell returned carrying a branding iron. "Which one of you wants to be first?"

Lu gasped and shook. This could not be happening again. She looked down at the brown boots covering her ruined feet.

"Leave her alone," Gabe spoke softly, watching in horror at the red-hot iron.

"You first then, Gabriel—you are such a gentleman. Where shall we start? I don't fancy taking off those great, big boots of yours. I bet your feet smell. So how about you just put that left arm of yours out in front of you and we'll see how that works. See if lovely Luce gets her memory back."

Before Gabe had a chance to make a move to protect himself, Lucas Cowell had shoved the bloody cardigan into his mouth. He pulled on Gabe's bloody hand and yanked his arm out and as quick as could be, Lucas pressed the still hot iron into the skin of his inner forearm. The skin sizzled and smoked.

"Once more before it loses its heat," he laughed as he pulled the iron out of the frying skin and pressed it in again. "Now you really do have something in common. Little L's are for Luce and big L's are for lover boy."

Gabe again could not believe what had just happened. His arm was burning. The flesh was sizzling. The smell of burning flesh and hair was revolting. He thought he might vomit except the bloody cardigan was still shoved into his mouth.

"It's a bigger size than what I use on Luce." He began singing, "Baby branding irons for girls, big branding irons for boys." He sniffed the air, "Don't you just love that smell. You're luckier than Luce, you know. The one I used on you is for branding cattle, although they use ear tags now. Luce was never so lucky."

Then he began to sing again, "L for Luce, L for Lucy, L for Lucia, L for Luscious, L for Lucifer, L for Love and L for Loot." He did a little dance as he turned off the gas stove and put the branding iron back down. He kept right on singing as he came back around and sat on the floor in front of them.

"Now, Luce, tell me truthfully—where is Grandfather?"

Lu was shaking in fear. Her eyes sought Gabe's. She thought she saw him nod. "He's dead," she stammered. "He fell under a train."

"Fell under a train! Grandfather fell under a train! Now why don't I believe you, Luce?" He looked over at Gabe, lying stunned and in agony on the floor.

"It's true," she cried. "He came to the station to pick me up. But he overbalanced. You know he had a big stomach. One minute he was there and the next minute he was on the track. Then the train came. It was awful." Lu had no trouble crying. There was no pretence. She could hear Gabe struggling with the pain.

Had she been brave enough, she would have screamed out to the heavens so that even the gods could hear her, but she dare not. His expertise in torture was too refined. Gabe might not survive much longer if she took a step wrong.

"Oh, well, you could be right. He was a silly, old bugger at the best of times." He looked again at Lu tied up on the chair. "Well, what about Grandmother?"

"She just died. Just up and died after her dinner. I think she had a heart attack."

"That would be right, the greedy, old pig. A fitting end, I say, serves her right. She caused such a mess. I'll never forget it. It took me hours to clean it up. It's not as though you can call the cleaners in for smelly, maggot-ridden grandmothers." He shook his hands in disgust at the memory of Grandmother lying dead on the floor in the happy bedroom.

"Well, what about the rest?"

"What rest?" she asked, knowing very well what he was referring to.

"Don't play games, Luce, or I'll get the branding iron again. It will be interesting to see how much he can put up with."

Lu knew their situation was hopeless. There was no white knight going to come through the door to save them. She tried to clear her head sufficiently so as to consider their options. Whatever she did, whatever she said, he would kill Gabe. He would either kill her as well or else take her back for more torture. Her preference was clear. She would much rather die right here beside her husband.

She smiled to herself as she looked at Gabe, still with the bloody cardigan shoved in his mouth. The time she had spent with him had been so short. They had so few chances to cement their love and their life together.

She shut her eyes and dreamed of the creek bank where she could have been loved by him. But it was too late now. She wondered what it would have been like. Would she have seen stars? Or been taken to heights of incredible feeling?

She looked over at him and felt such incredible love. He looked back at her and in spite of his pain she knew he felt the same. Uncle Lucas was yabbering away, but she had shut him out.

"I am talking to you, Luce, please do not ignore me. I can see now that you are far from being perfect. All those years, all that training and poof, it disappears, just like that. You are a great disappointment to me, Luce."

"It's under the house, Lucas. Just take it and go," she said as he walked back towards the kitchen.

"Thank you, Luce, now that wasn't so hard, was it?" He stopped and looked out the kitchen window and saw it was dark. "Well, it will just have to wait till tomorrow."

He kept walking to the gas stove. He lit it up again. The heat of the flames could be felt from where they were held. He returned some minutes later with the branding iron glowing hot.

"This time it's for stealing her from me—other side of the arm, please." Lucas pulled out Gabriel's already bleeding and burnt arm and pressed the iron twice more onto the anterior surface of his arm. He reeled in pain and then slumped totally to the floor. His right arm remained cuffed to the cupboard. His eyes closed.

Lu was in a state of shock but there was still a tiny speck of desire left in her to remedy their situation. She started screaming, as loud and as long as she could. After all, this was one of her areas of expertise, according to Uncle Lucas. How many times had he made his lovely, little home videos as she screamed and screamed as he branded her feet?

Her attempt to scream was abruptly stopped just as it had begun. Lucas kicked out at the chair that held her captive. It fell backwards. Lu could not break her fall. She landed heavily on her back with her head taking the brunt of the tumble. She saw her stars then, but not the stars that she had desired, but exploding stars of pain which led to unconsciousness.

Lucas Cowell was disgusted as he realised both his captives were out cold. There was little point left in playing more games. He went and checked his cameras and saw they were functioning correctly. He still could not decide what to do with Luce—treacherous, little thing that she had turned out to be.

He could not believe how it had happened that she had met up with a Farraday. He must remember to ask her tomorrow. She had been so young when grandmother, or Mrs Potter as she had been at the time, had taken her. She had never given any indication that she remembered who she had originally been—none, none at all. And yet, here she was married to one. How had that happened? You could live with someone, sleep with them, but marry, surely not!

He was thankful for his good memory. It was due to his expert memory that he had found her. He remembered that Grandmother had taken her from a place called Tewantin all those years ago. He remembered her name, Lucia Farraday. Apparently the Farraday name was quite notorious. They were bad apples, so Grandmother had said. He was beginning to think that his Luce was as bad as any of them.

So it had been an easy task to put two and two together and bingo, here he was in Tewantin, ready to regain his fortune. But how Luce had remembered the town called Tewantin, he could not fathom. He suspected his little gold mine was far smarter than she made out.

When Luce and Grandfather disappeared, he had checked with the school after getting rid of Grandmother. Initially he had been very perplexed, until he realised that it must have been clever Luce who had mimicked Grandmother's voice. But that was her big mistake, saying that they were heading for warmer climes. It didn't take a genius to figure out that Grandfather would be heading back to familiar territory. Lucas recalled that over the years Grandfather sometimes visited Mrs Potter for holidays.

What a tangled web it had turned out to be? And now here he was left with nothing to do until the morning. He didn't fancy trying to watch television with two unconscious bodies lying close beside him. That was not appealing for a relaxing night of TV viewing at all. Besides, once the smell of the actual burning of skin had abated, the odour was not nearly as attractive. He knew it would not be long before Gabriel Farraday began to smell.

Pity he didn't have the delicious, little home-movies to watch, which, if she could be believed, were hidden under the house. He could not wait to see Lu again as a little girl. It had been a wonderful time for all of them and very lucrative. But you couldn't stop time. They just got older. The biggest pity of all was that they could not stay as young children.

But they had all done their best. Give them their due, Grandmother and Grandfather had held up their end of the bargain. None of their clients ever realised Luce was much older than the skinny, undeveloped, young girl she appeared to be. They had stunted her development. Starvation and malnutrition could do that to a person. The five rules had been the best thing ever, especially the one about 'not eating'.

Lucas Cowell lay on the bed that he assumed was the marriage bed. He laughed softly. It had finished up being so easy. The Farradays were supposedly infamous. When he did a web search, there were sites for their various businesses. But there was nothing of a personal nature.

So where else would you look to find out what misdemeanours they had committed—from the court reports of course? From there it was a simple matter to sit in the background while the court was in session. He was proud of her. She was magnificent, crying and signing. She even had the magistrate sucked in. Outside the court house, all he had to do was to following them.

The wedding was what he could not fathom, not that he had seen it. He wished he had. In the courtroom, he had heard that Gabriel Farraday had a disabled wife. What a laugh! Again he was just so proud of her. She was that close to being perfect. She had pulled off an almost perfect escape. Just to be certain, he checked out the weddings that had been registered. There it was, undeniably true. Lucia Farraday had married Gabriel Michael Farraday. How bizarre was that?

Lucas slept like a baby. Gabriel suffered through a night of excruciating pain, alternating between crazy dreams, bouts of fever and shaking, as well as concern for his wife. His parents came to him often during that night. They seemed to be speaking to him. Then he saw his little sister, Sarina. Lu remained quiet and unmoving beside him for hours. Had he not heard her breathing, he would have thought she was dead.

Lucas swept into the room where they lay. He was as chirpy as a bird. He asked how they had slept, were they comfortable. Lu was now awake, but remained groggy. Gabriel could do nothing but look at his wife. He sent her a thousand messages with his eyes. He tried to tell her how much he loved her, how sorry he was that he could not protect her. Lu sent her messages back through her glazed-over eyes. She told him that she was happy because they were together. No matter what happened, she had never been as happy in all her life.

"Hurry up children. There's just so much to do this morning. Now who is going to crawl under the house and get the bags?" He surveyed the two horizontal figures in front of him. "Neither of you look too well. Another problem to be overcome—life is just so full of them."

Lucas walked out to the back veranda. He surveyed the back yard. Then he went and looked under the house. It was while he was there that a vehicle pulled up out the front. He quickly and quietly returned back inside and stood out of sight inside the front door.

"Hello Gabe. Are you there?" Mark Farraday called out as he walked straight through the open, front door.

It is always that first glimpse of disbelief that throws a person. His nephew was tied up and in obvious distress on the floor near the kitchen. There was another person there as well, strapped into a chair that had been pushed backwards. He could not believe his eyes.

Then he heard giggling behind him. Not the giggling of a young girl, but that of a male voice, giggling and snickering. "Who would believe it, another Farraday—and a big, juicy one at that?"

Mark looked around at the insignificant man who stood behind him pointing a gun straight at his head. "Just what the doctor ordered—a big, strong man. Well there's no time like the present. So get them both out the back, and hurry up about it."

"Do what he says, Mark," Gabe said as he saw the shock and horror on his uncle's face.

"No talking now, that's not allowed. That's rule number one, just ask Luce. 'I must not talk'. If you keep it up, there will have to be more consequences."

Mark looked at the man who was talking nonsense. It was as if he had walked into a movie scene—a horror movie. "What the hell do you think you're doing? Are you for real?"

"Oh, contraire, Mr Farraday, I am deadly serious and very real. Just take a look at your nephew if you don't believe me. Now lift up the chair with the lovely, little lady in it and carry her out into the back yard. When you've done that, come back and get lover-boy. Then we'll take it from there."

Mark Farraday had no option but to do as he was told as there was a gun still pointed at his head. He picked up the chair with the young woman in it and carried her outside. He sat the chair upright. As he did so, the young woman slumped forward. He did not miss the huge egg-like lump on the back of her head. He was certain she was unconscious.

"Now undo the cuff that connects lover boy to the cupboard and get him outside. Then you can tie him to the veranda railing."

Mark went to his nephew. He was appalled at what he saw. He was not sure what was under the bloody towel wrapped around his hand, but the deep and now suppurating burns on his arm were enough to sicken him. Mark cut the ties on his nephew's legs with a knife he found in the kitchen. He left the knife behind as he had been instructed.

Mark then helped Gabe to stand and guided him back outside. He did as Lucas instructed and used a plastic tie from the bundle he found on the veranda. He tied Gabe's right arm to the veranda railing.

"Well done, Mark. That wasn't too hard. The next part is up to you. If you want your nephew and his little lady to live, you'll crawl under the house and collect those two bags for me."

Mark was again shocked. "How am I supposed to get under the house? I'm not exactly small."

"That's up to you Mark. Turn yourself into an elf or grab a shovel and dig a trench and hurry up about it. Work it out for yourself. I'm getting tired of all these delays."

Gabe was trying to tell him something. His voice was weak. "There's a shovel in the shed," he said, just loudly enough so that Lucas could hear him. Mark, who was further away, did not hear him so he moved closer. "There's a shovel in the shed," Gabe repeated. Mark then heard him say in a whisper. "It's Lucia. If anything happens to me, please look after her."

Mark took some moments to realise what Gabe was saying. There was no one else around other than the young woman held captive in the chair. He wondered again if he had heard right. He was sure Gabe had said it was Lucia. He walked in a daze to the shed and retrieved a shovel.

Mark had not planned it, but as he walked past Lucas, he lunged at him with the shovel. Had it connected, it would have smashed his head in, but Lucas was too wily and quick for Mark. Instead, he kept the gun pointed at his nephew. "I could put another bullet in his other hand, but I have a better idea. Come with me, Mark, and I'll teach you about consequences."

He marched Mark back inside the house where he told him to light the gas stove and heat up the branding iron. "Make it nice and hot now, the hotter the better. I like to hear the sizzle."

With the gun still pointed at him, Mark returned outside. He still held the iron. Uncle Lucas shoved another towel into Gabriel

Farraday's mouth. With the gun now pointed at Mark's head, he took the branding iron and plunged it into the left side of Gabe's chest where his shirt had come open. He quickly repeated the action. Gabe slumped almost to the ground. His right wrist which remained tied to the veranda railing prevented him from falling all the way.

"Now that is a consequence, Mark, so I would suggest you get under that house and get those bags." Lucas sniffed the air, "Don't you just love that smell?" Gabe's chest was still smoking.

Lucas again started singing "Oh, the Farradays of Tewantin, they are so wilful and wanton."

Mark, while still in a daze, crawled under as far as his big body would allow and then began digging away at the loose soil so he could reach the black bag he could see not far from him. Once he held it in his hand, he backed out. His nephew looked to be semiconscious. Mark handed the bag to Uncle Lucas.

"Where's the other bag?" he asked, puzzled.

"There is no other bag."

"I am really tired of these games," Lucas was very annoyed. Lu was now awake and appalled at what had happened to Gabe. He went straight to Lu and pulled her head back. "Where is the other bag, Luce?"

"I don't know. I swear I don't," her reply was no more than a whimper.

"Leave her alone. She doesn't know," Gabe said. He was now fully awake. "But I do."

"More games. Then you better tell me where or we'll have to go through the consequences again. And you must be getting tired of them by now." Lucas kicked Gabe in the shins. "I'm waiting."

"In the dog kennels," Gabe gasped.

"You don't expect me to get into a dog kennel, do you?" Lucas was appalled at such a suggestion.

"It's under the dog kennels—it's buried."

"Another job for you, Mark, off you go now with the shovel." Lucas again sounded upbeat.

"I'll have to show him where to dig," Gabe said.

Lucas sounded impatient as he cut the tie that held Gabe attached to the veranda railing. Gabe struggled to stand. Mark held the shovel. Lucas held the gun. Lu remained tied to her chair.

Gabe walked behind Mark. Lucas followed. Gabe stumbled, almost hitting the ground. Lucas became annoyed again. He pushed at Gabe. Gabe turned quickly and plunged the knife he held in his right hand up into Lucas's diaphragm. Then he twisted it up under his left rib-cage.

34

As the knife pierced his heart, there was the sound of rushing legs and the image of brown-coated dogs as they flashed through the house and into the back yard. Gabe was slumping to the ground as one of the dogs leapt up and sunk its teeth into the throat of an astonished Uncle Lucas as he looked in disbelief at the knife sticking out of his chest.

The other dog went to Gabe and whimpered around him. It tried to lick the ooze that was coming from his chest. Mark stood in awe at the scene in front of him. Lu looked up as the dogs flew into the back yard. It was when she saw Gabriel fall onto the ground that she started screaming.

Her screams were more than loud. They were piercing. Their pitch reached up into the skies. The birds themselves were frightened. Small animals were alarmed. The birds commenced screeching. She screamed on and on and on.

Dr Zaylee Lang and her husband were getting out of the SUV that they had used to pick up the dogs from Matt. The screaming was so intense, they were momentarily stunned. Malcolm had apologies to make to his nephew but he had never expected to be met by the shrieking that was piercing his ears.

They both took off at speed, through the front door, out into the back yard. Zaylee took one look at the man on the ground still being guarded by one of the dogs. She knew it was her nephew. It was more than she could stand. For the first time in her life, Zaylee fainted. Her husband grabbed her as they both sank to the ground.

Mrs Lee, who lived close by, ran to her husband and yelled at him to call the police. He did as he was told. He too was deeply affected by the screams.

Andy Brown was pulling out of his driveway when he heard the screaming. He knew his screams. This was no ordinary scream. It was not a scream of a wife having a tiff with her husband or kids yelling at their parents. This was the ultimate scream of horror.

It took him only minutes to find the location of the screams. He saw the two vehicles pulled up in front of an ordinary-looking house. He rushed straight through to the back yard. That was when he stopped.

Again, it was that first glimpse of horror. He saw it all with incredulity. Mark was standing as still as a post in front of a dog guarding a man on the ground who appeared to be dead. There was another man who had a knife sticking out of his chest. There was a young woman tied to a chair who was sobbing quietly with a great, brown dog patrolling around her.

There was another woman whom he recognized as Dr Zaylee Lang out cold on the ground near the bottom of the stairs. She was being held up by Malcolm Farraday.

Andy Brown shook himself out of his moment of numbness. Then he was on his phone, requesting more police, ambulance and fire offices. He could detect the smell of something burning. The first responders were already on their way. Mr Lee had let the screaming do the talking. He had simply held his phone out and the operator was quickly convinced of the seriousness of his report.

Mark was beginning to regain his equilibrium. He saw the sergeant. He remembered him from years ago when his family had suffered catastrophe after catastrophe. He had little time for police but he had never been as pleased as he was now to see Andy Brown.

"You've got to get help for Gabe," he told the sergeant with fear in his face. "This maniac was killing him." He indicated the man with the knife in his chest. Andy Brown looked at Gabriel Farraday. The dog growled at him. He moved back but not before he saw the burn marks. The towel that had been around his hand had fallen off. He saw the bloody mess of his hand. His breakfast threatened to come up.

He looked around at the young woman tied to the chair. She had stopped sobbing and was staring out into space. She seemed to be murmuring. The other brown dog was walking around her, growling and with its hackles raised. Andy Brown had the presence of mind to take photographs of the whole incredible scene.

Mark was phoning his brothers. Matt was there very quickly just as the first police and ambulance cars arrived. He had been close by at the child-care centre. The shock on his face was a repetition of what Andy Brown had experienced.

The police could not get near Gabe or the woman tied to the chair because of the dogs. Matt eventually got them under control. He took them outside and put them into his SUV, with the windows half-way down for air. The paramedics started working on Gabe. It was clear the other man with the knife in his chest was already dead.

Zaylee was beginning to revive. Her husband still held her in his arms. He told her to put her head between her legs to get her blood moving. She did as he asked.

Andy Brown went over to the young woman and untied her. She was unaware of what he was doing. He listened to her mumbling. He listened time and again, not sure of what he was hearing, as she said, 'I must not speak, I must not laugh, I must not touch, and I must not eat. I must be perfect'."

He was again bewildered. He left her to the paramedics. Just then, big Mitchell Farraday arrived. Matt was filling him in with as much as he knew—which wasn't much. Mark was sitting down against the veranda. He kept hearing Gabe's words. He was still in shock.

He beckoned to his brothers. They went over to him. "Gabe said that the girl is Lucia." The other two brothers, equally shocked, sat down beside Mark. Shock was catching this day. "What do we tell Malcolm?" Mark finally asked.

"Damned if I know. What if it's not her? What then?" Mitch said.

"How about we say it might be her? That way it won't be such a disappointment if it isn't her." Mark was still trying to get the smell of burning flesh out of his system.

"It looks like Zaylee's coming round." The three of them went to sit beside their brother and sister-in-law.

There was no gentle way to break the news. "Gabe said the young woman is probably Lucia, Malcolm." Mark said it as gently as he could.

Both Malcolm and Zaylee looked at the three men at once. Zaylee again fainted. Malcolm looked like he was going to join her. They called the paramedics over. Zaylee was checked out and then placed on a stretcher. One ambulance departed.

The young woman was also being placed on a stretcher. She was still mumbling the incomprehensible words that made no sense to anyone who heard them. Malcolm went over to her. She looked straight through him. Space was a safer option to look at than more people.

He did not know what to think. Was this poor, skeletal, young woman his beautiful, little, golden-haired daughter whom he had loved so much? He could see no resemblance. He found he was shaking.

Mitchell Farraday was on his phone. He contacted Dax Webster who listened to the brief conversation. Dax then began organising a team of solicitors. There was a dead body in the yard of Gabriel's home. That was sufficient for concern, let alone the possibility that the young woman involved was Lucia Farraday.

Fire trucks were also present. Men in helmets and protective clothing were checking the house and grounds. The media had arrived. They recognized a big story was about to erupt. The number of police and ambulances was testimony to this. The Farraday name was usually good fodder.

One of the ambulance officers had overheard the name Lucia Farraday being mentioned. He was an old-timer. He remembered that Lucia Farraday had disappeared years go. The media soon heard of this revelation.

Raphael arrived just as his brother was being stretchered into the ambulance. He was devastated to see his brother in such an appalling condition. Before the ambulance door could be shut, a reporter managed to shove a microphone in Gabe's face and asked, "Can you tell us what happened, Mr Farraday?"

Gabe lifted his head, looked directly into the camera and said. "I can tell you one thing. If it takes me the rest of my life, I'll slit the throats of the fuckers who murdered my parents and sister." His parents had been very close to him during the night. He had heard them calling to him.

It was not the response that anyone expected. But it made for news-grabbing headlines. Then the name of Lucia Farraday was mentioned. They were unconfirmed reports, but it was enough to grab the public's interest.

Raphael went with his brother to the hospital. Mitchell Farraday informed the receiving hospital in no uncertain terms that his nephew, his sister-in-law and his nephew's friend were to receive the best treatment that money could buy. The hospital was to spare no expense. If specialists were required then they were to be flown in. The Farraday money-mill was up and working.

Andy Brown had managed to get the home roped off. He used his authority to ensure the scene was not contaminated any further. It became a crime scene. Forensic investigators were combing the grounds. After Lucas Cowell had been formally declared deceased, his body was taken to the morgue.

Mark was taken in for questioning, not that he was a suspect. He told them everything that had happened. He was as perplexed as any of the law enforcement personnel as to why his nephew had been tortured. He explained why he happened to be there at that hour of the morning. He was returning his nephew's vehicle after being serviced. His nephew had returned following his two week stint working in the mines,

He could, in all honesty, shed no light on the identity of the young woman or why such an atrocity had occurred. He had no idea who the dead man was except that he had been called Uncle Lucas and was a lunatic. He explained how he had seen his nephew branded with a hot, molten branding iron whenever the man became annoyed. He told them how he had been made to crawl under the house to remove a bag. He did not know what the bag contained.

He could not explain even to himself why he did not mention the second bag that was supposedly hidden under the dog kennels. He guessed it was a Farraday trait not to reveal all. He also did not mention that his nephew had said that the young woman was Lucia.

Andy Brown was feeling overwhelmed. He had his officers checking all leads. None of what had confronted him was adding up. The Farraday family history was again in the spotlight. Records, phones and computers were again being checked. Their business dealings were again under scrutiny.

He was waiting on autopsy results on the deceased man. He had yet to interview both Gabriel Farraday and the young woman. They were both too ill and receiving treatment. Mark again told him that he had no idea what the young woman's name was or who she was.

It became a huge story. Nothing could stop the momentum of a story of a young woman who allegedly disappeared many years ago being found. Everything was alleged. Andy Brown saw the news reports. It was everywhere. He had no idea how the story had originated.

He again contacted Malcolm Farraday who was still at the hospital with his wife. It turned out that Malcolm was equally dumbstruck at the rumour. He was aware that the young woman was in the same hospital. He had asked to see her, but the young woman was not talking except to keep repeating the same mantra she had been saying in the yard of Gabe's home.

No one seemed to know what the relationship between Gabriel and the young woman was. The Farraday's weren't sure either, at least those assisting with police enquiries, which were Mark and Mitch. Matthew had taken the dogs back to his home. He had collected Mitchell and Malcolm's children and had also taken them home with him.

The media barrage was ramping up. Further adding to the allegations was the fact that an unknown man had been murdered and Gabriel Farraday had undoubtedly been tortured. Media photographs were proof of this. How many times did the news readers comment that some viewers may find these images disturbing? The camera had clearly caught the burn marks on his chest and the carnage to his left arm

The most newsworthy report of all that had been captured by eager journalists was made by Gabe when he had made the threatening remarks about *slitting the throats of the . . . . who had murdered his parents and sister*. His black, determined eyes momentarily overshadowed the terrible wounds on his hand, arm and chest.

This again brought the history of the troubled Farraday family back into focus. It was a media scramble to retell old stories—all the deaths, the scandals, and the disappearance of the two little girls.

The woman in question, whose name had still not been ascertained and whom the media had initially reported as being a young girl, was refusing to co-operate with health professionals or the police. She would not answer questions. She refused any treatments. She refused any X-rays on her skull and she refused to have her blood taken. She had her rights and responsibilities. She had chosen to refuse all care.

When she did speak, it was to request that she be allowed to stay with Gabe. When told he was undergoing specialised treatment, she said he wouldn't care if she was with him. She wouldn't get in the way.

She kept repeating her mantra. No one understood it, but when she stopped eating, it was clear that something had to be done. So she was allowed to stay in the same room as Gabriel. She further astounded hospital staff by refusing to sleep on the bunk bed they provided. Instead, at night, she curled up with several blankets on the floor, as close as possible to the slowly recovering Gabriel.

When this was permitted, she then recommenced eating, much to the relief of the legal department of the hospital. It would not do for the young woman, who may or may not have been the missing Lucia Farraday, to die of starvation. She was already extremely thin.

Zaylee recovered quickly. Her first responsibility was to her husband who was again living a nightmare, not knowing if the woman found tied up in the back of his nephew's yard, was his long, lost and greatly-loved daughter.

When she explained that it was the same woman whom he had refused assistance to when she had brought the bedraggled woman to their home, his guilt was intensified. She didn't tell him about the severe illness the young woman had suffered as a result of being left wet and temporarily homeless.

No one had as yet discovered the trauma to her feet. This was because she refused to allow anyone to touch her. The torture was so far undiscovered. Zaylee Lang, even though she was still a patient in the hospital, insisted she be allowed to see the young woman, whom she said was called Lu and who was also her patient. As well as this, she also wanted to see her nephew.

The condition of the two of them horrified her. Gabriel was a feverish mess of bandages and pain. When he saw her, he smiled. "Thanks for coming. Will you make sure she's okay?"

Zaylee looked at Lu who was sitting on a chair beside Gabe. The young woman looked so frail that the merest breath of wind could have knocked her over. She allowed Zaylee to take her in her arms and comfort her. Lu began crying softly. Zaylee joined her. The doctor didn't ask any questions. It was too soon for that.

Gabe was happy to see that Lu had allowed someone other than himself into her private world. When the women were calmer, he spoke to Zaylee. "I think I'd like to see Mitch. Do you think you could arrange it? Maybe we'll see Malcolm later on."

Zaylee would have moved heaven and earth for the two of them, so these simple requests were the least she could do. She phoned Mitch immediately. He had been outside the hospital with his brother, Malcolm, so it was only a few minutes until he arrived. Francine also remained a patient in the hospital.

Gabe then asked Lu if she would go outside onto the balcony with Zaylee while the two men talked. Mitch was aghast at the condition of his nephew. All his anger towards Gabe for his drinking and driving offences disappeared as he looked at the carnage that had been perpetrated upon his nephew.

Then he remembered Gabe's father, his own brother, Michael. Michael had helped to care for his unknown daughter as well as the rest of the family for all those years while he escaped his own responsibilities. Mitchell owed Gabriel—big time.

Gabe gathered his strength before commencing. "It's about Lu, the woman who was tied up in the chair. Bad things have happened to her, real bad. From what the maniac said, I think she might be Lucia. He sang this stupid song and like everything else about him, he made little sense. But he did mention L for Lucia. That was when I twigged. She doesn't know who she is. She knows she has had different names, but for the time being, she's called Lu."

Mitch nodded his understanding before Gabe continued. "The thing is she killed a man so she could escape and maybe she killed a woman as well. I'm not too clear what happened. She's been tortured for years and years. You want to get a look at her feet sometime. Just ask Zaylee. The bastard used his branding iron on her and God knows what else he's done to her."

Gabe stopped to regain his strength. The pain was controlled with drugs but it still broke through from time to time. "She used to be called Luce Potulski. She's under the impression that the people who kept her were her grandmother and grandfather who she remembers were called Mr and Mrs Potulski. Then there's the psychopath, Uncle Lucas—God knows who he is or what his real name is. All I know is that he was a crazy bastard. He would have killed the two of us."

Gabe looked at his uncle. "I really do have to thank you for all those lessons you gave us as kids. It's probably what saved our lives. If I could, I would stick the sick bastard with a thousand knives. I hope it was the knife that eventually killed him and not the dogs. Please don't let them put the dogs down. They helped save our lives."

Mitch said he would move heaven and earth to save the dogs. Gabe again thanked him. He then continued, "The police can't find out about her grandfather or grandmother. Lu can't go through anymore. As it is, it's going to be another shit storm, especially if it gets out that she may be Lucia Farraday."

His uncle didn't have the heart to tell his nephew that the shit storm had already arrived. The media was all over the story that the woman was possibly the missing Lucia Farraday. It was all alleged. Mitch sat with his nephew until he fell asleep. He then beckoned to Zaylee and the young woman who may or may not be his niece. They returned immediately. The young woman went straight to Gabe and sat beside him holding his right hand. She did not look up or speak to Mitch.

It was not until Zaylee said, "I think we should be leaving now, Mitch," that the young woman looked up. She smiled at Zaylee. Mitch felt his heart leap in his chest. It was the same smile as his brother's.

Malcolm returned with his wife almost immediately. The young woman still sat holding Gabe's right hand. She looked at Zaylee as they entered the room, but she did not look at the man who accompanied her. As gently as she could she spoke to Lu, "This is Malcolm, Lu? He's Gabriel's uncle."

She briefly lifted her eyes then looked down again as she said, "Hello."

The five rules still ran through her head. She had been breaking them over and over and look what had happened. Uncle Lucas had returned and he had brought all his evil with him. How did she know which of these other people who were entering her life were not equally as evil? She decided again, then and there, that she would say nothing, or next to nothing, for as long as she could.

When it became clear that Lu was not going to say anything more, Zaylee took her husband outside. Nothing had changed for him. His heartbreak at losing his beloved daughter continued. If this young person was indeed his daughter, she was a totally different person. The word 'damaged' came to him. Whoever she was, she had been so damaged. Whoever she was, he would have to bear the scars of shame when he had refused her refuge when she had most needed it.

The Farraday family had much to think about and much to do. They were again living in a world of hurt.

Sergeant Andy Brown and his detectives had collected what evidence they could. They had found the hidden cameras. Even the strongest of them had difficulty watching and listening to the graphic scenes that had been played out. They could almost smell the sizzling and crackling as Gabriel's skin was cooked. The look of almost ecstasy that passed across the face of the man known as Uncle Lucas was appalling. His sniffing and lip licking were unbearable to watch.

Then the black bag was opened up. Some of the DVDs were obviously old. They were in numerical order. The first one was played. The first few scenes were very obscure. They showed a little girl in a tight, red dress who wore a head band with horns sticking out of it. Then the torture began. The long, sharp needles were shoved abruptly under her toe nails. The screams from the little girl were indescribable.

Then it showed the blood from the bleeding, little toes being sucked up by the mouth of a half-hidden man. The young child lay writhing in agony on a bed as the man then rubbed the little girl's bleeding foot against his genitals.

It was unbelievable viewing. For the police officers in the room, they were beyond words. Most of them had families. None of them wanted to watch any more. If this was number one of the set, what were the rest going to be like?

It was without doubt that the torture and abuse would only worsen and change. It would have to be left to officers who specialised in such things to view the rest. How anyone ever slept peacefully ever again was anyone's guess?

It was time for a break. Andy Brown badly needed one.

The day when she was to hear about Leon's grand plan was beautiful. Lizzie still retained some of the euphoria she had experienced when she had joined in with her family. She felt inured against anything that he might throw at her. *Bring it on, Leon,* were her thoughts on that beautiful morning.

Maryanne was again in her bedroom. She had enjoyed her morning coffee and contribution from Leon. Lizzie always went outside when Leon contributed to her mother's happiness. It was more than she could stand. It also caused her spirits to dampen—her poor, mad mother.

When she spotted Leon, he was looking very content. He beckoned Lizzie to join him. He was in the kitchen, drinking coffee. She noticed he had shut the door to her mother's bedroom. It was just a pity he wouldn't do this while he was contributing to her happiness, when she could see her mother's fat legs wound around him.

He asked did she want coffee. This was the last thing she wanted from Leon. She just wanted to hear about his grand plan and then get the hell away from him.

"So, what is your grand plan?"

"Oh, my bad, beautiful Lizzie, I can't wait to get started. It's just about your time."

Lizzie had been dreading this—the time for her once a monther. The thought of Leon and sometimes Bart as well, pawing over her body was more than she could stand. She gave thanks for her ability to return to her grey world. There was no colour left for her, not since Raphael had chased it all away.

His face was alive with excitement. "If this works out, which it should, you won't have to return to the club. Your pole-swinging days will be over."

She was not sure what he was up to. He would not easily give up on his lucrative, little earner. "This will be much easier. Besides, you're getting a little stale. You don't put enough of yourself into it any more. The customers need more. You just don't cut it any longer, Lizzie."

"How sad, Leon. I am just so upset," she replied with as much sarcasm as she could muster.

"Don't be upset, Lizzie." He seemed to have missed her sarcasm. "This next plan will be better for all of us. I just can't wait to get started. I have it all planned out. We'll spend the next few days at the house."

Lizzie knew very well which house he meant. "Don't you worry about your mother? I'll check every day that she's okay. I want you to be totally relaxed. Here, I've got something for you." He jumped up and pulled a package out from the kitchen cupboard. "I bought these last week. I should have started you on them sooner, but I've been so busy with planning."

Lizzie looked in amazement at the bottles of pills he pulled out of the package. "What are these for? They look like vitamins. I don't need vitamins. My mother might, but I don't."

"You can't be too careful, Lizzie. I've been reading up about it. You need to be as healthy as you can. Now be a good girl, get yourself a glass of water and take one of each."

Lizzie got herself a glass of water as instructed. Then she proceeded to open the bottles. There were several vitamins she was familiar with. Then she noticed one which belonged to the B group of vitamins. She tried to remember what she had learned about vitamins.

"Good girl, Lizzie. Now you have to take these every day. I know you come from a very healthy family but you can't be too careful. We want to have a good, healthy baby."

"What did you say? I thought you mentioned a baby." She was beginning to get a sick feeling.

"That's exactly right, Lizzie. We're going to produce babies. At least you are. Bart and I will just provide the little swimmers. Between us, we should be able to produce beautiful, bouncing babies."

"No, we're not, Leon. You must be out of your mind if you think I would ever want to have your baby or that creepy friend of yours." Lizzie could not believe what he was proposing.

She stood up to leave, but he grabbed her firmly by the wrist. "Well, it's either that Lizzie, or I'll put you out to all those hungry, throbbing penises that are just busting to try you out."

"You are so sick, Leon, and so despicable. Don't you have a conscience? There's no way that I will ever agree to either of your grand plans."

She pulled her wrist out of his grasp and made to leave. But he was very quick and grabbed her again. This time he had a knife in his hand which he used to nick her under the chin. "Oh, I have a conscience all right, Lizzie. Remember what your family owes me. You still have a long way to go before we're even."

She was aghast at the tiny trickle of blood that was dripping from her chin. "You keep saying that, Leon. But why does my family owe you? What have any of us ever done to you?"

"Why don't you ask your uncles? But never mind, this next little enterprise might just square us up."

"Know this Leon. I won't be having your baby and I won't be having intercourse with any sex-starved men. So you can just forget it." She wiped the blood from her chin. Her shirt was already spotted.

"No, Lizzie, we won't be forgetting anything and you will have babies, as many and as often as you can pump them out. I'd use your mad mother as well, only the result might not be too healthy. Rich couples only want perfect, healthy babies. So far, you haven't displayed any of your mother's madness. It's all in the genes, Lizzie. Not the jeans that cover that delicious, lower body of yours, but genes, the little threads that make us who we are. So we'll get started this week."

Lizzie thought she was going to be sick. He planned on selling babies, her babies. She was so shocked, that she sat right back down again on the kitchen chair. The blood was now dripping down her front. Her little bit of hope had just disappeared.

"We'll bake babies in your beautiful belly, Lizzie. I can't wait to start." He was staring at her with wondrous glee in his eye. "Show me your beautiful belly, Lizzie. I want to have a look at it."

She cringed and pulled back from him. He pulled out his knife again. "You remember what happened to your mother, don't you? She still has that delicious scar. I lick it every morning—such great memories."

She remembered her mother's belly being cut open, just as she remembered her hand being cut open. Slowly she stood up and lifted up her shirt. "Pull your jeans down further, Lizzie. I want to just savour this sight and this moment."

Lizzie saw the drops of blood that were dripping down her shirt. Slowly she stood up. She could not believe what he had planned. Her wits were deserting her. She stood in awe as he unbuttoned her shirt. He then pulled her jeans down below her hips. He was kneeling in front of her.

He reached up and brushed the now coagulating blood from below her chin and rubbed it against her stomach in the symbol of a cross. It was as if she were in a nightmare. He started licking the blood from her abdomen. She looked down at his dark head as he savoured her stomach. He sucked and licked. His murmurs of delight penetrated her ears.

She held onto the chair that she had sat on. It was beyond all belief. She looked down again at his black hair with its few streaks of grey. Ordinarily, when he and Bart enjoyed their monthly entertainment with her, their heads would be down further.

Lizzie then vomited. She had not eaten breakfast, but what was left in her stomach came back up. There was nothing she could do but deliver what was left inside her onto Leon's head.

This did not please him at all. Lizzie had to pay. He had been so enjoying her beautiful belly in anticipation of the beautiful babies that it would produce. He abruptly stood up and slapped her forcefully across the face. She fell to the floor.

He was very angry. "You are such a disappointment to me, Lizzie. I love you, do you know that? I have loved you since you were a little girl when I first made you mine. But you have changed lately, Lizzie, and I want to know why." He stopped speaking while he regarded her with suspicion. "Have you met someone? Have you been having sex with anyone else? You know what will happen if you have, Lizzie."

She slowly pulled herself up off the floor. He had the knife again back in his hand. "Tell me the truth, Lizzie?"

She tried to steady her shaking hands. "How would I ever be able to have sex with anyone? You watch my every move. You know where I am and what I am doing every second of every day, so no, I have not been having sex with anyone. Besides, I could think of nothing worse—once a month with you and Bart is enough for me."

Her conscience was totally clear as she spoke to him. Although why she should worry about lying to him, she didn't know. She didn't count the times with Arlo—that was just revenge. Raphael was another question altogether. At the time she thought it was making love. But that soon fell apart. Now she didn't know what it was. *One of life's great mistakes*, she supposed.

"You say the most hurtful things to me, Lizzie. It's not the best foundation for starting a family. But never mind, we just have to forge on. Now don't forget your vitamins. By the way, you can have the day off today. Get rested, go for a walk, and relax. I want you in top form over the next few days."

Lizzie felt a great sense of relief. She knew what her fate was now. She knew the grand plan. It was clear what she had to do.

"Can you answer me one thing, Leon? What sort of parents did you have? How is it that you turned out as you are?"

"What a strange woman you are, Lizzie, that you should be asking about my parents. But I suppose I can understand it. It's just as well to get the blood lines straight. Well, my father was probably your grandfather or his crazy half-brother. Who really knows? As for mother, that's a mystery. She was just some scrubber that Alan and Jack picked up. She was good breeding stock. Alan liked to have children. But alas, something happened, probably all those babies she was pumping out. Then she just disappeared—poof, gone, disappeared, never to be seen again. Strange thing, it was while she was on one of their trips down this way. She just never returned."

His telling of his mother's fate was so cold. It was more than she could bear to know this man was most probably her uncle and her mother's half-brother. Oh, what evil walked throughout her history? She had heard about the type of man her maternal grandfather, Alan Farraday, had been—a wicked man from all accounts.

But the poor woman who had been Leon's mother, what sort of a life had she been made to endure? She could well understand the utter relief she must have felt when she died. Lizzie just hoped it hadn't been too painful a death. Her decision was even easier now.

She stood up, gave Leon a small kiss on the cheek. "Well, it's all decided then. I'll just go for that walk now. Good bye Leon. Say goodbye to mum for me."

Lizzie returned to her own room where she picked up her pack of cards. She slipped a pocket-knife into her jeans pocket then left the house. She knew Leon watched her walk away. When she was out of his sight, she began crying.

She ran as fast as she could, stumbling over rocks, running through the tall gums, up into the hills, up to the Big Rock to her salvation.

Leon Jones watched his prize possession walk up the track towards the hills. It was surprising how easily she had acquiesced. All things considered, she was a great girl, was Lizzie.

He sat quietly at the table, considering his plan. He heard a small sound and looked around to see Maryanne standing at the door of her bedroom. One look soon convinced him that she was most probably crazier than ever.

"How are you, Danny?" she asked him sweetly.

"Maryanne, you know I'm not Danny. I'm Leon. Danny's dead. He passed away years ago."

Maryanne came out to the kitchen. She proceeded to make herself coffee. "You never change, do you? You lie, and lie, and expect me to fall for it every time. Well, not this time, Danny."

She calmly sat down beside him. She kept stirring her coffee. Strangely, she did not use a spoon but a knife. But this was not that unusual for Maryanne. She always said the fewer pieces of cutlery you used, the less work for Lizzie to do. You could use a knife to spread your vegemite on toast then reuse it to stir your coffee.

When she was in one of these moods, Leon knew it was easier to get her back into the bedroom where he could perform—a further contribution to her happiness. It was becoming exhausting though, all this performing.

But she had never spoken to him before as if he was Danny, the deceased husband—the pants dropper. What a day of mixed fortune that had been—two birds with the one stone. It should have just been Maryanne, but it turned out to be Danny and the little tart, Tiffany. In the end it had probably finished up all for the better.

"I never lie to you, Maryanne. I care for you. I look after you." He tried to sound conciliatory.

"If you cared about me, you wouldn't have been carrying on with that tart I just saw you with."

"That was Lizzie, Maryanne, your daughter." Leon was beginning to worry. Maryanne seemed to be losing it altogether.

"No, Danny, it was your little girlfriend, Tiffany. You didn't think I knew about her, did you? But I know everything, Danny." She laughed at him then. "Show me your arm, Danny. I want to remind you what will happen to you if you don't give up your philandering ways."

Leon was becoming very startled with Maryanne's behaviour. He wished Lizzie would return. She could usually get her mother to calm down, or give her a pill which might put her to sleep. This was an unknown Maryanne. She was nothing like the woman who sat and had coffee with him every morning and then waited for him in the bedroom.

He put his arm out for her to look at. There was nothing remarkable about his arm. She looked down at it, "See that scar, Danny. Do you remember when that happened?"

"No, Maryanne, I don't remember when it happened." He kept his arm out while she felt it.

"Well, I'll tell you what Danny, you'll remember this." Maryanne quickly pulled the knife out of her coffee cup and sliced it straight through the skin on the inside of his left wrist. She had aimed deep—deep enough to cause severe bleeding. "No more fishing for you, Danny boy."

Leon could not believe what had just happened. Here was poor, silly Maryanne slitting his wrist. They both looked in astonishment as the blood started to pour out. It began to gush in spurts. It was then that Leon realised she had cut his radial artery.

"For pity's sake, Maryanne, get a towel—anything. Call the ambulance. I'll bleed out here, so hurry up." Hysteria was creeping into his voice.

"No, no, Danny, there will be no ambulance, not this time, not yet. Tell you what, you come on outside and I'll fix you up properly."

Leon was now standing. He had grabbed a tea-towel from the kitchen and had wrapped it around his wrist. The blood kept gushing. He opened a kitchen draw and pulled out some more tea-towels. He kept trying to sop up the blood that was now lessening. He was unsure what Maryanne had meant when she told him to go outside. Maybe she had a change of heart and was going to drive him to the hospital.

She followed him outside onto the lawn near the front steps. He was feeling weak and dizzy. He was unaware that Maryanne had picked up the cricket bat that lay against the veranda wall. He was just turning around to see where she was when she swung the bat.

He tried to protect his head, but he was too slow. The bleeding wrist with the tea-towels wrapped around it, impeded his speed. Leon felt the crush against the left temporal area of his skull. He heard the sound. He had little time for any more thoughts. It was very bewildering. His last thought was that he would never see the baby being baked in Lizzie's beautiful belly.

Maryanne Smythe watched as Leon fell to the ground. "That will teach you, Danny. It will be a while before you're well enough to start fooling around with any more of your girlfriends. If you don't get a headache out of this, then I'll do it again."

Maryanne then sat on the veranda steps. She kept looking at Danny lying there on the ground. He wasn't moving, not that his lack of movement meant much. He was a devious bastard. She got tired of watching him so she went to the granny flat where he stayed.

He was so odd, Danny. Sometimes he did the right thing and slept with her, but then he would go to the granny flat and sleep there. She had no doubt it was where he kept his sluts. She hoped there was one hiding inside right now.

Well, if he's going to learn his lesson then he better learn it properly. Maryanne found the drum of motor-mower fuel, poured it around the granny flat, and then put a match to it.

She found the flames fascinating. They leapt up in brilliant yellow and orange colour. They moved very quickly. She had always loved the smell of petrol. It was nicer than perfume. She had often wondered why perfume makers didn't just fill their bottles with petrol. They could call them things like Fire and Flames, Hot and Smoky, Sizzling or best of all, Danny's Delight.

But then the smoke became thicker and the flames were so hot. She returned back to sit on the front steps of her home. Danny remained asleep. There were a few flies hanging around him. She concluded that he probably didn't have a shower—dirty bugger. So she got a bucket of water and threw it over him. Still he did not move.

"He must be just tired. All that sleeping around must have taken it out of him," she concluded.

So she went to collect a pillow and a sheet. When she tried to put the pillow under his head, she noticed the crack in his skull and the blood. This alarmed her. His eyes were open but not focusing. "Wake up, Danny. You can't lie out here all day. If the flies don't get you, the sunburn will." She covered him up with the sheet.

She returned to the stairs and sat a while longer. There was now far less smoke and the heat from the granny flat had died down. "I'll give it a while longer, Danny, and if you don't wake up, I'll just have to call Matt."

Maryanne went inside and made another cup of coffee. This time she drank it at the kitchen table. She wondered what the knife was doing there. She picked it up and stirred her coffee with it. The coffee had a different taste to it. She didn't really enjoy it.

Lizzie ran as fast as she could, away from the evil presence that was Leon Jones. She could still feel his tongue licking off the blood that had dripped onto her abdomen. She was breathless by the time she reached the top of the Big Rock. Her sobbing had stopped. She slumped down beside a paper-bark tree to catch her breath. She used some of the loose bark that had fallen around her to fan herself.

She thought she could smell smoke. It seemed to be coming from behind her. But she was not going to look back, not ever. If she looked back, then she might change her mind. She sat for a while longer.

She wished she had thought to bring a water bottle with her. But then she asked herself, *why did she need water?* Where she was going everything was laid on, or so she had been led to believe. Although when she thought about it further, it was only laid on for good people. Maybe she should have bought a water bottle after all.

There was no point in putting it off any longer. She stood up, brushed herself off, and tried to make herself look as presentable as she could. There was blood on her shirt. She wished she had stopped long enough to change it. She thought she could smell Leon on it. The water bottle would have been very handy. A few drops of water and she might have been able to wash some of the blood off it—too late now.

Her hair was a mess as she had not combed it when she got out of bed. She ran her fingers through it, trying to pull the tangles out of it. She looked down at herself and was satisfied she was as ready as she was ever going to be.

She walked to the edge of the Big Rock and looked over. It was quite a distance to the bottom. Surely, no one could survive a fall like that. Then she remembered the story about Jane Broadbent who was reputed to have been her paternal grandfather's lover.

What a bunch of amazing ancestors she had? All the men seemed to be randy old goats, dicking around where ever they could find it. And the women, how many of them had been long-suffering fools? Well, she wasn't going to be one of them. She would cut her losses and get out of here.

There was much to consider. Should she just jump feet first, fly over like an angel with her arms held out, or take a run-up like she was in the Olympics and in the triple-jump. She wanted to get it right. No mistakes like poor Jane Broadbent who must have been able to survive long enough to crawl into the cave and die there.

Lizzie wasn't having any of that. In spite of Rafe's rejection of her, she still had good memories of the cave. She certainly didn't want to cruel it for anyone else who might be lucky enough to make love there. Never mind sex, you could have that anywhere.

She thought she should practice. So she went to a smaller, flat rock that stood about half a metre off the ground. She stood on the edge of it and jumped off, feet first. It was quite easy to do.

Then she stood with her arms out beside her, ready to take the dive. No matter how much she wanted to, she couldn't bring herself to land head first on the ground below. Besides, her hair would be a dreadful mess, worse than it was now. So flying over the edge like an angel or bird was out. The angel part also put the spooks under her. She was about as angel-like as good, old Leon.

Then there was the run up for the triple jump. It didn't work because of the drop off the rock. All she managed was to fall over.

So now she had her answer. It was to stand on the edge and jump feet first. She took some deep breaths then calmly walked over to the edge. She decided she would not look down in case she lost her nerve. She looked up at the sky—the beautiful, blue sky with just a few puffs of white cloud. In spite of Leon and his grand plan, he couldn't change the day. It was a fabulous day to die.

She looked up at the sky and said the prayer out loud that she had been saying her whole life, ever since her dad had died. She had found it written on a scrap of paper in one of the books she cherished.

Be strong and courageous. Do not be afraid or terrified because of them. For the Lord your God goes with you. He will never leave you or forsake you.

She didn't know much about religious beliefs. But it sounded comforting. It had been written by some person called Deuteronomy, probably some old fogey who had lived way back in ancient times. *Well, Mr Deuteronomy,* she thought, *all your wondrous words have never worked for me.*

I'm none of these things, her thoughts were tormented. *I'm not strong or courageous. I am afraid and I am terrified. No God ever goes with me. Everyone always leaves me and I am totally forsaken.*

She stood on the edge of the Big Rock, looked up at the sky, took a deep breath—she was ready.

Then she heard the hiss. It was right behind her and frightened the daylights out of her. She turned around and there was Amazing Grace, hissing and standing up on his legs as if he wanted to attack her. She had heard stories of goannas running up people's trousers. Once more she thanked the fashion-gods for skin-tight jeans.

She got such a fright that she almost fell over the cliff but righted herself in time. She had to get rid of it. She picked up a few loose stones and fired them at him. "Get, scat, and push off."

The goanna stayed where he was. Lizzie eyed him off. What a dilemma? He didn't look like he was shifting. She was at a loss to know what to do. She supposed she could outwait him. Surely he would eventually go away. There was no way to get around him. If he intended to attack, she doubted she would be fast enough to get away from him. And for that matter, where would she run to? There was nowhere except over the edge.

Lizzie stood there looking at him. Amazing Grace was no longer up on his short legs. In fact he looked very comfortable, like he had settled in for the day. There was no more hissing. It was a staring contest. He looked at her. She looked at him. It was like when she had been at school, seeing who could look at someone for the longest time without blinking.

She thought it would never end, but then, just like that, Amazing Grace just up and ran away. She was so exasperated. How had she let a goanna outwit her? For a time she had even forgotten about her plan. But now, it just didn't seem worth it. Her momentum was gone. Maybe she would give it up for the day. She would go down to the cave and have a rest.

It was surreal walking into the entrance of the cave. She should have been dead, smashed up against the dirt and rocks not far away. Instead here she was, back in the cave. She pulled out the plastic sheeting that had been left there. She lay down on it. She could not believe how tired she was. It came to her that it was a very exhausting business trying to kill oneself. *It must be all that energy the brain needs to carry it out.* Lizzie fell fast asleep.

Maryanne tired of watching Danny just lying there with the sheet over him. He'd been there for hours. It was past time she had a nap. She was sick and tired of all of them, especially Danny with his womanising ways. She never saw her children. She was even sick of the taste of the coffee she had drunk so she went to her bedroom and fell asleep.

Someone had called into the fire department to say they could see smoke billowing in the direction of the Smythe property. The report was vague. It could have been the old Farraday property 'Sunshine' or it could have been the next property. It looked to be on the far side of the Big Rock.

The Smythe property was about the last along the road so there was no one to clarify just where the smoke was coming from. It could hardly be a grass fire because the country side was too lush due to the recent rain and the humidity was high. The ground was soaked. The only other explanation was that it had to be a building.

The fire service had been particularly busy that day. As there were no reports of specific damage, it was quite late in the day before a truck came to investigate the report. At first, the fire fighters could not detect anything. The Farraday property was clear. They moved onto the next property—the Smythe property. The smell of smoke from the dying embers was very strong as they drove in.

At first glance, it looked as though a shed had burnt down. There appeared to be no one home. They pulled up and were preparing to douse the smouldering remains when they saw the sheet. There was a pillow beside it. If they didn't know better, they imagined there could be a body under the sheet.

One of the men strode forward and lifted the sheet. "Good God Almighty," he shouted out. His colleagues came running. It was not every day that one saw a body lying flat out on the ground carefully covered with a sheet.

"Looks like he's had his head bashed in," one of the firemen said.

"Looks like he's slashed his wrist as well," another commented.

"Wonder which came first" another said.

"Poor bugger," said the fourth. He covered the man up again and phoned the police.

They then went to the source of the fire. It was a smouldering ruin, totally guttered. There were still hot spots to be put out. The men swung into action.

One of the firemen knocked on the door of the house, but as there was no answer, he went directly inside and started looking around. He noticed the blood on the kitchen table. The whole scene looked very suspicious. He went through the rest of the house. One bedroom had the door closed so he opened the door and marched straight in. The bed was ruffled up. He thought it was just an unmade bed with linen twisted around but then it all shifted as a woman sat up.

"Hello," Maryanne said, as though he were a long lost friend. "I was going to call Matt but I felt so tired I just went straight to bed."

The woman, who had initially sat up, then lay back down again. "I've been waiting all day for Danny to wake up. Is he still out there?"

This was a fire man, used to pulling people out of burning vehicles and fighting bush fires. He was used to dealing with many types of dangerous situations. He didn't think the current situation was dangerous but he certainly thought it was weird.

"Do you mean the man out in the yard covered with a sheet?" He was not going to be intimidated by some fat lady lying in a bed. Queer things happened all the time in his business and this was as queer as it got.

"He's very devious, you know. You can't trust him. He's been on with that little tart he keeps over in the granny flat. He didn't think

I knew about them, but I knew all right. You wait till he comes to his senses."

The woman spoke clearly and concisely. The fire man did not know what to make of it. His first thought was that there was another victim—another body, most probably burnt to death.

He left the woman in the bed. She didn't seem as though she was going to move herself out of it any time soon. He spoke to his fellow firemen. The hunt was on for another body. This one was most probably a smouldering corpse.

Andy Brown received notification of a body found on the Smythe property. He already had enough on his plate. But the name Smythe resonated in his brain. There was a relationship between the Smythe's and the Farradays. He remembered back to the bad, old days of their troubles.

When it came to anything to do with the Farradays, it was as well to be prepared and involved. It looked like there was another deceased person associated with the Farradays. He remembered that Danny Smythe had married Maryanne Farraday. Danny Smythe had been killed years ago in a motor vehicle accident in uncertain circumstances. He recalled that Maryanne Smythe had gone off her head at the time and had been carted off to a psychiatric unit.

The contingent of police cars arrived very quickly. Just as reported, there was a corpse, looking very much like the victim of a homicide. Andy Brown breathed deeply and knew there was nothing for it but to get on with it. He had just about had enough of policing.

He went in search of Maryanne Smythe who was still in bed just as the fire man had reported. She was lying flat on her back staring up at the ceiling.

He knocked and entered. "Hello Maryanne, my name is Andy Brown, do you remember me?"

The woman sat up. "No, should I?" He couldn't believe how much she had changed. She was no longer the slim, attractive woman she had been when her husband had died.

"I met you years ago when your husband died."

"I don't know how you could have managed that," she replied. "He's probably still having a lie down outside on the lawn—lazy

282 | *Claire Miles*

bugger. Anyhow I've just about had enough of him. As far as I'm concerned we're heading for the divorce courts." She looked at him with an all-knowing expression. "You know he's been carrying on, don't you? I think he's even been keeping his little tart over in the granny flat. But that romance is over now. I made sure of that."

Maryanne seemed to have exhausted her supply of information about her recalcitrant husband. Andy Brown looked at the young constable who stood beside him and shook his head. He told the constable to remain with the very obviously-psychotic woman.

Just as the fire man had reported, it looked as though there was a strong chance there was another body in the dying embers of the granny flat. It was happening again. Forensic officers were called in.

Andy Brown knew the Farraday men would be at the hospital with their nephew and the young woman who had been with him. Just as with that case, no one knew who this dead man was. He now had two deceased men and no identity for either. There was little point in asking Maryanne to identify the body. Her perception was that it was her no-good husband. Who the woman may be in the burnt-out granny flat was anybody's guess? If indeed there was a body there.

His call was answered by Mitchell Farraday. It's never easy reporting a death to anyone, especially under suspicious circumstances, like murder, and especially as it was more than likely the offence had been committed by a family member.

The Farraday men arrived en masse—four brothers and a nephew. Andy Brown noticed that the brothers had aged with some grey hair visible, but were generally all strong and fit-looking. He looked at the nephew. He was identical to the man who lay in the hospital bed, only in better condition.

They all shook hands. The brothers remembered Andy Brown all too well. It took them all back to the bad, old days. They were asked to identify the body. Mitch took one look and said it was their property manager, Leon Jones. He had no idea who his next-of-kin was or even if he had any. He had worked for the family for years, taking care of the two properties—the Smythe property and Miriam's Place.

"Where are Maryanne and Lizzie?" Matt asked.

"Your sister is in bed. I don't think she's very well. She thinks the body is that of her late husband, Danny Smythe. She needs to be in a hospital or else taken into custody." He let that sink in.

Matt was immediately shocked as were they all. But his despair was deeper. He knew of his sister's psychotic tendencies. Years ago, she had tried to kill their father with pills after practicing on the chooks in the hen-house.

Malcolm's anxiety levels were rising. He remembered the strange incident when Danny had suffered a huge gaping wound to his arm which he claimed was due to a fishing accident. Zaylee had stitched Danny up, but had always remained intrigued how the injury had occurred.

Then there was the worst incident of all when Maryanne stood out the front of the house brandishing a rifle. Andy Brown was well aware of this incident as he had been involved. The most horrifying of all was the image of their sister being strapped down onto a stretcher screaming obscenities at her deceased husband.

"Where's Lizzie?" Raphael asked with a trembling voice.

"From what Maryanne said, we think there might be another body in the burnt-out remains of the granny flat."

There was more shock etched on their faces. Raphael had to look away. He couldn't listen to any more. All he could think was—*not Lizzie, please God, don't let it be Lizzie.*

The brothers asked to see their sister. She lay staring at the ceiling. She did not speak to them. They were filled with immense sadness. Guilt was uppermost in their minds. They had all deserted her, all except Lizzie.

They could have all done more. They knew of her mental condition. But they had kept away as much as they could. None of them wanted to be touched by her madness. It had been left to Lizzie to be her main carer. The next big horror to be faced was whose body was in the fading embers next door. Had they failed the two of them?

Raphael walked away. He went up the track towards the Big Rock. His heart was breaking. She had asked for his help. He had rejected her. He had enjoyed her body and then like the coward he knew he was, had run away from her. His brother was laying half-dead in the hospital and now Lizzie, the only other really important person in his life, may be dead.

If he could, he would have walked forever, going through the tall gums, up as far as he could into the far-away mountains. But when he reached the top of the Big Rock, he was startled by the huge goanna that Lizzie had told him about. It was as big and as frightening as she had said. Amazing grace did nothing more than watch him pass by? It seemed like he had appointed himself the guardian of the Big Rock. It was his domain and he was in charge.

Raphael walked down the other side of the Big Rock, down onto the Farraday property. He thought he might go to the old home and spend some time in the prayer room. But then he looked up at the cave where he had loved Lizzie and then had walked out on her and broken her heart.

He thought of all that she had said to him, how she always seemed to be talking in riddles—about colours, and pretending. His heart was heavy as he walked into the entrance of the cave. That was when he was attacked by a wild woman. In that instant as he looked into the dimness of the cave, he realised that this person with a knife who was coming at him was Lizzie—his Lizzie.

"I'll never have your babies, never," she was screaming at him, brandishing the wicked looking knife that she was wielding around.

Raphael ducked but was not quick enough. She cut him on the upper left arm.

"Lizzie," he shouted out in the loudest voice he could muster, "stop it. What the hell are you trying to do, kill me?"

Lizzie stopped in her tracks. The face that looked at her was not that of Leon. It was Raphael. She dropped to the ground, still holding the knife. Her screaming had stopped but had been replaced by deep, racking sobs.

He walked over to her, took the knife from her hands and held her in his arms. She burrowed her face into his shoulder while he let her sob. He could feel the pain inside her. It seemed to be so deep. He could not imagine what it was that had caused Lizzie to break down.

He sat holding her for what seemed like hours, but was probably not that long. He listened as her sobbing stopped. Eventually, there was only their breathing to be heard. He knew his arm was bleeding. It was painful but not nearly as painful as what he knew Lizzie was experiencing.

"Tell me about it, Lizzie," he eventually said.

"Tell you about what?"

"Everything that's causing your pain," he said, still holding her.

Lizzie then told him everything. How it had started as a little girl? How she was his captive? How he would cut her, beat her, rape her, how he made her expose herself for the world to see? How he now had his grand plan? This was more than she could bear. How could she tell Raphael that Leon was going to bake babies in her beautiful belly and then sell them?

He kept quiet while she worked up the courage to tell him. When she finally told him, she cried again and he cried with her. His beautiful Lizzie had been at the mercy of a monster for all these years and no one had known. No one had suspected what was happening.

He held her, kissed her, and tried to calm her. He knew there would be much more required than a few kisses to ever erase what had been done to her. He also knew that her entire, extended family would never get over the guilt they would all feel for the rest of their lives at having left Lizzie Smythe as a little girl at the hands of a monster like Leon Jones.

"He's dead, Lizzie. He's gone. Leon Jones can never hurt you again. No one is ever going to hurt you again, Lizzie. I won't let them."

"I don't believe you. People like him don't die. They just keep going on with their destruction." She looked at him imploringly. "They destroy you, Raphael. They take away every vestige of self-worth that you have. That's what I am, Raphael. I am worthless. I have no worth. I am nothing."

"To me you are everything, Lizzie. You are all that is brave and beautiful. I promise you that he's dead. He'll never hurt you again."

"You better be right. I can't go through any more. I just can't. I tried so hard to jump over, but the goanna came along and it stopped me."

These words caused his heart to flutter. It was all starting to make sense now—all her unconnected sentences. She had been planning to kill herself. Raphael again felt deep shame. Here was another person he had failed. Even a goanna was more useful than he was.

"All I can say, Lizzie, is thank God for Amazing Grace. He saved you."

"I don't know what saved me. All I know is that I was trying to figure out what to do when you came into the cave. I was sure you were Leon coming after me. I was playing solitaire but the king of hearts did not come up. So it wasn't clear what I should do."

"What's the king of hearts got to do with anything?" He hoped that Lizzie was not reverting back to talking in riddles.

"Don't you remember? He's the suicide king. He's the one with the sword through his head. It was a joke when we were kids. Now I'm not so sure. Do you believe in omens, miracles, or whatever they are? I should be outside this cave with my head cracked open. Had it not been for the goanna, I should be dead right now. But it frightened the wits out of me again. I didn't have the time or momentum to do it, and then you come along while I was waiting for the king of hearts to turn up. Sometimes, I don't understand this place—all the terrible things that have happened over the years".

"Not all of them have been terrible, Lizzie. There's one thing that's happened that was the best thing in my life." He was still holding her but the feelings he was experiencing were no longer totally those of comfort.

"Raphael, are you flirting with me?" she asked and for the first time, he heard a hint of laughter in her voice.

"Not flirting, Lizzie, deadly serious."

"What about the priesthood?"

"It's not much good being a priest if all you can think about is a beautiful woman with magnificent breasts and what it's like making love to her."

"Maybe we could try it again someday," she said coyly.

"Maybe we could. I'd like that." He pulled her in close.

"I think I would too."

They sat together looking out at the world from the cave entrance while the sun faded in the sky. Lizzie was hungry, thirsty and tired.

"How about we go down to the old home and see what we can find to eat? And I'd better let the family know you're all right." He did not tell her about her mother, his brother Gabriel or the young woman called Lu. She had enough to deal with at the moment.

Raphael informed his uncles that he had found Lizzie. He said she was okay and would see them all the following day. The police were notified and were more than relieved to know there was not another dead person to be found.

The Farraday brothers watched in immense sorrow as they saw their only sister being taken away by ambulance again, this time with a police escort. They knew she would never again return home. Maryanne's life had been one of chaos and pain. Whatever or whoever had caused her mind to fracture had accomplished a fine job. There would be no coming back from the madness that had overtaken her this time.

Matt went over to the smouldering ruins of the granny flat where he had lived many years ago with Maryanne and Danny. This had been a happy time for both of them; probably the happiest Maryanne had ever been in her life.

But he was there for more than that. The photographs, recordings and camera given to him by the then Detective Denise Davidson for safe keeping, was his main focus.

It was the time when Sergeant Bill Boyd had tried to throttle her and she had recorded the entire incident. It was her bargaining chip to prevent her future husband, Michael Farraday, from being jailed for a murder which he did not commit.

Matt looked around at what was left of the building. There was no chance that any of these precious items had escaped the blaze. His memories lingered. Bill Boyd and some other prominent men in the area had been involved in paedophilia. His sister-in-law had discovered this crime and it was her agreement to remain silence about it that resulted in Bill Boyd arranging Michael's freedom.

Now there was no evidence left to prove that the sergeant, who had since risen substantially up the ranks of policing, had been involved in serious crime as well as trying to kill Denise.

Not that Bill Boyd would have any idea that the evidence had existed for all this time. Both Denise and Michael had been dead for years. Nothing had happened. There had been no contact from him. It was all dead and buried. Surely enough time had elapsed for Bill Boyd, if not to have forgotten, then at least to let it lie.

The search of the embers of the granny flat had not revealed a second body. The body of Leon Jones was taken away for autopsy although there was no doubt that he had been murdered and no doubt who had committed the homicide.

The questioning of Lizzie Smythe would have to wait till the following day. Andy Brown was tired. He had seen enough killing and torture. He checked on the progress of Gabriel Farraday who was reported as being stable. The young woman, as yet known only as Lu, although it was highly likely she was Lucia Farraday, remained in the same room as Gabe. She was refusing to leave his side or to speak to anyone except Dr Zaylee Lang.

Andy could not wait to lie in the arms of Rina Wright. He was working long hours, dealing with so many issues and with so many people. The media was relentless. When word got out that there had been another homicide and that this death was also connected to the name Farraday, it was almost beyond belief. They say things happen in threes. He sure hoped they were wrong.

One positive thing to come out of his long work days was that Rina went to his home each afternoon and cooked a meal for his children. Jude followed her through the dividing gate and sat with the old Alsation before walking up the stairs into the house. There he would sit beside Amanda and watch television. No one knew if he understood anything but he appeared content.

Andy had the best of everything in his home. Rina was delighted with his kitchen and with the amount of foodstuffs she found in his refrigerator and cupboards. She and Jude ate with Thomas and Amanda. She left him a cooked meal each night before returning back to her own home with Jude.

She was often jittery, never exactly sure why. She had full awareness of what had occurred on the day when Andy had found her under the bed and what she had told the doctor the next morning. She knew she had frightened the doctor. She felt bad about this. The doctor had been very kind to her, but all her senses told her that the 'end game' was underway. There was no point in pretending otherwise.

When he came to her later in the night, she held him close before she told him that it was not over for him yet. There was still more to come, more bad things were yet to happen. He had not told her anything about the homicides, the madness or torture he had seen happen. He didn't discuss his work with anyone other than his colleagues.

As usual her words disturbed him. He was beginning to accept that she was clairvoyant or something. She still woke screaming and terrified. If anything, the dreams were worse than ever.

Rina Wright often thought of the two young men she had met who had been so much alike. There was the man who had found Jude when she had first arrived in Tewantin and the other man whom she had met in Sundial Park. For some reason they were often on her mind.

She had been experiencing deep, intense feelings of dread about her friends from Sundial Park, Lu and Lizzie. They both seemed to have disappeared. She didn't know anything about praying, but she used her mind to send up messages to whoever might be listening to care for them. She always asked with her very strange and unpredictable mind to help them all through the dread that was to come. The dread seemed to be getting stronger.

Raphael slept with Lizzie that night. They lay curled up in the bed that had been his parent's. It was not a night of sexual coming together. Rather it was a cementing of what should have been. Raphael now knew his path. It was with Lizzie. He would always be haunted about what he should or could have done—for his sister, his mother and for Lizzie.

But life had to move on. Lizzie had to be protected and cared for. He vowed that night that he would always be there for her. He told her he loved, that he had always loved her since they were children. But she had been so far out of his reach, with her beauty and her allure. Lizzie did her best not to laugh at him when he said this. But he sounded so sincere. She felt that she had no beauty or allure, that it had all been sucked out of her by Leon.

She told him that she loved him too, that she had always loved him, right back to the time when she had first become aware of the difference between boys and girls. She told him she remembered the nights when she had been a little girl as they lay on the floor of the house at Sunshine. How he would lie beside her while they watched childhood movies.

The memories remained of his arm slung across her back protecting her from the vivid images that were meant to be funny. These images sometimes frightened her in spite of her best attempts to pretend otherwise. This was one of the first acts of kindness that she could remember.

Lizzie Smythe was taking the first small steps towards feeling whole again.

But there was always a next day when reality had to be faced. It was time for Raphael to switch his phone back on. He did not check his messages. He knew there would be too many. He and Lizzie had spent their first night together. He just hoped and prayed that there would be many more.

There was nothing for it but to tell Lizzie that most probably it was her mother who had killed Leon Jones. That it appeared she had become psychotic. She had been taken to hospital with a police escort.

Lizzie did not want to hear any more details about her mother and Leon. She put her hands over her ears and said to Rafe, "Let's get it over with, but promise me, you won't leave me alone with any of them, not the police, not your brothers, not any of the family and especially not Mitch."

"I promise, Lizzie. You've done nothing wrong. You have not committed any crime. You've been a victim for most of your life."

Lizzie did not altogether believe him. The law was a strange thing. Who knew what a smart lawyer could claim? After all it was only her word against a dead man. The police always wanted a perpetrator, although what they thought she might have been able to perpetrate, she had no idea. All she was good for was swinging around a pole half-naked.

They arrived at the police station at the scheduled time that had been arranged. The first person she saw was Mitch. She would not meet his eyes. But Rafe told her it was just as well that he was there. He had hired the best solicitors, just to be on the safe side. She couldn't think why she would need a solicitor.

Detective Senior Sergeant Andy Brown escorted her into an interview room. It was a stark room with little ambience. She did not know it, but it was the same room that her deceased uncle, Michael and her cousin, Gabriel, had spent time in.

After some preliminary explanations of what was to occur, she said that she would not talk about anything unless Raphael was present. She didn't care if the solicitors or Mitchell Farraday remained. It was agreed that Rafe could remain with her. She was aware that the other people in the room watched her with great interest, but she kept her focus on Andy Brown. She wanted to get this ordeal over with and disappear.

Andy Brown told her she was not a person of interest in the death of Leon Jones, but her input into the investigation was of paramount importance. She noticed that he had switched on his recording device. She held Rafe's hand under the table as he sat next to her. Then she commenced her story.

As succinctly as she could, she told how she had been left alone with her mother and Leon Jones when her mother had eventually returned home after extensive mental health treatment following the death of her father. She told them how Leon had come to her in the night, and had cut her hand open. She showed them the neat, white scar than ran from the tip of her left, little finger to her wrist.

She told them with her eyes closed and with shame on her face, how he had violated her. She had trouble saying the words. It had happened when she had been a little girl. She did not tell them how, on that very night, she had learned how to change her world from colour to grey. That would always remain her secret. That had been how she had survived.

She explained that he had coffee or tea each morning with her mother. After coffee, he would have sex with her mother. That was the time when the real horror began for Lizzie. She couldn't help but see what they were doing because the bedroom door was left open. The first time she had seen them together was the night that Leon had first come into her bed.

After that, he had come once a month for the rest of her life. If she objected, he would beat her or cut her. She showed them the many small nicks on those parts of her body that were not covered by her clothes. She told them that, if she didn't or couldn't enjoy it, he had forced her to pretend. She had been pretending her entire life—she was the great pretender.

Lizzie told them that if she ever said anything to anybody then her mother would also be cut. It wasn't a threat. She remembered with clarity the time he had cut her mother's abdomen in the shape of a cross. Her mother was so crazy at the time that she had thought it was funny. Lizzie had many, terrible memories of those years, not least the fact that she had to swing around a pole and expose herself for all to see.

Finally, she told them of his grand plan—the plan to *bake babies in her beautiful belly* and then sell them. If she didn't consent to participating in this plan, then he would pimp her out. Raphael held on to her hand under the table as if he would never let her go.

They all waited in expectation for her next words, but she had said enough. Other things that had happened were her business—or family business. She said no more. That was it, she was done. They believed her or they didn't?

There was silence in the room after the telling. She turned to Rafe. He put his arms around her. He asked if they were done. The police officer in charge, Andy Brown, managed to say that for the time being they were. He then added he might have to ask her more questions later on. Lizzie and Rafe left the room and disappeared.

Mitch was stunned by his niece's revelations. How was it possible that all this had occurred under their noses? He had no doubt it was true. What reason did Lizzie have to make up such a preposterous story? Again, he was filled with shame and remorse.

Andy Brown was sickened by her story. He thought then of Rina's words—*we're in the end-game right now.*

44

Maria Wright had regained her memory. It had slowly returned. She lived quietly in the secure-living unit where she had been placed when discharged from hospital after her failed suicide attempt. She remembered her history with all the dreadful incidents that she had experienced. Monsters predominated in her thoughts.

She no longer felt any fear. There was little in the way of cruelty that she had not experienced. Unfortunately, she had lived through the worst that the monsters were capable of—except death. So far, that had been denied her.

Vengeance was now her only recourse. She made a decision to return to the home she shared with Rina and Jude. If they weren't there, then she would hunt them down. How she would do this, she was not sure. When she was a small child, she recalled that her father often had guns in the home where she lived with her mother. The monsters that came to the house from time to time also had an array of guns.

Maria had always been a quiet person. She was the sort of person that no one noticed. Therefore it had been easy for her to return to the house where she had lived with Rina and the little monster. Neither of them was there which didn't surprise her. She had never heard from Rina, not once. The boy was always in her thoughts. He was the worst monster of the lot.

Everything was much as she remembered. After a quick check, the only things that were missing were their clothes and the backpack. This angered her. Rina had no right to its contents. She searched further and located her banking details. When she checked with the bank, she found that the money was still being paid into her account. It had been paid into her account for as long as she remembered. She expected that it had been left by her father.

Next she purchased a gun from a seedy-looking gun dealer who showed little interest in her. She had never fired a gun but she remembered watching her father and Jack Smith fooling around with them. She remembered how they used to pretend to shoot at her when she had been a little girl. It was another one of her fearful memories.

Maria was ready for her journey north to Tewantin. That would be her starting point. It was as good a place as any. She had no idea where Rina might have gone. Rina had never given any indication that she remembered where she had lived as a child. But who knows what remained of memories even in very young children. Again, she travelled by bus.

There were many holiday units available so this is where Maria stayed. She gave herself time to familiarise herself with the area. When she had lived there with the monsters, she seldom had the opportunity to see much more than the streets which surrounded the house of shame and horror where she had lived.

But she had time on her side. There was nothing else of interest in her life but to find the monsters, Rina and the little monster. She had no difficulty in finding the house where she had lived. It was much unchanged except for becoming more dilapidated.

There was little evidence that anyone lived there any longer. The granny flat where so much carnage had occurred stood dark and gloomy at the back of the house. Maria looked down at her ruined hands with the two missing fingers. She wondered if there were more who had suffered the same fate.

Thoughts of Francine and Sarina came back to her. The image of amputated fingers and excruciating pain penetrated her mind. She wondered what had happened to Francine; if the monsters had murdered her or if somehow she had managed to survive. Maria wasn't too concerned that the monsters would recognise her as she had aged considerably, looking more like an old woman instead of being in the prime of her life.

Her hair was now grey and her stance was no longer upright. *All the better*, she thought. Whether she found an old monster or the little monster made no difference. Whichever one she came across first would feel her wrath. They had all ruined her life as had Rina.

Stealth was required. With any luck she might find the lot of them. If she could dispatch them all to a worse place, then she would do it. After that, she could always find another bridge and take herself out of this life once and for all.

Maria frequently visited Sundial Park. She usually went in the early morning. When she spent time in the park, the memories came back with force. The second-hand shop was one of the places where she had a few moments of enjoyment in her horror life. This became part of her day. She would visit the shop and buy simple things like figurines and old books.

It was while she was reading one of these books in the park when she realised that the day was half gone. She packed up and was walking back to her holiday unit, when she glanced over to the playground area in Sundial Park where she spotted the little monster.

There he was sitting on the ground with an old dog beside him. She had no difficulty in recognizing him as he had not changed much. She stood and watched and sure enough, there was the treacherous Rina beckoning to the little monster to sit on the swing.

Maria felt both rage and satisfaction. She was on the right track. It wouldn't be long before she could commence her revenge. All that was required was a little more surveillance and planning.

Chaos—there was no better description. The Farraday's were in shock. It was like the old days, when Jack Smith had been shot, their father had hung himself and then again, years later, when five members of their family had died and two nieces had disappeared. There was also the chaos when the brothers had entombed three men.

It was happening all over again. It had never stopped. Would they ever be free? Guilt and shame were felt by all of them. Why hadn't they done more? The brothers were now held together by their sins of omission. These sins had been carried over to their children. What do you do next? Just get on with it? Be like Lizzie and pretend.

Gabe was stable, as the medical professionals were prone to say. They issued oblique statements like critical but stable. Lu wasn't saying a word but remained by Gabe's side, not talking but still eating. Lizzie had disappeared with Raphael. Maryanne was a homicidal maniac. Nothing much was known about the two men called Lucas and Leon—only that they were both bad men and thankfully dead in the morgue.

The media frenzy continued especially about Lucia Farraday. The DVDs would keep crime squads busy for months, if not years. So far the name Potulski had not cropped up. Who knew when the police would figure it out?

Zaylee Lang had recovered and wanted to return home. Her husband was refusing to leave the hospital so as to be near the young woman who may be his daughter. Mitch said he would take Zaylee back to her son who remained with Matt and Mia. His wife,

Francine, was also ready for discharge following her seizure. She had not experienced any further symptoms.

Francine was very quiet. Zaylee could see she was still very fragile. Her sister-in-law was somewhat of a puzzle. She was a stunning-looking woman but she could not bear to be apart from her husband.

Francine tried hard, but whatever had happened to her when she had been abducted, she had never really recovered. It was as if she was always looking around for danger. No amount of reassurance could ever bring back the person she once was. It was not only her memory and finger that had been lost during the terrible time of her abduction but part of her spirit as well.

Zaylee was bothered about more than Francine. She could not forget the words the woman called Rina had said to her about the end-game that was coming for all of them. Like a coward, she had not gone back. She had made a crazy promise to look after her disabled son. Zaylee wondered, not for the first time, how she got mixed up with so many strange people.

Her conscience would not leave her alone so she asked Mitch if he could stop for a moment so she could do a quick check on a patient. Francine remained sitting beside him in the vehicle. He could tell his wife was agitated.

"What's wrong, Francine? Aren't you feeling well?"

"I don't know. I feel well. It's something else. There's something wrong."

"Do you want to go back to the hospital?"

"It's nothing to do with my health. It's something else."

Mitch glanced back at Zaylee who was almost ready to leave his vehicle to visit her patient. Zaylee was also feeling that something was wrong. So much had happened recently. It was probably just nerves, a left over from all that had happened.

"I won't be long," she said as left to go through the front gate to Rina's house. She knocked on the door. There was no reply. She knocked again, still no reply. She had done her bit. Her attempt at salving her conscience was done. But Rina's words came back to her, "There's nothing you can do for me until it's over."

Zaylee almost ran back to the car. "No one home," she said.

Mitch drove off, intent on picking up his children and getting his wife home. He had driven around Sundial Park when Francine spoke.

"You have to go back."

"Back where?" Mitch asked.

"Back to the woman; you have to make sure she's all right."

"What woman?"

"The one who lives in that house," she replied.

Zaylee was listening in. Her heart was hammering in her chest. She wondered whether she might again faint. "How do you know it's a woman who lives there?"

"I just know," Francine replied.

Mitch pulled up. He sat quietly looking at his wife. It was beyond him. He had never understood his mother with her strange ways. He remembered it was a family story that Sarina had been much the same as his mother. Now his wife was saying strange things. It was all too much. He saw Zaylee in his rear vision mirror, sitting curled up in the back seat, looking like she had the hounds of hell after her. Of all people, the doctor was the last person to be spooked.

He turned his vehicle around. If it placated his wife, he would go back to the house and break in if that was what it took to calm her. He pulled up, got out of his vehicle and marched up the front stairs. He knocked, again there was no answer. He thought he would give it a few more minutes before leaving. It was then that he heard a noise. It was indistinct. He listened again. There it was again. Then he saw the dog come around the corner to greet him.

He bent down to pat the dog. It looked very old, with grey around its head and mouth. "What is it, old fellow?"

The dog whimpered and started scratching at the front door. It reminded him of the time he had been to a cottage at a place called Sandringham Creek when he had discovered he had a half-sister and a bunch of half-brothers.

He had not forgotten his skills he had used back then. He soon had the door open and was inside with the old dog close behind him. The house was in almost total darkness except for a couple of candles. He couldn't see anyone. The old dog ran off towards a bed room. Mitch followed. The dog was sitting at the feet on a boy. The boy was sitting on the side of his bed, not doing anything but staring down at the dog.

"Hello," Mitch managed to keep his deep voice quiet so as not to frighten the lad. The boy looked at him then back at the dog but did not speak. "Are you all right?" Mitch asked.

There was no reply. "Are you alone?" Again there was no response. It was becoming weirder. Mitch was beginning to understand why Zaylee had looked spooked. If the boy was not going to speak, there was nothing for it but to look around the house to see who else might be present. He went to the next bedroom and nearly fell over. There was a woman sitting on the side of a bed sucking her thumb.

He knew he would never forget this sight.

She took her thumb out of her mouth, and in a tremulous voice asked, "Are you a monster?"

He was rattled. Not since the day when Francine had been returned by the kidnappers, had he felt so alarmed. *Get it together,* he told himself. *This is not Afghanistan. This is just a woman sitting on the side of a bed sucking her thumb. It might be weird, but there was no law against it.*

"Why would you think that I'm a monster?"

"Because they are coming back again," she looked up at him, staring into his dark eyes. "You look like you could be one."

"I promise you that I'm not a monster."

"You could be lying. But please don't hurt Jude. If you want, you can have another finger, or two, or the whole lot for that matter, but please leave him alone."

His blood almost froze. What was she talking about fingers for? His wife's finger had been brutally amputated when she had been taken. Did this woman know something about what had happened to her? Except that she was weird, there appeared to be nothing really wrong with her. It was no crime to suck your thumb. She wasn't doing anything wrong. He wanted to get out of the place.

"If you're sure you're all right, I'll be leaving. Is there anything I can do for you?"

"There's nothing anyone can do for me until it's over. I told the doctor that. The end game has started but you probably know that."

He couldn't speak—the end game. What was she talking about? Surely there was nothing else that could go wrong. There was nothing he could say. He nodded to her as he left the room.

"Tell the doctor not to forget her promise," the woman said as he slammed the door shut.

Mitch hurried out to his vehicle. He sat still, not looking at either his wife or Zaylee. The two women stared at him, noticing how freaked out he was. "Is she all right?" Francine asked.

"What do you know about her, Francine?" he asked, ignoring Zaylee.

"I'm not sure. It's all mixed up in my head." Francine put her hands around her head and then put her thumb in her mouth. Mitch almost choked.

"Francine, what's happening to you?" He could not believe his eyes. He was aghast. Mitch put his arms around his wife and held her. He looked back at Zaylee. She saw the tears in his eyes. He was shaking his head in despair.

"What happened?" Zaylee softly asked. "Is the woman all right?"

"It's a bit hard to tell. She was very weird. There was a young lad there. She said some odd things. She said that there's nothing anyone can do for her until it's over. Then she said that the end game has started, but that I probably already knew that."

"She said much the same to me. She spooked me out. Can we please leave?"

Mitch continued to hold Francine who still had her thumb in her mouth as he spoke to Zaylee, "She said to tell you not to forget your promise."

Zaylee almost choked but before she could speak, Francine spoke. "I have to see her."

"I don't think that's a very good idea, Francine. Both you and Zaylee have just come out of hospital. You should both be home." Mitch turned on his motor.

"No, I have to see her. I think she's the answer." Francine opened the door. Mitch was bewildered. This was his wife who was always nervy and anxious, who never wanted to leave his side. Here she was walking up to the door of the house where he had been as fearful as at any time during his life.

Both Mitch and Zaylee followed her. Francine entered the house. She looked around. The boy was still in his room with the old dog. Mitch was behind her. Zaylee was looking around.

"Where is she? She was here a few minutes ago." Mitch was walking through the house.

"I think I might know." Zaylee walked into the bedroom where she had previously talked to Rina Wright.

"I know what to do. I'll sort it out," Francine interrupted, pushing her way in front of Zaylee. She lay down on the bed.

Mitch and Zaylee stood at the door entrance and stared at Francine as she lay on the bed.

"The monsters have gone. Would you like to lie on the bed with me?" Francine was holding her left hand as she spoke. Mitch and Zaylee thought she was off her head.

"Are you certain they've gone?" The voice was faint and fearful that came from under the bed.

"You can come out now. It's safe." Francine moved over to the side of the bed.

Rina Wright crawled out from under the bed. She was holding her left hand in her right. She lay on the bed beside Francine.

There was movement coming from the side door. Both Mitch and Zaylee looked up to see Andy Brown walk through the door. He was about to demand an explanation before Zaylee put her fingers to her lips so as to silence him. He was astounded to see big Mitchell Farraday as white as a sheet standing there with the doctor. When he looked into the bedroom, he was as perplexed as the rest of them.

He wanted to ask a thousand questions. His daughter had phoned him to say that there were strangers going in and out of Rina's house. She was worried. As she spoke to her father, Amanda burst into tears. "I don't understand what's going on, Dad. I love Rina and Jude, but something's not right. Please come quickly."

Andy stood at the door of the bedroom where he spent his nights with Rina. Only this time, he was just in time to see her crawl out from under the bed and lay beside an unknown woman. This was his Rina being bizarre, but it was his right and his right only to witness her bizarre ways. He wanted to shout out, to take her away from all these marauding eyes, but big Mitch Farraday signalled to him to be quiet. His wife was his main concern. She had been an anxious person for years, but had never been crazy.

Three sets of eyes watched the interplay between the two women lying on the single bed.

"Is the pain really bad?" Rina asked.

"Yes, it's intolerable." Francine replied.

"It does get better eventually. See mine. It's healed. Your hand will heal in time." Rina held up her left hand with the missing fifth finger.

"Mine still pains me," Francine replied. She held up her hand and showed Rina the missing ring finger of her left hand.

Rina took Francine's hand in her own and held it. "If you like, I could hold you until you go to sleep. Would you like that?"

"Yes, yes I would very much. I feel so incredibly tired. My head hurts." Francine felt Rina's arms go around her, hugging her like she was a small child.

"You go to sleep now. If the door rattles, I'll put the gag back in your mouth and crawl under the bed." Rina held Francine close as they both closed their eyes.

The three people who watched this incredible scene take place were in awe. No words could express what they were feeling. No words could explain what was happening. Andy was incredibly tired but knew he was facing another crisis. He signalled to the other two to follow him outside.

As they left, they checked that the boy was still in his room. Now he was on his bed. The old dog was on the floor beside him.

"I don't know what's going on here, but I want some explanation?" He directed his question to Mitch.

"You and me both," Mitch replied. "All I can tell you is that my wife insisted she see the woman who lives in this house. You saw the rest of it. I don't know what any of it means."

"What did Rina mean when she said that if the door rattles, she'll put the gag back in and crawl under the bed? That must mean something to you. She's your wife."

Mitch and Zaylee looked at each other. It was time to speak up. The sergeant wanted answers. "Some years ago, my wife was abducted. We paid a ransom and then she was returned minus a finger. We never heard from the kidnappers again. I don't know if this has got anything to do with what happened all those years ago. Francine also suffered a severe head injury and had no memory of what happened to her. Maybe it's all coming back to her. I'm not sure."

"How come the police knew nothing about this? You didn't think it was important enough to let us know?"

"They said they would kill her. As it was they sliced off her finger and did god knows what else to her. Just as well she lost her memory. She's never really been the same since."

"Did this happen when the two little girls disappeared and three members of your family were murdered?"

"Yes, around the same time," Mitch answered softly.

"How does Rina fit into all this?" Andy was visualising Rina's missing finger. His mind was leap frogging to so many scenarios. "How come you know Rina?"

"I don't. I've never seen her before. It was my wife. She insisted on seeing her. We stopped because Zaylee wanted to check on her patient."

"This is totally bizarre. For your information, Rina is my woman so if there's any looking after to be done, I'll be doing it. Why don't you take your wife home? I'll look after Rina and the boy."

"I'd like nothing better, believe me, but it's really up to my wife. There's something going on with her?"

"No kidding," Andy said as he returned inside.

The two women were sleeping, holding onto each other. Mitch told Zaylee to take his vehicle and go home as he would not be leaving Francine. The sergeant also said that he would be staying the night. The two men had little to say to each other. It had been a very wearing day. Zaylee said she would return the next morning and then left. There was nothing for the men to do except sit and wait.

They must have dozed. Early morning light was visible outside the windows. The door rattled. Francine woke with a start. "Get under the bed, Sarina, hurry."

Both Mitch and Andy woke at the same time and looked at the front door. It was like an apparition. There stood a wild looking, grey-haired woman in dark clothing with a gun in her hand pointing straight at them.

"What, more monsters? You're not supposed to be here." she said. "I don't remember you two. But it's the little monster and Rina that I want. Why don't you go get the two of them? Then I'll deal with you pair later."

The two men were stunned as the woman looked mad enough to pull the trigger. "One of you better hurry. Get the little monster first unless you want a bullet in your brain."

It was at this moment that Zaylee walked through the door to be confronted by the incredible scene of a wild-haired woman holding a gun pointed at Mitch and Andy. Mitch tried to signal to her to run, but Maria swung around and indicated that Zaylee join the two men.

Andy was standing, not quite certain what this crazy woman wanted. Just then Francine came to the door. "Hello Maria, what are you doing here?" Mitch was astounded at seeing his wife talking to this woman.

The woman looked started. "Francine—I wondered what happened to you. I thought they probably killed you. Looks like you got lucky. If you do as I say, you might remain lucky. Where's Rina?"

"Where do you think? She's right where you taught her to hide, Maria."

"Then you'd better get her out. She's got to pay, you know, just like the little monster."

There was more noise in the bedroom as Rina crawled out from under the bed. She was trembling as she said, "What are you doing here, Mother? What happened to you? Did the monsters find you?" Rina was at the bedroom door beside Francine.

"I think you've turned into a monster, Rina. You had no right disappearing. You left me." Maria still held the gun on the two men and Zaylee. They were all equally stunned by the scenario being played out in front of them.

"I thought you must have found a boyfriend or something. I didn't know what had happened to you." Rina sounded very frightened.

"No, no boyfriend and no death. But after I deal with you and the little monster, if I can't find the other monsters then I'll be ready for death again. I was almost there you, know."

Just then Jude stumbled out of his room with the old Alsation following him. Mitch and Andy stood in silence watching the woman. There was almost a look of glee on her face. Rina went to the boy and stood beside him.

"Please don't hurt him, Mother. He's only a boy. He's not a monster."

Francine remained at the bedroom door, her eyes glued to Maria. "Maria, you saved me, you saved Sarina. Why do you want to harm anyone now?"

Both Mitch and Andy stared in disbelief as Francine spoke. The name Sarina was resonating in their memories. Zaylee was shaking her head. Again she thought she might faint.

"You should know. Both of you should know what monsters are capable of. They never leave you alone. They come back in different disguises. The little monster is proof of that."

Mitch was processing all that he was hearing as fast as he could. Was it possible that Rina was Sarina? Was she still alive after all these years? The talk about monsters confused him at first but then he thought of the men who had been entombed. He took a chance, hoping these men were the monsters she was referring to.

"There are no monsters left, Maria. They're dead. They can't hurt you anymore."

Maria swung around to look at him. "Just how would you know that?"

"I know because we killed them. I swear to you they are all dead." Mitch was unaware of Andy's close scrutiny. Zaylee was remembering all she been through when Francine had been returned after her kidnapping and was so very critically ill. The Farraday brothers had all been in shock.

Maria still held the gun pointed at the two men. "It's not that easy to kill a monster, unless you shoot them through the head. I don't know how else you could get rid of them."

Mitch was taking a chance. "That's exactly what happened."

"What? You shot them? How many did you shoot?"

"All of them are dead. Doesn't really matter how they died? They're gone. They can never hurt you or anyone else again."

"I asked you how many? Anyway I don't believe you. There's a monster right there in front of me. He's the biggest monster of the lot and he's got to go. He caused me more grief than the rest of them put together."

"Please don't hurt him, Mother. He's my son. He hasn't hurt anyone." Rina was becoming tearful and begging mother to leave Jude alone.

"Oh, shut up Rina, or Sarina or whatever else you're calling yourself now. He's not your son and you know it."

"But he is my son, Mother. You were there when he was born. Please leave him alone."

Maria looked at Francine and Zaylee. "She's crazy, you know. She was always so gullible, and stupid, always sucking her thumb when she was a kid. But I'm tired of all this talk. It's time."

Maria gave them all one last look then changed her stance and lifted the gun towards Jude. Rina's senses were on high alert. She knew what mother was capable of and her intention was very clear. She flung herself in front of the boy just as her father had years ago when he protected her mother.

The bullet struck her. Rina fell to the floor. Jude looked at Rina lying on the floor. The old Alsation was whimpering, trying to push Jude out of the way, but Jude sat down on the floor beside Rina.

Both Andy and Mitch tackled the woman who was being called both Mother and Maria. Maria landed with a thump on the floor. Francine was screaming. Zaylee was in shock. For a moment she thought she was going to faint again, but she fought the light headedness and rushed to Rina.

Andy left Mitch holding the woman down while he phoned for more police and an ambulance. He kept his eyes on Rina as blood pooled beneath her. His heart was thumping rapidly at fear of losing her. Zaylee had come out of her shock and was giving first aid, trying to stop the blood that was oozing from Rina's left side abdomen.

Mitch yelled at Francine to find something to tie the woman up. Francine gave him the scarf that she had worn for her return home from hospital. Mitch quickly had the woman trussed up with her hands behind her back and his foot in the middle of her back. He looked up at Francine when he had done this.

She looked at him and he saw that she was crying. "Please be gentle with her, Mitch. She saved both our lives. She went through so much for both Sarina and me."

He could not believe what she was saying.

Just then a young girl came rushing through the door yelling out, "Dad, what's happening?"

Andy was with Rina. Zaylee was doing her best to staunch the bleeding. Andy looked at his daughter. "Stay outside the door, Amanda. I'll see you soon." Amada did no such thing. She ran to Rina and Jude. The old Alsation had not shifted from Jude's side. When Mitch looked over, he could see very little other than the cluster of people surrounding the bleeding woman.

Rina lay very quietly on the floor. It was a very weird feeling as the blood drained out of her. There wasn't pain as such in her side, it was more like a burn and that she was floating away. She kept her eyes open for as long as she could. She looked up at Andy and Zaylee and said, "It's not over yet. There's still more to come." She then closed her eyes.

There were police and paramedics rushing through the door. Sergeant Andy Brown had to drag himself away from the unconscious woman on the floor as paramedics came to her aid. He spoke to his officers and did his best to explain what had happened to his neighbour and the crazy woman who was trussed up on the floor. But more than anything, he wanted to speak to his daughter. He called her over.

"I want you to do something for me and not tell anyone. We're going to go into Rina's bedroom and I am going to give you a backpack. I want you to put it on as though it's yours, like you're going off to school. I want you to take it home and put it in my wardrobe. Will you do that for me?"

Amanda's eyes were full of concern. "Is it for Rina and Jude?" Her father nodded. She followed him into the bedroom where he made pretence of searching for identification. He pulled out the backpack and gave it to Amanda. She slipped it on. She didn't have to pretend she was upset, she was out-rightly crying.

"Go home, Amanda. It's almost time for school." He spoke loudly enough for all to hear.

There were more sad scenes as Rina Wright was taken away by ambulance. The woman known as both Mother and Maria was taken by police officers. Andy Brown remained in the house, still confused and trying his best to keep his emotions under control.

Mitch, Francine and Zaylee sat outside, giving police room to begin their investigations. Amanda returned and was about to take both Jude and the old Alsation home with her. Zaylee watched the young girl take the odd boy by the hand when she remembered the promise

Never in her wildest dreams had she given this promise any credence. It was almost more than she could manage as she staggered towards Amanda. "Would you and Jude like to come home with me? I promised Rina I would take care of Jude if anything happened to her."

"I'll have to ask dad. If he says okay, then I suppose it will be all right." Amanda told Jude to stay with the dog as she went to the door to speak to her father. When she returned, she said they could go with Zaylee as long as the dog could go with them.

The sergeant then came over to the trio and said Zaylee could leave with the children as long as she was available to give a statement later. Zaylee was feeling too overwhelmed to do anything else. She drove off to Matt and Mia's house with two children and an old dog.

Bewilderment—the word hardly seemed adequate to describe what had just happened. Mitch sat with his wife on the grass outside Rina's home. Francine was very quiet. Her hands were still around her head. He knew there had to be a million crushing thoughts swirling around in her mind.

Could the woman called Rina be his niece who had reputedly been murdered all those years ago? Was it possible? Both his wife and the mad woman had both called her Sarina.

"Are you feeling better, Francine? Do you feel like talking?" She looked at him. For the first time since he had met her, she looked strained, like age had crept up on her. "The police will want to talk to you, to both of us. If it's Sarina, it will be another shit storm."

Before she could speak, Andy Brown came out of the house and walked towards them. Mitch spoke quietly to his wife. "If you don't feel up to it, Francine, just say so. I don't want you getting sick again. From what I could make out, this is all to do with the time you were abducted. Maybe it might be better if you say nothing until we have some legal representation. I think I'd better phone Dax and the brothers."

He wasn't quite sure how to say that another missing niece may have returned. There was no easy way. He phoned Dax and told him that it was possible that they had found Sarina and would he let the rest of the family know. He didn't have to add that they would need the solicitors again.

Mitch and Francine waited for the sergeant. "I haven't got long. We'll have to talk privately about what else is going on here. I don't know what you Farradays are hiding now, but I'll do what I can to help you, but only for Rina's sake, remember that." Then he added, "In case she is Sarina."

Another officer joined them and then the questions were set to begin. They were taken to the police station. It was awkward for all concerned.

Mitch wanted first and foremost to protect his wife. He also wanted to protect himself and his brothers. What they had done all those years ago was a terrible deed. He did not know what to think about the two unknown women. His wife's mental state was his main focus.

For so many years he had wondered what had happened to her during her kidnapping. Her memories of this time had been erased by the severe head injuries she had sustained. At least that is what he thought had happened. But maybe she had just blocked it all out.

Francine was not coping. The police station with all its various personnel and equipment was freaking her out. She asked to be excused and went to the toilets where she vomited. When she returned, she was as white as a ghost. Mitch explained that his wife had just returned from hospital and was not well enough to assist in any way.

Dax had the solicitors in place, grim faced men who were willing to deflect any suggestion of wrong doing when it came to the Farradays. They were well apprised of the complexities of the Farraday history. They had all been there before and knew that the Farraday money was well worth all the hours and the billing.

Francine was taken back to Matt and Mia's house. There was no doubt she was very unwell. There were no more seizures, but there were noticeable tremors of her hands and her eyes stared unblinking at all those in the interrogation rooms. No one wanted to be responsible for having to deal with further seizures.

Mitch tried his best to answer Andy Brown's questions. It was very awkward for both of them. They both had their secrets. They both needed to keep quiet about many things. It eventuated that Mitch told his tale as simply as possible.

He said his sister-in-law who was a medical doctor wished to check on her patient, Rina. They had gone into her home where the woman did not appear at all well. His wife had been overcome by the woman's plight and had decided to stay the night. The lad called Jude had remained in his room. He did not know either of these two people. The lad had not spoken. Yes, Mitch did wonder why this was so.

He explained that he had stayed the night because his wife was so concerned about the woman, Rina. He reiterated again that he didn't know the woman and neither did his wife. But that was what his wife was like. She was a concerned and caring person and when she saw how distressed the woman was, she had decided to stay the night. The woman had not objected.

Mitch explained that he stayed with his wife as she had just been released from hospital following a severe seizure. Zaylee, his sister-in-law, had recommended that the woman, Rina, not be left alone. The doctor had gone home as she too had been unwell.

In all honesty, he could give no insight into why the woman called Maria had entered the house and had threatened them with a gun. Andy Brown kept asking questions. Mitch did not give any indication that the Detective Senior Sergeant of Police had been there for the entire interlude. Mitch kept answering questions as simply as he could.

His top-notch solicitor stood by giving direction and advice. No mention was made of the name Sarina Farraday although minds and hearts were breaking to find out if it was truly Sarina.

After the possible location of Lucia Farraday and the aftermath of what had followed, if this woman called Rina was actually Sarina Farraday, the fall out would be mammoth. There would be so many questions and so many ghosts to deal with—ghosts that needed to remain buried.

So far the name Sarina Farraday had not been mentioned but there was little doubt the woman called Maria would soon be telling all, including many references to his wife. Would this lead to the bodies they had entombed? He didn't want either of these two things to happen. So Maria also had the best solicitors that money could buy.

Maria was in a maniacal state, but she was able to comprehend from her solicitor that she was not to answer any questions. It was clearly evident from her behaviour that she was mentally unhinged. There was little credence given to her ravings.

Forensic officers were all over Rina's house. Andy knew both his and his children's fingerprints would be everywhere. But he had a good excuse for this. The woman looked after his children, or at least his daughter, whenever he was working late. She cooked meals for them and sometimes if he was very late and his daughter was asleep, they would stay the night. He made it clear that he did not know the woman called Rina at all well. She was a friend of his daughter.

Hard floors were something he would never get used to, but for once he was pleased that he had never slept with her in the bed. The blankets under the bed were easily explained. These were used when either he or his children slept at Rina's house. Not that it was anyone's business who he might have slept with, but he did not want to be excluded from the investigation. Conflicts of interest were best avoided. There was too much at stake.

As soon as he could, Andy went to the hospital. He knew she lived. Now it was just a matter of time until she recovered consciousness from the surgery that had removed the bullet. He tried his best to remain professional but it was becoming very difficult especially when he saw her being returned to the intensive care unit. She was so still and white. He knew he couldn't see her or be with her yet, but he had every reason to be concerned about her. After all he was the man in charge.

The doctors advised him that she would not be able to be questioned at least until the next day. In many ways, he was glad about this as it would give him time to visit the Farraday brothers. There was more to this story than the shooting. Before he left, he went to see Gabriel Farraday and the skinny woman who remained by his side. He could not believe his eyes as he walked into the room to find her lying on the floor.

"What's going on?" Gabe asked as the sergeant came into the room looking very rattled.

"There's been a shooting. A young woman has been badly injured." Did he dare say that she might be your sister? Just then Lu got up and sat beside Gabe.

"You might as well tell him," she said to Andy. He looked again at the frail woman who had just been through her own ordeal, or a lifetime of them.

"Tell him what?" the sergeant asked. Again those feelings of alarm were skirting around in his brain.

"Tell him that the woman is Sarina."

Both Gabe and Andy stared at her as if in a daze. Andy was shaking his head. "We don't know that yet. We don't know anything."

"What are you saying, Lu? Is she Sarina? How do you know?" Gabe was breathing rapidly. He could feel his heart beginning to gallop.

"It's something that happens. You must know what it's like when someone talks to you in your mind." No, neither of the two men knew what this was like. "She used to be called Sarina. She used to speak to me a long time ago but then she went silent. I heard her again tonight. She said she had been injured but was going to be okay. Then she told me that it isn't over yet—the end game. I don't always know what she means."

The sergeant had to sit down. Sweat was pouring off his brow. Here were Rina's words being spoken again by this skeletal woman. Andy watched Gabe stare up at the ceiling as if he was seeing ghosts. The young woman kissed Gabe on the cheek and went back to her blankets on the floor.

The hairs were standing up on his arms as he said goodnight. There was no reply from either of them. He wanted nothing more than to go home to bed and sleep for a month. But he had to be better prepared if the woman was Sarina.

47

Andy Brown took a chance that Mitch Farraday would be at his youngest brother's home. There was also his daughter and Jude to consider. Tom was with friends. When he arrived, it was to a plethora of vehicles. It looked like the entire clan had gathered.

He didn't knock but walked straight in. They were sitting together in the kitchen—big men, now all getting older and going grey, but impressive all the same. Four of them were drinking whisky and coffee. There was more noise further inside the house. He could hear women's and children's voices. The four men looked at him as he stood at the door.

"Come and have a drink. Take the edge off. You look like you could do with one." Mitch pulled out a chair.

"You want to tell me what's going on and I don't need you to piss me around? Tell me about your wife and the monsters? If Rina is Sarina, I need to be prepared. Just so you know I've been sleeping with her for months. So I have an invested interest in making sure she's protected."

He didn't mention the million dollars as he filled his glass for a second time. He didn't think there was enough whisky in the world to take the edge off.

The brothers were unsure what to say. How to tell the tale that had been going on for years? Their silence lasted a few minutes until they all indicated their agreement. Mitch began the narrative. The brothers drank steadily while he spoke. The women and children remained out of sight. They were now quiet, some sleeping, some remembering, some questioning.

"You told the woman, Maria, that the monsters were dead, that *we killed them*. What did you mean by this?" The sergeant was clearly fascinated by what he was hearing.

"That's right. I killed two of them and Denise shot the third. Do you remember her?" Andy nodded.

"What did you do with the bodies?" His blood felt it was curdling as he listened to the details of the Farraday family lives.

"We buried them. You don't need to know where. They had killed Danny, Tiffany and Carrie. As far as we knew, both Sarina and Lucia were dead. What would you have us do? Tell them to go away like good, little boys and behave themselves. Francine had been taken. You saw what they did to her. When she was returned, I thought she was dead. They would have killed me too except for the detective—Denise."

They all took a breather. Matt found another bottle. Glasses were refilled.

Mitch continued. "Then Michael was murdered and Denise was dead. I don't know how this happened. I always wondered if there was another one out there, and it seems there was. From what we can make out from Lizzie, he was one of them. I've no doubt it was this man who may have murdered Denise and somehow had Michael killed. If these two young women are Lucia and Sarina, then it looks like we were all wrong. There had to be others involved in their disappearance. That's another part of the story that's still unfolding. Now you know about as much as the rest of us."

"What about the woman who shot Rina?" The whisky was wearing off. Andy Brown was very tired.

"The woman is most probably one of them. I don't know for sure. My wife seemed to remember her. She called her Maria. Francine lost her memory during her abduction. It seems to be returning. You saw the interplay between Francine and Rina. It was very eerie. It spooked all of us."

"Still does," Andy replied. "If it turns out that Rina is your niece, what happens then? I know your wife called her Sarina but there will have to be DNA evidence to prove it. Heaven help us all, if she is Sarina. The media will be in frenzy. She will need to be shielded from the press. She's very fragile. I wouldn't put it past her to disappear again. I won't let that happen."

"None of us want that," Matt replied. "If she is Mick and Denise's daughter, then she'll need her family. She'll need stability. What about Gabe and Rafe? Do they know?"

"That's another story. I don't know where Raphael is. The young woman with Gabe as much as said Rina was Sarina. She spooked me. I don't understand it, but she seemed to be clairvoyant, psychic or something. Rina is the same. Gabe didn't say a word, just stared up at the ceiling. She also said that Rina told her that it's not over yet. Do any of you know what this means?"

Their blank expressions indicated they had no idea. The men were silent until Malcolm said, "We have to find out if she's my daughter. It's driving me crazy. This whole business is enough to drive anyone around the bend."

"Whoever these two young women turn out to be, they are going to need a lot of help as well as Lizzie and Francine." Mitch then added, "As well as Gabe. They have all been traumatised and brutalised. God knows what else has happened to them. We'll need the best head doctors that money can buy. It could take years." Mitch stood to leave. He had said enough. The bottles were empty.

"You can all camp here tonight if you don't mind sleeping on a mattress. I don't think any of us is sober enough to be driving. The women and children are already asleep." Matt indicated that Andy was included in the offer. His daughter was already asleep in the large lounge room along with Jude, Emmet, Finn and Rosa. Harry was still awake with ear phones keeping him company while he watched television.

It was a large house with many bedrooms purchased years ago when Matt and Mia had taken on the care of Gabe, Rafe, Arlo, Hope, Lizzie and Harry after the destruction of their parents.

It was a strange feeling for the sergeant to be bunking down on the floor of another home, but at least he had a mattress to sleep on. It was better than a hard floor. After the hospital reported Rina was improving, he slept far better than expected.

Before he dropped off, he thought about the four Farraday brothers. He had always thought of himself as being a man of integrity and honesty. Now all his values were being compromised— and all for a woman.

He thought of each of the brothers and wondered again if they were men of peace and good will. They seemed like they were. He was no longer sure how one managed to go through life maintaining peace and goodwill what with all that life threw at you.

Now he was privy to the knowledge that three men had been slain and buried—all done by the Farradays. Could he live with that?

Rina opened her eyes. Her mind was clear. She remembered everything that had happened. There was no pain. The hospital room was very quiet and secluded. There were some outside noises but nothing too penetrating. She had a room with wide windows so that she could look out and see the gentle swaying of many trees. She felt at peace.

Hospital staff came and went. They were all very caring and treated her with tenderness. Then he came into the room, accompanied by another officer. A solicitor was also there stating that he was there to represent her. Mitch Farraday stood in the background.

Her eyes locked on Andy's. He looked very tired. Rina gave him a small smile. His heart did a triple jump. It was her Mona Lisa smile, the one that had grabbed him and stolen his very being.

"What do you remember?" The sergeant gently asked.

"All of it," she replied. "When I saw Francine it all started coming back to me. I know I am Sarina Farraday. I know I was taken when I was a small child. I used to call the men who took me 'monsters'. Maria saved me. When they sliced off my finger, they tied me up in a garbage bag and threw me into a dumpster. Had it not been for Maria, I would have died. Then they took Francine and they cut off her finger. I used to hide under the bed whenever the door rattled. Then they took Francine away again. She was very ill. I thought she had most probably died. Then Maria took me out of the room and we drove away."

"Stop if you're too tired. We can do this later on if you wish."

"No, I want it to be finished or at least as much as it can be. There's more to come, you know." Andy looked at Mitch. There were the words again. They both felt the chill that went up their spines.

She continued her story about Maria and about Jude being born. She said that she had always believed Jude was her son because Maria had told her this many times. This was how she had become two people—one before Jude was born and the other after he was born.

She explained how she had reared him when she was just a little girl. Maria had by then become her mother and then she began to change. She was no longer the gentle woman who had saved both herself and Francine.

Maria hated Jude. Rina remembered back to the day when she found her mother with her hand across his face. After that happened, Jude never cried again. Mother had always told Rina she had to be invisible so that the monsters would not find either of them again.

Rina shut her eyes as she relived her memories. She spoke for a long time. She related how one day mother just disappeared and never returned, so she decided she would leave with Jude. Andy Brown was fearful she might speak of the money but she made no mention of it. How would she be able to explain a million dollars?

She was tired and said she needed to sleep. The solicitor and the other officer left. Mitch went to her and told her he was her uncle and that he would take care of her. He left her with Andy who stayed with her until she was asleep.

Mitch went to Gabe's room. The young woman called Lu was curled up in a chair. Raphael and Lizzie were also in the room. They were all silent as he came in.

"I need to tell you all something—it's about Sarina. It looks like she's been found. She's here in the hospital. She was shot yesterday but she's going to pull through. It's another horrific tale. I don't know where to start."

"It's all right, Uncle Mitch. Why don't you go home to Francine? You look so very tired. We'll find out soon enough." Lizzie's feelings of guilt were magnified. She wondered how she would ever be able to confess to what she had done. How did she even know if what she had read in evil Leon's documents were true?

Lu and Lizzie looked at each other. In their hearts they knew that Rina was Sarina. Had they in some way suspected this when they had met in the park? They had looked at each other's scars. None of them had confessed how these had been acquired. Their wounded spirits had such enormous scars it seemed like they would never be healed. Yet here they were, with life becoming better, with something more in their hearts than the pain, fear and shame that they had endured for so many years.

It was not a time for words. Lizzie sat holding hands with Raphael. He could not take his eyes off her. He had told her so many times that he loved her so that she now believed him.

Gabriel was improving. Youth and good health were great healers. His hand would never be as adept as it was once, but he had movement in it. The burns were also healing. They would always be deep and noticeable. The hospital spoke of further surgery, skin grafts. But he didn't think he wanted this. All the L's that were now imprinted on his body would be his tribute to Lu. He couldn't call her Lucia yet.

All Lu wanted was to be by his side. Fragments of the five rules still came back to haunt her but she was learning to drive them from her mind. Zaylee had been to see her and had told her that when she had done the blood tests when she was so very ill, she had checked her DNA and it was certain that Malcolm was her father. It would take time for Lu to come to terms with this knowledge.

*

Zaylee had her own secret. She wanted to tell someone as she was so full of excitement, but who would she tell and what would it prove. It would probably just dig up more stress for everyone. But what it did do was to fulfil her. She might never know who her birth mother was but she now knew who her father and half-brother had been. She had only met Michael once, when he had been consumed with grief at the loss of his daughter.

She escaped to the peace and quiet of Miriam's Place where she welcomed her brother into her heart and then mourned him. But now she had a bonus in her life, three of them. She had two nephews and now a niece all of her own blood line. She had her own son as well. She had found her heritage.

*

There was a reunion of two brothers and a sister. Rina was nervous but when she saw them she could not keep the smile off her face or the laughter from her voice. Instantly, she remembered them. She had met them both before, one outside the Royal Mail Hotel and the other in Sundial Park. The twins could not believe they had both spoken to her and had no realisation of who she was. How strange was fate? They hardly spoke, just sat quietly looking at each other. There was so much to say. Where do you start?

"Do you still play solitaire?" Gabe asked.

"Not that often," Rina replied.

"Lizzie plays it all the time. Sorry, do you remember Lizzie, Sarina?" Raphael's enthusiasm was bubbling over. Lizzie never left his mind.

Rina smiled at them both. "I know both Lizzie and Lu. I'd like to see them some time when they're up to it." They talked of insignificant things, nothing deep. Nothing was discussed that would cause any of them more bad dreams.

Then Lu and Lizzie arrived. They had given the twins time to reunite with their sister. They kissed and cried. Three women united again. This time none of them showed their wounds. This time there was no need for shame.

How do you announce it to the world? It couldn't be kept quiet much longer. There was as much protection provided as the hospital would allow. Her privacy was guaranteed. After the isolated life she had led, it would be a long time before she would ever have the confidence to confront a hungry media.

Then Mitchell Farraday called a press conference. Detective Senior Sergeant Andy Brown was also there. It was left to the solicitors to be the spokespersons.

Headlines flashed across newspapers, internet and television screens. Murdered girl, Sarina Farraday, found alive—how could this be? What had happened to her? Where had she been all these years?

Then the question of her father being jailed for her murder was brought into focus. How had the police got it so wrong? Andy Brown felt the full force of media and police scrutiny which is what he had expected. He knew his time had come. His policing days were over.

As Rina improved, he handed in his resignation. He still had to maintain the proprieties. He still had his children to protect as well as Rina. It was hard staying away but she understood. It was as if she could read his mind. When he thought about it, he realised that she probably could. He would just have to get used to it.

There would have to be further court cases. The Farradays were facing so many. There was Lucia, Gabriel, Lizzie, Maryanne, and now Sarina. There was also the woman called Maria. What the brothers also wanted was that Michael's name be cleared. It would take years. Finally, it could all be put behind them.

Francine had escaped scrutiny. There was never any hint that three other men had been killed. None of the brothers was quite sure why they had never been reported missing. Why, in all the years the man, who had kept Lizzie as a slave, had never come forward?

When she was well enough, Rina was discharged into her family's care. She disappeared during the night. The Farradays had enough property in the area to hide a person for years. But there were the medical visits. Although they were fearful of anyone delving into their subconscious, the three young women were eventually convinced by Dr Zaylee Lang of the need for such therapy.

So the healing began. It would be long and arduous. It was not easy talking about the graphic details of the horror they had been through, especially for Lucia. Some things they kept to themselves but overall it was therapeutic. Whether it was the psychological intervention or father time, it didn't really matter.

Mitch was learning about the terror that Francine had lived through. As with Rina, it was all coming back to her. She cried in his arms every night, cried for the little girl who had tried to shield her, cried for the woman who had cared for her but who had also lost her mind. He listened to her words and her description of the revulsion that Maria had to face on a daily basis.

He knew who this woman was. She was the daughter of Geraldine Wright and Alan Farraday, his half-sister. Like his brother before him, he vowed he would do everything he could to help this woman. She was probably the biggest victim of the lot. Alan Farraday's secrets, sex and lies were still haunting them. None of the lies, lust and silence had ever really gone away.

Weeks went by and with time, life settled down. If it could be called settled what with ongoing police investigations, court hearings, various enquiries, medical care, counselling and sorting out the lives of so many who had been touched by this latest spate of terrible events.

Hope, Lizzie and Harry visited their mother, not often, but occasionally. Memories remained hurtful. Maryanne still lived in another world. Danny was sometimes the evil one or else he was her beloved. A ruined mind was piteous to observe.

Francine got up the courage to visit Maria. She took her husband with her. Maria seemed calm. They spoke about how she was feeling. Francine was uncertain if she should mention Rina's name, fearful that Maria would again start raging. As they were leaving, Maria did ask about Rina but she never mentioned her own son, Jude.

"Give it time, Francine. It might take years before she accepts him as her own. It might never happen. All we can do now, is make sure they are both okay."

Jude remained with Matt and Mia. He became part of their household. Matt had him doing outside chores. Harry treated him like a younger brother—a slow, younger brother who needed a lot of attention and pushing to get him moving, but a brother all the same. Finn and Rosa often stayed as well, as did Emmet.

Andy Brown's children, Tom and Amanda, had also become frequent visitors and slept there most nights. Their father had left the police but he still drove away each evening and returned the next morning. His children weren't stupid. They knew he went to stay with Rina.

There were times when Jude looked lost. They all knew he was missing Rina, the only mother he had ever known. He was also being given specialised educational assistance. He saw Rina as often as was safe. She was still healing. Rina remained hidden away from the media spot light while her slow recovery continued.

Zaylee had kept her promise that Jude would be looked after, but it was Matt and Mia who were doing this. Zaylee had her own husband who she was concerned about as he tried to establish a relationship with his lost daughter. She continued to feel unwell.

Gabe and Lu were back living at Gabe's home with the two dogs. He still had a long way to go, as did Lu. But they were happy. Their time seemed to fly by. There was so much rehabilitation. There were also the dogs to be looked after. They often went back to Matt and Mia's place and fooled around with their young cousins. The dogs looked on haughtily but they were now used to the children.

Malcolm visited whenever he could. Lu was becoming used to him. She would smile when he entered the room. Black devil was the clincher. He saw her holding it in her arms. Gabe kept his distance. They had to find their own path. It happened while they were visiting with Matt and Mia.

"Can I look at the bear, Lu?" Malcolm asked. He dare not call her Lucia. He was taking small steps, a little bit at a time.

"Why?" she asked. Next to Gabe, black devil was her most prized possession.

Malcolm looked at her. Now that he knew for sure that she was his daughter, it was all he could do not to take her in his arms and cuddle her as he had as a child.

"Your mother and I gave you two bears one Easter. Your mother gave you a black teddy bear and I gave you a brown one. You really loved them. They were so big, you could hide behind them. Do you remember that?"

Lu looked at the bear, so old and worn with his missing arm. She stared at him. She remembered what she had done to him, the times she had thrown him against a wall, had stuck her fingernails into him. She remembered how she had hated him. But then she would always take him back, apologise and she would love him all over again.

She looked at her father and started crying. Gabe knew this was a defining moment between father and daughter. "Your mother loved you so very much, Lucia. We both did. You were our life."

"I don't know what I remember," she replied in a weak, tremulous voice. "But I think I would like to be called Lucia again. Would you mind calling me Lucia instead of Lu?" She looked at Gabe first and then at her father.

"I would love to," Gabe replied. "That's who I married—Lucia Farraday. That's who I will always cherish."

Malcolm looked in astonishment at both Gabe and his daughter. "What do you mean?"

"It's pretty simple. We got married. Lots of people do. Lucia is my wife."

Malcolm again stared at the frail woman who was his golden-haired daughter of years ago. He looked at the man who had saved her from more torture and who had ultimately married her. He had to walk outside. His emotions were about to overwhelm him.

"Go to him, Lucia," Gabe said. "He really needs you."

She walked outside and smiled at her father. It was not the time for great demonstrations of love and affection. Instead she took his hand and stood beside him as together they looked at the young cousins playing cricket in the yard. James and Boag stood guard. The old Alsation lay curled up under a tree watching the game progress. Black devil was left with Gabe to be looked after.

Gabriel eventually had to speak to his wife about what had occurred on that fateful day when Uncle Lucas had come to visit. He had never seen the DVDs. He didn't want to. But he did ask her about the second bag. The one he had buried under the dog kennels.

She smiled at him as she said, "That's my gift to you if you want it."

"You're my gift, Lucia. I don't need anything else."

"You might. You probably won't be able to do heavy work again because of your hand. You're not as strong as you once were. Maybe in time, you will be. What's in the bag is ours. It will help with our future."

"Do you want me to dig it up?"

She shrugged her shoulders. "It's not doing much good where it is now."

The dogs followed him as he found a shovel. They looked on with curiosity. Gabe was exhausted by the time he found the bag wrapped in plastic. It was substantial in size. He dusted it off. Lucia was looking amused.

"Do you want me to open it?"

"Sure, but maybe we better go inside."

He carried the bag inside. He took some time before he removed the plastic that covered it. He looked up at her in amazement as he opened the bag. They looked at the contents together.

"Wow, I don't believe it." He put his hands into the bag filled with bundles of notes. "Wow" he said again. "How much is here?"

"A lot, it's mine, I earned it. Not that I ever want to remember how. Now it's ours. We can do whatever we like with it. You won't have to be dependent on anyone if you can't work like you used to."

They sat together on the back steps, talking about their future, what they would do. "We'll have a honeymoon," he said.

She looked away from him. "We could start the honeymoon back at the creek bank at Sunshine," she kept her head down. She felt too shy to look at him.

"How about we get started now? Sunshine will have to wait until I'm all healed up." He kissed her gently on the lips.

*

Gabe and Rafe were both very contented men in spite of having to live through the fall out of the recent events in their lives. Gabe asked his brother to drive him to Sunshine as there was something he needed to do. He was mindful of the court order banning him from driving. He also had limited use of his left hand. Rafe was only too happy to oblige.

The twins were spending more time together. They had more in common than ever. The women in their lives had very close bonds. It was a fine, sunny morning as they drove around winding roads that took them to their old home.

It was also the same fine, sunny morning when Rina woke up beside Andy, again screaming in horror. He could scarcely believe it. Ever since her shooting, she had been able to sleep through.

They had even progressed to a mattress on the floor. Life had been progressing well. She was becoming stronger; could walk almost upright again and had embraced electricity. They had even spoken about the money in the backpack.

"What is it, Rina?" he asked, holding her until her trembling stopped.

"It's my brothers. They're in trouble. You have to help them, Andy."

Not again, did it never stop? His thoughts were conflicted as he looked deeply into her dark brown eyes. Just for a moment he wanted to run, to put as much distance between the two of them as he could. The brown eyes held him and he knew they would hold him forever.

"Do you know what's wrong with them?"

"All I know is that they are in terrible danger. I don't know more than that. Please help them, Andy. I promise I won't ask anything of you again. You can have all the money if you'll help them. Please, please, help them. If you can't, then will you please get my uncles, get somebody, please."

"Okay, Rina, I'll do what I can. Do you know where they are?" He pulled on his jeans as he saw her shake her head.

"Try Lucia," she said. She watched him on his phone, heard him speak a few word to Lucia. He went back to her and kissed her goodbye. "This is it, Andy, this is the end of it—the end game."

Her hands were around her head. He could almost see the turmoil in her mind. The red scarring on the edge of her left hand was more vibrant than ever. As he left her, she seemed to be talking to someone. He thought he heard her mention her parents.

*

Sunshine was lush and green when Gabe and Rafe arrived. They talked about what it would take to do up the old house. The gardens were blossoming. There were flowering shrubs everywhere.

"Mum and dad would love this," Rafe said as they pulled up. Gabe made no comment. He found it hard to talk about his parents.

He told Rafe he was going up to the Big Rock. Rafe said he would spend some time in the prayer room. He had a lot to be thankful for. Gabe did not comment. He was learning to control his judgements of others. Conscience was a funny thing—each to his own. He, of all people, was the last to judge. How many hard lessons had he learned during this recent period of his life?

Rafe sat in the prayer room. He thought of Lizzie, how much he loved her. He had it in his mind that he would ask her to marry him. His mind swirled around the intricacies of getting married and once he was wed, what he would do then? Gabe and Lucia had done it and they were getting along pretty well. Not that Gabe was up to working yet. There was a lot to think about.

His parents floated back to him. It was so unfair how their life had turned out. They would never know their daughter lived. Then again maybe they did. He felt very close to them as he sat on the lounge chair staring at the blind statue as he listened to the creek flowing outside.

He was very deep in thought because he didn't hear a thing until he heard footsteps behind him. *That was quick. Gabe was back already. God only knew what he found that was so fascinating up at the Big Rock.*

The whisper came from behind his left shoulder. "If you know what's good for you, Mr Farraday, you'll stay where you are."

Raphael almost jumped out of his skin. "What the heck? Who are you? What's going on?"

He was about to turn around, when he felt what he thought was a gun being shoved into the back of his head. His fear was paramount. It was another nightmare. It was beyond belief.

"I'm making sure that you're not able to slit anyone's throat. You're just like your mother, full of yourself."

"I don't know what you're talking about. I don't know who you are. What do you want?" Rafe was doing his best to control his nerves. At that moment he wished he was more like Gabriel. That he had his killer instincts. That he had the guts to turn around and belt this person who was threating him.

"I'm the person who did your mother and father. I'm the person who is going to do you. Did you think you could get away with your threats? Not likely."

Raphael knew he was in a dire predicament. All he could think to do was to play for time. Maybe Gabriel would return. Although what he could do was beyond him. He only had one useful arm and still suffered the pangs of his healing burns.

"What do you mean when you said you did my mother and father?"

"Just what I said, I got rid of the two of them. Your mother was easy. Come to think of it, so was your father. It's amazing what a few pills and a few privileges will do. Anyway, enough with the talk, I don't have much time. Have you got any last words?"

"I sure do," the voice behind him was low and menacing. There were no more words spoken. The knife that Gabe held in his hand pierced the right carotid artery of the man who held a gun to his brother's head.

"I promised you when I was a boy that I would slit your throat and that's just what I'm about to do. You just said you did my mother and father. Well, I'm doing you."

The man lifted the gun slightly as he fired. Raphael was unclear what he felt. He slid to the floor. There was something very wrong with his head.

As the man fired the gun, he swung around to see an identical face to the one he had just shot looking straight at him. He felt the knife in his neck. He could feel blood pouring out as Gabriel pulled the knife out from the right side of the neck and then drew it from left to right until a gap appeared that partially separated his head from the rest of his body.

Gabe held the man up with his injured left arm. He pulled the knife away from the bleeding throat. Neither brother was sure where the bullet had gone. Raphael could still feel and hear the bullet reverberating throughout his head. He remained on the floor but as he looked around he was astonished to see an unknown man with blood pouring down his chest.

Raphael could not believe his eyes.

Gabriel still held the man with his left arm. The knife remained in his right hand but was held out to the side of the dying man as Gabe slowly lowered the man to the floor.

Strange things went through Gabe's mind as the blood pooled and the room became a mess. He remembered back to another time when he had made a mess of this very same room. It was when his parents had been murdered.

Raphael was now sitting upright on the floor. It was a moment of disbelief. He had heard the words the man spoke. Here was the killer of his parents. He looked up at his brother. Their eyes locked.

Gabe left the man and went to sit beside Rafe. They held each other as once before they had held each other while lying under palm fronds in Sundial Park while two men tried to hunt them down.

"You better check my heads still on properly. It doesn't feel too good." Raphael managed to say. Gabe looked through his brother's hair. When he removed his fingers, they were covered in blood.

"Looks like you've got a helluva groove there, but it doesn't look like it's too deep. I think you'll live although you'll probably have a permanent part in your hair."

The brothers sat looking at each other until Rafe said, "You've done it again, Gabe. You've made another mess of the room." The brothers started laughing. Rafe had blood pouring down his face and shoulders. Gabe started to shake. Rafe put his arms around his brother's shoulders. They sat that way until the shaking stopped.

"What do we do now? Is he dead?" Rafe asked as Gabe helped him stand. They looked at the man on the floor.

"He sure looks like he's dead to me. I wonder who he is. You heard what he said, didn't you? He's the bastard who killed our parents."

Gabriel again looked at the man bleeding out on the floor of the prayer room. Then he went out into the kitchen and sat at the table. Raphael followed him. Gabe had tears in his eyes. Raphael sat beside him. "That's two men I've killed," he said. "I don't understand any of this. Why does it keep happening?"

"I don't know. But if you hadn't, either one or both of us would now be dead. But we need some help. I'm going to call Mitch. You wait here, Gabe. Make some tea, something."

Raphael left his brother and walked outside. Mitch answered on the first ring. "You've got to come to Sunshine, Mitch. You've just gotta come now."

Mitch did not question his nephew. Had it been Gabe he would have had a million questions, but Raphael was not Gabriel. He was the steady one, not the risk taker.

It seemed a long time that the twins sat on the front steps of the house at Sunshine. But Mitch had moved quickly. The words his niece had spoken still haunted him. She had said there was more to come. As he pulled up, he took one look at his nephews sitting on the front steps and immediately knew more had come. Was this the end game?

"What's up?" Mitch asked, startled at seeing the blood on the brothers.

"I had to kill him. He's the one who murdered our parents." Gabe had a haunted look in his eyes.

Mitch walked inside. The blood spots were an easy trail to follow. He went into the prayer room. The twins heard him swear. A man lay on the floor. The wide gash that partially separated his head from the rest of his body was clearly visible. He looked up at the blind statue. It had stood there for so many years. He wondered just how much it had seen, how much it knew.

He stayed for a few minutes before returning to the twins. Again he could not believe his eyes as he watched Andy Brown get out of his vehicle. "What do you want?"

"Rina asked me to check on her brothers. They don't look so good. What's going on?" A blind man could see the twins were a mess.

"Not your business," Mitch replied. "The boys will be all right. I'll see to that. You can go now."

"I don't think so. I told you I have a vested interest. Rina is their sister. She told me that something is wrong. I want to know what it is."

"You don't need to know anything," Mitch replied. "Just go. I need to contact my brothers."

Andy gave no indication that he intended going anywhere. The twins looked on as the two men fought their verbal battle. "Was it the fourth man? Is that what's happened?"

Mitch started swearing. "Why don't you just go? It's not your business. Haven't you got enough going on dealing with Sarina? You don't need anything else coming down on your head."

The former sergeant of police pushed past him and walked into the house. He vaguely remembered it from when Sarina had disappeared all those years ago. He too followed the blood trail.

When he looked down at the man lying dead on the floor of the prayer room, just as Mitchell Farraday had, he started swearing, only more forcibly. The words could be heard from outside. It wasn't long before he joined them.

His silence lasted a few more minutes while he sat on the steps beside the others. "Bloody hell, do you know who that is?"

Their blank looks were answer enough. "It's the deputy commissioner of police. What in the hell has happened here?"

Words were beyond them. Why had this man wanted to destroy them? They looked up as more vehicles approached. The brothers had arrived—big, grim men who expected the worst.

For a moment, Andy Brown was alarmed for his safety. Hadn't these very same men already been involved in the killing and burial of three men? Was he to be included in their grim deeds?

But then he thought again. No, it was impossible. He couldn't be made to disappear. Rina knew where he was. They wouldn't do anything to harm their niece, not after all she'd been through. His ace up his sleeve was her clairvoyance. The thing that had been putting shivers up his spine for months would surely be his salvation if push came to shove.

The brothers assembled before their nephews. "What's going on?" Mark asked. If they were surprised to see the former sergeant of police present, they made no comment, merely looked at him.

"The man inside in the prayer room was the one who murdered our parents. He was going to shoot me through the head but Gabe came along just in time and slit his throat. He died." Rafe kept his story short and sweet. He wasn't up to long speeches. His head ached. There was no further bleeding only the drying blood that was caked over his face and neck.

The three brothers went inside. They returned quickly. "He's dead all right," Malcolm said. "You did a good job, Gabe. Who is he?"

"He's the frigging deputy commission of police." Andy answered. "We're facing the biggest shit storm of all now."

The brothers looked at each other until Matt spoke. "Maybe not, we've done it before. We don't have much option. He killed

Mick and Denise so as far as I'm concerned, it's no more than he deserved. I say we get on with it. We'll think out the repercussions while we do it."

Matt never thought he would be grateful for a violent death. Relief swept through him knowing this man who had been responsible for killing the two people who had cared for him during his childhood and youth, had met a brutal death.

For so many years he had kept the evidence hidden just to see it go up in smoke when the granny flat at the Smythe property burnt down. He had all but given up on justice for Michael and Denise. To think it was their injured son who had to be the one to bring justice for their deaths.

"We better get a move on. I'll get my tools." Mark hurried back to his SUV.

"Is this the part where you bury them?" Andy Brown was beginning to sweat at the thought of what he was mixed up with. It was one thing for these Farraday men to kill and bury three bad arses but it was altogether another to kill and bury the deputy commissioner of police.

"How about you lend a hand instead of fighting with your conscience? Gabe and Rafe aren't much good to us. Gabe's only got one good hand and Rafe's got the mother of all headaches."

Mitch was as yet uncertain what to make of Andy Brown. Sure they had covered for each other when Sarina was shot. But how much could he be trusted with this current circumstance?

"I don't understand you lot. I never will." Andy took the spanner and crow bar that Mark handed him.

After that, not much was said. There was a job to be done and the quicker the better. Andy was directed to follow Mark, Malcolm and Matthew. It was no easier than the last time. The bolts were rusting into the floor. The old monstrosity of the iron bed remained, just older with the paint flaking off that Matthew had applied all those years ago when they had entombed the three men.

Mitch didn't want to do it, but he needed his nephews to get a hold of them-selves and help him wrap up the body, hose off the blood and clean up the mess. As they worked away, he told them what had happened all those years ago when Francine had been kidnapped. How he thought they had killed her. How they had been going to kill him. How their mother had shot one of them and he had cracked the neck of a second man and cut the throat of a third.

At mention of this, Gabe looked away. In that instant, uncle and nephew were bonded forever in the blood of men whose throats they had cut. It was something no one should ever be forced to do. Gabe asked himself if he would ever feel normal again. Mitch smiled at him then, and he knew that all things could be overcome. There could be life after such horrendous events.

"Was that the day when mum got out of jail?" Raphael didn't know how much more he could take. His head was thumping. Now he was hearing what his mother had been forced to do.

She had been given no time at her beloved Sunshine. She had killed a man on the first day of her release from jail and been murdered on her second day home. Nothing was fair. Their father had been jailed for the murder of Sarina and this man had orchestrated his murder.

"Geez, I can't take this anymore." This time it was Raphael Farraday who kicked the body that was lying wrapped in a blanket and then went outside to the front veranda where he belted the railings of the front steps.

Like Gabe had done all those years ago, he would have run up into the mountains except the skies had darkened and rain was falling. The fine, sunny morning had disappeared.

After a few minutes, Gabriel went out to get his brother and then they dragged the body into the bedroom that had been their grandparents. The brothers and Andy Brown had shifted the heavy, iron bed. They all stared at the opening that led down meters into the ground under the house.

"Who wants the privilege?" Matthew asked. He didn't know why he asked. It wasn't as though anyone would want to go down into the hole of death.

"I'll do it. I'd love to," Gabe said.

"No you won't," Matt replied. "This is my job. Besides you need two good hands for a job like this."

It never got any easier. The bones crackled beneath him. The blankets that the three bodies had been wrapped in were falling apart. He thought of the fourth body that had lain there for so long. For some reason he imagined it was female.

He dragged the body of the deputy commissioner of police as far along as he could then he made sure the blankets covered him. He crawled back to the entrance where his brothers and Andy helped him out.

Matt brushed himself down—never again did he want to go down into that dark space. This time he was taking out extra insurance. "Before we put the cover over, there's something I need to do."

He went over to the jewellery box where he had left the bone fragment of the first person who had lain in that dark tunnel for so long. He knew his mother had kept a small book of Psalms there. He pulled it out. It was very old and faded. It took him a few minutes to find it. Then he started reading.

The Lord is my shepherd; I shall not want. He maketh me lie down in green pastures; He leadeth me beside the still waters. He restoreth my soul; He leadeth me in the paths of righteousness for his name's sake.

The men stood silently as they looked down into the dark hole where five bodies now lay.

Yea, thou I walk through the valley of the shadow of death, I will fear no evil. For thou art with me; thy rod and thy staff they comfort me. Thou preparest a table before me in the presence of mine enemies; Thou anointest my head with oil, my cup runneth over; Surely goodness and mercy shall follow me all the days of my life, And I will dwell in the house of the Lord for ever.

"Let that be the end of it. No more, never again. None of us should ever have to walk through the valley of the shadow of death again." Matt said. "We'll put the bed back and get the hell out of here."

There were many hands to help so it did not take long.

"What happens now?" Andy asked. "It's not as though he's unknown. The deputy commissioner of police can't just disappear. He's an important man."

"A prime minister disappeared once as I recall. He went for a swim and was never seen again," Mitch replied as he helped to clean up the blood and grime left in the bedroom and prayer room. "Does that give you any ideas?"

"I don't know what you mean?"

"Come on. You were a copper not so long ago, so think. This man we entombed had no identification on him. He's in a hire car. When he came out here he had murder on his mind. Gabe had made a threat when he was shot, that he would get whoever had murdered his parents, so he knew Gabe had to be silenced. He didn't know what evidence was left behind. For all he knew, the photographs and video of what happened when he tried to throttle Denise still existed. He knew where Gabe was. How did he know that? Pretty simple, it was because he followed him. It's hardly likely he would have told your buddies at the police station what he planned to do. So he liked to swim alone. Many people do. How's anyone going to know the difference?"

"So what are you saying? We plant just enough evidence so that everyone thinks he just happened to go for a swim and was drowned, or was taken by a shark. It doesn't gel."

"How is anyone going to prove otherwise? Do you think anyone gives a stuff that he murdered my brother and sister-in-law or tried to kill my nephews? You, of all people should know better."

Mark listened to Mitch speak. No one was too sure about what to think of Andy Brown. He was an unknown. Sure he had helped their niece, was caring for her, sleeping with her, but was that enough to ensure his loyalty? He had even helped to entomb the deputy commissioner of police. But would he develop a conscience?

"We'll get rid of his vehicle tonight. We'll leave it at one of the isolated beaches. Eventually, someone will report it. The hire car company will be tracked down and they will be able to give a description of who hired it." Mark looked at Andy Brown. "How about you give me a lift home after its done? Gabe and Rafe aren't up to it. Both Mitch and Malcolm have got sick wives. Matt is already looking after Jude and Amanda. That just leaves you and me. So what do you say? I'll meet you here at midnight and we'll get rid of the car."

Andy Brown was trapped. He had no option but to go along with the plan. He felt sick. This was beyond anything he had done in his life. But when he thought about it, Bill Boyd would have killed Rina's brothers in cold blood. He knew he would lose her for sure if she ever knew he had failed her request to help the twins. He nodded his head and told Mark he would meet him at Sunshine at midnight.

"How about we have a beer together tomorrow?" Matt suggested. "Mia will soon whip up something to eat. Bring the women. You never know, it might be fun."

"We can always get a taxi home," Gabe commented. He was still thinking about the backpack and gun that had disappeared from the cave at the Big Rock. It was the thing he had set out to bring home, to share with his brother.

It was ironic that the anger he had felt when he saw they were gone was the catalyst that had brought him running back down the hill in swift, short time. It was his anger that had saved his brother. His anger at the disappearance of the money had turned out to be the best thing that could have happened.

It was another fine, sunny day when the Farraday family gathered at Sunshine. There was huge reluctance by the Farraday men to return there but Lizzie was insistent. After all, this was the place where Raphael had first broken her heart and then mended it.

It was a big event. None of the Farraday weddings had been as big a splash as this one. In fact, none of them had even caused a ripple. Low profiles had always been the order of the day. As long as the festivities occurred outside and not in the house, the brothers went along with it.

The ceremony was over. Lizzie was radiant in her cream and coffee coloured dress. Raphael was devastatingly handsome in his dress suit. They couldn't keep their eyes off each other. The younger cousins were all involved. Finn and Emmet were in charge of keeping the bridesmaids and best men on track.

Harry made sure Jude knew what he had to do. Andy Brown's children, Tom and Amanda enjoyed every second of the festivities. Their father was almost as dreamy eyed as Raphael as he kept looking at his new wife.

Mr and Mrs Lee catered for the event. They were in their element. They would do anything for Gabe and Lucia. There were red baskets full of sweet treats for all involved.

Even Mr and Mrs Baxter had been flown from Sydney for the occasion. They had the offer of a house for whenever they felt the need of a holiday. It had been a very emotional reunion for Rina. They had been her only friends and support while she had lived her bizarre life with Maria and Jude. When Maria's name was mentioned, they had little to say. They had always considered her to be a little off, to say the least.

During their short courtship, Lizzie had brought Raphael to Sunshine and made him climb up through the man hole. He wasn't too keen on doing this after the experience of the tunnel under his grandparent's old bed. But love did strange things to a person, so he wriggled through and pulled out the backpack.

She opened it up. Like anyone else in similar circumstances, he was flabbergasted. Lizzie did not mention the stand that held the blind statue. As far as she was concerned, everything that it held could stay there. Harry had the key. If one day he discovered its treasure, then so be it.

Lizzie threw her bouquet of roses over her shoulder and Amanda squealed with delight when she caught it. She and Roza giggled at this romantic experience. Mark held hands with the new lady in his life, a nice lady called Susan. Arlo and Hope were pretending not to be making eyes at each other.

Lizzie knew she could not put it off any longer. She should have done it before. She found her uncle standing alone. "I have to tell you something, Uncle Mitch, and I'm really sorry. I guess I was just so angry at you, at everyone really."

"It's okay Lizzie. I understand why you did it. When you were a little girl, you used to help me cook right here in the kitchen at Sunshine. You probably don't remember. But I always remembered thinking if I had a daughter, I wished she could have been like you. You stole my heart all those years ago and then I deserted you. I left you to that monster."

She felt better now she had his forgiveness. "What about Francine? I found some papers that Leon had and it seemed to say that . . . you know."

"It's a puzzle? But Francine is my wife, nothing more. You frightened the hell out of me, so I had some DNA testing done. I don't know who my daughter is or even if I ever had one. So it's over, Lizzie. Go and enjoy your honeymoon."

Gabe and Lucia sat with her father and Zaylee. Malcolm looked like a renewed man. He held the hands of both his very pregnant wife and his beautiful daughter. James and Boag were dressed for the occasion with new, shiny collars. They keep a keen eye on the proceedings. They eyed off the old Alsation just to be sure he kept track of Jude.

Zaylee looked over at Francine and Mia, giggling like young girls. They had been friends most of their lives. Since Francine had regained her memory and danger no longer stalked her, she was a different person.

Zaylee thought again of what Lucia had once said about Mia, about what was wrong with her. As Zaylee watched Mia, she noticed there were slight changes happening. There was the minuscule shake of her head that she had never noticed before. One day she would ask Lucia just what she had meant, but not today. In the meantime, Matt and Mia could not be happier.

Visits to Miriam, Maryanne and Maria were becoming more regular. They were all as well as could be expected. But the day was for happiness and not to relive the old hurts and haunts of days and years gone by.

After a time, as the festivities were winding down, Lizzie, Lucia and Sarina sat together, all looking beautiful in their new colourful clothing. Three, little girls had grown up to be three, lovely women who were trying hard to be whole.

Their torments were behind them. As they sat together, Lizzie pulled a pack of cards out of the small bag she carried. It wasn't really the occasion for solitaire, but there were times when she couldn't help herself. The spades kept coming up—fire and swords. This alarmed her so she packed her cards away.

There had been too much sin which had almost destroyed them. The desire for better days was stronger than ever. They were experiencing a taste of how good life could be. The danger, deceit and mystery that had surrounded them for so long no longer existed.

The weather remained fine and sunny. It had been a wonderful day for all concerned except for Maxwell Bartholomew who sat up high in the hills with his strong binoculars watching the Farradays pack up after the happy bride and groom had driven away.

He had both moments of sadness and black rage. Should he not have been with them? Wasn't he a Farraday or a Smith or any surname he chose to have? Life was seldom fair. He was alone in the hills above Sunshine, but maybe that could change. He decided to drive north to see how his other venture was progressing.